by A. J. Cronin

A Song
of Sixpence

A Song of Sixpence

by A. J. CRONIN

LITTLE, BROWN AND COMPANY • BOSTON • TORONTO

A Song
of Sixpence

1

EVERY EVENING at six o'clock a sense of expectancy filled
the house, brightening the long, vague and dreamy afternoon. As I went into the front room my mother, moving about the kitchen preparing our supper, began to sing.
It was something about a miller's daughter who lay down and
died. She sang these sad Scottish songs in so lively a manner
and with such natural cheerfulness they sounded gay. I stood
on the hassock to look out of the window. Although I was to
go to school next week I still had need of the hassock.

The road to the village station was empty except for Mac-
intosh's dog, asleep in the shade of the sycamore tree outside
the smithy. Beyond the station with its beds of sweet william
and yellow calceolarias lay the wide sweep of deserted shore,
and beyond that the Clyde estuary, enlivened at present by a
white-funneled paddle steamer, a Broomielaw boat, going
downstream. Presently a figure appeared, not the expected
one but still a friend — indeed my only friend, Maggie, or as
she was called most unjustly by the "bad" boys, Mad Maggie,
a big awkward girl of thirteen who, festooned with milk cans
from Snoddie's farm, was now squeezing through the bars of
the shut gates of the level crossing. This was a short cut so
strictly forbidden me I watched reprovingly as she dragged up
the road on the start of her evening milk round. Passing our

house, one of four little villas primly in a row, she saw me at the window and, with a dull clank of cans, waved an arm in greeting.

I had begun to wave back when there came a shrill whistle. My eyes, diverted from Maggie, picked up a plume of steam beneath which a dark maroon serpent snaked slowly round the curve of the railway line. Painfully, as though out of breath, it puffed to the single platform. In the year 1900 only the slowest North British trains stopped at Ardencaple village.

As sometimes happened, my father was the only passenger to get off. He walked briskly, with the step of a man who likes to get home, an alert figure, conveying, even at that distance, an unmistakable and distinctive sense of style. He was wearing his brown suit, with dark brown shoes, a brown bowler hat with a curled brim, and a short fawn coat. As he drew near, the dog looked up and, being unaware of the prejudices of the village, raised the dust with its tail. Then I saw, with increased anticipation, that Father was carrying a parcel. Quite often when visiting his customers in Winton he would bring home to Mother and me something for supper that rarely failed to excite us: perhaps a bunch of choice Colmar grapes, or a cut of Tay salmon, or even a jar of Canton green ginger, exotics which seemed to indicate that Father was himself not averse to having good things to eat and which, of course, went so far beyond the modest standards of our daily life that, unveiling them casually with one eyebrow critically raised, he secretly enjoyed our startled looks.

The door clicked open and Mother, plucking off her apron, ran to meet and hug him, an action I did not altogether approve but which unfailingly took place. Father took off his coat and put it on a hanger — he was always careful of his clothes — then came into the kitchen, lifted me up in a detached manner and set me down again. Mother put the soup on the table.

It was Scotch broth, a dish Father particularly liked but of which, unless pressed, I would eat only the peas, arranging them first in a circle on the rim of my plate. There was boiled beef to follow. Against the native custom — and this was only one of our many failures to conform to the strict usages of the community in which we lived — we took our main meal at night, since Father, on the move all day, seldom had the opportunity for more than a sandwich. Meanwhile, with an air that I felt to be unusual, even slightly strained, he was slowly unwrapping his parcel.

"Well, Grace," he said. "It is all settled."

Mother stopped ladling the broth. She had turned pale.

"No, Conor!"

He looked at her with a smile, affectionate yet ironical, and touched up the ends of his short blond moustache.

"I had the final meeting with Hagemann this afternoon. We've signed our agreement. He's taking the boat back to Holland tonight."

"Oh, Con dear, you can't mean it."

"See for yourself. There's the first sample. Before your eyes."

He placed a round glass container on the table, sat down calmly, took the soup plate from her unresistant hand and picked up his spoon. I thought that Mother, unbelievably, was going to cry. She sat down weakly. Dimly aware that something terrible, a crisis, had occurred, disturbing the peace of my home, I could not take my eyes off that round glass bottle. It contained a yellowish powder and had a printed label with a red, blue and white flag. With a great effort Mother handed me my soup.

"But Conor," she said pleadingly. "You're doing so well with Murchison's."

"You mean I have done well for *them*."

"Of course. At the same time, they are such sound people."

"I have nothing against Murchison's, my dear Gracie, but I'm tired of wearing my boots out selling their flour. I've given them five good years of my life. Mind you, they've been fair with me. In fact old Murchison advised me to take the agency."

"But Conor . . . we are so comfortable now . . . and so safe."

Father raised that single eyebrow, but not on this occasion to present Colmar grapes. This mysterious bottle must surely be a bombshell.

"We shall never get anywhere by remaining comfortable and safe. Now, do eat something like a good lass, and I'll give you the details later." He leaned forward and patted her hand.

"I'm too upset." Mother got up and placed the boiled beef on the table.

Unaware that I had not touched my broth, she removed my plate without scolding me. Father, with his invariable air of aplomb, carved the beef, calmly and elegantly. With his slight figure, his russet hair and warm complexion, his hazel eyes and even white teeth just showing beneath his curled moustache, he was a handsome man. I admired him intensely and was often spellbound by the unpredictable and daring audacities he would "bring off" without turning a hair. But in the full meaning of the word I did not love him. I belonged entirely to my mother. Soft, timid, kept back by a chain of illnesses that began with mumps and ended with diphtheria — I could still taste the carbolic glycerine Dr. Duthie had used to paint my throat — and forced by the remarkable circumstances of our life into ties with Mother and my home that were especially close and emotional, I fully merited that deplorable epithet, a mother's boy. Yet who would not have been with such a mother, at that time not more than twenty-four, rather short and soft in figure, with regular features, soft brown hair, eyes of a deep gentian blue, and in all her movements a kind of natural grace which, to my childish mind, seemed to explain her name. But above all, it was her look of sweetness that held me captive.

Now, with her chin cupped in her hand, she was listening to Father, who alone was doing justice to the beef.

"You must admit," he was saying reasonably. "The mustard, thank you dear . . . that I could not miss this chance. We are on the eve of a revolution in the baking industry. The old-fashioned barm method is on its way o-u-t, out." When Father wished to be impressive he would often spell a word before he said it.

"But Conor, the bread we get is perfectly good."

Father, chewing with relish, shook his head.

"You don't know how often I've seen barm go sour. Bub-bling out of the casks. And a whole batch of loaves completely spoiled. Ruined. After all, it's only distiller's scum. The new process will make cheaper and better bread. And it won't go wrong. Think of the opportunity, Grace, with my established connections. Why, I know every baker in the West. I'll be first in the field. And working for myself."

Mother was being persuaded.

"You're quite sure of Mr. Hagemann?"

Father nodded with his mouth full.

"He's straight as a die. I can import from him in Rotter-dam on most favourable terms. Besides, he's advanced half the money to give me a start. Would he if he didn't believe in me?"

A faint gleam of reassurance appeared in Mother's eye, suc-ceeded by a remote look of expectancy. When supper was over she did not rise to clear the table. Nor did Father follow his usual habit of devoting half an hour to me — an elastic period often extended by my importunities — before I went to

bed. Beyond the short stroll he occasionally took before re-
tiring, Father never went out at night. After a long day spent
in the society of men who were his friends he seemed perfectly content to be, as he put it, at his own fireside. Besides,
there was no inducement for him to go out. Though he had
bare acquaintances, he had never sought, let alone made, a
friend in the village. Ardencaple was for him, indeed for all of
us, a hostile camp.

Our evening communion was partly educational — it was he
who had taught me my letters, and he would instruct me to
read out, for our mutual benefit, recondite facts from his favourite compendium, *Pear's Encyclopedia* — but in the main,
and especially since my illness, he had sought merely to enter-
tain me. With an amazing fertility of imagination, he invented
and related a whole series of fascinating adventures in which a
young protagonist of precisely my age, small and rather delicate, but intrepid almost beyond belief, performed feats of
outstanding bravery in tropic jungles or on desert islands
amongst primitive tribes and man-eating savages, meanwhile
interpolating from time to time side remarks to my mother
which related usually to the natural appendages and accoutre-
ments of the dark-skinned female members of the tribe and
which, while I did not in the least understand their significance, made her laugh.

Tonight, however, as my parents continued to be absorbed
in talk, I perceived that the prospect of my being regaled with
a cannibal feast had faded and, meeting Father's eye when he
paused in what he was saying, I suddenly demanded, in the
tones of one wronged and neglected:

"What is in the bottle?"

He smiled with unusual benignancy.

"It is yeast, Laurence. To be specific, Hagemann's Royal
Dutch Yeast."

"Yeast?" I repeated, in bewilderment.

"Just so." He nodded graciously. "A living substance composed of innumerable living cells. Yes, a form of life itself, one might say, an organism that grows, buds, turns starch into sugar, sugar into alcohol and carbon dioxide gas, and so leavens our staff of life. Prepared," Father went on, in his best vein, "in mineral salt-sugar solution — as is my Royal Dutch Yeast — a modern technique far superior to the grain mash method, it offers a unique opportunity for introducing an entirely new process that will reorganize the Scottish baking industry."

Father sounded as though he himself had discovered yeast and for long afterwards I believed he had. His exposition, obviously prepared, left me speechless. Mother, too, seemed to find it overpowering or at least quite enough for me at present. She rose and, although the clock on the mantelpiece assured me it was well before my usual hour, suggested in a tone not to be disputed that I should go to bed.

This was ordinarily a lengthy process, prolonged by every pretext by which I sought to detain my mother, and complicated by all sorts of fetishes and rituals that I had built for my own protection and which, while unworthy of enumeration, may be imagined from my first action, which was to satisfy myself that a boa constrictor was not concealed beneath my bed. Tonight, however, the advent of the yeast distracted me from all my ceremonies and shortened everything in a highly disagreeable manner.

Even when I was in bed and Mother had said good night, leaving my door ajar according to custom, this strange substance, mysterious invader of our home, kept fermenting in my mind. I could not get to sleep. As I lay with closed eyes I saw the yeast working in the flask, bubbling and frothing until it burst upwards in a swelling yellow cloud, overhanging our house, taking the form of the genie from the bottle in one of my father's stories. I stirred uneasily. Was this the beginning of a dream of some strange vision of the future?

Although they spoke in low voices, the resumed conversation of my parents came in snatches through the unshut door of my narrow bedroom. From time to time I heard impressive and disturbing phrases: "away from this confounded village" . . . "take up your music again" . . . "he could go to Rockcliff, like Terence" . . . And finally, just before I fell asleep I heard Father declare, in his most serious and decided tone:

"You wait, Gracie, we'll show your folks . . . and my lot too . . . that they can't go on treating us like this. One day they'll make it up to you. And soon."

2

FOR WEEKS I had longed to go to school, an adventure skilfully built up for me in the most glowing terms by my father, and deferred only by my susceptibility to the commonest germs. But now that the day had arrived, my state of mind verged on panic. As Mother put the finishing touches to me, buttoning up my new blue serge trousers and pulling down my jersey, I begged her with tears in my eyes not to send me. She laughed and kissed me.

"You'll be all right with Maggie. See, here's your new satchel. Strap it on your shoulders like a real boy."

The satchel, although empty, did help to brace me. I had begun to feel stronger when a knock at the back door made me jump.

Maggie was there, standing on the doorstep, with her usual expression, humble and lowering, her tangled locks falling over eyes which had that dull yet appealing look seen in young Highland cattle. She was the daughter of the village washerwoman, a known slattern whose husband had long since made his escape from her abusive tongue and who, while bewailing the lot of her deserted bairn, made a drudge of her. Dressed in an old cut-down tweed skirt my mother had given her, with a darn on the knee of one stocking, Maggie had few outward signs of grace. Self-acknowledged to be stupid, and with a heavy, depressed air that bespoke overwork and ill-usage at home, she was mercilessly teased with shouts of "Daft Maggie" by the boys of the village, who nevertheless were wary of her, for she had a strong arm and a sure aim with a round pebble, gathered from the shore and always handy in her pocket. But to me she was both confidante and mentor. I truly trusted her, as did my mother, who liked Maggie and was good to her in many ways. Despite the numerous duties imposed upon her — and after school hours one rarely saw her without a bundle of laundry or her armour of milk cans which, after her round, she must scald and scour at the farm before her final task of feeding the hens — she had been during the long summer holidays a kind of nursemaid to me, taking me for walks in the afternoon during my periods of convalescence. Our favourite pilgrimage took us along the shore, passing on the way an isolated, sadly broken down little cottage with a rotted green trellis, misnamed Rosebank, where, to my everlasting disgrace, it appeared that I had been born. How so momentous an event could have occurred in so deplorable an edifice I could not comprehend, yet presumably it had, for as we passed Rosebank, Maggie would launch into a fearsome yet compelling description, derived doubtless from her mother, of my arrival in this world on a dark and dreary Sabbath night when it had rained torrents and the tide had risen so high that my father, desperately seeking Dr. Duthie with his little black bag, had almost failed to reach the village.

"And to beat all," Maggie turned her commiserating gaze upon me, "ye came into the wurrld the wrong way round."

"The wrong way! But how, Maggie?"

"Not head first. Feet first."

"Was that bad, Maggie?" I demanded, petrified.

She nodded in sombre affirmation.

After this humiliating disclosure Maggie would revive me

by taking me further along the estuary to the Erskine Rocks, where, enjoining me not to tell my mother, who would have been shocked to hear that her spoiled darling was upsetting his stomach with such "trash," we gathered fresh mussels which she roasted, nut-sweet, on a driftwood fire. The novelty of this repast alone delighted me, since I was, if anything, over-nourished; but for Maggie, sadly ill-fed, it was welcome sustenance, and by way of dessert, taking off her battered boots and the long black stockings, one or other of which despite the darns usually sported a hole, she would wade into the grey waters of the firth and, feeling in the muddy sand with her toes, uncover little fluted white cockles which she devoured like oysters, raw and quivering.

"But they're living, Maggie," I protested, dismayed at the pain these innocent bivalves must suffer under her sharp teeth.

"They don't feel anything," she assured me calmly. "If you bite them quick. Now let's play shop."

Maggie invented all sorts of games and was full of country skills. She could make a willow whistle, fashion intricately woven harvest plaits of a pattern that my fingers could never master, and magically unfold tight little paper boats that we sailed down the Gielston burn. She could also sing, and in a hoarse but tuneful voice would offer me current favourites like "Goodbye, Dolly Gray" and "The Honeysuckle and the Bee."

But the game Maggie liked best undoubtedly was "shop" and she never tired of it. When we had collected and set out on the shore our varied symbols, chips of shells, seeds of wild fennel, burdock tips and sea pinks, white sand, bladders of seaweed, marbled pebbles, each representing a different commodity, Maggie would assume the airs and responsibilities of the proprietress while I became the customer. This gave to

Maggie, so poor and neglected, a sense of security, even of wealth. Looking round her shop with the pride of possession, counting her store of good things — tea, sugar, coffee, flour, butter, ham and of course black-striped peppermint balls — she could forget those days when she must stave off hunger with salt cockles, a raw turnip lifted from one of Snoddie's fields, or even the skins from the dog-rose and hawthorn berries that we called "hips and haws."

We were happy together, and I felt her fondness for me until, glancing upwards suddenly during our game, I would find her eyes bent upon me with the wondering expression of one whose attention is drawn repeatedly to some incomprehensible singularity. I knew then what must come, for presently in a tone half puzzled, half commiserating she would soliloquize:

"When I look at you, Laurie, I still can't credit it. I mean, you're not much, but you don't seem any different from *us*. And your mother and father too, they're so nice you would never dream they were *that*."

I hung my head. Maggie, in her blundering, good-natured way, had once again uncovered one of the hidden shames that seared my early years and which, without further pretence, must be confessed. I was, alas, a Roman Catholic. A boy bound hand and foot to the grinding chariot of the Pope, miserable acolyte of the Scarlet Woman, burner of candles and incense, potential kisser of the big toe of St. Peter. Not only so, my parents and I were the sole adherents of that reviled religion, and worse, the only ones ever to have established themselves in the staunchly, exclusively true blue Protestant village of Ardencaple. We were as conspicuously out of place in that tight little community as would have been a family of Zulus. Equally, we were outcasts.

Whatever the public attitude towards my father, which he

delighted to provoke rather than to appease, I suffered nothing beyond that certain pitying or even sympathetic curiosity bestowed upon an oddity. Nevertheless, on this Monday morning when I faced the prospect of school, this had its part in lowering my morale. And when, after final admonitions from Mother, Maggie grasped my hand firmly and we set off up the road to the village, my mind was in a dither. A horse was being shoed in the smithy amidst an enticing fume of burnt hoof, yet I scarcely noticed it. The windows of the village store, against which I liked to press my nose, investigating the rich display of boiled sweets, peppermint oddfellows, slim jim and apple tarts, was passed unseen. It was a dolorous way, made more harrowing by Maggie's low-toned recital of the fearful punishments exacted by the schoolmaster, Mr. Rankin, whom she designated by the name Pin.

"He's a cripple," she kept deploring, with a shake of her head. "And a stickit minister. No more nor that! But he's a terror with the tause."

Although we went slowly, only too soon did we reach the school.

This was a smallish old red brick building with an open yard of beaten, stony earth in front, and here, but for Maggie, I should certainly have run away. In this playground a mimic battle was being waged. Boys darted about, struggled, shouted, kicked and fought; girls, flailing with ropes, skipped and shrieked; caps were torn from heads and sent skimming through the air, tacketty boots slid and scraped, sparking living fire from the stones, the din was ear-splitting. And suddenly noticing me, the biggest of the "bad" boys let out a wild and ribald yell: "Look wha's here. *The wee Pope!*"

This sudden elevation to the throne of the Vatican, far from sustaining me, produced in my innards a further apprehensive sinking. In a moment I should be surrounded by a crowd seeking to exact more from me than my apostolic blessing. But from this and other dangers, pressing through with her sharp elbows combatively extended, Maggie protected me until suddenly a clanging quelled the tumult, and the schoolmaster appeared, bell in hand, on the steps of the entrance.

Undoubtedly this was Pin, his right leg deformed and sadly shorter than the other, supported by a twelve-inch peg fixed to a queer little boot by an iron stirrup, the lower end capped with rubber. Surprisingly, he did not strike me as alarming. He was, in fact, though given to sudden explosions and choleric rappings of his desk with his knuckles, a mild, prosy, defeated little man of about fifty with steel-rimmed spectacles and a short pointed beard, seen always in a shiny black bobtailed suit, a celluloid dickey and a tucked-in black tie, who in his youth had studied for the ministry but, by reason of his deformity and a tendency to stammer, had failed repeatedly in trial sermons and become in the end a melancholy example of that supreme Scottish failure, the "stickit minister" turned dominie.

However, it was not to him that I was delivered. Pushing away from the main turbulent stream, Maggie finally entrusted me to the assistant mistress in the lowest class, where with some twenty others, many younger than myself, I was given a slate and seated on one of the front benches. Already I felt better, since I had recognized our teacher — a warm-looking girl with soft brown eyes and an encouraging smile — as one of the two daughters of Mr. Archibald Grant, who kept the store. Her younger sister Polly never failed to give me a butterscotch drop when I went to the store on errands for my mother.

"Now, children, I'm glad to see you back after the holidays and to welcome the new pupils," Miss Grant began, and I thrilled, fancying that her smile dwelt on me. "As Lady Meikle will be making her usual opening day visit to the school this morning, I expect you all to be on your best behavior. Now answer your names as I make out the register."

When she called out "Laurence Carroll" I imitated the others with a "Present, miss," which, however, was so uncertain as to suggest that I doubted my own identity. Nevertheless it was accepted, and after we had all given our names and Miss Grant had entered them in the big book on her desk she set us to work. The class was at different stages. Soon one section was droning out the two-times table, another copying sums from the blackboard on their slates, while a third struggled with block letters of the alphabet. To me all this appeared such manifest child's play that my earlier apprehension began to fade and to be replaced by a tingling consciousness of my own worth. What infants, not to know a *B* from a *D!* And who, amongst these older boys, had dipped, like me, into the mysteries of *Pear's Encyclopedia* with the picture of the tramp on the frontispiece announcing that for five years he had used no other soap? Surrounded by such evidence of juvenile ignorance, I felt the power of my superior knowledge, the distinction of my new clothes; I wanted to display my talents, to shine.

The screech of the slate pencils had not long begun before the door was flung open and the command given.

"Rise, children."

As we clattered to our feet Pin appeared and deferentially ushered into the classroom a stiff, self-important, overdressed little woman with a bust so swelling and aggressive as to give her, in conjunction with the tuft of feathers on her hat, a marked resemblance to a pouter pigeon. I gazed at her in awe. Lady Meikle was the widow of a Winton corset manufacturer who, behind the blameless but intriguing slogan: "Ladies, we use only the finest natural whalebone," plastered on the

hoardings of every railway station — an advertisement that to
me ranked in interest equally with "The Pickwick, the Owl,
and the Waverly Pen, they come as a boon and a blessing to
men" — had advanced to considerable wealth, then, after a
long term as provost of Levenford, to a knighthood, a distinction that had induced him to purchase and retire to a large property in the vicinity of Ardencaple. Here he had leisure to
indulge his hobby of cultivating orchids and tropical plants
while his spouse lost no time in assuming the duties and assert-
ing the prerogatives of the lady of the manor, although with
her down-to-earth ways and lapses into broad Scots idiom she
was not, and freely admitted this, to the manner born. Yet
Lady Whalebone, as my father named her, was a decent
woman, generous to Ardencaple — she had given the new village hall — and charitable to the entire county. She had moreover a characteristic grim sense of humour and a strong dash
of sentiment, since besides giving her lamented husband a
magnificent tombstone, replete with many awesome urns, she
faithfully maintained and had indeed made famous the orchid
collection he had instituted before his decease. Strange though
it may appear, while I had never exchanged a word with so
exalted a personage, I had good reason to be familiar with her
estate in all its extent, with its woods and river, the avenue a
mile long winding through the park between giant rhododendrons to the big house with its enormous adjacent conservatory.

"Be seated, bairns." She swept forward. "This room is unco'
stuffy. Open a window."

Miss Grant hurriedly complied while her ladyship, keeping
a formidable eye upon us, conferred with Pin, who, bending
forward, his deformed limb drawn back, half concealed behind the sound leg — a posture I soon saw to be habitual —

made submissive murmurs of acquiescence. Then she addressed us, in the broadest Doric, beginning thus:

"Bairns, ye're a' young and fushionless, but I hope and pray that so far ye have come to nae harm or tummelt into evil ways. Now ye a' ken the interest I take in the village and in a' of *you*, for what ye are, or may be, so see ye pay heed to what I'm about to say."

She continued in this fashion at considerable length, exhorting us to work diligently, to improve ourselves and to maintain always the highest standards of good behaviour and moral conduct, implying that it would go hard with us here and in the hereafter if we did not. Her address completed, she pursed her lips and favoured us with a dignified yet half humourous smile in which might have been detected a trace of slyness.

"As yet ye ken nothing. Virgin soil, that's what ye are, virgin soil. But I am going to test your nat'ral intelligence to see if ye have any gumption or for that matter anything in your heads at a'. Miss Grant, a pencil."

The pencil, yellow in colour, was immediately presented, and poising it before us for a moment, she threw it, with a dramatic gesture, to the floor. We held our breaths.

"Now," she resumed impressively. "Ye have no hands. None of ye have hands. *But I wish that pencil picked up.*"

Whatever prompted this extravagant experiment — perhaps she had been visiting one of her many charities, a home for paralytics in Ardfillan — the result was silence, dead silence. The class was stumped. Suddenly inspiration struck me. As in a daze, I got up, weak from my own boldness, tottered into the public gaze and, prostrating myself before the yellow pencil, snatched at it with my teeth. But the pencil was round and smooth. It escaped my feeble incisors, shot far ahead on the dusty and uneven floor. I followed, crawling face down, like a tracking Indian. Again I tried and again failed. The pursuit continued. Every eye remained rivetted upon me. Now the pencil had discovered a crevice between the floor boards. I nudged it forward with my chin, coaxed it to a favourable position, only to see it roll gently into a deeper crack beside the blackboard where a dust of chalk had already fallen. But my blood was up. Sticking out my tongue, I licked my quarry from its hold, then before it started to roll bit hard and true. The class gave a long sigh of applause as, whitened by chalk dust, my nose skinned and raw, I staggered to my feet, with the pencil impaled, clenched between my jaws.

"Well done!" cried Lady Whalebone, clapping her hands enthusiastically, then placing one upon my head. "Ye're a verra clever wee laddie."

I reddened all over, bursting with pride. To be commended thus by the lady of the manor before my teacher, before the schoolmaster and, best of all, my classmates! And on my first day at school. A very clever boy. What joy to tell my mother.

Meanwhile, as Miss Grant dusted me off, her ladyship, with the air of a phrenologist, still maintained a benevolent hand upon my cranium.

"How old are ye?"

"Six years, m'am."

"Ye're unco' small for six."

"Yes, m'am." I yearned to tell her of the illnesses, almost fatal, that had dwarfed me, probably for life, but before I could proceed she went on, encouragingly, a real patroness.

"Ye must sup your porridge, with plenty of milk. Not skim, mind ye. And never turn up your nose at the staff of life. Ye ken what I mean by the staff of life?"

"Oh, yes, m'am." Hot with triumph, conscious of my superior knowledge, recollecting my father's use of the same phrase in connection with the bottle, I gazed at her brightly, answered confidently, loud and clear: "Hagemann's Royal Dutch Yeast!"

A timid titter, swelling uncontrollably to a shout of laughter, rose from the class. Utterly dismayed, I saw my patroness's face alter, approbation supplanted by a heavy frown. Her grip on my skull tightened.

"Are ye darin' to make fun of me, boy?"

"Oh no, m'am, no!"

She studied me narrowly for a long moment while my insides seemed to liquefy. Then, repudiating me, she removed her hand with, at the same time, a forward thrust that impelled me forcibly towards my seat.

"Go! I see I was mistaken. Ye are nothing but a doited clown."

Humbled, disgraced for life, in fact once again an outcast, I sat for the rest of the morning with bowed head.

On the way home, seeking the hand of my true protector, blinking water from my eyes, I mourned:

"It's no use, Maggie. I'm no good at anything, just a doited clown."

"Ay," Maggie answered with despondent satire, apparently having had a bad morning in her own class. "We're a braw pair."

3

❀❀❀

D ESPITE Mother's misgivings, and the public humiliation
it had caused me, the business of the Royal Dutch
Yeast had made a most auspicious start. Undoubtedly
the opportunity was there, and my father, naturally clever,
with a sharp and far-seeing business eye, was the very man to
seize it. His intimate knowledge of the baking trade, the connections he had established throughout the West of Scotland
during his five years as a salesman for Murchison's, his attractive personality and easy manner, which he could attune exactly to the status of each customer and which made him generally popular, above all the aplomb with which he would
fling off his jacket, tie on a white apron and actually demonstrate the new process in the bakehouse, all marked him for
success.

Evidence of this was manifest after the first few months, in
a family expedition to Winton when Father, having shown us
with pride his new little office in the Caledonia Building, took
us to a matinee of *Aladdin* at the Theatre Royal and afterwards to the famous Thistle Restaurant. Always an open-
handed man, he was more than usually generous that Christ-
mas. In addition to a new winter outfit which did not greatly
interest me, I received a sledge of that superb variety,

equipped with a steering bar, known as a Flexible Flyer, while for Mother there arrived one December day from Winton in a big two-horse van something she must have longed for ever since her marriage, a gift whose unexpectedness, since Father characteristically had not breathed a word of its coming, doubled and redoubled Mother's joy. An upright piano. Not one of these yellowish cottage affairs with plush insets, such as we marched to in school, that twanged like an old banjo, but a brand-new, solid, ebony-black instrument, bearing the magic name Bluthner, with twin gilt candlesticks and shining ivory keys that on the merest touch emitted deep and vibrant chords.

Mother, still quite dazed, sat down on the revolving stool that had come with the piano and, while I stood at her shoulder, after running her hands up and down the keyboard with a discerning mobility that amazed me, remarking at the same time, "Oh dear, Laurie, my fingers are all thumbs," she paused for a moment to collect her thoughts, then began to play. So vivid is my recollection of this scene I remember even the piece she played. It was Chaminade's "Danse des Echarpes." To say that I was stunned and spellbound is no exaggeration, not only by the delicious sounds that fell upon my eardrums, but because of the miracle that Mother, whom I had never before heard strike a note and who from loyalty to Father — unable until then to afford a piano — had never introduced the subject in my presence, should after these silent years suddenly produce this unsuspected and accomplished talent and enchant me with a sparkling stream of music. The two porters, having each received a shilling and already with their caps on, in the lobby, had been arrested on their way out. Now, with me, as Mother ended, they applauded spontaneously. She laughed joyfully but shook her head.

"Oh, no, Laurie, I'm so terribly rusty. But it will soon come back to me."

Here, in this remark, was another enigma to add to those others, still unsolved, that complicated and disturbed my early years and that, when I pressed Mother for an explanation, caused her merely to smile and to make some evasive answer. Meanwhile nothing could detract from this new joy. Father was not musical and although sympathetic did not really care for the piano; this indeed — for I had begun to *know* Father — may in some degree have delayed its delivery. His idea of music was a stirring melodic mélange from a good brass band, and to this end he had provided himself with several pink Edison Bell phonograph cylinders of the famous *Besses o' the Barn.* But to Mother, particularly in our *apartheid* state, the beautiful Bluthner was both consolation and refinement. Every afternoon when she was "dressed," after she had finished the day's housework and satisfied herself that all was shining and in perfect order, she would "practice," leaning forward from time to time, since she was naturally a little short-sighted, to study a difficult passage, then, before resuming, brushing aside her soft brown hair which, waved in the middle, fell across her brow. Often when I came home from school and always if the weather was wet, I would come silently into the front room and seat myself by the window to listen. I soon knew the names of the pieces I liked best: Chopin's "Polonaise in E Flat," Liszt's "Hungarian Rhapsody," followed by Schubert's "Moments Musicaux," and my greatest favourite, to which perhaps the name contributed, Beethoven's "Sonata in F Minor," which beyond all the others induced in me a precocious sadness, fostering visions wherein under a shining moon I saw myself leading lost causes in distant lands and reaping the soul-satisfying reward of a hero's lonely grave and from which, resurrecting myself, I would run into the kitchen to put the kettle on the range and make hot buttered toast for our tea.

That was a happy winter which nothing subsequently could destroy. Our little ship, sails set full to a favourable wind, rode the tide buoyantly on its safe though solitary course. Father was getting rich. At school I had been moved to a higher class and, although regretting Miss Grant, was agreeably surprised to find myself drawn to my new master. Pin, so unjustly condemned by Maggie — his outbursts were the result of a nervous affliction rather than ill-temper — might be a failure in the pulpit, but as a teacher he excelled. His education had naturally been superior to that of the average village dominie and he had that invaluable knack of putting things in an interesting way. Surprisingly, he seemed to become interested in me. A wry appreciation of our common inferior standing in the village may have appealed to him, or perhaps, though he never overtly made this evident, he had hopes of converting me in the manner of a brand plucked from the burning. Whether or not, I experienced more good than I deserved from this despised and rejected little man.

How swiftly those months slipped past! I barely realized that spring was on the way till Father, who had what he referred to as a "bronchial tendency," caught a heavy cold in March due to his sardonic Irish disregard of the old Scots aphorism: "Ne'er cast a clout till May goes out." But he threw it off as the smithy sycamore began to bud and suddenly we were in the green days of April. A soft west wind was blowing, hearing on its wings the news of our increased prosperity. Was this, perhaps, the cause of that rare event, a surreptitious visit from my cousin Terence, a boy of sixteen, who from his earliest years had been blessed with a nose keenly receptive of the lightest airs of affluency?

Terence was a cool, long-legged, unusually good-looking

fellow, endowed with more than his share of the Carroll charm. His home, which I had never seen, was in Lochbridge, only twelve miles away, where his father owned an establishment curiously named the Lomond Vaults. While I did not then comprehend the implications of that occult word "Vaults" beyond its suggestion of subterranean depths, Terry's great distinction, enviable in my eyes, was that he attended the famous Rockcliff College in Dublin as a boarder. At present on his Easter holidays, he rolled up to the front gate on a shining new Rudge Whitworth bicycle. He was wearing well-creased grey flannel trousers, from which he negligently snapped off the clips, the blue Rockcliff blazer and a rakishly tilted straw hat banded with the school colours. An Olympian, straight from Parnassus — the Vaults? — he dazzled me.

Mother, ardently hospitable and long starved of visitors, was delighted to see Terence, although put out at being caught unprepared.

"My dear boy, if only you'd let me know you were coming, I'd have had such a nice lunch for you." She looked at the clock, which showed twenty minutes to three. "Tell me what I can get for you now."

"As a matter of fact I've had my lunch, Aunt Grace." I could see that the term of kinship pleased my mother. "Still, I could do with a snack."

"Just say what you'd like."

"Well, I'm rather partial to a hard-boiled fresh egg, if you have some in the house."

"Of course. How many would you like?"

"Should we say half a dozen, Aunt Grace?" Terence suggested carelessly.

Fifteen minutes later he was seated at the table gracefully making contact with six hard-boiled eggs and several slices of

thickly buttered cottage loaf, while at the same time recounting to us, in an offhand manner and an accent tinged with the intonation of upper-class Dublin, his notable triumph of the past term, a win in the hundred-yard sprint at the school sports. Impossible not to admire, and we did, although Mother seemed to wilt slightly as for the third time Terence repeated:

"The way I left them in my final burst they might have been standing still."

Indeed, it was she who suggested later on that Terence take me for a short walk, pending the return of my father. As we set off, up the road to the village, I put my hand in his and rapturously burst forth:

"Oh, Cousin Terry, how I would love to be at Rockcliff with you!"

Terrence looked at me fixedly, then, producing a quill toothpick, began absently to work on his teeth.

"Don't mention it to your mater, who's a doat, but one of these eggs was a trifle off."

He burped slightly to emphasize his point.

"Oh, I'm sorry, Terry. But did you hear what I said about Rockcliff?"

Terence shook his head indolently, but with a finality that chilled me.

"My poor little caper, you'd never stand the ferrula. Rockcliff would kill you stone-dead. Good God, what's that object over there?"

I spun round. It was Maggie, on one of her slavish errands, with a big bundle of laundry flapping on her head, uncouth, unkempt, and waving to me, waving wildly in friendly recognition. My skin contracted. To acknowledge Maggie before Terence? No, no, it was unthinkable. Guilty of the first of the two great acts of apostasy of my childhood, I turned away.

"God knows who it is," I mumbled, in a feeble imitation of

my cousin's manner, then walked on, leaving Maggie stricken, one arm frozen in mid-air.

At the head of the road Terence paused outside the grocery store. In the window, on a glass stand, lay one of Grant's special dessert apple tarts. Beyond, within the shop, bent over a book with her elbows on the counter and her back towards us, was Polly Grant. Her posture, which certainly presented us with a notably curvaceous view of the part usually sat upon, seemed to amuse Cousin Terence. He lounged in an athletic way against the window, his gaze wandering from the apple pastry to the unconscious Polly.

"That's not a bad-looking tart," he commented.

"Oh, yes, Terry. Simply spiffing."

"Very well rounded?"

"They're always round, Terry."

To my surprise Terence laughed, and Polly, disturbed in her reading, stood up and swung towards us. Meeting my cousin's eye, she reddened and closed her book with a bang.

"We could do with something to sweeten our mouths, after the eggs," Terence resumed. "I daresay you have an account here."

"Oh, we have. I often do messages for Mother and have them marked."

"Then suppose you nip in for the pastry and have it charged." He added airily: "I'll square up for it later."

Enthusiastically, I obeyed. Polly seemed unnaturally disturbed. She even forgot to give me my usual butterscotch drop.

"Who is that young fellow with you?" she inquired, with still heightened colour.

"My cousin Terence," I answered proudly.

"Then tell him from me he has a pretty good cheek."

Naturally I could not think of conveying such a message

to my cousin, who, surveying the prospect as I came out with the tart, suggested that we should stroll across to a shady corner of the village green, known locally as the Common.

Here he settled himself comfortably with his back to a chestnut tree and undid the paper bag, releasing a delicious fragrance of crisp puff pastry.

"It's not so big when you see it close," he remarked, inspecting the tart, which to my eye seemed much larger at near view. It was at least nine inches in diameter, oozing lovely juice and snowy with sifted sugar.

"Hmm," said Terence. "You wouldn't have a knife?"

"No, Terry. I'm not allowed one yet. For fear I should cut myself," I apologized.

"Pity," said Terence thoughtfully. "We can't go tearing this apart or we'll have the innards all over us."

A pause, during which Terence, frowning, seemed to ponder more deeply, while anticipation of those rich inner flavours made my teeth water.

"There's only one thing for it, man," he declared at last, resolutely. "We'll have to toss for it. You're a sport, aren't you?"

"If you are, I am, Terry."

"Good, man!" He produced a penny gravely. "Heads I win, tails you lose. I'll give you all the benefit. You make the call."

"Tails, Terry," I ventured timidly.

He uncovered the coin.

"And tails it is, more's the pity. Didn't you hear me say tails you lose? Well, better luck next time."

In a way, although my eyes blinked, I was not too unhappy to have lost. Watching Terence eat the tart slowly and with every sign of relish, I enjoyed it vicariously, down to the last flaky crumb.

"Was it good, Terry?"

"Fair," he decided critically. "But too rich for your young blood."

Without disturbing his reclining position, he eased a gunmetal cigarette case from his pocket, extracted a gold-tipped cigarette and, while I watched reverently, lit up.

"Wild Geranium," he explained.

"Terry," I said. "It's so nice you being here. Why don't you come more often? And why can't I come to see you?"

"Ah," he said, bringing smoke down his nose. "Now you're getting into a bit of family history."

I seized the opening eagerly.

"Tell me about it, Terry."

He considered, half hesitated, as though about to consent, then made an airy gesture of negation.

"You're too young to be bothering about that sort of nonsense."

"But I do bother, Terry. There's all sorts of things I don't understand. Especially why we never see any of our relations."

He glanced at me sideways. Couldn't he sense my anxiety for news of the unknown members of my tribe?

"Don't any of your mother's folks come to see you either then?"

"No, Terry. At least only one of Mother's brothers. The one at the University, the youngest one, called Stephen. And then only once in a very long while."

There was a pause.

"Well, man," Terence said at last, pontifically. "There's a certain situation, I will admit. And as you're bound to be told one of these days, there's no harm in giving you a slant on it now."

He lay back, puffing at his cigarette, while I waited intently, then he suddenly began.

"First of all," he spoke impressively, almost accusingly, "if it hadn't been for the Caledonian Railway Company you wouldn't be sitting here today. In fact you would never have existed."

This unexpected statement staggered me. I gazed at him fearfully.

"You see," he went on, "every evening when Uncle Con came back from his work in Winton he had to change trains at Levenford to take the Caley local to Lochbridge, where he was living at that time. But for that he'd never even have set eyes on your mother."

This contingency seemed so incredible that my alarm deepened. Pleasantly conscious of my rivetted attention, Terry resumed with easy nonchalance.

"Usually Con would go into the waiting room with the *Winton News* — for the Caley train was always late. But one of these evenings he found something, or rather someone, better to look at."

"Mother!" I gasped.

"Not yet, man. Don't rush me. At the moment she's just Grace Wallace and sweet seventeen." He frowned reprovingly. "She came regularly, carrying a music case, to meet her brother, a schoolboy, coming back on the Caley train from the Drinton Academy." He paused. "Now Conor, your father to be, always had, if you'll excuse me, an eye for a pretty girl. Yet this was different. Although he wanted to speak he was afraid he'd offend her. But one evening he up and did. And at that moment, man," Terry exclaimed sensationally, "as they looked into each other's eyes, the damage was done!"

"What damage, Terry?" I whispered faintly.

"Her parents were dyed in the wool Presbyterians, true blue, couldn't have been stricter, and she was the apple of her old man's eye, who, to make it worse, had a Scotch pedigree that went right back to the original William Wallace, if you ever heard of him. So here was a lovely girl, well thought of in the town, helped her mother in the house, sang like an angel in the church choir, never put a foot wrong." Terry shook his head sorrowfully. "When they found out she was going steady with an upstart Irish R.C., blood brother to a publican and, God help us, a priest, hell's bells, man, did they raise the roof. Prayers and tears. For weeks there was the devil to pay while they tried every mortal thing to keep them apart. It couldn't be done, man. In the end, with never a word, and although Con hadn't a fiver to bless himself with, they just up and off to the registry office. She knew her folks would never speak to her again and Con knew he'd be the bad boy of his lot for not getting tied up in chapel, but never mind, they got spliced."

"Oh, I'm glad they did, Terry," I cried fervently, for I had followed his recital breathlessly.

Terry burst out laughing.

"At least they got you here on the right side of the blanket, caper."

For a moment he sat studying me, as though trying to read my face, in which there was now only blankness. Perhaps what he had related did not altogether surprise me; I must have vaguely sensed something of my parents' situation. Yet suddenly an extraordinary depression fell upon me, intensified by the lively unconcern with which Terry treated a subject that affected me so deeply.

"So now you know." He broke the silence. "Only don't let on I told you."

"I won't, Terry," I said, numbly. I was less happy than I had hoped to be, and to cheer myself up I said:

"So I actually have two uncles?"

"It's three you have, on our side. There's my father, your Uncle Bernard in Lochbridge, and his reverence your Uncle

Simon in Port Cregan, not to speak of your Uncle Leo in Winton, though nobody knows much about him." He rose to his feet and hauled me up. "Time we were getting back. I need a box of vestas, so I'll stop at the shop. Come on and I'll race you there."

He set off springily, bent on showing me his style. I was not in the mood for running, yet now I felt strangely combative towards my incomparable cousin. I ran as hard as I could, so hard that Terry, glancing over his shoulder, was obliged to drop his clean-cut air in an effort to increase his pace. Perhaps the apple pie and the hard-boiled eggs incommoded him, possibly the report he had given of his prowess at the Rockcliff sports was coloured by a native talent for drawing the long bow. When we reached Grant's store he had not shaken me off, I was exactly at his elbow. After we had regained our breath he looked at me for the first time with a shade of respect.

"You're fast, man. I couldn't have believed it. Of course, you know I wasn't going all out."

While I waited outside he went into the shop and spent a very long time selecting his matches. Polly, who served him, did not seem at all displeased by his reappearance, or by his fastidious taste in vestas. As I watched through the window Terry appeared to be making her laugh a great deal. It was a way he had, careless and carefree. Could Terry really love anyone . . . let alone a poor little caper like me? I felt my throat tighten unaccountably.

My sadness persisted all the way home, deepened during the delicious chicken dinner Mother had prepared and which I could barely swallow. Father, in one of his best and most entertaining moods, showed a marked fondness for Terry, tipped him a sovereign, which Terry seemed to expect and which perhaps had been the purpose of his visit. Then, lighting his carbide bicycle lamp, my cousin swung himself on the machine and set off for Lochbridge.

When he was out of sight I went into the kitchen.

"Mother," I said, coming close to her. "I may not be much, but at least I am a sport."

"Are you?" Mother said, without enthusiasm. "I don't know that I want you to be a sport."

"But it's a good kind of thing. Terry said I was one when we tossed for the apple pastry."

"The apple pastry?" Mother turned in bewilderment, her hands covered with suds. "Was that why you ate no dinner?"

"No, Mother. I didn't eat any of the pastry. Terry ate it all."

"And where did this famous pastry come from?" Mother was now inspecting me very strangely.

"Why, Mother, it's the one I bought and charged to our account."

"What! You charged it!"

Mother was stupefied. But Father, who had come back and had been listening, suddenly said:

"How did Terry toss?"

"He was quite fair, Father. He tossed heads I win, tails you lose."

Father burst into a fit of laughter, so prolonged it brought on his bronchial cough.

"The young rascal." He choked. "He's a regular Carroll."

"I don't think it's at all amusing," Mother said frigidly. "I'll talk to you seriously about it in the morning, Laurence. Now you'll go straight to bed."

I undressed slowly, sadly. The afternoon, welcomed with such joy, was bitter in my mouth. A weight lay upon my mind, and upon my conscience too. Had I not openly rejected Maggie, dear Maggie, my friend and protector, yes, cut and repudiated her, and all for a cousin who thought no more of me than, well, than a box of Swan vestas? Above all, the mystery involving my parents which Terry had unveiled for me, the isolation in which we were compelled to live, pressed me down. I turned to my pillow and let the willing tears flow.

4

Autumn came early that year. The leaves of my favourite tree, fringed with gold and scarlet, had begun to flutter down, weaving a royal carpet at the entrance to the smithy. Morning mists drifted in from the firth leaving dewy crystals on the feathery grasses of Snoddie's field. The soft air held a sense of change, and of something intangible that made me dream of far places, strange unvisited kingdoms where I still felt I might once have been in other long forgotten days.

But today was Sunday, an actual day which, whenever I woke up and sniffed the revealing odour of frying bacon and eggs, brought always a more practical consideration. Father, from tradition and belief, was what I must call an affirmative Catholic, contumaciously so in the fact of opposition, despite certain unorthodox reservations of his own, but as a performer he could only be classed as indifferent. If the sun shone on the seventh day and the weather promised fine he would hire farmer Snoddie's pony and trap and drive to St. Patrick's, the nearest Catholic church, in Drinton, nine miles away. Mother, despite her Evangelical upbringing, amicably went with him. Such was her attachment to Father I am convinced she would have willingly accompanied him to a Hindu Temple had he professed that faith. I, of course, was taken along and, like Mother, held my breath at Father's amateur handling of the reins, a recklessness ill-disguised by a pretence of high expertise that deceived neither of us nor, for that matter, the pony. With a flick of its hooves as Father shaved the corners it would turn round and, craning its neck, stare at him with indignant wonder. A rare motor car was now being seen on the roads, usually a red Argyle from the Lochbridge motor works, and as one sped past in a cloud of dust, missing us by a miracle, Mother, clutching her wide-brimmed hat, would exclaim chokingly:

"Oh, dear, these horrible machines."

"No, Gracie," Father replied coolly, tugging at the shying pony. "They are wonderful inventions. Since I mean eventually to have one, don't run them down."

"They may run us down," Mother murmured in my ear.

But there were many Sundays when Father felt that God did not require him to expose his family to the hazards of the road and, reading his face as he inspected the mellow grey sky and sniffed the soft west breeze that hinted rain, I knew this autumn morning to be one of them, that it would be for me another Sunday of high excitement, sharpened to a fine edge by alarm. And indeed, after breakfast, which he took in his dressing gown, Father turned to Mother.

"Perhaps, my dear lass, you'd make a few sandwiches for the boy and me." Father usually said "my dear lass" when he wanted something done for him.

He went upstairs and presently came down wearing his usual get-up for our expeditions: a thick grey Norfolk knickerbocker suit, stout boots and knitted stockings, and a mackintosh cape, like a poncho, that fastened at the neck with a metal clasp.

We set off, up the Station Road and through the village, where the bells of the parish kirk had begun to ring. In answer to this summons the *natives* — as my father insisted on naming them — universally in sober black and armed with their black Bibles, were moving towards the church in a slow, solemn, God-fearing stream.

"Black beetles!" came the disgusted ejaculation from beside me.

Father, I am sure, wilfully selected this precise moment so that as an R.C. outsider he could outrage the Scottish Sabbath convention. It was his way of defying the tight-lipped prejudice against us in the village. Nowadays, when an enlightened liberalism seeks to promote unity of the churches, it is difficult to conceive of the bitterness that existed then against Catholics, particularly against Irish Catholics, in the West of Scotland. These descendants of unwanted famine refugees, many of whom had as yet failed to raise themselves above the level of the labouring class, were referred to as "the dirty Irish" and were universally despised and execrated, both on account of their nationality and their religion, which was publicly referred to in such terms as: the Roman harlot, drinker of the cup of abomination, or the whore that sitteth upon the seven hills of sin. I myself had trembled as I spelled out the notice of a sermon to be preached in the village parish church: "Rome, the seat of the beast, according to Rev. 18, 19."

But Father's nature, unlike mine, was combative and it amused him to evoke shocked looks and pursed lips and to ignore contemptuously the general dour air of reprobation created by our appearance. Now, as always, he traversed the village with a springy, almost jaunty step, head in the air, manner aloof, a scornful smile curving his lips, which from time to time he rounded in an affected whistle. For me, trotting at his side and dreading disaster, the ordeal was racking, only slightly relieved by the hidden, envious glances from other boys for whom Sunday was a penance, banefully filled by a two-hour sermon, a day of excruciating tedium, wherein the forgetful raising of the voice was a desecration, laughter a crime, and the passage of the one slow train known as the "Sunday-breaker" which defiled the sanctity of the day, an instance, publicly proclaimed, of the evil that was bringing the world to perdition.

I began to breathe more freely as we reached the last village landmark, Macintyre's sawmill, and came out to open country. Here, presently, we passed the entrance to the Meikle estate, a noble gateway with tall pillars each bearing a green bronze eagle flanked by twin lodges of cut stone built in the Scots baronial style. The avenue wound upwards between massed rhododendrons through the park, apparently to infinity. The sight of this privileged magnificence had already caused me a preliminary tremor which was intensified when Father, some two hundred paces further down the country road, took a cautious look round and, motioning me to follow, plunged through a break in the hedgerow. We were now in the wooded, rigorously forbidden policies of Lady Whalebone. I quivered at the thought. Father, however, quite unperturbed, steered a familiar course under the beech trees — the beech nuts crackling much too loudly under our boots — and brought us out to a bracken-covered glen. He then circled a plantation of young larch and entered a thicker wood, bushed with undergrowth and echoing with the sound of running water. This was the Gielston River, strictly preserved, and noted for its run of sea trout.

Arrived at the river bank, immediately below the falls, Father's next move was to remove a two foot canvas case from beneath his cape and to assemble therefrom the short sections of a greenheart rod. The reel was fitted, the line threaded and presently he had begun to cast into the creamy spume at the head of the pool. As a boy, living near the shores of Loch Lomond, he had passionately fished every burn that fed the

Loch and now, as I watched intently, allowed at intervals to take the rod, that same ardour was communicated to me.

I wish I might boast of Father as one of the elect, a dry-fly purist, or even simply a fly fisher. He was not. He fished with brandling worms dug for us at the farm by Maggie, and which I disentangled, wriggling and rank, from the Van Houten's cocoa tin I carried in my pocket. Father's object was to catch fish and he held to the method that served him well in his youth. Today, however, it seemed as if we should have no luck.

"Not even a nibble." Father was annoyed, he did not like to be beaten. "Yet the sea trout should be up. We'll leave our line in the water and eat our lunch."

Mother's sandwiches were always good, especially the to-mato ones. We sat down in a little clearing under a silver birch tree that diffused a soft silver-green light. The river splashed and twinkled through the tall grasses and reeds. The hum of the woods set a fearful privacy upon the place. The sudden chatter of a jay made me start. Now, as on all our ex-peditions, I was dreadfully scared that we should be caught by the gamekeeper or, worse, by the owner, that redoubtable little woman who had scorned me on my first day at school and whom, in my mind, I had come to designate concisely and with odium as *her*. This was the terror that salted my de-light. Father, meanly, or perhaps to harden me, would pretend sometimes to give the alarm: "Hist! There she is!" causing me to turn pale while he shook his head disparagingly.

When our picnic was over Father lay back, hands behind his head, hat tilted over his eyes. He had that slightly drugged look which suggested to me that he was about to take a nap, a suspicion confirmed when he murmured drowsily:

"Go and pick yourself some rasps."

The raspberries grew wild everywhere in the wood. No

need to go far, there was a great patch of them quite near. Once I was amongst the tall stiff canes, safely concealed, the spirit of adventure pricked my scalp. Transformed in a flash, no longer Terry's poor little caper, I became the hero of Father's evening stories. Picking the honey-sweet berries, staining my face and hands with the crimson juice, I sustained myself on desert islands, staved off hunger in untrodden jungles, quenched a burning thirst at desert oases whither I had been borne on the backs of camels.

Suddenly, a series of earsplitting splashes sent me running back to Father. He was standing on the bank, rigid with effort, his rod, gripped in both hands, curved in an incredible arc while a big fish tore madly about the pool, twisting and plunging, leaping into the air and restriking the surface with thunderous detonations.

For interminable minutes the struggle continued, while the pool boiled and I quivered in an anguish of suspense lest the prize should escape us. At last, slowly, the lovely fish came in, all spent and defeated, its silver made golden by the peaty water, and Father, with a quick but gentle pull, slid it onto the pebbled sloping bank.

"Oh, what a beauty!" I shouted.

"A fresh run sea trout." Father too, was breathing with difficulty. "At least five pounds."

When we were calmer and had admired our trophy from every aspect, Father decided we had done enough for the day, since the sun had now broken through strongly. Really, he was dying to show the fish to Mother, who was often openly diverted by the size of our catch. He bent down, passed a stout cord through the trout's gills then, lifting the fish till it was suspended at waist level, tied the cord securely round his middle.

"What the eye doesn't see, the heart won't grieve for," he observed jocularly, putting on his cape. "Let's be off, boy. No, not that way . . ."

Father, enchanted by his success, was clearly in his most exalted mood. Cordoned by the heavy fish beneath the hampering but necessary cape, I saw that he had decided against the long detour through the woods. Ignoring my alarmed protests, he declared that we would take the short cut through the fields after crossing the main avenue below the big house. I could only follow.

"Sunday afternoon." He calmed me as we approached the shrubbery bordering the drive. "There won't be a soul about."

"But look!" I pointed to the lion standard above the house. "The flag's up. *She's* there!"

"Probably having an after dinner snooze."

He had barely spoken when, emerging from behind a clump of rhododendrons, we almost collided with a short, plump figure in a light muslin dress who, from the shade of her lace edged parasol, stared at us in shocked surprise. I almost fainted. It was *her*. I wanted to bolt, but my legs refused their function. Father, on the other hand, apart from an involuntary start and a momentary loss of his natural colour, was managing to conceal his discomposure. He removed his hat and bowed.

"Your ladyship." He paused and gave a slight cough. I knew he was racking his brains as to how he could get us out of this frightful disaster. "I trust you won't regard this as an intrusion. If I may explain . . ."

"Ye may," came the reply in the broadest Scots, mingling suspicion with extreme displeasure. "Whit's your *wull* in ma policies?"

"Gladly," Father exclaimed, rather pointlessly, and coughed again. Then, by some sleight of hand and without disturbing the folds of his cape, he produced one of his business cards from his inside breast pocket. "Madam, if I may introduce myself," he said, politely yet winningly, pressing the card on the little woman. She took no notice of it whatsoever. "The fact is that my partner, Mynheer Hagemann of Rotterdam . . . you see his name on my card . . . is by way of being something of a horticulturist. A Dutchman, you understand they are all gardeners there. When in conversation the other day I chanced to mention your famous collection of orchids he asked, indeed begged me, to seek an appointment for him. He expects to be in Winton some time next month. And so, if you could be so gracious . . ." He broke off.

Silence. Lady Whalebone's gaze, passing from one to the other, had come to rest on me and in her eyes I saw a fateful recognition. Finally she put on her pince-nez, suspended from her neck by a fine gold chain, and studied the card.

"Hagemann's Royal Dutch Yeast." Her eyes again sought mine. "A close relation of the staff of life."

"Yes, madam," Father acknowledged with the modesty and assurance of one who has made his case good. Standing easily, almost playfully, he was quite unconscious of the mysterious yet steady drip, drip of water which was already forming a sizeable pool exactly between his feet. My heart sank. Had *she* seen it? And what in heaven's name would she make of it?

"So your partner is interested in orchids." She meditated. "I thocht the Dutch grew only tulips."

"Certainly, tulips, m'am. Fields of them. But orchids also."

The ghost of a smile playing around Lady Meikle's lips gave me hope. Alas, it was illusory.

"Come awa' then." She spoke with decision. "I'll show ye my collection and ye can tell your fancy Mynheer all about it."

"But m'am, I only hoped for an appointment," Father protested. "We could not think of deranging you *on a Sunday*."

"The better the day, my dear sir, the better the deed. Indeed, I insist. I'm rather interested to jalouse how both of the two of ye will react to my orchids."

Father, for the first time, looked thoroughly taken aback, at a loss for words. But there was no escape. We were led by our cicerone up the avenue, along the terrace that fronted the imposing mansion and into the conservatory, a great high Victorian erection of glass and ornate white painted ironwork that adjoined the far wing of the house. We entered this crystal palace through double glass doors that were closed carefully behind us and, greeted by a waft of humid air, were immediately in the tropics. Towering palms rose to the high roof mingling with giant ferns spreading enormous fronds far above my head, banana trees with bunched fingers of miniature fruits, strange twining creepers, spikey yuccas, great lily pads the size of tea trays floating on a pool, masses of luscious greenery of which I could not even guess the names, and amongst all this, coloured wickedly, gleaming like brilliant jungle birds, the orchids.

In my normal state how ravished I would have been by this gorgeous materialization of so many of my dreams. Even now my anxiety was half forgotten. I gazed in wonder, dreamily following our guide as, in a manner which had turned discursive, even pleasant, she demonstrated her specimens to Father. It was hot, extremely hot. Already I was beginning to sweat. Deep banks of pipes ran everywhere, emitting a rising steamy vapour, and was it my overstrained fancy that wherever the access of calefaction became most intense Father was made to stop, examine, and listen? Looking at him directly for the first time since we entered I saw that he was suffering. Yes, suffering acutely, in his heavy woollen clothing. Great drops of perspiration were running down his face which, while not as yet matching the colour of the tomatoes in Mother's sandwiches, had taken on the hue of stewed rhubarb.

"Ye find it a trifle close, maybe. Will ye not remove your cape?"

"Thank you m'am, thank you, no," Father said hurriedly. "I am not at all inconvenienced. I rather enjoy a warm air."

"Then take a look at this verra special cataleya. There . . . ye'll get closer if ye bend forward over the pipes."

Unlike the other orchids, which hitherto had been unremarkable for their odour, this cataleya seemed to emit a most distinctive smell. It smelled, in a word, as father leaned over, of fish.

A fresh horror struck at me. Our trout, habituated to the chilly waters of the ocean, was not taking kindly to this equatorial pyrexia.

"Beautiful . . . extremely beautiful . . ." Father now scarcely knew what he was saying as, surreptitiously, he sluiced his drenched brow with a back handed flick.

"My dear sir," broke in our tormentor solicitously, "ye're positively sweltering. I insist on ye taking off that heavy cape."

"No," Father gasped in a hollow tone. "The fact is . . . we are really grateful but . . . an important engagement . . . already late . . . time getting on . . . we must be going . . ."

"Nonsense! I'll not hear o't. Ye havena' seen but the half of my treasures."

And while our temperatures mounted and the torrid emanations increased, this terrible little woman made us complete the slow suffocating circuit of the conservatory, forced us even, while she stood below, to climb the white painted iron stair that spiralled to the roof where, intensified by its ascent, the killing heat produced a mirage in which the prospect we had been enjoined to view assumed the appearance of a deep green swelling sea with cool enticing waves in which Father, at least, would willingly have plunged.

At last she opened the double glassed doors. Then, as we

stood weakly in the blessed fresh air she bestowed, first on me, then on Father, a grim yet somehow amiable smile.

"Don't fail to give my regards to your Dutch friend," she said, almost with benevolence. *"And this once ye may keep the fish."*

Father walked all the way down the avenue in total silence. I dared not look at him. How frightful must be his humiliation — the crushed abasement of a man whom I had hitherto believed capable of anything, of coming out top in the most embarrassing and alarming situations. Suddenly I gave a start. Father was laughing, yes, he had begun to laugh. I thought he would never stop. Turning to me with a look of complicity he clapped me companionably on the back.

"The old girl got the better of us, boy. And I'm hanged if I don't like her for it."

With these few words he reinstated himself. My faith in him was restored. That was always Father's way — he had the knack of snatching victory from defeat. But just before we reached home he put a finger to his lips and lowered his left eyelid.

"All the same, we'll not say anything to your mother."

5

⚜ ⚜ ⚜

I HAD MADE my peace with Maggie, an act of amendment for
which, afterwards, I had cause to bless my mother.

Consulting with her on the most appropriate means of
atonement she suggested that I should spend my Saturday
penny on whatever my betrayed friend liked best. I accordingly purchased, at Luckie Grant's, a ha'penny worth of black-
striped balls and the same amount of coloured transfers and
carried these gifts to Maggie's home on the far side of the railway line.

She was seated by a dull fire in the dark little stone-floored
kitchen that smelled of soapsuds. She had a sore throat and
wore a woollen stocking fastened round her neck with a safety
pin. Perhaps because of this, she received me gently, so gently
that I gave way to remorseful tears. For this weakness Maggie
reproved me mildly in words I have never forgotten and which
were so painfully true I must record them in Maggie's own
native idiom.

"Och, Laurie, laddie, ye're a fearfu' greeter. Yer tear-bag is
awfu' near yer e'en."

Maggie's mother was out, to my great relief, for I could not
bear her, not alone because she nagged Maggie, but because,
calling me "love," and other endearments which I knew to be
false, she sought to pump me about my home with insidious

questions such as did my mother get on with my father, what had she paid for her new hat, and why did we eat fish on Friday?

All that afternoon Maggie and I sat together at the wooden table and stuck the coloured transfers on our hands and arms while sucking the black-striped balls. Cementing our restored amity I gave her a lucky medal which I said would cure her throat. Actually this was a little silver St. Christopher medal of the size and shape of a sixpence, but as I dared not invoke the religious element, I made it out to be a charm. Maggie, who liked charms, was delighted and when we parted repeatedly assured me that we were friends again.

In spite of our mutual pledge I did not see much of Maggie that winter. My poor friend was never free. Nevertheless, as I sat at my homework I was pleasantly aware, listening with one ear to my parents' conversation, that good things were being prepared for Maggie and for her betterment.

As our circumstances improved, Father had been urging Mother to seek some help in the work of the house. He had never liked to see her scrubbing or sweeping although I must confess that he rarely offered his assistance in such undertakings. Mother, I truly believe, in spite of the apparent absurdity of the statement, enjoyed housework, and the deep satisfaction of creating a spotless, shining, well-ordered home. She was what the Scots term "house proud" and I well remember how, on those days when she had washed the kitchen and scullery floors, I was made to take my shoes off and tread in my stockings on the spread newspapers. Hitherto she had demurred at Father's suggestions, but now twin circumstances induced a change of mind: the new piano demanded better care of her hands, and Maggie, now fourteen, was leaving school at the end of the month.

Mother had a tender heart. She was sorry for Maggie and had grown fond of her. She now made a suggestion to Father which he instantly approved and of which I became the instrument when Mother instructed me:

"Laurie dear, when you see Maggie tell her I'd like to speak to her mother."

Next day when Maggie stopped at our house during the lunch hour to say that her mother would "come round" on Saturday evening, Mother took the opportunity of sounding her out. Naturally, I was not present at the interview, but Maggie's expression, as she departed, was proud and happy. When I saw her at school that afternoon she had a new air, an important and entirely superior personality as, pausing only to beam a smile towards me, she confided to the other girls in her class that, freed of the tyranny of these everlasting milk cans, she was to be our maid, to have the small attic bedroom, a new dress and a good wage.

Next day was Saturday. In the afternoon, following her weekly custom, Mother put on her best dove-grey costume and, taking me by the hand, proceeded to the village in the open and friendly manner she invariably adopted on such occasions and which was of course completely the reverse of the attitude affected by her husband. Father's public attitude was really inexcusable. I believe he had been badly hurt in some way, unknown to me, during those early difficult days at Rosebank and he was not one who readily forgave an insult. Mother was different, amiably disposed towards all the world, willing to overlook a slight, eager to make friends, and she sought always to modify Father's "touchiness," to disarm prejudice and soften hostility. These Saturday excursions, although ostensibly for the practical purposes of shopping, envisaged this other objective and during our promenade, while holding herself in readiness to accept and return the few acknowledgements made to her, Mother, moving in a glowing ambience of good feeling, would maintain a lively conversation with me on all sorts of subjects, thus conveying to the village an impression of our strong social instincts.

On this particular afternoon she spent a very agreeable half hour at Miss Todd's, the milliner's, chosing a dark dress and also a new pair of stockings and house shoes for Maggie. Thereafter she had a good gossipy talk with Polly Grant, who now never failed to ask after my cousin Terence, then, emerging from the grocery, she actually received a bow from Mrs. Duthie, elderly wife of the village doctor. Things were looking up for Mother. And this was not all. As we turned to go home, we encountered Pin Rankin, who pegged hard across the road to intercept us.

"Have you a moment, Mrs. Carroll?"

Naturally Mother had as many moments as were desired. Pin, a batchelor, was always shy with women. He took a quick breath, which I knew to be the prelude to a longish speech delivered with the same involvement that, no doubt, had marred his sermons.

"You have a bright boy, m'am. Some of his compositions are outstanding. I read them to the class. But it's not that I wish to speak to you about. The fact is, Lady Meikle is organizing a charity concert for the Children's Home, to be held in the village hall on the fifth of next month, and I wondered, *we* wondered if you would consent to perform a piano solo. I, we would be so pleased and grateful if you would favour us."

I looked sharply at Mother. She had blushed deeply. She did not answer for a moment.

"Oh, do, Mother," I cried. "You know how beautifully you play."

"Yes," she said, in a low voice. "I will play."

On the way home Mother, ordinarily so discursive, remained completely silent. Yet from that silence I knew how deeply this recognition, so long delayed, had gratified her.

In the kitchen Father was brewing some herbal tea at the stove. His cold was apparently not quite gone and he had taken to dosing himself with a concoction of his own. Now, he looked seedy and in a mood that was far from propitious. When Mother disclosed her great news he stared at her. I could see that he was going to throw this precious invitation back in the teeth of the village.

"Naturally you told them to go to the devil."

"No, Conor." Mother shook her head firmly. "It's a good thing. It means that they're taking to us at last."

"They've only come to you because they need you."

But Mother had known he would be difficult. She was determined to have her way. Countering all his arguments, she talked Father over. In the end, he became reconciled, in fact quite puffed up with the idea. Realizing that Lady Meikle was "behind it" he was inclined, with the vanity of a reformed lady-killer, to attribute the invitation to his influence upon her, the result of that memorable meeting.

"You see, boy," he gave me a conspirator's nod, "she hasn't forgotten us."

That jocular glance of Father's seemed to set a seal upon the new pattern of our life. We were getting on in the world. Father was prospering, Mother was to play at the concert, I had been praised by Pin for the little essays he set for the weekend homework and to crown all, in the village people were actually beginning to like us. What a lucky boy I was, and how shining a future stretched before me.

That evening, as we were seated by the fire, variously engaged, the front door bell pealed. An unusual sound. Looking up from the pursuit of knowledge in *Pear's Encyclopedia*, I wondered, in mild alarm, who had come to breach our little castle. But Mother, knitting placidly, merely said:

"That'll be Maggie's mother. Run, Laurie, and ask her to come in."

I went to the door, and presently returned.

"She says she'd rather not come in."

Mother looked surprised but, rolling up her knitting and spiking it with her needles, she immediately got up. I followed her half way to the door. Already I surmised that something was wrong but nothing had prepared me for the violence or the virulence of the attack.

"You're not to have my Maggie."

Mother seemed dumbfounded.

"If it's a question of a little more money . . . I'm quite willing . . ."

"Not all the money in the world will buy my Maggie."

Was she drunk? No, peering into the darkness, I saw a face possessed, distorted by rage and spite. I shall not attempt to re-create the stupid and malicious abuse she launched at Mother. When I first contemplated this story of my childhood I pledged myself to record no ill of anyone. But Maggie's mother was that unfortunate creature, a woman so envenomed by misfortune she sustained herself on hatred. Maggie had always been her drudge, the outlet for her rankling grudges, the living, ragged evidence of her own ill usage. She could not bear to think of her escaping to a happier and more comfortable life. Mother was trembling now under a fresh tirade in the midst of which, after the words "you and your papist medals," I saw something thrown, a small silver disc, that hit the floor and rolled on its edge to my feet. The lucky charm I had given Maggie. As I picked it up I saw that Father had come silently forward, still holding the *Herald* which somehow increased his air of studied calm.

"My good woman." He spoke moderately, without rancour, yet in a voice of ice. "You have said enough. We are all fond of your daughter here. Anything we have done or proposed to do has been with the best intentions. But as you so obviously dislike and distrust us, we can only yield to your wishes. And now will you please withdraw."

She was silenced. She had expected invective and was prepared for it, not for this dignified restraint. Before she could collect herself, Father quietly closed the door.

How I admired Father at that moment. Knowing him to be capable of the most inflammatory tempers, of truly majestic displays of contemptuous satire, he might well have reduced the incident to a vulgar brawl. But we ourselves were unduly silent for the rest of that evening. On Mother's account Father was obviously put out, the measure of which was that he lit a cigarette. He did not smoke — he hadn't the inclination, or perhaps he was vain of his beautiful teeth and did not want to discolour them — but in rare moments of stress he would resort to a Mitchell's Special No. 1. And now, puffing inexpertly, with one eye half closed against the smoke and the other directed at intervals reassuringly towards Mother, he sought to compose himself and her. Next day at school news of Maggie's predicament had reached the playground and obliquely, from the corner of my eye, I could not fail to note the ring of her tormentors. But Maggie, though downcast, was tough and could give back as good as she received. After class she waited and, taking my hand, walked down the road with me.

"Anyway, we're still friends, Laurie. And one of these days I *will* come and work for your mother."

But Mother was still upset. She had not the heart to practice for the concert. However, on the evening of the last day of the month, after she had prepared supper, she went to the piano while waiting for Father's return. I was in my place at the window, yet so absent in my thoughts that the whistle of Father's train reached me from another world. Yet vaguely I had begun to be aware that he was a long time in coming from the station when I heard the familiar nightly click of the front door. Mother immediately broke off and went to meet him. As I turned away it was almost dusk outside. Suddenly, through the side window, I saw two men moving slowly up the road. Pressing close to the glass and rubbing away the mist of my breath I made out Jim, the station porter, and the signalman who worked the level crossing gates. They were passing now very slowly, in single file, with bent heads, carrying something between them. Was it a long plank, covered with a blanket? At first I did not take it in, yet I received so sinister an impression from that sagging elongated thing and from the slow pace of the men who bore it that suddenly I was terribly afraid. I ran to tell Father. He was standing in the lobby with Mother. He had not taken off his hat or coat. His face was white with shock. In a voice I did not recognize he was saying to Mother:

"Her foot must have caught in the points, the train comes in so slow. But, Grace," his voice broke, "if you'd seen the poor thing we lifted up."

Mother, with a terrible cry, covered her face with her hands.

Dumb with horror, I knew no immediate pain, only that Maggie had done with the milk cans for good.

6

ᎦᎦᎦ

How SAD and confused, above all how unforeseen, was the period that followed. Even now, disentangling it from memory, I still cannot view it without pain. Surely no one could have blamed Mother for Maggie's death. On that same night Father had gone back to the level crossing with a lantern from the signal box and found, wedged in the switch "points" of the rails, the torn off heel of Maggie's boot. My poor friend, trapped in this vice, had clearly made a frantic effort to free herself. At the inquiry the procurator fiscal had made it clear that if Maggie had wished to destroy herself she would not first have carefully inserted her foot in the switch then tried to tear it loose. And I knew too from Maggie's last hopeful remark to me that no such intention had ever entered her mind. And yet, despite the evidence, the certainty of accident was rejected by the village in favour of the more awful alternative and Maggie, exalted by tragedy, became a martyr to our interference.

The theme was played with variations. Father, bitterly reporting the latest gossip as we sat at dinner, did not spare us. If we had not come between a devoted mother and her only child, dangling false promises, arousing illusory hopes, if only we had "let the poor girl *be*" she would still be alive and happy. And, of all people, what need had we of a servant!

Mother, who had not stirred from the house for days, and who now at our evening meal was barely touching her food, pressed her hands together.

"We'll have to leave, Conor."

"Leave?" Father stopped eating.

"Yes. Get away from this wretched Ardencaple. You've always wanted to."

"What!" Both Father's eyebrows shot up dangerously. "Run away! Bolt like a rabbit! What do you think I am? There's nothing wrong with Ardencaple *itself*. I like the place and country here. Now especially, nothing would make me leave. Besides . . ." He spoke slowly, with special meaning. "Don't forget you have an engagement at the concert."

"That!" Mother cried, all the softness in her nature shrinking from the mere idea. "I'm going to no concert, never, never."

"But you are, Grace."

"No, no. I can't face it."

"You must."

"I'm not capable of it. I'd break down."

"You won't."

"But, Conor . . . to be up there, before them all, alone."

"You won't be alone. I'll be with you. And so will Laurence. Don't you see, lass," he was looking at her grimly, "if you don't go it'll be a clear admission of guilt. We are utterly blameless for poor Maggie's accident. So we *must* go, all of us, stand up for ourselves, and show that we don't give a tinker's curse for what they say."

Already I was shaking at a prospect that had suddenly reached out chilly arms towards me. Yet while, like Mother, I sat dismayed, Father faced us with a calm, remote determination.

"You'll see," he said, as though talking to himself. "Yes, you . . . will . . . see."

On the afternoon of the concert Father came home by an earlier train. Under his arm he carried a long stiff cardboard box, the contents of which were revealed to me when, at half past six, Mother came slowly, almost unwillingly, downstairs looking lovely, but oh, so fearfully pale, and wearing a new blue silk dress, cut low in the neck and with a long pleated skirt.

"Yes," Father said in a hard voice, after studying her critically. "Exactly the colour of your eyes."

"It's beautiful, Con," Mother said faintly, "and must have cost a ransom. But oh, I feel so nervous."

"You won't, lass," Father said, in that same gritty tone. Then, to my amazement — for I had never seen such a thing in the house before and knew my father to be of a most temperate habit that rarely took him beyond a glass of beer with his customers — he produced a flat bottle distinctly labelled: *Martell's Three Star Brandy*. Carefully, as though measuring out a medicine, he poured a substantial draught into a glass, added a sudden generous splash, then held it out to Mother.

"No, Con, no."

"Get it down," Father said implacably. "It'll put new heart in you."

While Mother hesitated there came the clop-clop of horses' hooves and the rattle of a cab drawing up at our gate. Trembling at the sound, she feverishly snatched the glass and, while I watched, wide-eyed, emptied it at a gulp that made her choke.

The darkness of the cab brought a temporary relief. I sat on the edge of the seat, stiff in my starched collar and Sunday suit. Father was wearing his best clothes too, and his moustache had been trimmed and curled so that the points had a combative upward sweep. At least we were showing a brave front to whatever lay ahead. And suddenly, as the red glare from the smithy fire lit up the interior of the cab, I saw Mother reach out and press Father's hand.

"I'm not afraid, now, Con. I feel all warm and strong. I know I can do my best."

Father laughed softly, yes, to my shivering amazement the man actually laughed.

"Didn't I tell you, dearest lass?"

"Yes, Con darling." Mother's voice held a strange note. "Only . . . I feel I want you to kiss me."

Was the woman mad too? To my shamed horror, unmindful of me and of the chasm that confronted us, they embraced each other closely, after which Mother gave a sustained, comforted sigh.

It was a minor relief to get her safely delivered at the performers' side door, then Father took my hand and we went round the building to the front entrance. The hall was full, already people were standing at the back, but at the front, immediately beneath the platform, places had been reserved for relatives of the performers. Towards there Father advanced, with his head high in the air, so high indeed, that while himself conspicuously visible, he need recognize nobody. However, despite this strategic posture, he had not failed to note the crowd, made up mostly of young men, at the back of the hall, for he hissed cryptically into my ear:

"Outsiders from Levenford . . . there'll be trouble."

Our entry had been well timed. We had barely taken our seats when the proceedings were opened by Lady Meikle, who bustled on to the stage, made a short speech indicating the purpose of the concert and asked the audience to be receptive towards the artists.

Piper Finlater, Piper Finlater,
Played the Cock o' the North!

While the last verse still vibrated against the roof more applause burst out, stamping of heavy boots, and repeated shouts of " 'core, 'core." And now Mother was in full cry. Scarcely hesitating she broke into what I can only call a medley, or rather an improvisation — since she played many of them by ear — of the old Scottish airs: "Ye Banks and Braes," "Green Grow the Rashes, O," "Over the Sea to Skye," and ending with the local favourite, "The Bonnie Banks of Loch Lomond." The effect was tremendous, even those most unresponsive in the body of the hall, whom I had thought to be our enemies, were conquered, beating time now, nodding and humming, swept away by this brilliant melodic surge of sentiment and national spirit.

I was glowing with pride, my palms hot with clapping in homage to this wonderful mother whose undreamed of cleverness and skill had saved the day for all of us.

And they wanted more. Even when Mother rose from the piano they would not let her go. Someone unseen in the wings must have signed to her to yield. What would she play now? The answer came quickly and it seemed that her eyes had sought us out. She struck the first chords of Moore's "Far from the Land," a tribute, not to her old loyalties, but to the new. And she was singing it, too, calmly and confidently, as though she were sitting at the piano at home. I scarcely breathed as her voice rose, clear and sweet, in the perfect attentive stillness of the hall.

Father, leaning back, twirling his moustache, and with a strange rapt smile, had kept his gaze rivetted on Mother as though he could scarcely believe his eyes. And when at last, after a final curtsey, she left the stage, he rose abruptly and, demonstrating in every action that the event of the evening was over, he took me by the collar, steered me down the aisle and out of the hall.

We had not long to wait for Mother. She came hurrying down the steps of the upper entrance wearing her coat, with a fringed white shawl round her head, and ran straight towards us. Father gave her such a hug it lifted her off her feet.

"Gracie, Gracie . . ." he murmured in her ear, "I knew you had it in you."

"Oh, Mother!" I was hopping with delight. "You were splendid."

Mother gave a little gasp.

"It was an awful hash of sentiment but I fancied it was the only thing, and I think they liked it."

"They loved it, Mother," I shouted.

"Couldn't have been better," Father purred.

"I didn't want to go on so long, but Lady Meikle made me."

"Ah," said Father, with a satisfied click of his tongue. "I knew the Whalebone would be on our side. But what made you think to do it in the first place? Did she give you the idea?"

"No."

"Who, then?"

Mother gave him a sly glance.

"It must have been your Mr. Martell."

Shouts of delirious laughter from all three of us. What joy, what bliss! What a triumph for the Carrolls.

"Oh, we mustn't, Con," Mother said suddenly. "Think of poor Maggie. You know, all the time I was playing, somehow at the back of my mind I felt I was doing it for her."

We walked back together under the shining moon, Mother and Father arm in arm, talking, talking as though they would never stop, but I did not feel jealous or that I was at all excluded, for Mother with her free hand had found mine and snuggled it into the pocket of her coat. There she held it cosily, all the way home.

How bright the moon was, how clear and high. And our star, the Carroll lucky star, was rising too, yes, rising again, clear and high, to join the galaxy above.

7

THE NEXT DAY was Sunday and, perhaps in a spirit of
thanksgiving, we went to Mass at Drinton, coming home
to a late and rather special lunch of roast duck followed
by the trifle, with crystallised cherries and whipped cream,
that Mother made so well. In the dwindling winter afternoon,
after Father had had a nap, Mother suggested a stroll along
the shore. The golden aura of yesterday still lingered about
her and, in addition, a kind of happy langour which, from
the dreamy reminiscent glances she directed towards him, I
somehow associated with the attentions of Father. Already I
had begun to sense the strong physical attraction that existed
between my parents which in the beginning, overcoming
every conceivable obstacle, had brought them together almost from different worlds and which now endured in a close
responsive union. In later years, when I came to read the
records of other childhoods so often marred by constant
parental strife, by conjugal incompatibility and mutual hatred,
I became more fully aware that in their marriage my mother
and father were uniquely fortunate. Although there were sudden minor storms, provoked by Father's quick temper, they
never lasted more than a few hours and ended in spontaneous
reconciliation. And always between them, even in their si-

lences, there existed a mutual understanding that made my home a safe, warm place in an often threatening world.

This feeling was palpably in the air as, having been to Geddes Point, in the direction opposite to Rosebank, which for reasons I dimly glimpsed Mother always shunned, we were returning slowly through a soft mist gathering on the dead, deserted estuary. The air was so still that the sob of the tide came like the faint echo from some distant sea shell. Mother idled in front, accompanied by Darkie, the Snodgrass farm cat, which often attached itself to her on these excursions. Father and I had fallen some paces behind, competing in a game of "skiffers" and being cautioned, though indulgently, by Mother for our shouts as we counted the skiffs when the flat stones, smoothly polished by endless tides, went skimming and leaping over the calm grey water.

Suddenly, as he threw, Father gave a short wincing cough, straightened, and put his handkerchief to his face. I looked up in surprise, then, with the air of making an announcement, called out importantly:

"Father's nose is bleeding!"

Mother turned round. I saw her expression change. I saw too that the handkerchief was covering Father's mouth. Mother came near.

"Conor, it's your cough."

"It's nothing." He had moved the handkerchief and was staring almost stupidly at a small scarlet stain. "Only a spot. I must just have strained myself."

"But you coughed," she persisted, in concern. "You must sit down and rest."

"It's nothing. Just a stitch in my side." By way of evidence he produced a very slight artificial cough. "See, it's all gone."

Mother made no answer. Her lips came together in a manner more determined than submissive, and as we resumed our way, though she glanced at Father from time to time, there was no languor in her eyes, and her silence persisted until we reached our house.

This cough of Father's, appearing intermittently, particularly in damp weather, and dismissed in his offhand style as "a touch of bronchitis" or even, with a sort of possessive pride as though it were an attribute peculiar to him, as "my bronchial tendency" and alleviated by herbal remedies of his own, had come to be accepted in the family, despite occasional protests by Mother, as a natural phenomenon. I thought nothing of it, and its relation to that absurdly small spot of crimson which Father had himself made light of seemed so improbable or at least so unimportant that immediately we got home I went off whistling to the farm with Darkie to fetch the milk, an evening task that had now devolved on me.

In the byre the milking was still in progress and for perhaps twenty minutes, while the hot milk squirted and frothed into the pail, I waited, amused by the antics of the cat as it caught and lapped the driblets that splashed to the stone flags. Sauntering up the road with my jug of milk I was totally unprepared for the sight of Dr. Duthie's gig standing outside our house, a shock heightened by the fact that the gig lamps were already lit and, magnified by the misty dusk, seeming to typify the personality of the village doctor, were glaring at me like two enormous eyes.

This Dr. Duthie was a formidable figure, and not to me alone. A fierce old red-faced man, past seventy, dressed invariably in corduroy breeches, shiny brown leggings and a baggy velveteen jacket, he stamped in and out of sick rooms like a Highland bull, discharging his diagnosis in a voice comparable to the Erskine foghorn, so forcibly indeed that when he had attended me I was often hit by a spray of saliva upon my cheek. By all the canons of romantic fiction this rough exterior should have harboured a heart of gold. It did not. The doctor was coarse and often brutal with his patients. Caring nothing for public opinion, he was generally admitted to be "a hard nut to crack." He had a farm in the back country where he reared saddle back pigs and was often heard to declare that he preferred them to his patients. If he had a weakness, beyond the bottle of whisky he drank daily and which served him as an *elixir vitae* — for he seemed to grow more potent with every dram — it was for a pretty woman. He squeezed the dairy maids at all the farms he visited while they giggled and pretended to protest, bumping them against the steading wall with his knee. While his manner towards her was less amorous, since he had the wit to know where to stop, I always felt that he had a soft spot for my mother.

Of course, I dared not enter my home while this ogre was in possession. I had suffered enough at his hands. Creeping into the shadow of the wall I peered cautiously into the lighted parlour. Father lay on the sofa, stripped to the waist, while Dr. Duthie, with his ear on a short wooden tube, bent over him. Never had I seen my audacious parent at such disadvantage, so subdued, dominated, almost possessed. The sight was unbearable and, turning away, I slid down and sat with my back to the wall, supporting the warm jug of milk between my knees.

A longish interval elapsed before the front door opened and Dr. Duthie and my mother appeared on the threshold, both figures clearly visible against the lighted lobby. I crouched lower as the doctor's voice boomed out:

"Send to the surgery for the medicine. I'll let ye have the cod liver oil and malt as weel. But mind, woman," he pressed Mother's arm, giving point to his words by a series of reproving yet caressing shakes as though trying to turn her towards him, "the main thing is to get him out of here. Didn't I tell you at Rosebank to keep away from the shore? It does nobody good to spend their lives on damp mud and silt. Forbye, river fogs are fair poison for a man with his chest."

I did not properly interpret this pronouncement, I was too fully occupied in watching Dr. Duthie safely off the premises and into his gig. Nor, when I went into the house, was Mother disposed to elaborate upon it. Her mood was not communicative and, relieving me of the milk jug, she quietly set about preparing our tea.

For two days Father remained at home, restively and with a very ill grace, then went back to work. And although I did notice the conferences, yes, and arguments, that began, and were continued, between my parents, if I gave any thought to them at all, I assumed them to be connected with the business of the yeast. Everything seemed to have returned to a happy normality. Father, energetic as ever, soon, in typical fashion, discarded his bottle of medicine and consigned the jar of cod liver oil and malt to the dustbin. I was quite unprepared when one April afternoon, as I came rushing in from school, Mother, wearing all her best clothes and with the air of having returned from a journey, took me aside.

"Laurence, we are leaving this house next month and moving to Ardfillan." Quickly, reassuringly, seeing my look of consternation: "To such a nice place, dear. Really a move for the better."

This sudden prospect of change, always alarming to a child, quite disconcerted me. All at once Ardencaple had never seemed more attractive. I was now altogether at home in school where I had moved up two classes. I liked Pin, and had become friendly with a few of the boys. Last Saturday I had caught two speckled trout in the Geilston burn. And we were to leave all this when everything was going so well for us.

Mother must have read this in my face, for she put her arms round me, smiling at me confidingly, in such a manner that I knew all this to be her doing and that she was deeply pleased with it.

"Ardfillan is a lovely town, dear. And our new flat is high up on the hill and not far from the moors. I'm sure you'll like it."

8

THE REMOVAL was accomplished with surprising ease and, as Mother had promised, our new home proved to be a great advance upon the little villa we had relinquished. Like the town of Ardfillan, it quite overcame me with its splendours. Reaching up hill from an expanse of estuary so wide as to be almost open sea, Ardfillan was a fashionable place, a select resort with a discreet pier, promenade, and bandstand, yet, at the same time, a residential town favoured by wealthy Winton business men who utilized the fast train service to the city, and by others, of equal or greater affluence, who had retired. Big houses, pretentiously styled and surrounded by large enclosed gardens, studded the hillside, making the most of a choice view of the Gareloch and the Kyles of Bute yet in no way intruding upon the wide sweep of heather moor that reached up behind to Glen Fruin and on to the shores of Loch Lomond. There were many superior shops, a private circulating library, and two of the most exclusive schools in Scotland, one Beechfield for boys, the other St. Anne's for girls. I soon discerned, too, a particular well-bred manner of speech, an accent rather, that stamped and distinguished this society, was indeed obligatory for admission to its membership. There existed, in short, an air of "tone" which

Mother immediately liked, which Father ignored, and which at first intimidated me.

Prince Albert Terrace enjoyed a good situation well up the hill amongst some excellent neighbouring mansions, and although slightly dimmed, still maintained much of an earlier elegance. Built of finely cut stone, in a semi-Georgian, part Victorian style, with elaborate double entrance porticos and wide bay windows, it consisted of a number of large luxurious maisonettes with separate, roomy flats above. These maisonettes had finely proportioned high-ceilinged rooms, an attractive ornamental garden in front and the privacy of a long walled-in lawn behind. Naturally we could not aspire to such grandeur, but in the storey above, in flat number seven, all freshly papered and painted, we had ample accommodation, and here we faced a future that seemed favourable, especially to my father who, responding to the change of scene and the briskness of the air, which he inhaled deeply in breathing exercises morning and evening at the open window, was full of sanguine expectation. Yet I was troubled by something altogether new in my mother's expression, when she paused in her arrangement of the house, a subtle harassment which, when aware that I was looking at her, she would banish with a smile.

In Ardfillan there was no excuse for Sunday self-indulgence. We had in the lower town the double advantage of St. Mary's Church and its parochial school in Clay Street. Moreover the first person to call upon us one afternoon, and to win us utterly by his frank gaiety and unselfconscious charm, was the young parish priest, Father Macdonald, a Highlander from Invernesshire who had studied at the excellent Blaires College in Aberdeen. Angus Macdonald was the kind of man whom, as my father put it, even the staunchest Orangeman must have liked. Mother, still a little scared of priests, whom she had never seen at close quarters, could not believe her eyes, when after tea, he got up and, to my unrestrained delight, demonstrated the Highland Fling. In due course, under his tactful persuasion, certain technical adjustments, which I scarcely understood, were made in my parents' marriage which reconciled them to ecclesiastical orthodoxy. Moreover, without in any way deploring the inadequacy of my own religious knowledge, which was extreme, he suggested that, at least for the present, I should attend the parish school. So to St. Mary's, the following week, I was sent.

I am obliged to confess that while gratified by my advancement to the third class where my teacher, Sister Margaret Mary, seemed prepared to make much of me, I missed my old friend Pin and was not, on the whole, entranced by my new school. To get to Clay Street I had a long walk by a back road that led down hill to the poorest part of the lower town, which was in effect the working class district of Ardfillan. Here in a narrow street, with a tenement building opposite, were the precincts of St. Mary's — church, school, and presbytery, all of raw red brick construction, practical, but starkly indicative of restricted means. So too, amongst the school children, did this sad note of poverty prevail. They came almost entirely from the poor, immediate neighbourhood of the church, many of them children of despised Irish "tatie howkers" who had come to work in the Clydeside potato fields, and some, alas, in a very ragged state. They played odd games which I did not understand, the makeshift games of the underprivileged, using clay marbles, tin cans, chalk-marked walls, balls made of paper and cloth tied together with odd pieces of string. The truth is that Ardfillan Catholics who had the means sent their children to other schools, to Levenford Academy or to the Jesuit College in Winton, though never, of course, to Beechfield, an establishment which remained supremely and exclusively patrician. And so, despite the goodness I found there, the general effect of St. Mary's was depressive. A feeling of social inferiority was immediately implied and communicated to me, a sort of spiritual wound, deriving from my religion. When I tried to convey something of this to Mother, who had other more serious preoccupations, she would try to comfort me.

"It's for your good, dear, and it won't be for long. You must just put up with it for the time being."

Lack of companionship was my greatest cross. I use this phrase since I was by this time learning the idiom of the saints. Whatever their moral excellence, Mother could not bring herself to allow me to be friendly with boys who, as Father put it, had no backside to their trousers. And so, feeling myself neither fish nor fowl, I mooned around during my leisure hours in boredom and solitude.

My sole recourse, though it served merely to increase my discontent, was to wander across the hill to the beautiful green playing fields of Beechfield School. Peering well concealed behind the surrounding hawthorn hedge, I watched the games in progress with a burning, envious longing. Here was everything that I craved, twin white goal posts flanking well marked green pitches on which the players, many as small as I, in their varying fascinating house colours ranging from scarlet to vivid blue, thudded balls about, ran, passed, tackled and scrummed, in a manner to be expected of boys who would go to Fettes, Glenamond, Loretto, or even, as some did, to the best English public schools. When I could bear it no longer I turned moodily for home, kicking imaginary goals so wildly that I stubbed my toes against the kerb, thus causing Mother to complain that I was ruining my new boots.

One Saturday, when at a particularly loose end, I was attempting to amuse myself by taking pot shots at imaginary targets in the road outside the front garden of No. 7. Suddenly one of the stones flew sideways out of my hand and, describing a lethal parabola, crashed through the front window of the maisonette above which we lived. The icy splintering of falling glass horrified me. I dashed upstairs to Mother.

"You must go at once and apologize. The lady's name is Miss Greville. Say that you will pay for it. Come and I'll give your face a quick wipe." She called after me as I went out: "Mind now, your best manners."

Agitatedly, I pressed the bell of Miss Greville's front door. Out of the corner of one eye I could see the big jagged hole in the window. An elderly maid in a neat cap and uniform admitted me. She had grey hair and, I thought, a discouraging expression.

"Wait here," she told me, when I had explained the nature of my visit.

As I stood in the hall, I was struck by the remarkable sight of two crossed oars on the wall, both cut down in size, and with the blades painted bright blue. Other unusual objects were catching my eye, notably a pair of foils, but now the maid had returned and was showing me into the front room where Miss Greville, standing by the fatal window, turned to take a good look at me. I, in turn, looked at her.

She was a tall, solid woman of, I guessed, about forty-five, full bosomed and exceedingly erect. She had a pale, full face, its fulness exaggerated by her light coloured hair puffed out at the sides under pads, and by her tight, stiffly starched collar fastened with a stud. Her dress was simple, even severe: a grey trailing skirt and white blouse over which dangled the thin chain of her pince-nez. She looked what she was, unalterably a gentlewoman, and also what she had been, a school mistress. I had heard my mother say that she had taught, at one time, in St. Anne's Girls' School. She would have been to me at that moment a formidable figure but for a certain absence of manner, an air that detached her from the more sordid realities of life amongst which I was one.

"Please, miss, I have broken your window."

"So it appears." She spoke in a high, clear voice, her accent not of Ardfillan, but rather what the local accent unsuccessfully affected. "At least it was honourable of you to come of your own free will."

I accepted the unworthy compliment in silence.

"How did it happen?"

"I was throwing, please, miss."

"Young Carroll . . . I assume you are young Carroll . . . do not address me as thought I were the girl in a teashop. You may call me Miss Greville, at least until our intimacy develops. What were you throwing."

"Stones, Miss . . . Greville."

"Stones! Good heavens, what a depraved habit. I shouldn't mind you breaking my window with a ball. But stones! Why?"

"If you want to know," I answered, beginning to warm up, "it's because I've a pretty good aim. I can hit any post on the other side of the road you like."

"You can?" she exclaimed, with a show of interest.

"Shall I show you?"

"No, not with stones." She paused. "Don't you ever throw a ball?"

"No, Miss Greville. I haven't got one."

She studied me, almost with pity, then, telling me to sit down, she went out. While she was gone, I sat on the edge of a stool and looked about me. The big room baffled yet awed me. Strange pieces of furniture, the like of which I had never seen, not dark and shiny with French polish like our best mahogany suite from the Emporium, but mostly of a faded, honey colour, the chairs with seats worked in coloured threads, an inlaid cabinet revealing china patterned in yellow and gold, the carpet a soft grey with a central design of faded pink. Flowers were in the window space and also in a great blue bowl on the piano which, bearing no resemblance to ours, was long and flat.

My vision had travelled to the mantelpiece on which stood a considerable number of small silver cups, when Miss Greville came back.

"You may have this." As I stood up she handed me a ball. "It has a history, which probably wouldn't interest you. It belonged to my brother."

"The one with the oars?" I asked, feeling myself inspired.

"No, no. Not the wet bob. The other younger one." She smiled absently, and though not unkind, it was to my regret unmistakably a smile of dismissal. I had not wished to come but now, strangely, I did not want to go. These mysterious references to wet and presumably dry Bobs intrigued me. I made an effort to prolong the conversation.

"Doesn't your young brother want the ball himself?"

"He doesn't want anything now," she rejoined impersonally. "He was killed two years ago at Spion Kop."

"Oh, Miss Greville," I exclaimed in a burst of sympathy. "He gave his life for his King and country."

She considered me with inexpressible repugnance.

"Don't be a sentimental little prig, or our acquaintance, hitherto brief and uneventful, will cease forthwith." And she rang the bell for me to be shown out.

My mother, although distressed that I had forgotten to offer payment for the window, evinced both interest and pleasure when I gave her an account of my visit, from which I tactfully suppressed the final passage. Ever since our arrival she had been politely curious about our neighbour. But the ball, on inspection, seemed rather profitless. Hard, covered in leather, with a sewn seam, it did not bounce and was in every way unsympathetic to my usual practices. That evening I showed it to Father.

"It's a cricket ball," he explained. "And it's been played with."

"She told Laurence it had a history," Mother interposed interestedly.

"No doubt." Father gave her his ironic smile. "According to the house agent, she's full of history. They were very grand people at one time. A big estate near Cheltenham. But her papa went through most of it, and she took up teaching. First at Cheltenham College, then at St. Anne's. But she's given it up now."

"I wonder why?" Mother meditated.

Father's smile deepened.

"I am led to believe," he murmured in his best manner, "that in certain of her manifestations she is inclined to be a trifle pec-ul-iar."

He gave to the word an intonation it had in a popular song of the day which began "Oh, isn't she pec-ul-iar."

"Nonsense," Mother exclaimed defensively. "That's just idle gossip. She seems a perfect lady to me, and she was exceedingly kind to Laurie. I mean to bow and thank her next time we meet."

In this way, through the broken window, our momentous acquaintance with Miss Greville was begun.

9

HE ACKNOWLEDGEMENT, correct in every way and even
reserved, that Mother made towards Miss Greville some
days later met with an agreeable response. Our neighbour, living alone and with, apparently, a restricted circle of
friends, seemed disposed to an acquaintanceship. She called
and left her card. Ten days later Mother returned the call and
was given afternoon tea, an entertainment from which she returned flushed with pleasure and teeming with exciting
news.

Miss Amelia Greville, she reported to Father and me at
supper, was charming, and very much, Mother stressed the
words, a lady. Her furniture and silver, which had come from
the family home near Cheltenham, were lovely, in fact everything in the house was in exquisite taste. She was artistic, fond
of music, played the 'cello, and hoped to arrange duets with
Mother. An enthusiastic botanist, she had displayed a wonderful album of pressed wild flowers. She often had gone climb-
ing in Switzerland. Her parents were dead. She had two
brothers who had been educated at Eton, the surviving one
now farming in Kenya. She attended St. Jude's, a church notably High Anglican, and was therefore well disposed towards
Catholics. She was most . . . Suddenly meeting Father's eye,

bent on her with more than usual ironic indulgence, Mother had broken off.

"Yes," she blushed slightly, "she was nice to me. But quite apart from that, I like her. And you know, Con, I have missed having a woman friend, especially with you away all day."

"Then I'm glad you've found one," Father said generously, "only don't . . . well, don't push too hard, lass."

I did not in the least agree with Father. Miss Greville had deeply impressed me. Indeed I had fallen into the habit, when I returned from my ragged school, of hanging around the front garden in the hope, which so far had proved illusory, of attracting her attention. Now, thinking of those fascinating blue oars, I said rather wistfully:

"It must be nice to have had a brother at a school like Eton, even if you didn't go there yourself."

Father laughed, as if he found something in my remark, or my manner of making it, to amuse him.

"Don't worry, my boy. St. Mary's is only a stopgap. Things are going to turn up trumps for you pretty soon."

He was in excellent spirits these days. The change of air undoubtedly suited him. He enjoyed the express, luxurious train service between Winton and Ardfillan for which he had a first class season ticket. He was rising in the world, an unmistakable promise of prosperity was implied in his words, his manner, his elegant, well groomed person. He seemed quite recovered from his strange mishap on the Ardencaple shore and did not fail to remind us that his own efforts were mainly responsible for this happy result. When we left Ardencaple Dr. Duthie had given him a note of introduction to a colleague in Ardfillan. This was Dr. Ewen, a thin, stooping, soft stepping, elderly little man with hollow cheeks and a tuft of grey beard always carefully trimmed to a point. With his silent approach, almost on tip-toe, his manner maintained a gravity unvaryingly professional, and he was known to be clever.

At first sight Father disliked him. "He has a graveyard face," he reported to Mother and thereafter, although periodic examinations had been advised, he reduced his visits to the doctor's house to a minimum, and had recently allowed them to lapse altogether. Mother half suspected that some sort of disagreement had occurred, that Father had, as she put it, "fallen out" with Dr. Ewen. On the other hand, on principle, he had never liked doctors; his amused and sceptical distrust of the profession had long been a feature of our household. "Burnt sugar and water," he would scoff with a shake of his head, indulgent towards our gullibility, as he watched Mother — who had a steady belief in tonics and administered them to me regularly — measuring out a tablespoonful of my Parrish's Chemical Food.

He believed in nature and in the natural restorative powers of the body. Thus, while conforming to the rules of hygiene imposed by Dr. Duthie — whose strong words, which had probably shaken him when they were delivered, still retained some force — he followed confidently a health regime of his own. He had evolved an elaborate system of breathing exercises, and a diet rich in butter and cream supported — though he was always a temperate drinker — by Guinness's stout. He slept between blankets with the window open, wore woollen underwear next the skin, and red rubber soles to his shoes.

So all was going well with Father, and with us. Yet gradually it dawned on me that Mother was not altogether satisfied with Father's interpretation of his own condition. How was this made evident? Perhaps in her extra solicitude towards him, yet more probably by those moments of abstraction when she would pause suddenly in her work as though a sudden anxiety had dispossessed her happiness, and a play of shadows and reflections would flit across her face, imperceptible almost, yet revealing to one who translated everything, even her most obscure expressions, with complete and intuitive fidelity.

One evening, as I sat at the table doing my homework, Mother, who was knitting by the fire, said reflectively and with a casual air, that did not deceive me:

"Conor, dear, isn't it about time you were looking in on Dr. Ewen again?"

Father, reading his *Evening Times* in the easy chair, did not appear to have heard. Then slowly he lowered the paper, looked fixedly at Mother over the top edge.

"I beg your pardon?"

Nerving herself now, Mother repeated her remark, which undoubtedly Father had heard. He studied her.

"Is there any apparent reason why I should go to see your Dr. Ewen?"

"No, Conor. Still, you were advised to have an examination once in a while. And you haven't been to see him for ages."

"True," said Father, in his most sententious tones. "However, as I can't stand the man and always felt worse after I'd been to him than before I went, I decided, reasonably and sensibly, to stay away. In plainer language, I have no faith in him."

"That's rather odd. He's very highly regarded in the town and has a first class practice."

"Yes, he caters for the idle rich and panders to them accordingly. He may have a practice but he's not *practical*."

"How can you say such a thing?"

"Because I found him so." Father spoke heatedly. "If you can believe it, he actually wanted me to knock off work for three months and take a long sea voyage to Madeira. Sea voyage indeed! That may be all right for the old ladies he looks after but it's no use to me."

He broke off, looking as though he had said too much, and attempted to resume his paper. But Mother forestalled him.

"Yes," she said equably, still knitting and revealing nothing of the shock she had received, "I admit Ewen is fussy. Still, there are other doctors. And I do think you ought to find one you can like."

"But why?"

"Well . . . to find out how you're getting on. After all, you haven't quite got rid of your cough."

Father was frowning at her uneasily.

"It's nothing, I've told you a dozen times I've always had that tendency."

"Still . . ." Persuasively, Mother lowered her knitting and leaned forward. "Isn't there a doctor you know of in Winton who could occasionally look you over?"

There was a silence. I waited, my eyes on my book, expectant of an indignant outburst, or at least a dignified and magniloquent refusal. Instead, Father yielded, though half grudgingly:

"Well, lass, if it pleases you . . . there's a chap near my office. Medical Officer for the Caledonia Insurance Company, I run into him occasionally. Since you're so insistent, I might drop in one day and see him for you."

Ignoring the onus Father had skilfully put upon her, Mother gave a soft sigh of relief which, though suppressed, was still audible.

"Then go, Conor. Why not go tomorrow?"

Father, having resumed his paper, apparently took no notice.

On the following evening when he returned Mother met him at the door in the usual way. As they came in together I noticed nothing wrong in Father's expression except that he seemed tired. But often, when he had been unusually busy, he looked tired. During dinner, which was nicer than usual, with the beef stew Father liked, he ate with a good appetite. No reference was made to the conversation of the day before. When I had finished I moved to my seat by the window with a book. Only then did I hear Mother say, in a low voice:

"Well?"

Father did not immediately answer. When he did, his voice was calm, rather thoughtful.

"Yes, I went. Dr. Macmillan. A very decent sort. It appears that you were right, Grace. Apparently one of my lungs is slightly affected."

"Affected? But with what?"

"With . . . well . . ." Father did not want to say it, but he had to. "A bit of a touch of T.B."

"Oh, Con . . . is it serious?"

"Now don't get alarmed. After all, it's nothing unusual. A common complaint. Lots of people get it. And they get over it."

I heard Mother's breath go out in a long troubled sigh. Then she reached slowly across the table and pressed Father's hand.

"At least now we know where we stand. You'll give up now and really get well. Go to a sanatorium or take a sea voyage, like Dr. Ewen advised."

"Yes, I'll go. It's to be a sanatorium apparently. I'll go like a shot. I promise you. But not quite yet."

"Conor! You must go at once."

"No."

"You must."

"It's impossible, Grace. Simply can't be done. Every penny we've got is in the yeast. I've even borrowed from the bank. And all my plans are just coming to a head."

"What does money matter at a time like this?"

"It's not the money. I'm doing well. But the business is young, you know it's a one man affair, and there's something extra special come up with the U.D.L. that I *have* to be there for, I simply can't leave, with the next few months going to be so critical."

"Oh, Con . . . Con . . . I don't know what you're talking about, with your U.D.L. It's you, and your health, that come first."

"Now, Grace, we must be sensible. For your sake and the boy's, as well as my own. U.D.L. is United Distillers Limited, one of the biggest companies in the country, and they're definitely, yes positively, interested in my yeast. I'm sure I can bring off an amalgamation in a matter of three, perhaps only two months. Such a short time, lass. After that I'll be free to take a six, even nine months' rest to get well. In the meantime, I can work shorter hours, take an extra day off once in a while. I'll be careful, extra careful in every way. I've thought it all over in the train coming home. I'll do everything you say except throw away all I've worked and sweated and hoped for. It would be madness just when I'm in sight of the chance of a lifetime."

In their intensity of feeling they had both forgotten me. I stole a fearful glance at Mother. Tears were beginning to bud beneath her eyes. I knew that she was beaten and that Father would have his way.

Yet for once my sympathies were with him. At that moment, and all through the period that followed I never for a moment doubted my father. My confidence in his astuteness, judgement, and general aplomb, confirmed by scores of instances in which I had seen him carry off a difficult situation without turning a hair, remained absolute and unshakable. Even in his few failures, he had somehow managed to remove the implication of defeat by a final attitude of amused or careless indifference. His two phrases "leave it to me" and "I know what I'm doing," uttered calmly and confidently, had become for me the touchstones of triumphant achievement.

Mother no longer sang as she went about her work. I failed to understand her constant air of stress. In her worried state, she had been driven to confide in Miss Greville and to seek relief in our neighbour's sympathetic response. Yet as the days slipped past, all was going according to plan. Father certainly did not look ill. His colour, always ruddy, remained good, his eye was bright and he had suffered no loss of appetite. As he had promised, while never affecting the attitudes of invalidism, he was taking care of himself, avoiding the worst of the weather, and taking things easy during long weekends. If he still coughed, expectorating surreptitiously into the little flask he now carried for that purpose, then in only a short time, a matter of weeks, he would go away — Switzerland, suggested by Miss Greville, was now definitely agreed upon — and be quickly cured. Meanwhile he was persisting with his own herbal remedies, periodically he called upon Mother to massage his chest with olive oil and one evening he came back from the city with a strange appliance, which he introduced to us confidently as a medicated inhaler. This consisted of a metal canister with a spirit lamp beneath and a length of rubber tubing fitted with a mouthpiece above. Water and a special mixture of herbs, supplied with the apparatus, went into the canister, the lamp was lit and when the hot medicated steam hissed out Father faithfully breathed in. And all this, and the rest, was carried out with a sanguine assurance of recovery that would have been comic if, in the light of what followed, it had not proved to be so tragic.

In later years, when I came to analyze this obstinate folly, the reasons were not far to seek. Father was an ambitious man who constantly took risks. He knew the danger of delaying his cure but, since his business had reached a crucial stage, which if successfully passed would elevate him to a position of real importance, associated, as was later revealed, with his mention of the U.D.L. — letters which, to my youthful mind, assumed a cabalistic significance — he was prepared, in his own phrase, "to chance it," for all our sakes. There was courage here, yet beyond this natural hardihood the superabundant optimism of his Irish temperament betrayed him into the belief that his gamble must come off. But above all, his conduct could most truly be explained by a strange and characteristic manifestation of the actual malady itself and which, years later, I came to recognise as the *spes phthisica*, a false and persistent hope, engendered in the nervous system by the toxins of the disease, the false illusion of ultimate cure and complete recovery.

Father had this to a marked extent and, inevitably, communicated it in varying degree to Mother and me. We were quite unprepared for the calamity that followed.

The month was March, as far as I remember the second week, and it must have been towards two o'clock in the morning that I awakened. Through persistent mists of sleep I had the dim and unreasoning sensation that Mother was calling me. Suddenly, as I was about to turn over, I heard her voice, very loud, and charged with such a fearful urgency that I immediately sat up.

"Laurence! Laurence! Come here!"

I got out of bed. My room was dark but when I opened the door the lights in the hall were on. The door of Father's bedroom was half open and from within Mother called again. The dread of some terrible disaster held me back, but I went forward and into the room. It is a moment I have never forgotten.

Father lay on his side with his head over the edge of the bed. He was coughing, coughing and coughing, as though he would never stop, and from his lips a bubbling scarlet stream gushed out. His face was the colour of clay. Mother knelt by the side of the bed. One hand held Father's head, the other with difficulty supported the big white basin from the wash-stand. The basin was half full of that scarlet froth which, all at once, sick with horror, I knew to be blood. There was blood everywhere, on the sheets of the disordered bed, spattered on Mother's nightdress, even on her hands and face. Without changing her position or taking her eyes from Father, Mother spoke to me, in that same strained note of anguished command.

"Laurie! Run for Dr. Ewen. Go now. Immediately. Hurry, for pity's sake."

I turned and ran, ran from sheer shock. Without stopping to put on my jersey and trousers, a sensible act that would have delayed me not more than a half minute, I ran straight out of the house into the street in nothing but my nightshirt. Bare-footed I scudded along the pavement of the Terrace, my heart already beating against my ribs. The darkness made my speed seem beyond all human speed. I knew that never before had I run so fast. At the end of Prince Albert Road I swung into Colquhoun Crescent, then down hill to Victoria Street where, ahead of me, half way to the Esplanade, I saw the red lamp outside Dr. Ewen's house. A square, ornamental lamp em-bossed with the town arms — he had once been Provost of Ardfillan. Not a soul was in sight. The empty silence was broken only by my gasping breaths as I ran and ran, into the doctor's driveway at last, not caring for the hurt of the gravel on my feet, and up the steps of his front porch. I pressed the night bell long and hard, heard it buzz loudly within the house. For some painful moments of suspense nothing stirred, then as I pressed again a light went on upstairs. Presently the door was unlocked. The doctor stood there in his dressing gown.

I guessed that he would be angry at being disturbed since, from my parents' conversation, I knew him to be a difficult man. Worse still, had not Father quarrelled with him, cast him off and ceased to be his patient? Before he could speak I gasped:

"Please, Dr. Ewen, come to 7 Prince Albert Terrace at once. Father is bleeding terribly."

Yes, he had meant to show annoyance, even anger, that exasperation experienced by a doctor knocked up in the middle of the night after a hard day's work. But instead he compressed his lips and stared at me in a kind of wonder.

"Please do come, sir. You know my father, Carroll is the name. Never mind anything else. Just come."

He still stared at me.

"*You* come," he said. "Out the cold."

I followed him inside.

"Is your father coughing much?"

"Oh yes, sir, very much."

He muttered something under his breath.

I sat in the hall while he went upstairs. Above the hall stand a stag's head mounted on the wall stared down at me with glassy implacable eyes. I heard the slow pendulum beat of a clock from another room.

The doctor was not long in dressing. When he came down he was carrying a pair of carpet slippers and a tartan travelling rug. He tossed these to me.

"Cover yourself."

He watched while I draped myself in the plaid. I did not feel cold but my teeth were chattering. The slippers were old but they fitted not badly — Dr. Ewen was a little man — and I could shuffle along in them. He picked up his black bag from the hall stand. We set off.

On the way up hill, though he kept glancing at me from

time to time, he said not a word. But as we drew near the Terrace he unexpectedly exclaimed:

"You seem not a bad sort of boy. Don't *you* ever be a fool."

I did not grasp his meaning. With my mission accomplished I felt limp and spent and could only dread this return to the nightmare disruption of my home. I had not closed the door of our flat when I rushed out. It remained open. We entered. I dared not look, but as Dr. Ewen went into Father's room and was greeted by Mother's cry of relief, my head, by a kind of reflex, came round. Mother was still kneeling by the bed, still supporting Father, but the basin, already fixed in my consciousness as the atrocious frothing symbol of unforgettable horror, the basin had gone.

I slipped into my own room, discarded the plaid and shoes, and crept into bed. For a long time I lay shaken by occasional tremors, listening to the movements about the house, interspersed with the muted voices of my mother and Dr. Ewen. How long the doctor was staying! I wished with all my heart that Mother would come to see me before I fell asleep, to take me in her arms and tell me that all was well. Above all, to praise me for my splendid, breathless run. But she did not come.

10

⚜⚜⚜

THE LITTLE paddle steamer splashed gaily through the
sunlit waves. She was the red-funneled *Lucy Ashton*,
playing across the firth between Ardfillan and Port
Cregan. On deck, the passengers were promenading, sniffing
the sparkling air, or sitting in groups, laughing, talking, listening to the lively music of a four piece German band. Below, in
the deserted, plush-upholstered saloon, smelling of stale smoke,
Miss O'Riordan and I sat alone, in silence. Since, until that
day, I had never set eyes on her, I ventured an appraising
sidelong glance from time to time, although hampered by the
roughened edge of the stiff collar that went with my best suit.
She was a reddish fair woman of about forty-five with full
watery eyes, pointed features and a tendency to pale freck-
les. Her expression, manner and general appearance all seemed
to convey a sense of pious resignation to a life of sacrifice and
suffering. I had begun to wonder why it should be my fate
always to be in the charge of women and, in particular, such a
holy woman as this, when she broke the silence.

"Your father being so ill, dear, I didn't think you ought to
be up there with that band. Besides I'm a poor sort of a sailor."
She paused. "We might put up a prayer to pass the time. Have
you a rosary?"

"No, Miss O'Riordan. I did have one, but it broke."

"You should be more careful of a sacred object, dear. I'll give you a new one when we get to the presbytery. His reverence will bless it for you."

"Thank you, Miss O'Riordan."

I perceived, with some dismay, that my Uncle Simon's housekeeper was even holier than I had feared. Beyond this, the motion of the boat seemed so little to agree with her that eventually I was constrained to inquire:

"Are you ill, Miss O'Riordan?"

"Ill, dear?" She leaned forward, half closing her eyes and pressing a hand into the small of her back. "The good God knows I'm never well."

As she did not speak again I had leisure to brood rather dejectedly on the changes in my life. Was I actually going to stay with a priest? Yes, I was. Father's desperate illness had induced a reconciliation with his brothers, of whom the youngest, Simon Carroll, had considerately proposed that it would greatly relieve my mother in her self-imposed duties as nurse if I should spend at least several weeks with him. Although when he came to visit Father I had liked Uncle Simon very much, looking across at Miss O'Riordan whose lips were moving in silent prayer, I had begun to feel that the prospect was forbidding, when a bump and a creak indicated that we were alongside Port Cregan Pier.

However, as we disembarked Port Cregan seemed to me a nice sort of place with interesting shops and lots of movement on the front. Like Ardfillan, across the firth, it was built on a hill, and on top of the hill, which Miss O'Riordan, a hand to the favoured spot in her back, climbed with extreme slowness, stood the church and rectory, both small but pleasingly built of cut grey limestone. We entered a darkish hall panelled in oak, smelling of candle grease and floor polish, then Miss O'Riordan, having first regained her breath by a prolonged series of gasps, inquired in a discreet whisper if I wished to "go," meaning, I assumed, to the lavatory. On my replying in the negative she led me to the sitting room at the side of the house. This was a large room opening on to the garden and well lit by a bay window with an exciting view of the harbour. As we came in, Uncle Simon had been sitting at the roll top desk against the far wall. Now he got up, came forward and took my hand.

As he smiled, I saw immediately that he was shy, and I knew that I should like him more than before. He did not speak but, still holding my hand, looked inquiringly at Miss O'Riordan who gave him a long and detailed report on our journey. While she talked I had a chance to re-examine my uncle. Of the four Carroll brothers two were fair, two dark. Simon, the youngest, at that time not more than twenty-six, was a dark one, black haired and blue eyes, so tall that he stooped slightly as though to avoid hitting things like chandeliers with his head, and boyishly, almost alarmingly, thin in his long soutane.

"And Conor?" he asked in an undertone, when she had finished.

She did not answer, but with a meaningful glance that passed over my head, silently compressed her lips, imperceptibly shook her head and left the room.

"Miss O'Riordan will be bringing up our tea. I expect the sea air has given you an appetite," my uncle said cheerfully. He put me into one of the two old and rather battered leather chairs on either side of the fireplace, and went and stood at his desk. "Just let me finish what I was doing. I'll be with you in a minute."

I felt instinctively that he was giving us both time to settle down. Certainly these were strange surroundings for me. Beyond the chairs and the roll top desk, on which stood a large blue and white statue of the Madonna, there was little furniture and less comfort in the room. The drab curtains were shabby, and the carpet, like the chairs, was badly worn, as though trodden by many feet over many years. On the mantelpiece a biretta and a long row of pennies arranged in little piles caught my eye. On one wall a black and ivory crucifix hung. But what startled me was a large engraving on another wall of a long-bearded, half naked, hairy old man, perched on top of a high stone pillar.

"Do you like him?" Uncle had risen and was watching me with a faint smile.

"Who is he?"

"One of my favourite saints."

"But whatever is he doing up there?"

"Nothing much." Uncle was really smiling now. "Just being a peculiar person, and a saint."

At this point, with an air of supreme effort, Miss O'Riordan brought in a black japanned tray on which the tea things and a large plate of thick slices of bread and butter were set out. Although accustomed to much better fare, I barely noticed the absence of cake. My mind was so filled with this amazing old man on the pillar that whenever the housekeeper had gone I broke out:

"How high was he up, Uncle, and how long?"

"Thirty-six cubits high, on top of a mountain too. And he stayed up for thirty years."

It was so truly astounding I choked on my first slice of bread and butter.

"Thirty years! But how did he get his food."

"By lowering a basket. Of course he fasted a lot."

"Why didn't he fall off when he was asleep? I know I would have."

"Well, he was a very miraculous old man. And probably he didn't sleep much. Perhaps his hair shirt kept him awake."

"Good gracious, Uncle. A hair shirt!"

He smiled.

"I can't see why he did it," I said at last.

"Well, Laurence." I felt a throb of pleasure as he used my first name. "Simeon lived long ago, in wild mountainous country, amongst savage tribes. As you may imagine, great crowds came to see him. He preached to them, often for hours on end, healed the sick, became a sort of judge, worked miracles, and in this way made an immense number of conversions to Christianity."

There was a silence.

"Is that why you have him in your room?"

He shook his head.

"When I was at college in Spain I got to know of him. And as his name was like mine I felt rather flattered. So you see it's just vanity on my part after all."

I gazed warmly at my uncle, enchanted by our conversation which, instead of the expected references to my father that might have made me blubber, had raised me up to rare historical and intellectual heights.

"I wish I might see a miracle, Uncle," I said thoughtfully.

"They're happening every day, if we only look for them. Now tuck into your bread and butter. It's Mrs. Vitello's day off and we won't get much more before breakfast tomorrow."

I wanted to stay with this newly discovered uncle for further talk about pillars, but he told me he must go to the church to hear confessions, adding however, and so whetting my expectation, that he would be free after Mass tomorrow to show me something interesting. And so, when Miss O'Riordan came for the tray she claimed me. After she had again satisfied herself that I did not want to "go," we went down a short flight of stairs to the kitchen. Here she produced a bot-

tle with a label depicting a huge cod with its mouth wide
open.

"I'm putting you on Purdy's Emulsion, dear. A tablespoonful
three times a day. It's wonderful for the chest."

She slowly decanted the creamy fluid which, though well
disguised, tasted of cod liver oil.

"Now," she said, when I had gulped it down, "let's look
what you've on." Prodding my shirt open with a forefinger
she gave an exclamation of distress. "What! No flannel, dear?
You should have flannel next the skin. God knows we don't
want you to go the way of your poor father. I'll see to it for
you before you're a day older."

She then released me, telling me to go into the garden and
play, but not to catch cold or spoil my clothes. I went out.
The garden was a square of green, bordered by a shrubbery in
which a little grotto had been made with a large statue of Our
Lady wearing a coronet of stars and standing upon a pediment
of sea shells. A narrow concrete path traversed the grass, giving access to the side door of the church. I longed to go there
to look for my uncle but held back, aware that he would be in
his little grilled box.

I hung about with my hands in my pockets, thinking of a
great many interesting things about the man on the pillar, and
wishing that I had witnessed the many miracles he had performed. What a splendid sight — a miracle — and they could
be seen, too, if one looked out for them. I thought also that, although the fading light made me long for my mother, I might
do very well here with Uncle Simon, if only Miss O'Riordan would let me alone.

Alas, as the town clock struck six, she appeared at the
back door of the refectory, and beckoned me in.

She had made porridge for my supper and a plateful, with

its attendant glass of milk, steamed on the kitchen table. As she sat down opposite to watch me sup she may have observed in my expression a flicker of discontent. She said:

"We never turn up our noses at good food, dear. We live very plain here."

"Plain, Miss O'Riordan?"

"Yes, plain, dear. The church is fair loaded with debt. And your uncle, poor soul, is fair killing himself to pay it off."

"But how could the church get in debt?"

"It was the rebuilding of it, dear. Fifteen years ago, when I first came here. I won't mention names, but a certain reverend gentleman had ideas that went more than a trifle beyond his station."

"But don't the people pay, Miss O'Riordan?"

"Pay, dear?" she exclaimed with a scorn that lashed nameless congregations. "Have you seen the coppers on your uncle's mantelshelf? That's how they pay. Pennies and halfpennies and, God save us, sometimes farthings too, the brutes. Why, with the debt redemption and the interest, and what he does for charity, there's scarcely enough for the poor man to put a decent shirt on his back. But he's a clever one, and a good one, and with God's help, and mine, he'll do it."

These startling revelations, while depressive, had enabled me to finish my porridge without noticing that there was no salt in it. Later, I discovered that she was a firm advocate of a saltless diet being, as she put it, easier on the kidneys. We rose from the table.

"I have your rosary now, dear," Miss O'Riordan confided, in an intimate tone. "We'll just say five decades in your room before I put you to bed."

Upstairs, we knelt down in the bare bedroom that seemed to exhale the austerity of the many missionaries it had harboured, going and coming between the port of Cregan and the interior of Africa.

"We'll take the five sorrowful mysteries," Miss O'Riordan whispered. "And remember. Our intention is for your poor father."

She began: "First sorrowful mystery: the agony of Our Lord in the Garden:" and first moving my lips noiselessly I finally joined in. Despite our intention I did not think about my father. I was sorry for him. I deplored his pitiable state. But that fearful midnight scene which kept recurring in grotesque forms throughout my dreams had made him taboo during the daytime when my will, such as it was, could exercise command. Instead I thought about Mother, and as I was then, and have been since, a visual, her face rose vividly before me. I saw her look of strain and sadness, mingling with tenderness and sweetness when she said goodbye to me that morning. I thought on no other agony but hers. And suddenly, though she had begged me to be brave, while I continued to pray mechanically, a flood of tears defiled my cheeks. I did not care that my companion's eyes were glued upon me — this, indeed, increased the flow. At last we finished. Miss O'Riordan got slowly to her feet, still viewing me and with — could it be? — a new interest and respect.

"Before God, dear," she said solemnly, "you pray well. Such piety! I will certainly tell his reverence. Never have I seen a child so touched to the heart over his beads."

I reddened guiltily. But in an odd way, I felt comforted.

"Look, dear," she went on persuasively, when I had undressed. "Here's a little something I've run up for you. It'll keep your poor lungs nice and cosy."

She produced a sort of chest protector made of red flannel and fastened it on with tapes round my neck and back. I found it hot and uncomfortable but was now so worn down by her ministrations I had not the strength to resist. This is my hair shirt, I thought sadly, and Miss O'Riordan is my pillar.

When I had closed my eyes in simulated sleep, but still keeping a faint chink through which I could warily observe her, she stood for a few moments looking down at me. Then she made the sign of the cross over my bed and turned out the gaslight. Suddenly, in the darkness I felt the press of lips on my forehead, not the soft warm lips to which I was used, but dry, stiff, strangely unaccustomed lips. Still, a kiss — and from Miss O'Riordan. I heard the door quietly close behind her.

Poor Miss O'Riordan, I must never permit myself to record anything really unkind of you. What harder thing is there in all the world than to be a frustrated, lonely, self-martyred, hypochondriacal, spinster housekeeper of forty-five, with only a daily Italian cleaning woman for help, in a struggling parish rectory? Nothing, unless perhaps to be the priest.

11

M Y STAY at St. Joseph's was to prove longer than I had
foreseen and although, unlike his housekeeper, my
uncle did not at the outset overwhelm me with attentions, I soon sensed that he welcomed my presence in the
rectory and that my companionship, absurd though this may
seem, relieved that special and very human loneliness enforced
by his vocation, the more so since he could not fail to observe
that I was beginning to be attached to him. This was not difficult. Simple goodness, so different from Miss O'Riordan's re-
ligiosity, is always attractive and, for all his self-imposed discipline, there was a softness in his nature, a fine sensibility,
that must have won any child.

He was, like my father, naturally clever, with the same in-
born distinction, an attribute which, I was soon to discover, had
not been bestowed by heaven on their two brothers, Bernard
and Leo. At an early age he had been sent to the Scots College
at Valladolid in Old Castile where, during seven formative
years, he had lived and studied with outstanding brilliance.
Spain had educated, moulded him, imbued him with its tradi-
tions and culture. He loved Spain, and deeply admired its people — I well remember one of his phrases, "the nobility of
the men, the grace and purity of the women." In his dark

clothes, with his thick black hair, dark eyes and sallow skin, his clerical cape drooping from his shoulders, he had indeed a Spanish look which rather consciously he sought to emphasize by many little mannerisms. And how often, in a nostalgic way, did he speak to me of the happiness of his life at Valladolid, the lovely city of Cervantes and Columbus that was saved from the Moors by Sanchio de Leon, evoking not only the dramas of history, but more personal images of sunsplashed cloisters, a white-walled study facing on distant ochre mountains, and of the College gardens, scented with orange trees, leading to a special arbour of vines under which he took the midday siesta, and from which the small honey-sweet grapes fell, as he put it, almost into one's mouth. To be transported to a raw, run-down Scottish parish, amidst uncouth accents and the din of nearby shipyards, seemed to me a sad dismissal from Eden.

But Uncle Simon did not mind. He was completely at home in his parish, knew all the children, and most of the old women, by their first names, and seemed actually to enjoy the many parochial duties and demands, in my view dull and fatiguing, which, from six o'clock in the morning when he rose to prepare for his early Mass, complicated a day often extending until late at night. Because I enjoyed his society and missed him when he was away it annoyed me that he should place himself at the disposal of everyone, especially since, in addition to his normal routine, he now devoted a half day every week to crossing to Ardfillan to see my father, visits from which he returned with a fictitious cheerfulness that did not deceive me.

Nor did I approve his readiness to respond to every distressful story. I sensed that he was being imposed upon, a view vigorously shared by Miss O'Riordan, who was especially critical of what she called the Beggars' Procession. Every Wednesday afternoon a string of needy petitioners presented themselves with unfailing regularity at the kitchen door, to be rewarded with their established perquisites. Watching from the open window of the kitchen with Mrs. Vitello, the daily woman, while Miss O'Riordan dealt with the queue, I suspected that not a few were impostors and of these, one especially seemed the worst, an old crone with a shifty eye named Sarah Mooney who hobbled on a crutch, dragging one leg, with many wails and groans, and who never was satisfied that her "peck" of tea and canister of sugar contained full measure. In my suspicion I was fully supported by Miss O'Riordan, and time and again I heard her protest to my uncle against Sarah's depredations on the larder.

Uncle Simon, however, despite the handicap of youth, had a way with his difficult housekeeper who through long tenure had come to believe herself the keystone of the parish. He let her have her head in many directions, tolerated her foibles, did not interfere in the management of the house, and above all, endured her atrocious cookery without complaint. Of Miss O'Riordan's culinary skill I may say that never before or since have I known anyone inflict more harm on a simple mutton chop or an inoffensive joint of beef. But unlike me, Uncle had apparently slight regard for what he ate, his only indulgence being a large cup of black coffee after the one o'clock dinner, with which he smoked a thin, curved cigar with a quill at the end selected from a box sent to him by a colleague in Spain.

By this forbearance in matters which he considered of small account, he not only earned Miss O'Riordan's regard but was able to assert himself without interference in all that pertained to his ecclesiastical office. Quietly and with firmness he interposed on my behalf, and while he could not defeat all her ministrations — notably those directed against my bowel, for she purged me relentlessly, nor must I omit the large camphor cross which for hygienic reasons she hung round my neck and which, impregnating my skin, made me smell like an animated mothball — he negatived her untimely religious plans for me, too ambitious steps to saintliness that would have compelled me to make my first confession, take the order of the Brown Scapular, and learn by rote the Latin responses so that I might serve my uncle's Mass within the brief compass of my visit. If she had had her way I believe this devoted woman would have had me ordained, tonsured, perhaps even canonized before she had done with me. But Uncle Simon would not have it. He had both the sense and the sensibility to realize the psychological shock I had sustained, and to see me as a nervous, highly strung and physically undeveloped child, often tormented by nightmares that awakened me in a cold sweat and which, since they were centered always on grotesque variations of my father's haemorrhage, I referred to as my "red dreams." How grateful I was for the time he somehow managed to devote to me. In the evenings we played draughts, a game I already knew. He taught me the rudiments of chess, and engaged me without his queen. Our conversations were always interesting since he never laughed at my naiveties, and I recall that we touched on further notable eccentricities amongst the saints, while on another occasion we had a very reassuring talk on the subject of hell. On several Mondays, his least occupied day, he hired a row boat and took me out to that part of the firth known as the Tail of the Bank. But our greatest diversion was the entertainment he had hinted at when we first met.

One morning, when he had said his office immediately after breakfast, he led me up to the attic and there amidst the lumber of years stood a model locomotive, covered in dust, but a real working model, so big, so full of magnificent potential that I jumped at the sight of it.

"I've no idea how it ever came here," Uncle meditated.

"The remnant from a jumble sale perhaps. And I don't believe it works very well. But we might have a shot at it."

We took it down to the garden, placed it on the concrete path outside the back door. I ran into the kitchen to Miss O'Riordan for dusters. Cleaned, revealing gleaming driving wheels, double cylinders and pistons, and a shiny green tender, it was an engine to thrill the heart.

"Look!" I exclaimed, pointing to the bronze letters on the casing of the driving box: "The Flying Scotsman."

It was actually a scale model of that famous locomotive. What joy to fill the boiler with water, to charge the little fire-box from the bottle of methylated spirit Uncle had thought-fully provided, to light — with matches obtained over Miss O'Riordan's protests — the well-trimmed wick and then to stand back, holding one's breath, expectant of immediate action. Alas, when all this was done The Flying Scot refused to fly. The water boiled, promising steam floated from the fun-nel, even the tiny whistle emitted its shrill and fascinating note, but for all its inner agitation, and mine, the beautiful ma-chine remained indifferent and inert.

"Oh, Uncle, we must get it to go!" In my eagerness I scarcely noticed that I had used Miss O'Riordan's classic phrase.

He seemed to be of the same mind. He removed his coat and knelt down with me on the bare concrete. Together we oiled the engine with the oiler from his bicycle kit. We examined in detail all its working parts. Vainly we unscrewed nuts and re-tightened them. Lying flat now, with dirty smears of oil on his face, Uncle was blowing hard on the spirit flame with a view to intensifying the heat when Miss O'Riordan suddenly appeared.

"Your reverence!" Her hands and eyes went up in horror.

"In your shirtsleeves. And such a state. And Mr. and Mrs. Lafferty waiting for you in the church with the poor unbaptized innocent infant, a good half hour."

He got up, with an apologetic smile to Miss O'Riordan, looking rather like a guilty schoolboy. But as he hurried off he gave me an encouraging glance.

"We're not beaten yet, Laurence. We'll try again."

We did try again. We tried repeatedly, and always without success. The reluctant engine became, for us, an absorbing hobby. We discussed it daily, in unmechanical terms, determined not to be beaten.

On Wednesday of the following week we had just had dinner, Uncle's coffee had been brought in, he had selected and lit his thin cigar. He always smoked this in a dreamy manner with half closed lids as though transporting himself back to his beloved Valladolid. How surprised and saddened I should have been had I known that within a few months he would in fact be transferred back to that city to become a member of the College staff. But this afternoon I did not know nor, I am sure, did he. Mellowed by the coffee and cigar, there was a quizzical look in his eye.

"The Flying Scotsman?"

"Yes, Uncle," I shouted.

We brought the engine out from the toolshed. While Miss O'Riordan watched disapprovingly from the kitchen window, making remarks under her breath to Mrs. Vitello, we fed it oil, spirit and water, saw it boil furiously to bursting point. And all without effect. It simply would not "go."

With our heads over the straining machine Uncle said, in a voice wherein, at last, I detected a note of pessimism:

"It must be blocked somewhere. Try giving it a shake."

I gave it a despairing shake, a hard, a violent shake, and finally, in a temper, I kicked it. Immediately there was a sharp explosion. The boiler, from its internal parts, shot out a blob of viscous matter. Steam hissed from an unsuspected valve. The wheels spun violently and The Flying Scotsman shot away from us like an arrow.

"Hurrah!" I yelled. "It's going. Look, Miss O'Riordan, look!"

Straight down the concrete path it sped, gathering momentum with every thrust of its powerful pistons, wheels racing, steam flying, its firebox sparking like a comet's tail. A glorious, stupendous sight!

"Oh, heavens," suddenly exclaimed my uncle.

I followed his eyes. Sarah Mooney had come out of the church and, with her head down and her bad leg dragging, was hobbling towards us on her crutch.

"Look out, Sarah!" shouted Uncle Simon.

Sarah, absorbed by the prospect of tea, did not hear, and the engine, bearing down with an accuracy almost inspired, struck her crutch fair and square. The crutch flew into the air in a perfect arc and broke with a resounding crash. Mrs. Mooney sat down on the concrete, while the engine, emitting billows of steam, spun over on its side and lay panting hoarsely on the grass. For a moment Sarah sat stupefied, enveloped in a heavenly cloud, then with a screech she scrambled to her feet and ran, ran like a hare, to the safety of the church.

"Well, thank God she isn't hurt." Uncle turned to Miss O'Riordan, who had now joined us.

"But Uncle Simon," I clutched his arm, finding my voice at last, "didn't you see? She ran. No crutch. Actually ran. It's a miracle."

He looked at me thoughtfully, but before he could answer Miss O'Riordan, who for once was looking pleased, interposed.

"If she's not back tomorrow with two crutches that *will* be a miracle."

Uncle still said nothing, but he was smiling now. I think he had enjoyed Sarah Mooney's twenty yard dash.

The Flying Scotsman, after its brief moment, never was the same again, and without any attempt at repair, was retired to the attic. Indeed, from that day on, the whole complexion of my stay at the rectory changed. I was told nothing, but from Miss O'Riordan's expression and my uncle's manner, which became serious and more concealed, the news from Ardfillan was obviously much worse. Simon began to cross the firth more often, returning with a sad face which he tried, not always with success, to lighten when I appeared. In the kitchen too, I would break in on muted conversations between Miss O'Riordan and Mrs. Vitello, to be greeted with excessive and too obvious endearments, but not before I had heard the two ominous, often repeated words, "galloping consumption," words which immediately and vividly created in my mind's eye a vision of my father, pale as on that unforgettable night, galloping madly to destruction on a great white horse.

I never understood or sought to explain to myself why the horse should be white, but I knew then, knew absolutely, and with a strange apathy, that my father would soon die. Had I not sensed, unconsciously, on that night of blood that he would not recover? I hung about the house, feeling neglected, hearing with impatience the whispers of "another haemorrhage," resentful of the gravity and preoccupation of the others, chilled by the loss of the warmth that had enveloped me.

One evening, some ten days later, I had coaxed, perhaps tormented my uncle into a game of draughts. We were at the board and he had permitted me to crown a man when I heard a door bell ring, a sound I disliked since it usually was the prelude to a sick call. But when Miss O'Riordan entered, she had a telegram in her hand. My uncle read it, turned pale, and said:

"I must go to the church, Laurie."

Miss O'Riordan went out of the room with him, leaving me alone. Not a word to me. Yet I had known instantly. I did not cry. Instead a dullness, a kind of heavy dreariness descended on me. I looked at the draught board, regretting the untimely ending of the game where, with my crowned man, I held a winning position. I counted the piles of pennies on the mantelshelf, twelve pennies in each pile, studied again my friend, the old man on the pillar, then went down to the kitchen.

Miss O'Riordan was weeping and, with many fervent ejaculations, saying her beads.

"I have a headache, dear," she explained, concealing the rosary under her apron.

I felt like saying: "Why tell a lie, Miss O'Riordan?"

But I gave no sign of grief until the following morning when Miss O'Riordan, deputed for the occasion, led me to the window of the sitting room, put an arm about my shoulders and while we both gazed distantly to the harbour where a Clan Line ship was in process of unloading, proceeded, by a series of low-toned graduated remarks, to break the news gently. Then, because I felt I must, that it was expected of me, I burst dutifully into tears. But they were quickly dried, so quickly that Miss O'Riordan was able to remark several times in the course of the day, and with a complacent air of self-achievement: "He took it well!"

In the afternoon, having dressed herself "for the town," she took me into Port Cregan and bought me a ready made black suit which, being chosen, as she put it, for my growth, was a shameful misfit. The jacket hung on me like a sack, the wide trousers, unlike my own neat shorts, sagged half way down my calves, giving the impression of a man's long trousers, amputated well below the knee. Determined to make me a walk-

ing example of grief the good Miss O'Riordan completed the
outfit with a black bowler hat that extinguished me, a black
tie, a crape band for my arm and black gloves.

Next morning, in this hideous panoply of death that made
me look like a miniature mute, I said goodbye to Miss O'Riordan who, in embracing me, calling me "her poor lamb,"
bathed me with her incomprehensible tears. But perhaps she
foresaw better than I what lay ahead of me. Then, accompany-
ing my uncle, I departed in a cab for the Ardfillan boat.

We sat on deck where the same German quartette dis-
coursed the same lively Viennese waltz tunes. My heart
lifted up at the music to which some children were skipping
around. I wanted to jump up and join them, but sombrely conscious of my attire which, in fact, had drawn upon me much
sympathetic attention, I dared not.

12
❦❦❦

THE FUNERAL took place privately in Lochbridge where, in the local cemetery, a family plot had been honorably provided by my father's humble yet eminently worthy parents. It was in this industrial town that Laurence and Mary Carroll, driven from their Irish croft by the great potato famine, had settled to lead out their lives in pious obscurity, here my father had lodged in batchelor rooms before his marriage, and here too was Uncle Bernard's establishment, the Lomond Vaults, now revealed, to my surprise and chagrin, as a rambling, run-down public house, above which my uncle and his wife resided with my two cousins, Terence and Nora.

The afternoon was grey and drizzling as the cortège set out from the church. But I was not there to view it. To my immense relief Mother had ruled that I must not attend the burial. On the previous day, over my frantic protests, I had been induced by Uncle Bernard to take what he called "a last farewell" of my father in his coffin. This was my introduction to death, and I had been frozen by the sight of Father, so young, so handsome, a perfect waxen image of himself, stretched in the sumptuous, embossed, richly cushioned shell that Uncle Bernard himself, with extravagant sentimentality and against Mother's wishes, had ordered. Prepared immaculately for the grave, hair brushed, moustache clipped, Father was groomed, as he himself would have ironically phrased it, "to a hair." Then, as Uncle Bernard, oozing tears, lifted one of those flaccid, clay cold hands and placed it in mine, tightening my skin with horror, I noticed at the same instant on the dead chin, cleanshaven by the undertaker only the day before, a faint reddish beard beginning to sprout. With a shriek I tore myself free and dashed so wildly from the room that I cut my head on the jamb of the door. So now, with a bandage round my brow, but freed from the further terrors at the graveside, I waited with my new cousin Nora in the back yard of the Lomond Vaults.

The yard lay between the railway line and rear premises of the red brick Vaults, a strange, unbelievable yard, enclosed by broken wooden palings, a no man's land, littered with lumber, with wooden cases, with stacks of empty and broken bottles and their rain-sodden straw casings. A heap of coke blocked the cellar door, in one corner there was a dilapidated poultry hut before which hens scraped, pecked and cackled, in another a range of dog kennels that seemed held together by a tangle of rusted wire. And all this existed in such a state of wild disorder, contrasting with the spotless order of my own home, with all that I had known or seen before, it actually became invested with a fearful and attractive charm.

Something of this must have shown in my face as I glanced around, for Nora favoured me with a mischievous, inquiring smile.

"It's not very tidy, is it, man?"

"Not very," I agreed tactfully.

"That's how things are here. We're always in a mess." She added carelessly: "The whole property's condemned."

"Condemned?" The word had a sinister sound.

"Ordered to be pulled down. By the town council. If it doesn't fall down first."

At that moment a Caledonian train roared past, perhaps the very train that my poor father had taken in his youth, and in the thunder of its passage, as though bearing out Nora's words, the entire yard rattled, boxes fell off the top of the pile, the hens scuttled for shelter, while the house itself, quivering and vibrating throughout its aged structure, loosed a small piece of mortar that fell exactly at my feet. I gazed at her apprehensively.

"But what will you do then, Nora? When it's pulled down?"

"We'll just go bankrupt, I suppose, like we nearly did before."

Was she joking? No, apparently she was serious, yet she did not seem to mind a bit, and with complete unconcern was smiling at me again. I liked her smile, so full of a careless ease that was beyond me. Indeed, although I had known my cousin only a few hours, I was inclined to like all of her, especially her thin, delicate, vivid face which, despite the bereavement in the family, was bright and full of fun. Her skin had a creamy colour, her eyes were almost black with long curling lashes and her hair, which she kept tossing about, was a glossy black also. Although almost three years older than me, she was small, still about my height, and very skinny, with thin elbows and legs. She had been dressed for the occasion in a smart new braided black voile dress with fetching pleats which, contradicting her protestations of financial insolvency, had a most expensive look.

"That's Terry's dog. The Joker."

As though anxious to stir up our lagging conversation she had resumed her air of cicerone, pointing to a long, lean, mouse-coloured hound with melancholy eyes and a thin curved rat-like tail that silently materialized in an elongated manner from the recesses of the kennel, a dog of a species I had never seen before and which bore absolutely no resemblance to the

aristocratic canines that I had hitherto observed being carefully walked out in the privileged Ardfillan thoroughfares.

"Is it a mongrel?" I inquired.

"God, no. Don't you know a whippet when you see one?
The Joker's a valuable animal that cost a mint of money. And
has made a mint for Terry. You'll not beat Terry at the races,
dog, horse, or man."

My expression of total incomprehension must have made
her want to give me up. Yet although she shook her head she
was not easily defeated. She chose however a simpler gambit.

"Well," she commented, breaking the silence, "they'll soon
be back. But not Uncle Simon. He can't get out of his appointment with the Bish."

Not to be behind her, I nodded agreement, although I had
not the faintest idea what she meant or who the Bish might
be. Before leaving for the cemetery Uncle Simon had talked
privately with my mother, but I had no idea of the nature of
their conversation.

"Naturally the old Bish is against it," she went on, "but he'll
have to give in. You understand it's a great honour for Simon."

"Oh, yes," I lied. This little wretch seemed to have the inside track on everything. Only a fearful curiosity made me
ask:

"Who is the Bish, Nora?"

She stared at me.

"The Bishop, man, old Mick Macauley in Winton. Don't you
know that they want Simon back to teach at the College in
Spain?"

I gazed at her in shocked dismay. So Uncle Simon would
be leaving us, just when I had become so fond of him. And
Mother had been counting on him too.

"Uncle Leo will be coming back though," I said, after a

pause, anxious not to lose the stabilizing presence of this other uncle whom I had never seen until today.

"Oh, yes," she said indifferently. "Leo'll be back, he has to wait for his train. He's a queer one."

"Queer?"

"And deep . . . You'll see for yourself. Terry calls him a cold-blooded bastard."

This unmentionable word uttered with such casual aplomb she might still have been referring to the Bishop, shook me to my heels. But I persisted.

"What does he do, Nora?"

"He has a warehouse in Winton. Sells cloth wholesale. But Uncle Conor used to laugh and say that no one ever knew what Leo was up to."

Since the day before I had been in a highly agitated state and this unexpected reference to my father, alive and laughing, brought a sudden rush of tears to my eyes. She frowned at me protestingly.

"God, don't start that again, just when I was beginning to take to you. Here, come on and I'll show you the hens."

Grasping my arm she dragged me forcibly into the hen house, bent on distracting me at all costs.

"See, there they are. Chookey, chookey, chookey. We had a dozen but two died. That one's broody, I have to chase it off the nest. Get off, there, you old devil. And here's an egg, a brown one too, we'll take it up and I'll boil it for your tea."

She held up the smooth, brown, slightly speckled egg enticingly. But it was no use. The startling change from daylight to the dim mysterious interior of the hen house, redolent of straw and other more acrid odours, had increased my woe.

"Will you stop it, man, for the love of God."

Holding the egg, she pushed me against the wall of the hen house, and with one arm firmly round my neck and the other braced above me against the wall, she began to butt me hard with her head. The brush of her hair against my cheek, the warmth of her nearness, the determined encirclement of her arms, all this was strangely soothing. When, at last, rather short of breath, she paused, I felt a sharp regret that her restorative treatment had not continued longer. I had begun to smile wanly when suddenly I became conscious of a sticky coagulation on the top of my skull that was now running down the back of my neck.

"Oh, God, the egg's broke," she exclaimed. "Quick, give us your hanky. There now, never mind, never mind, it's a grand shampoo, nothing better for the hair."

What could I do but submit to her ministrations as she mopped me up.

"Anyway, that's knocked the water out of you," she declared, examining me critically. "But you could still do with a sup of something on the way up."

Docilely, I permitted her to lead me across the yard to the back door, then along a narrow passage into the saloon bar. While I gazed with a neophyte's wonder at the ivory beer pulls, the rows of bottles on the shelves, the sawdust thickly strewn on the floor, making round islands of the brass spittoons, she remarked:

"Out of respect we're closed till the evening."

She advanced calmly to a small china barrel on the counter emblazoned with the words RUBY PORT. Turning the little nickel tap she expertly drew off two full glasses of the wine.

"Here," she said. "Put this down. But don't tell. It'll stiffen you up."

I was now clay in her hands. While she sipped her portion, I "put mine down." Then I followed her up the back stairs to the parlour, a big room full of good but knocked about furniture and, in its own way, almost as untidy as the yard. Above the fireplace, before which some towels hung drying, was a large coloured photograph of Pope Leo XIII, with some strips of yellowish palm stuck in at the top, and at the bottom, a pink notice for the June Ayr Races. A treadle harmonium with broken keys stood at the far end of the room, and in an adjoining corner were some odd shoes, a split bag of dog biscuits, some battered prayer books, and a pair of old striped braces. It seemed inconceivable that Uncle Bernard should be so different from my father, who hated slovenliness and in his own person, and in all that applied to hygiene, was almost excessively fastidious.

As I entered, feeling perceptive and extremely light on my feet, Mother was busy helping Bernard's wife, whom I now knew as Aunt Teresa, to set the long mahogany table for tea. Mother's activity and resolved air of cheerfulness astounded me. True, she was much thinner, but when I returned from Port Cregan I had expected to find her prostrate with an inconsolable grief. I had failed to realize that, whatever reaction the future might bring, for the present she had no sorrow left. Worn out by months of nursing, knowing that my father must die, she could only feel relief to see his suffering end.

"How nice your breath smells, dearest," she said, kissing me. She had kissed me a great deal since my return. "Have you been sucking sweets?"

"No, Mother," I said virtuously.

At that moment Aunt Teresa wandered in with a platter on which lay a huge red boiled ham.

"Didn't I hear the cab?" she said, smiling and nodding to me. "If so, we may as well dish up."

Nora's mother was a gentle, wavering little woman who seemed wrapped in an air of abstracted wonder. Her bosoms, swelling visibly under a rich black satin blouse, gave me the odd notion — was it promoted by the port? — that for comfort she had removed her stays or perhaps forgotten to put them on. Her face, naturally pale but faintly flushed now from the stove, had a dreamy remoteness as though years of these condemned Vaults and the disorder that reigned there had in the end exalted her to a supernatural plane where she drifted peacefully, isolated and immune.

"There they are now," Nora confirmed. "On the stairs."

Almost as she spoke the door opened and my two uncles entered. Bernard came first, a heavy, round shouldered, flabby figure, half bald, with a full, sagging face and pouches under his eyes which, although he could not have been more than forty-five, make him look much older. Since already I had observed in him an emotionalism so acute that he seemed unable to contain it, I was not surprised to see his black-bordered handkerchief still in his hand as he approached my mother and laid a consoling arm upon her shoulders.

"My poor girl, the hand of the Lord has been laid upon us. But you must be brave, it's over now, he's at rest under the sod, with his own kith and kin, and we can only bow our heads to the will of the Almighty. God's will be done. But I tell you, it fair broke my heart as they lowered him down, Conor my own brother, so young, and well favoured, with most of his days and his future before him. And to leave you and the boy, ah, that must have been the bitterest cut of all. But God help me, I'll see that you don't want, neither of the two of you. I swore it at the grave, and by your leave I'll swear it again. Now, dear, you must keep your strength up, so sit down and we'll have a bite. When we've had our tea we'll go into everything and see what's to be done for you."

Bernard's affirmation, delivered almost in one breath with lyrical intensity, and which my mother listened to with averted head, touched me deeply. I glanced expectantly at Uncle Leo, but to my surprise and disappointment he remained silent. This uncle, a few years younger than Bernard, was tall and extremely thin, with a long pale cleanshaven expressionless face, topped by a plastering of smooth black hair. Unlike the others he gave no evidence of mourning, being dressed in a plain navy blue suit, so tight fitting and shiny with use that he seemed to have grown into it. While Bernard was speaking his features remained completely blank except for a slight, yet most peculiar twitching of the corners of his lips which, but for the fact that his personality seemed so reserved, repressed and distant, might have been the vestige of a sarcastic smile.

At this moment my cousin Terence came bustling in, looking smarter, more handsome than ever, quite a man of the world in fact, and when Bernard had said grace we all sat down.

The lavishness of the repast provided me with a further indication of Bernard's generosity, all the more commendable in the face of his own financial difficulties. As Aunt Teresa kept drifting in and out, absently bringing fresh hot supplies from the kitchen, sausages, white puddings, a boiled fowl — never had I seen such quantities of food — Bernard repeatedly pressed us to eat and, considering his grief, sustained himself with remarkable fortitude. Mother had not much appetite nor, indeed, had I. The ruby port was taking its toll and my head felt as if it were stuffed with cotton wool, an extraordinary yet not unpleasant aerial sensation that made me forget my earlier miseries. Most curious of all, however, were the table manners and gastronomic proclivities of Uncle Leo, who at the outset of the feast had resolutely reversed his plate to preclude all possibility of the funeral meats being placed upon it and, avoiding like the plague Aunt Teresa's steaming dishes, contented himself with a glass of milk, a plain wheaten scone, masticated with extreme thoroughness, and four tablets taken from a little bottle which he extracted from his waistcoat pocket.

"And now, my dear Grace," Bernard gazed at Mother with admiring sympathy, "if it's agreeable to you, should we have our little family chat about your future? From what I can gather, our poor Con didn't leave you with too much of the ready — if I may put it that way without offence."

"Almost everything we had went into Conor's business," Mother answered quietly. "And to very good purpose. He had paid off every penny he owed, both to Hagemann and the bank. He was his own master."

Uncle Leo, who had so far said nothing, had a strange way of not looking directly at anyone. Now his gaze travelled well over Mother's head as he asked despondently:

"Was he insured?"

"No. I believe he tried eventually, but was refused a policy."

"What exactly is in the bank?" Leo persisted, still viewing the ceiling.

"A matter of two hundred pounds." Mother flushed as she answered. "And of course there's the doctor's bill and the funeral expenses."

Bernard raised a restraining, benevolent hand.

"Not a word more about that, dear. As I told you before, I'll take care of the funeral, every penny of it. And we'll throw in the doctor's bill as well."

"Even if that's done, two hundred won't take you far," Leo said gloomily. "In my opinion the first thing you'll have to do is sell some of your furniture and get out of that big expensive flat."

"I have already arranged to do so."

I wanted to cheer Mother for that calm, composed answer,

and such was my elevated state, I would probably have done so had not Leo immediately resumed.

"Next, you must try to sell the agency."

Mother shook her head.

"No."

"Why not? It must be worth something . . . if we can find a buyer. Even if the U.D.L. have cooled off they'll make some sort of offer."

"I don't want a buyer."

I reached under the table and found her hand. It was cold and trembling slightly. But she went on firmly:

"Conor made the business. It was all his idea, and a wonderful one too. Apart from my loyalty to him, I'm not going to see it thrown away. It's essentially single-handed work. I believe I can do it. And I'm going to try. I'm going to carry on the agency."

There was a silence, then Bernard thumped the table enthusiastically with his fist.

"And you'll do it, too. You'll have sympathy on your side. You'll get orders for that alone, not to speak of your pretty face. By God, you're a brave little woman. But what about the boy? You'll be in Winton all day. Shall I send him to Rockcliff for you, like I did my Terry?"

"He'll go later, perhaps," Mother said. "I can't part with him now. I've arranged with a neighbour, the lady downstairs, to rent three rooms in her house. She'll keep an eye on Laurence when he's not at school."

So we were going to Miss Greville! Following on Mother's previous announcement, for which I had been equally unprepared, this news gave me a real start in which apprehension and excitement had an equal part. While Bernard continued to praise Mother with the most optimistic prognostications of her success, I tried to foresee the possibilities inherent in our new lodging and, although I failed, somehow sensed they would be profound. The discussion between Mother and my uncles went on, but I had now passed beyond the stage of coherent attention, although from time to time I was vaguely conscious of the note of pessimistic protest in Uncle Leo's voice.

"Well," he declared finally. "If your mind is made up, there's nothing more to be done."

In the pause that followed Uncle Bernard made a special sort of sign to Terence who nodded and got to his feet.

"He'll open up below," Bernard explained with a sigh. "Life must go on."

"I'll feed the dog first," Terry said. "Get his dinner, Nora. Like to come?" he added, with a glance that casually took in me.

We descended to the yard by an outside stair I had not noticed before. Repulsing the Joker's frantic leapings and quiverings with the words: "Down brute," Terence dusted off a convenient box and seated himself judicially.

"Well, caper, here we are again."

"Yes, Terence."

"And not under the best of circumstances."

"No, Terence."

A pause while he looked me up and down.

"As a matter of interest, who slapped these duds on you?"

"Miss O'Riordan."

"I thought as much." He shook his head in slow disparagement. "You know, caper, if you don't watch out women'll be the ruin of you. You've got to learn to stand up for yourself, and not let them run you, or you'll be under their thumb for the rest of your life."

Terence's homily was not altogether comprehensible but

as it seemed to manifest some interest in my welfare I took it as a compliment to my bereaved state. He seemed indeed to be on the point of offering me further sage advice; however, at this point Nora appeared with a plate on which lay a thick outsize slice of prime raw steak.

"You'd better hurry, Terry. There's a crowd outside with their tongues hanging out."

"Ah, let them wait, it'll strengthen their thirst. I want to show caper the Joker." Holding off the hound whose whip-like tail lashings had now become intense, he took the plate from Nora, placed it on the ground and in a solemn tone of warning said: "Friday."

The Joker, already launching himself on the steak, was stopped by what had every appearance of a lethal electric shock. Curved in an acute parabola over the plate, saliva drooling from his jaws, he fixed one intense imploring eye on Terence.

"You see," remarked Terence, lighting a cigarette in a manner so leisurely as to exacerbate the Joker's anguish. "That's a good Catholic dog. He'll not touch flesh meat on days of abstinence."

"But today isn't Friday, Terry," I objected.

"For the Joker," Terence said, "my word is good enough. Yes, man, for that dog I'm as infallible as the Pope. In a minute I'm going to tell him it's Saturday."

I was deeply impressed until a thought struck me.

"But how do you manage in Lent, Terry? Practically every day's a fast day then."

"In Lent," Terence appeared to reflect. "In Lent we get him a dispensation. Yes, man, that's a very holy dog. Strange too, when you consider I bought him from a Jewish gentleman by the name of K. Q. Fink. I had a bit of trouble getting him out of his Kosher habits but in the end, thank God, we converted him. And has it paid off, man! Now he's just full of piety. You ought to see him play lame just before I match him in a race."

Where this remarkable dialogue would have led us is impossible to determine. Certainly it appeared to cause Nora a series of suppressed internal spasms. But it was interrupted by a violent banging on some outer door and a voice shouting:

"Open up, will ye, for the love of God. We're all parched out here."

At this Terence lounged to his feet and released the Joker with truly apostolic gesture and intonation.

"There's proof for you, caper," he remarked as he went out. "The Joker never fails me."

In three swift snaps the steak had gone.

A somewhat hollow silence followed this remarkable demonstration. It was broken by my mother calling me from the head of the stair. Apparently we had been pressed to stay the night with Uncle Bernard but to my disappointment, since I harboured an extraordinary inclination to resume my acquaintance with Nora in the hen house, Mother had declined. And now, as it was past four o'clock, she said we must leave for our train.

While she was getting her coat and hat Leo, who had not spoken to me once, had not even appeared aware of my existence, came slowly towards me. While his tall, sad, enigmatic presence loomed above me, he produced from his shiny trouser pocket a short handful of silver amongst which, after a diligent search, he found a threepenny bit.

"Here, boy," he said. "Don't waste it. It's hard-earned money. And always remember this. Your best friend is your own bank book."

So far I had not been at all favourably impressed by Uncle Leo but now, discovering him to be so poor — a suspicion I had already entertained — yet willing to spare me this coin, albeit the smallest in the realm, and as I now observed, thin, darkish in colour and slightly bent, all of which made me dubious of its negotiability, I felt a twinge of sympathetic pity and thanked him profusely.

"It seems Bernard has you in hand," he said impassively, though his lips were twitching again. "There's no end that he means to do for you. I've a poor sort of business myself, but if ever you should need a job or want to learn a trade, come to me. I've told your mother."

Without saying goodbye he turned and went off.

Nora and Terence, now released from duty by his father, came with us to the station. How pleased I was when Nora took my hand, swinging it as we walked along. I reddened with gratification when Terry asked me if I could still run fast. It was good to be in the open again with a fresh breeze to blow away all the strange and conflicting impressions so summarily forced upon me. Mother's step seemed lighter too, as though she had not been at ease in Bernard's house, and that while she had supported it with calm and fortitude the day had been for her a fearful ordeal.

Seated together in the corner of a third class compartment she did not speak. Gazing intently into her face I felt sadness descend upon her. What were her thoughts? Of my father no doubt, and perhaps of how blessedly different he had been, as was Simon too, from those other brothers. Or did she think of the strangeness of her life, contrasting her upbringing and early background, both so proper and correct, with all that she had experienced and endured today? I could not guess. Then, all that mattered was that she held me close to her as the train rumbled past the Lomond Vaults and, gathering speed, bore us through a pale serene sunset towards the darkening valley of the Fruin beyond.

13

IN THE second week of April Mother and I moved down to
Miss Greville's house — a memorable transition, not in dom-
icile alone, but also in our lives. The accommodation so graciously offered was pleasing and, everything considered, well
suited to our needs. At the back of the first floor of the spacious
maisonette we had two nice rooms, not large but well lit
and cheerful since both overlooked the lawn, and an adjoining
smaller room, actually a deep alcove which Miss Greville, by
installing a gas cooker and a porcelain sink, had converted to
a small but practicable kitchen. A bathroom, too, was conveniently near on the half landing. Care had undoubtedly been
taken and thought expended to make us comfortable and while
I had no exact knowledge of the sum Mother paid in rent it
must of necessity have been disproportionately modest, representing, in my view, Miss Greville's wish to help us, rather
than any sordid desire for gain.

Here, then, in this miniature lodging, our new iife began.
Every morning Mother rose at seven o'clock and made our
breakfast. Usually I had a cereal called grapenuts, then we
each had a boiled egg and hot buttered toast. I drank a glass of
milk while Mother had several cups of very strong tea. She
confided in me that she could never do without her morning

tea. It seemed to brisken and fortify her, although she still looked sad. She had not yet lost the pinched look that startled me when I returned from Port Cregan.

After breakfast she washed the dishes and I dried them, then, while I finished dressing, she put on her new business suit, a costume of dark grey material, and how relieved I was to see her out of that sinister funeral black, which she had wisely decided would be prejudicial to her work. At quarter past eight we left the house together, Mother resolutely to take the eight-forty train for Winton, I reluctantly, to go to school. I need hardly add that I was still attending St. Mary's — our position at the moment was too uncertain to justify any change to a better school.

Nevertheless, if that cherished dream seemed deferred, I was amply compensated by a new and striking departure from my dull routine. Since my poor mother was away all day, did not in fact get home until six o'clock at night, and made the best of some kind of lunch at one or other of the city tea rooms, Miss Greville had suggested, had indeed insisted, that I take my midday meal with her. Lunch with Miss Greville became then the fascination and, at least in the beginning, the bane of my existence.

On the first day, when I arrived breathless at half past twelve, having hurried all the way back from school for fear of being late, she was waiting for me in the dining room, standing erect with her thumb in her waistband. She glanced at the curious bronze and porcelain clock on the mantelpiece.

"Good. You are punctual. Go and wash your hands. And brush your hair."

When I returned, she indicated my place. We sat down. The food, served by Campbell, the silent elderly maid who behaved as though I did not exist, was delicious, hot, and startlingly strange. The table appointments, among which twin silver pheasants were outstanding, no less than the arrangement of the heavy silver cutlery, embarrassed and intimidated me. I dropped my stiff napkin and had to grope under my chair. When I had retrieved it Miss Greville addressed me pleasantly.

"We are going to have our first little talk, Carroll. You observe that I call you simply Carroll. As you are now the only Carroll in this vicinity you have no claim to be known as *young* Carroll."

To a boy endearingly denoted Laurie, and only on the strictest occasions referred to as Laurence, I could only regard this repeated use of my second name a brutal assault on my feelings.

"To resume. When we go to table you must in future withdraw my chair and see that I am properly seated before *you* seat yourself. Do you understand?"

"Yes, Miss Greville," I said, abjectly.

"Again, during our lunches, which I trust will always be agreeable to you, we must cultivate the art of conversation. We shall talk of current events, of sport if you wish, of natural history, books, music, and of people. The first person to be discussed, Carroll, is you."

I turned hot all over.

"To begin, I assume that you have no desire to become a confirmed brooder. You know, of course, what that is?"

"Some kind of a hen," I faltered.

"Apt, Carroll, if erroneous. A creature perpetually wallowing in self-pity. Would you wish to be like that?"

"No, Miss Greville."

"Then you must stop being sorry for yourself. Fond though I am of your mother I regard you as suffering from an excess of maternal leniency. I therefore propose to introduce you to the Spartan ideal. Doubtless you know of the Greek city of Sparta, where weak children were simply exposed and left to perish? Or better still, simply thrown over the cliff."

"Oh, no," I gasped.

"I," said Miss Greville coldly, "have seen the actual cliff. Now, Carroll, do you want to be thrown over the cliff or to live like a real Greek boy?"

"And how *did* he live?" I tried to express contempt.

"From the day he went to school at the age of seven he spent a considerable part of each day exercising under trained supervision, in the palaestra. He wrestled, ran, punched a ball filled with fig seeds, rode bareback, learned to throw missiles and ward them off, his interest being kept alive by innumerable competitions for boys of different ages. But enough of history. For the present it will suffice to suggest to you the virtue of a cold bath every morning, of strenuous exercises, of endurance tests that harden the body and summon up the blood. The uncomfortable truth is, Carroll, that I find you a soft, spoiled, spineless, and abnormally solitary boy."

Outraged beyond belief, I felt my eyes fill with water.

"If you weep, Carroll," she said firmly, "I shall, from this instant, utterly disown you."

Repressively, I bit my lip hard. Cruelly maligned though I was, I did not, strangely, wish to be disowned. Besides, indignation was beginning to seethe in me. The phrase "abnormally solitary" stuck in my throat.

"Perhaps you will tell me," I said carefully, so as not to break down, "how a boy in my position can help it. Who can he not be solitary with?"

"With me. I am going to take you in hand." Miss Greville regarded me calmly. "Do you know anything of botany?"

"No, I don't," I answered sulkily.

"Then tomorrow, as it is Saturday, you shall begin to learn. Be ready at nine sharp. And now you must have another cutlet.

Only, remember that your fork is not a shovel. The prongs are to be utilized. Do not scoop. Impale."

Having thus reduced me, Miss Greville now appeared to withdraw into herself. With a faint, peculiar smile on her lips, her mood seemed focussed on the invisible. Her eye, however, remained on the clock. When it struck one she rose and, taking the cup of coffee that had been served her, advanced to the window. Spellbound, I watched her take her stand behind the long lace curtain where, partly concealed, she slowly sipped her coffee. Suddenly the cup was arrested, her smile deepened, remained. At last she turned and with a satisfied, almost a gay expression, put down her cup.

"You may go now, Carroll," she said pleasantly. "And don't forget. Tomorrow morning at nine."

That afternoon in school, instead of attending to Sister Margaret Mary who was endeavouring to instruct us in the principles of compound fractions, I brooded darkly, almost heroically, on the insults I had received, and in the evening, when Mother returned from Winton, I informed her that I wished to be no party to the plans Miss Greville had conceived for me.

"I think you should go, dear," Mother said soothingly. "I'm quite sure Miss Greville means well by you."

Thus it became apparent that Mother was in league with my detractor.

Next morning, between apprehension and expectation, I kept my appointment. Miss Greville presented a somewhat singular figure. She was wearing an oatmeal Harris tweed skirt much shorter than I thought proper, revealing muscular calves encased by a strong pair of weather-beaten high laced brown boots. Her green Tyrolean hat, turned up at one side and perched on her head, sported a bushy ornament indistinguishable from a shaving brush, and over her shoulder was rakishly slung a curious black japanned container.

"*That*," she explained, reading my expression, "is a vasculum. And *this* is our lunch. You may carry it."

Handing over a bulging knapsack as weather-beaten as her boots, she helped me to strap it on my back, then we strode off at a cracking pace along the terrace and into Sinclair Road which led straight up the hill, Miss Greville using a curious spiked walking stick covered with little silver badges. I wanted to ask what they were, but so furious was her assault upon the slope, I thought it wiser to save my breath. Besides, I was horribly conscious of the odd glances directed towards us by the passers-by, looks of amused recognition which my companion disdainfully ignored.

Up we went, without a word exchanged between us. Soon we had passed the last big villas that were widely spaced in their extensive grounds among the first of the big pine trees. Civilization now lay behind us. We were totally in the pine woods. Sweat had started to run into my eyes, my breath made a sharp whistling tune, and when I saw that even this remote wood was not far enough, that she meant to take me to the high moors, I almost wilted. But I would not give in. Whatever puny spirit I possessed had been ignited by this abominable yet absorbing woman. I meant to show her that I was not the sort of boy to be chucked offhand over that Spartan cliff.

With a dry throat and a pumping heart I kept on, sometimes at a half trot, refusing to lag behind, and when at last we broke out of the woods on to that great wide expanse of moorland that ran on and on for many miles, free and undefiled across Glen Fruin to the shores of the Loch, I was still, though completely blown, at her side.

Here, mercifully, she drew up, looked at me, then took her watch out of her waistband.

"One hour and twenty minutes," she announced. "Not altogether bad. We'll do better as you progress. Are you fagged?"

"Not in the least," I lied.

Inspecting me closely, for the first time, she actually smiled.

"Then we'll start on the real business of the day." She spoke with animation. "It's been an open winter and with luck we should find some interesting things for your collection."

Without enthusiasm, I followed her as, with bent head, she stalked off slowly into the heather.

"You know, I'm sure, the commoner heath flowers. The ericas, not yet out, the yellow gorse, the broom and the cotton grass — these white tufts blowing in the wind." She paused. "But have you seen this?"

"No, I haven't," I said sourly.

Kneeling down she had parted the grass and exposed a delicate little plant with pointed green leaves and starry, bright golden yellow flowers.

"The bog asphodel. *Narthecium ossifragum*. One of the *Liliaceae*."

Quite against my wishes and inclination, I was impressed, not only by her manifest erudition, but by the sudden uncovering of this hidden, sparkling and wholly unsuspected flower.

"Shall we dig it up?"

"Decidedly not. But we'll take one raceme for pressing." And she snipped off a single stem which, rather to my surprise since I had decided not to cooperate, I accepted and tucked away in the vasculum.

We proceeded for some minutes without incident, then she stopped again.

"Here is something rather striking. The round-leafed sundew. *Drosera rotundifolia*."

As I gazed questioningly at the graceful little rosette, she went on.

"Each leaf, as you see, bears several rows of crimson hairs, terminating in rounded heads, like a sea-anemone's tentacles.

Indeed they serve a similar purpose. They secrete a clear sticky fluid which entraps small insects crawling over the leaf. Their efforts to free themselves irritate the hairs which bend over the insect so that it is secured, digested and assimilated by the plant."

"I say!" I exclaimed, in a tone of wonder. "A fly-eating plant!"

"Precisely. We shall dig this one up — I have no love for the sundews — plant it in peat moss and you may observe it in action at home."

"May I really, Miss Greville?"

"Why not?"

She allowed me to wield the trowel taken from the vasculum and, when the plant was safely stowed, made a gesture of liberation.

"Now that you're launched, Carroll, you may go off on your own. Call me if you find anything that looks exciting."

I started off, with a willingness I would not have believed possible, eager to demonstrate my tracker's skill. To my chagrin, although Miss Greville seemed to be having success, my untrained eyes found nothing. But at last, suddenly, I stumbled on a splendid bloom, starting up from amongst the withered grass, big as a hyacinth and of a deep glowing purple.

"Quick, Miss Greville," I shouted. "Please come quickly."

She came.

"Do look, Miss Greville. Isn't it a beauty?"

She made a generous gesture of assent.

"The *Orchis maculata*. Tubers palmate, bracts green, three nerved. A first-rate specimen. I congratulate you, Carroll. If only we can find its neighbour, the *morio*, we may count ourselves fortunate."

I blushed with pride, watching as she carefully snipped two flowers from the spiky stem and, with some other specimens she had collected, permitted me to stow them away.

We were now in a grassy saucer of the moor, probably an old sheep dip, sheltered on one side by a marbled ridge of rock. She glanced upwards. The pale sun was now directly overhead.

"Does this strike you as a suitable spot for lunch, Carroll?"

I immediately approved the terrain.

"Then see what Campbell has given us."

I unpacked the knapsack, reverently handling the damp, napkin-wrapped packages, noting with enthusiasm that several homemade sausage rolls were included. Finally, tucked in beside the flask of coffee, a splendid bottle of Comrie's lemonade was revealed. This foresight touched me so acutely that involuntarily I exclaimed.

"Oh, Miss Greville, you are terribly kind."

"Campbell," she replied calmly.

"But Campbell does not like me."

"Campbell does not show her feelings."

"But Miss Greville, Campbell does not answer when I speak to her."

"Campbell is not naturally predisposed to conversation. Besides, she is rather deaf."

With Campbell disposed of, we began lunch. As this exceeded my expectation I ate a great deal, an indulgence made possible by the fact that Miss Greville herself appeared rather indifferent towards the sausage rolls. She had removed her hat and, sitting erect with closed eyes and that faint withdrawn smile, had surrendered herself to the spirits of the moor. From time to time, while eating steadily, I gazed at her with awe. The wind was singing in the heather, overhead curlews were circling and calling against the blue sky. No other sound but the faint hum of an early bee.

"May I tell you something, Miss Greville?" I ventured, taking up the last egg and cress sandwich. "I think I am going to like doing botany very much."

Imperturbably, she inclined her head.

"Then we shall do some more presently. We still have to find an *Orchis morio* to match your *maculata*."

After we had rested for a while we started off again, not deeper into the moor, but across, towards the road. Charged with botanical ardour, I surpassed myself. We found the *morio* orchid, and specimens of bog myrtle, yellow pimpernel and St. John's wort, for all of which Miss Greville knew the Latin names. She also showed me a lapwing's nest with four eggs, and a bed of whortleberry shrubs that in a few weeks would yield us fruit.

The afternoon was fading into an umbered haze as at last we struck the road. But now, though long, it was all down hill. My legs were tired but my chest felt full of fresh air. This inflation and an intoxicating sense of achievement supported me during an unexpected encounter — which otherwise might have unnerved me — with Mr. Lesly, the vicar of St. Jude's, Miss Greville's church. Although I felt myself automatically suspect by all clergymen of denominations other than my own, this was a pleasant man to whom, when questioned, I identified myself as a Papist in a manner Miss Greville subsequently commended.

"Mr. Lesly is exceptionally gifted. Broad minded too." She continued in the same strain of praise. "And of course, Carroll, we Catholics at St. Jude's are in many respects in accord with you Romans, although naturally celibacy is not imposed on our clergy."

After that we were soon home. With effusive thanks I parted from Miss Greville and dashed upstairs with the vasculum.

"I've had such a time, Mother. I found a rare orchid. We got a plant that actually eats flies, and all sorts of other specimens. Miss Greville's going to show me how to mount them, and to cut sections too, for her microscope."

She was seated at the table, adding figures on a sheet of paper. As she raised her head, her expression remained so pre-occupied that I called out:

"Mother, what's wrong? Didn't you hear me?"

She recovered herself immediately.

"Yes, dear, of course I did." Drawing me towards her she held me tight. "And what fine red cheeks it's given you. Now sit beside me, very close, and tell me all about it."

14

D URING THAT spring and summer I spent entrancing hours
of happiness and well-being on the moors, sometimes
with Miss Greville, more often alone. My passion for
natural history had at least the merit of improving my health.
Or perhaps this was due to the light dumbbells Miss Greville
had placed in my room and those morning cold baths which,
though Mother demurred, I now persistently endured under
the admonitions of my patroness who, with compelling instances of the austerities endured by runners training for
Olympia, continued to fire me with the Greek ideal.

"You have not been endowed with too remarkable an anatomy, Carroll. You must make the most of it."

While no visible muscular bulges appeared, and it was morti-
fying when Miss Greville sought vainly for the first sign of my
biceps, nevertheless, I did at last begin to grow. And beyond
this, I became absurdly expert in moorland lore. I knew, and
had found, practically every wild flower between Ardfillan and
Glen Fruin, could spot the subtle difference between a Cinque-
foil and a Tormentil and, when I wanted to show off, could
even cut and stain sections to demonstrate to Mother on Miss
Greville's ancient Zeiss microscope.

My solitary wanderings through the heather had failed to
afford me my greatest wish, the congenial companionship of

someone my own age, but they had brought me, incredibly, the friendship of that spectre of my early childhood, a game-keeper. After a painful introduction when, observing my fig-ure against the horizon, keeper John Mackenzie had come strid-ing in pursuit to charge me with "herrying" grouse eggs, the contents of my vasculum had partially reassured him, and the botanical jargon which I gabbled in excuse probably convinced him that he was dealing with an oddity. On subsequent occa-sions, watching through his stalker's telescope, he must have assured himself of my innocence and took occasion to meet up with me, to sound me out and, when later on he found me useful in locating outlying nests for him, to have a companion-able chat. As keeper for Glen Fruin his task was to provide a maximum of birds for the twelfth of August. I think in the end I earned his respect for he took trouble to tell me many inter-esting things about his work, which provided me with stimu-lating topics for my lunchtime conversations with Miss Gre-ville.

"Do you know something, Miss Greville?" I would begin, having sampled with relish my first spoonful of a red soup which was apparently called *bortsch*.

"I know a great many things, Carroll, to which of these do you refer?"

"Grouse, Miss Greville."

"Yes," she replied meditatively. "I am fairly familiar with that bird, both on and off the table. My poor father shot a great many of them on the Yorkshire moors."

"But do you know, Miss Greville, that when the young bird flies only five days after hatching it couldn't exist without two things."

"The young green shoots of the heather?" she suggested.

"And?"

She shook her head.

"Midges!" I exclaimed.

She looked up from her soup.

"Good heavens, Carroll. You startle me."

"I thought I should," I said triumphantly. "That's one of the reasons the old rooty heather must be burned off, and the damp patches kept on the moor as a breeding ground for the protein-rich insects." I was rather proud of that word "protein" — Mr. Mackenzie was quite a learned man. "Water is needed too, Miss Greville. The hen bird drinks a lot when she's sitting. Of course the sheep are Mr. Mackenzie's greatest curse, he's always counting them."

"Does he sleep badly?" she inquired, blandly.

"Oh, not that, Miss Greville. The sheep grazing on the moor. Only a certain number are supposed to be allowed and they eat the young heather day and night. They're worse than the hooded crows. They never lose their appetite."

She at last allowed herself to smile.

"Well, I'm glad you haven't lost yours. Have some more soup."

In these adventures, I should have been happy all through the long school holidays but for the change, that suddenly became apparent to me, in my mother. Because I loved and trusted her best in the world, I had always taken her for granted, and I had imagined that she had "got over" Father's death. Nor could I guess what deprivations she endured beyond the loss of Father's companionship and support. Absorbed in my own pursuits, I had barely noticed her lost look when she returned from Winton in the evening, or how at times she would sit, her gaze detached, a finger pressed against her cheek, her lips moving slightly, as though she were talking to herself.

"Come, Grace," Miss Greville would remonstrate, making a sudden appearance upstairs. "This melancholy moping won't do at all. You must come down to me. Miss Gilbraith and Alice Charteris have called and we're going to have music."

"I'm rather tired," Mother would say, "and don't really feel like it. You'll manage very well without me."

"Nonsense, dear Grace. We all want you. And it will do you a world of good."

These friends of Miss Greville's were mistresses at St. Anne's, desirable in every way, and when she yielded to persuasion, these musical evenings did take Mother out of herself.

Yet there were responsibilities of which I realized nothing, that could not be relieved by a Haydn quartette. To me it seemed simple and natural that Mother should have taken over Father's business. Everything was settled, going well, and would continue as before. Not a breath of financial stress was in the air.

One evening the post brought a letter for Mother, an event unusual enough for me to wait expectantly while she opened and read it. Suddenly I heard her gasp, saw her press a hand to her forehead.

"Oh, dear," she exclaimed, in a pained voice. "This is too bad."

"What is, Mother?"

Overcome, she sat down, holding the letter.

"Your Uncle Bernard has sent me the bill." Mother was almost incoherent, but I saw that she must speak to me. "Before your father died he told me he wanted, yes, insisted on a simple burial. But Uncle Bernard would not have it. He took all the responsibility. So we had all these unnecessary, hateful, expensive trappings. And now the unpaid bill, that I thought was settled long ago, has come to me, with the threat of a summons.

"Is it much?"

"Terribly much."

I felt myself go hot all over with indignation.

"He must pay it. He promised he would. I heard him say so."

Mother was reading the letter again.

"He says he can't. That they've condemned his property, that he owes other people, that he's very hard pressed."

"What a beastly thing to do. Mother, he must be a . . . a perfect cad." This was a word I had learned from Miss Greville, and was in this case entirely misapplied. My Uncle Bernard was a soft, muddled, impractical, self-indulgent man, always in debt and skirting the edge of disaster yet somehow managing to live well and to do well for his children. Moreover, like others of his sort, he was full of good intentions. His fulsome promises and extravagant ideas of doing good were genuine. Not only did he believe at the time that he would fulfil them but often, by a sort of hallucination, became firmly convinced that he had done so. Perhaps Mother felt this, for she sighed.

"He meant well, I suppose, and I daresay he hasn't the money. He says he may have to go bankrupt. His affairs are in a bad way."

"He always seems to be going bankrupt, Mother." I was still unforgiving. "And doing very nicely out of it, with lots of good food and fine clothes, and all sorts of comforts, like we saw at the funeral."

"Some people live like that, dear. Anyway, it is my responsibility, I'll settle it at once." Mother spoke slowly, and she added, to herself: "My poor Conor, there will be no mean squabble over your grave."

Bernard's letter must have made Mother feel very much alone. Uncle Simon was cloistered in Spain. We never by any chance heard a word from Leo. It was natural for her to seek encouragement elsewhere. Although she never once wrote to her home, she could get in touch with Stephen, her youngest brother, at the Winton University Union. Such a letter was sent; I posted it for Mother.

Stephen came on a Saturday afternoon and was exactly as I remembered him on his rare visits to Ardencaple — a pale, quiet and thoughtful young man, with well-cut, regular features and a fine intellectual forehead inclined to furrow in a studious frown, not saying much, but so glad to see Mother, holding her hand for a long time and looking questioningly into her eyes. Only to see them like this was to be made aware of the affection that existed between them.

A good high tea with cold ham and potato salad had been prepared, and when we had finished Mother gave me money and said I might go to the town for a box of Eman's toffee. I knew they wanted to talk so I did not hurry, but when I got back they were still talking, with their heads bent over a pile of papers on the table.

"You really mustn't worry, Grace," Stephen was saying. "Things are going quite well." He had a pencil in one hand and with the other was ruffling his black hair, sending little sprays of dandruff on to his jacket collar. "When everything is paid off, including the defaulted bill, you'll still have one hundred and fifty pounds in the bank."

"It's little enough. With Laurence's education to think of."

"But you have your job. Hagemann's been very fair in guaranteeing deliveries on the same terms as before. The business, as I see it, is extremely easy to run. And your orders have more or less kept up."

"They only give them because they're sorry for me. And because they liked Conor so well."

"They'll like you too."

Mother shook her head, yet not so despondently as before.

"I can't go in and be hail-fellow-well-met with them over a bottle of beer, like poor Con."

The idea of Mother with a bottle of beer was so comic I gave a shout of laughter which made them both look up, and in a moment Mother smiled back at me. She gathered up the papers.

"Did you know that your clever young uncle has taken his degree with honours and won another special research bursary at the University? You'll do that too, won't you, dear?"

I had no doubt that I would do it.

Stephen stood up, looked at his watch, a plain five-shilling Ingersoll like mine, and said it was time for his train. Then, with a guarded look at me he said, in an undertone, to Mother:

"I don't want to press you again, Grace. But won't you reconsider Father's offer?"

"What's the use?" Mother said. "Am I to go back and pretend that I'm sorry, that I made a terrible mistake, but now I'll be good and make up for it?"

"I think I could promise you'd be welcome. You'd have a comfortable home again, your own folks around you."

"But on their terms? I couldn't bring myself to accept them."

"Is that one point as important to you as all that?"

Mother, looking down, seemed to be debating some question with herself.

"Oddly enough it is. And certainly it is for . . . you know whom. What in all the world would he think of a mother who suddenly recanted and said, now you've got to forget all you've been brought up to and knuckle under and become something else? Besides being cruel, it would be an act of horrible disloyalty to . . . to the dead." Mother shook her head. "What's done is done. I don't regret it. And there's no going back on it."

There was a longish silence. Then Stephen said:

"I believe you're right, Grace. I respect you for it."

This conversation which I did not understand had nevertheless made me feel extremely uncomfortable. I was glad when Stephen asked me to walk with him to the train.

On our way to the station he encouraged me to stick in at my lessons. He had heard that I was clever and for any boy who hadn't a father behind him hard work was the road to success. He told me he was going to have a shot at the Indian Civil Service, not necessarily to go to India, for if he got a high enough place in the examination he would be kept at home. But he was modestly pessimistic about his chances.

Finally, just before the train pulled away, he said to me, in his cautious way:

"Don't worry your mother, Laurence, for things you don't actually need. She has enough to look after at present. And she's making quite a few sacrifices for you."

I promised faithfully to be considerate, prudent and vigilant. Yes, in all possible ways, to cherish Mother. Did I not love her with all my heart? Alas, my promises were easily made, and soon I was careless of them. Now that the weather had finally broken and winter was drawing near, a new passion had begun to absorb me.

15

MISS GREVILLE had an extensive library, inherited from her father, to which I had free access. It was, I imagine, a typical English country house library of the period, well bound, full of things both good and bad, and with a sporting flavour. During that cold, wet and sleety winter — climatic conditions normally found at that season in such latitudes — I read with ever increasing voracity.

In the recollections of those who, like myself, have ventured into descriptions of their early years, nothing has bored me more than those long, tedious, and particularized listings of the books the author has read and which led, in the end, to the formation of a literary taste that was demonstrably excellent. For this reason I refrain from presenting a catalogue and state simply that I read everything.

But the manner of my reading may be worthy of note if only because it was so bad. Lying flat on my face in a secluded and therefore dark corner of the room with my nose pressed close to the volume, I read at a great pace, a technique of speed that increased with habit. Not only did I skip mercilessly, I acquired the unholy knack of getting the sense of a page by the almost express absorption, through my flickering vision, of certain key words and phrases. I vividly remember racing through *The Scarlet Letter* in the space of a short forenoon, getting Hester Prynne with child — by obscure processes entirely beyond me — almost burning her at the stake, and finally interring her safely in the old burial ground, all between breakfast and lunch, a performance of assimilation that even the most expert professional critic might envy.

Whatever the mental results of these endeavours, and my imagination seethed with hectic visions amidst which I strayed as in a trance, the physical effects were soon apparent. My eyes stung and reddened, I had headaches, developed a permanent crick in my neck and tossed my bed into disorder when asleep. Yet I persisted, would not, or rather could not give up, so firmly was I in the grip of the drug.

One Saturday in March when the first pale fingers of spring sunshine were feeling their way into the room, I looked up mistily from my prone position on the floor. Miss Greville was observing me with distaste.

"This won't do, Carroll."

"What won't do, Miss Greville?"

"This bookworm business. Don't you see that the sun is out? Where is my Spartan youth?"

"Yes, but this is so awfully good, Miss Greville. Mr. Jorrocks has just taken a terrible toss in the bog."

She relented slightly.

"Yes, Jorrocks is good, isn't he? And James Pigg. Still, there's a limit, Carroll."

She went out. Relieved, I rejoined Mr. Jorrocks in his chase for his horse.

However, in the afternoon, just as I was again nicely settled, she returned.

"You still have that ball I gave you."

"Yes." I had in fact never used it. "In a drawer in my room."

"Get it," she commanded.

With great unwillingness I obeyed, submitted while she led me to the garden.

Three cricket stumps had been pitched at the far end of the lawn while a fourth, against which a bat reclined, stood at the house end. Advancing, Miss Greville picked up the bat and flourished it.

"This is now yours, Carroll. See you keep it well oiled. Mind now, only pure linseed oil."

When I had accepted the bat she removed her long cardigan and with a businesslike air rolled back the sleeves of her blouse, unexpectedly revealing arms as muscular as her calves. She then silently extended her palm, upon which I placed the ball, an action that afterwards supported my claim to have begun my cricketing career with a ball used at Lords in the Eton and Harrow match.

Meanwhile, however, I had been motioned to my stance at the batsman's wicket. Although my knowledge of the game was rudimentary, I knew I had a good eye, and the bat felt extremely comfortable in my hands. As Miss Greville's grand manner had put my back up and I had resented being taken from Surtees, I resolved to hit her out of the garden and, if possible, since she would be responsible, through a window.

"Play," she called, and with a short, fierce run, bowling underhand, launched the ball towards me.

I took a vicious swing, missed, and found my wicket in ruins.

"That was a sneak," I protested.

"A yorker, ass."

My humiliations during the next fifteen minutes were acute. She had been brought up on cricket, had played with her brothers as a girl, had attempted even to introduce the game at St. Anne's, an unapproved act that may in part have contributed to her resignation from that prim establishment. She bowled leg breaks, off breaks, lobs, more yorkers at which, enraged, I swiped crookedly and in vain. Only when, in this manner, she had convinced me of the necessity of a straight bat did my instruction begin and with such good effect as to enable me after a further quarter of an hour to experience the delight of striking the ball sweetly with the bulge of the bat and driving it hard beyond her all the way to the back door steps.

One of the qualities of this remarkable and, alas, unfortunate woman was her ability to communicate her enthusiasms to me. I fell madly in love with the game of cricket and played endless games with Miss Greville, a willing victim, throughout that mild dry spring. She had introduced me to the *Captain* magazine wherein, with envious rapture, I studied photographs of public school elevens, exclusive, immaculate, Olympian groups in white flannels, gay blazers and striped or quartered cricketing caps. Gone now were my expeditions to the moors, my ambition to excel in natural history. I wanted to be a famous cricketer, like George Gunn of Notts., whose name was on my bat and whose scores I followed with a passionate interest in Miss Greville's *Winton Herald*, sharing his triumph whenever he scored a century, bitterly downcast when he made a duck.

One afternoon in early June, after I had made a particularly handsome square cut that buried the ball in the currant bushes, Miss Greville looked reflective and, although she made no remark, I observed her that evening in conversation with my Mother, who seemed pleased. Afterwards Mother said to me:

"Hurry back after school tomorrow, Miss Greville wants you."

Next day, in expectation of our usual game on the lawn, I got home in good time. Miss Greville was waiting on me, but she was dressed, though sportingly, for the street, and her bicycle, with my bat strapped on the carrier, stood at the gate.

"Hop on the back step when I get going," she told me.

Miss Greville's bicycle was a Dursley-Petersen, a first class and expensive machine but one with its unusually high seat and unorthodox frame so distinctly original in design as to compel attention on the road. With Miss Greville aloft, in her Tyrolean hat, pedalling hard and myself hanging on by the back step, we were soon afforded evidence of presenting a unique combination to the public gaze. But these amused stares were easily ignored when at the west, superior end of the town I discovered that she was taking me to Willow Park, the ground of the Ardfillan Cricket Club.

Miss Greville swung through the open gate into the select, immaculately mown enclosure. We dismounted at the neat white pavilion. With appalling disrespect Miss Greville leaned the Dursley-Petersen against the flagstaff. In the middle of the green oval a man in yellowish white flannels and an old sweater was slowly pushing a roller. Cupping her hands to her mouth Miss Greville shouted:

"Heston!"

He came over, hastening and touching his peaked blue cap when he recognized my companion.

"How are you, Heston?" She held out her hand.

"Pretty spry, thank you m'am. Haven't seen much of you lately. Not since you had me over to St. Anne's."

He was a brown, thick set, close cropped, tight lipped little man, just short of middle age, whose skin seemed made of tough leather. He combined, as I well knew, the duties of professional and groundsman to the Ardfillan Club.

"You're still doing a bit of coaching, Heston?"

"Oh, yes," he admitted. "Quite a few of the Beechfield boys come round. Especially in the holidays."

"I want you to take on this boy. Give him three or four nets a week and send the bill to me."

He looked at me, and under his doubting eyes I felt my chin quiver.

"He's small, Miss Greville."

"You are not large, yourself, Heston."

He gave a faint, dry, self-contained, rather sad smile which as I afterwards discovered was his nearest approach to a laugh. No, never once did I see Heston laugh.

"All right," he said, in an offhand manner. "We'll have a look at him. Now, if you like."

We went into the pavilion, where he tossed me a pair of boy's pads. On the inside, printed in ink, I saw the name Scott-Hamilton and beneath, Beechfield School.

"Put these on. Or one of them. No, not the right leg."

I buckled a pad on my left leg, so nervous I could scarcely fasten the straps. The pad was too big for me, it felt difficult and flapped as I walked to the practice ground. Miss Greville was already there, behind the net.

Heston began by tossing me some ridiculously easy balls, clearly indicating his opinion of my ability. The first was a soft full pitch. I attempted feebly to block it, missed completely and it hit the off stump.

"Don't be an ass, Carroll," said Miss Greville encouragingly.

I stiffened my shaking knees, determined not to be an ass. More than anything I had ever longed for in my life, I wanted to have the entry to that cricket ground and I knew that if I made a fool of myself with Heston I should be returned to the nursery of the back garden.

I began to hit out at everything. For five minutes Heston continued to bowl at an easy pace, then he increased his run and bowled faster, so fast indeed that I flinched away from the crease. Now it was not a question of hitting, although I made one good hard square cut off a short ball, but of keeping my wicket intact. At the end of the half hour Heston had knocked out my stumps only three times and I saw with satisfaction that he was sweating.

I knew that I had done well and fully expected praise or at least congratulation. But although Heston had a private talk with Miss Greville, whom he seemed to regard with favour, to me he said no more than:

"We'll have to teach you not to run away from the fast stuff."

But this indication, grudging though it was, that I could continue with him was enough to raise me to the heights. On the way home the Dursley-Petersen seemed to soar. Arrived, I rushed upstairs.

"Mother, Heston's taken me. Not counting the full toss he only bowled me twice." I considered myself justified in subtracting one I had played on to my wicket.

She had just come in and, still in her outdoor clothes, was beginning to make our tea. She looked even more pleased than I had expected. Amongst her other anxieties she had been worrying about the summer holidays and what she should do with me during the long two months of the school vacation, a situation complicated by the certainty in her mind that we could not afford to go away for a change of air.

"So you can go to Willow Park in the holidays?"

"Yes," I said boastfully, and with unutterable selfishness. "You'll not see much of me, Mother. I mean to go there every day."

16
❧❧❧

THE SUMMER was unusually fine. The long, sunny days diffused a golden light. In the boundary wood of the cricket field honeysuckle flourished, twining wild over bush and hedgerow, and whenever I drew near to Willow Park the scent intoxicated me with the promise of the afternoon.

By some further quite unrecognized personal economies Mother had bought me in Ardfillan a second-hand Raleigh bicycle that gave the impression of being almost new. From Winton one evening she brought and unwrapped a parcel containing white flannels, a navy blazer and a blue and white cricket belt with a silvered snake clasp. Alone in my bedroom I tried on this rigout and studied myself carefully in the looking glass — Miss Greville had instructed me never to say "mirror." I decided that my general aspect was that of a cricketer, and although hitherto I had entertained grave doubts of my own appearance, often wondering how two such handsome parents could have had so insignificant a child, regretting especially the green colour of my eyes even to the point of discovering in *Pear's Shilling Encyclopedia* that this almost invariably was the unhappy fate of offspring of blue and brown eyed parentage — despite all this I was rather taken with this unusual reflection of myself. Did my eyes look a trifle less green, picking up the shade of the blazer and tending rather towards blue? Perhaps not, but I had grown a bit in a straight sort of way, my hair was a soft russet brown, and I had at least inherited my father's fresh complexion and sound white teeth.

Was it this new look that falsely established my status at Willow Park, that select preserve of affluence and snobbery? More likely my sponsorship saved me from being regarded, and possibly discarded, as an interloper. Despite her eccentricities Miss Greville had a definite status in the town. Amongst the members of the club I passed as a visitor, staying with her, perhaps her nephew, for the holidays. The keenness with which I fielded and made catches won an approval that sanctioned this view.

With the Beechfield boys my situation was more critical. Many of these boys, whose parents were stationed with the army in India or elsewhere in what was then proudly referred to as the Empire, remained at the school during the holidays, and there were others living in Ardfillan, notably the boy called Scott-Hamilton, whose pad I had worn, and his younger brother, who came often to the ground for a scratch game. At first their attitude was stony, but one day, after I had held a particularly hot return, Scott-Hamilton, a strong tall boy of thirteen who was captain of the Beechfield eleven and like myself, a cricket maniac, lounged over with his brother.

"Would you care to join us in a game? You're here for the holidays with your aunt, aren't you?"

"Yes."

"By the way, what school are you at?"

This was a question I had long anticipated and to which, with premeditated cunning, I had prepared the answer, knowing that if in effect I had admitted to attending my unspeakable little school in Clay Street I would be damned and cast off on the spot.

"I have a tutor," I lied calmly, yet excusing myself with the thought that after all, Miss Greville, if not my aunt, *was* a sort of tutor.

"Oh, I say," said Scott-Hamilton in a tone of sympathy. "Have you been ill?"

"Chest." I tapped my ribs in an offhand manner.

"Hard cheese!" murmured the younger brother.

"Anyhow, it hasn't jolly well interfered with your cricket," said Scott-Hamilton. "Let's pick sides."

I breathed again. It had come off. I was accepted.

Heston, of course, could have given me away. But beyond the fact that I often came down in the mornings to help him with the roller, mark the crease, or put up a new net, Heston was on my side of the fence. The sense of equality between the amateur and the professional that developed half a century later was then not even dreamed of, and Heston's position was that of a paid servant who must inveterately "sir" his masters and be subject to their command and abuse: "Heston, blanco my boots, will you," or, "Heston, give me half a dozen on the off side." "Damn it, Heston, where the devil have you hidden my sweater?" But Heston, if he suffered, was imperturbable, the most impassive man I had ever known. He had just failed to get his Hampshire county cap and, coming north to coach, had married the very pretty young waitress who served the teas at Willow Park. They had a baby girl, he was provided with a cottage and a garden, his home life was happy. Beneath that unconcerned exterior, I felt that he thoroughly despised the snobbery and "side" of his employers, some of whom, at least the newly rich, had all the affectations of the parvenu.

All that summer I played cricket with the Beechfield boys, in whose companionship the sweet sound of bat on ball became sweeter still. At last I had friends, the kind of boys I had always wanted as my intimates. The sun burned me a deep

Indian red, real muscles appeared on my arms and legs, I had never felt or played better. Most delicious of all, an achievement beyond my wildest dreams, was the patronage, verging on friendship, with which the elder Scott-Hamilton, my senior by three years, had come to favour me. Friendship existed on my side, a longing for affection and companionship, but it was never returned in kind. He had a code of casual, superior, slightly bored indifference that must never be infringed. His favourite epithet of disparagement was the word "toad." Demonstrativeness or gaucherie of any kind was met by: "Don't be a toad, toad." He repeatedly enjoined all of us not to be toads.

Inevitably, there were dangerous moments, but I carried everything before me. Miss Greville, who from the first failed to esteem my cricketing belt with the snake clasp, had suggested a more stylish support for my trousers, and to this end she gave me an old tie of her brother's — after his death a great many of his belongings had been returned to her.

"I say," commented the younger Scott-Hamilton, who was more impressionable than his brother, "Carroll's sporting an old E. tie."

I then elaborated further, ignoring Spion Kop but bringing in Kenya, creating relations, all with a fertility of imagination and an offhand use of Beechfield slang that quite startled me. Was I a snob? No. I was elevated far above myself. But most of these boys boasted, arrogantly and quite naturally, Douglas bragging of his father's steam yacht, a yellow-funnelled monster that lay in the Gareloch, and young Colquhoun never failing to remind us that his parents kept fifteen servants in Bengal. I had nothing to boast of, so instead of exaggerating, I invented. But all that I said and did was defensive, the fervent, ridiculous and pathetic expression of a lifelong longing for social acceptance and equality.

I could not bear to think that autumn would bring the cessation of my joys, yet as the season drew to a close that sting was palliated by the thought of the final game, the traditional annual fixture between the boys coached by Heston and the second eleven of the club. Scott-Hamilton had picked our side: ten Beechfield boys and myself. True, I was last man on the list, but that did not seem to matter. I was in the eleven. From now on, as the afternoons drew in to early dusk, our practice at the nets became intensive. Although his attitude was casual, verging between boredom and a kind of sleepy indifference, I knew that Scott, as I now called him, wanted desperately to win this match. Not only was this his last year at Beechfield before going to Fettes, he had a special animus, amounting to a vendetta, against one of the Beechfield masters, Cunningham by name, a "complete outsider," according to Scott, with no chin and buck teeth, who was captain of the club eleven.

17

THE MORNING of the match was crisp and sunny with only a faint autumnal haze, which gave promise of a fine still day. It was of course a single innings game, and was due to start at eleven o'clock. To my sorrow, Miss Greville was debarred from seeing me perform by an engagement at the vicarage where Mr. Lesly, with extremely bad taste, had chosen this particular day for St. Jude's annual garden party. Yet, in a way, I felt slightly relieved at this enforced absence of my "aunt," since there was always the horrid possibility that one or other of her more outspoken observations might expose the true nature of our relationship. It was enough that I carried her good wishes with me as, at ten o'clock, I set out for the club ground.

Now the game of cricket is presumably not a matter of passionate interest for every reader of this book, nevertheless this particular match was an exciting one, and since its upshot proved even more memorable, I must briefly describe it.

A coin was spun in front of the pavilion and Cunningham, having won the toss, elected to bat first. Our opponents, with a jocularity that we found offensive, were prepared to treat us lightly. They began by offering catches in the deep field which to their surprise we accepted. When they settled down to be serious it was a different matter. But our bowling was steady. Douglas, son of the yachtsman, had a particularly deceptive off break, and our fielding, of the swift dash and one handed pick up variety, kept the score down, besides bringing frequent bursts of hand clapping from the spectators. Although Cunningham, unfortunately, carried his bat for fifty-seven, which included eleven boundary hits, they were all out just after one o'clock for a hundred and thirty-nine.

Mrs. Heston had provided an excellent buffet lunch which was taken standing up, people moving about with plates of chicken salad and cold veal pie, in a general air of heartiness. All my running had made me extremely hot so that I did not feel up to eating much which, in view of the excellent fare, was rather a pity. But I had a ham sandwich and several glasses of lemon squash. As I went up for my final squash Mrs. Heston, who must have known of me from her husband, said in my ear:

"I do wish you a good knock, Laurence."

After the luncheon interval it was our turn to bat. Scott, a first class batsman and good all rounder, had bowled without change at one end. Now, with Bethune, he went in to open our innings. How I admired him as he walked elegantly to the wicket and calmly took centre. He played the first over confidently, scoring two off the last ball.

Seated on the pavilion verandah with the others, applauding that strong, clean, cover drive, I felt a rising hope — despite Mrs. Heston's good wishes — that I should not have to go in. Although in my usual fashion I had built extravagantly on a spectacular performance, now that deeds might be demanded of me, the prospect of that lonely walk to the wicket had begun to intimidate me. Thus far, while I had made no catches, I had fielded extremely well. My reputation might rest on that with safety. Bethune, having taken middle and leg, was now set to receive an over from Cunningham who, taking an alarmingly long run, delivered his first ball. Fast and well pitched up, it knocked out Bethune's middle stump. One out, and only two on the score board — it was a shock.

When Bethune returned, to averted glances, while I entered a painful nought in my scoring card — which I have retained to this day — Colquhoun followed. Next to Scott he was our soundest bat, one who could be relied upon to stay. Unfortunately, on this occasion, he remained for a bare ten minutes and a stodgy nine. The next batsman's effort was equally short and even more uneventful. He contributed three. A chill air of despondency had now settled on the verandah bench. My agitation was increasing by the minute. Once the rot started the sorrowful procession continued and was held up only by Hailey, our wicket keeper, who made a solid ten, all singles, before being caught and bowled by Cunningham. A final, momentary respite was provided by Douglas, the spin bowler who, hitting out at everything, scored fourteen including three wild but valuable boundaries that sailed over second slip's head.

When Douglas left, out to a catch at long leg, the score stood at no more than eighty-two for eight wickets, of which Scott-Hamilton had made forty-six. And now I shivered as the younger Scott-Hamilton, who immediately preceded me on the batting order, went swaggering out to the pitch in a manner that made me envy his cheek. There was a good deal of the clown in Harry, he liked to raise a laugh even if against himself. On this occasion he succeeded. After taking guard in exaggerated fashion he walked up and down patting imaginary imperfections in the bone dry pitch. Having succeeded in amusing the spectators, who as the afternoon wore on had grown in number, he took guard again and faced the bowler. The ball was a slow leg break. Harry turned to pull it to leg, missed his footing and sat down on his wicket. The result was an enormous shout of laughter in which, irresistibly, even the fielders joined. So in this atmosphere of hilarity I would have to go in. My pads were already on. With a frightful hollow in my stomach I put my bat under my arm and stumbled down the wooden steps of the pavilion into that wide green arena.

Scott came to meet me half way to the wicket. Pale with anger and disappointment he greeted me with a string of scarifying bad words.

"The bowling is absolute blank, blank tosh. These blank, blank toads have simply got themselves out. Just keep your blank end up and let me do the scoring."

These profane injunctions did little to fortify me. I was so wretchedly nervous when I went to the wicket that I forgot to take guard. The game had degenerated into farce and in the interests of cricket must be terminated at once by my dismissal. The first ball shaved my wicket, the second hit me a sad crack on the elbow. It was then the end of the over.

While the field changed Heston, who was umpiring at my end, strolled towards me, hands in the pockets of his long white coat.

"Straight bat," he said mildly. "Don't run away from them."

In the events that followed Scott-Hamilton was the hero, I merely the accessory to the fact. It is enough to report simply and briefly that, with incredible good fortune, I stayed there for more than three quarters of an hour, surviving by the skin of my teeth, while Scott hit up another thirty-eight runs. His score was eighty-six, my total no more than a miserable nineteen, but beyond keeping my wicket intact I had one moment of glory when, off what proved to be the last ball of the match, I ventured on a square cut that somehow sped past cover point then trickled to the boundary. I did not realize that it was the winning hit until I saw Scott waiting for me to walk to the pavilion.

In the pavilion, as we took off our pads, he brushed off all congratulations.

"I never believed I would have the misfortune to know such a blank collection of blankety toads. You, Harry, were the toadiest of the lot. Lucky there was one toad," he announced, "who wasn't altogether toadish." Then turning to me: "You'll come home to tea with me, won't you, Carroll?"

The invitation went to my head like wine. This was the final accolade, an honour and an intimacy I had never hoped to attain. My powers in the game had already raised me well above myself. Now I floated, disembodied, an elected member of the élite.

When we had changed we set out, Scott, Harry and I, sauntering towards their house, which stood quite near, in a secluded position, behind the wood. On the way over we discussed the match, Harry with his usual sense of fun, Scott mockingly amused at Mr. Cunningham's discomfiture. To me the master had not appeared at all upset at the defeat of his side, rather the contrary, and apart from his unfortunate teeth he seemed a genuinely nice sort of man. He had clapped me heartily on the back and said "Well played" as we came off the field. But it was enough that for reasons of his own Scott detested him. Strolling along easily in my new-found arrogance I derided the unhappy Cunningham, inventing comic names for him, of which one, "Rabbit Teeth," won approval. Scott said that it would *stick*.

The grounds of the house were imposingly large. We went along an avenue of chestnut trees that revealed a paddock on one side and distantly on the other the fruit and vegetable garden, where two men were working, and beyond which I made out an inviting row of glasshouses. A shrubbery and a rock garden appeared next before finally we came to the house, a half timbered mansion draped in virginia creeper, fronting a wide stretch of lawn flanked by twin herbaceous borders.

A woman, tall, thin, with greying hair and a distinguished look, was crossing the lawn as we approached. She was wearing gardening gloves and carried a trug in which lay a profusion of full blown roses.

"Mother," Scott said, "this is Carroll. I've asked him to tea."

She smiled pleasantly, viewing us all, not with the outgiving affection my own mother would have shown, but with a certain aristocratic, faintly amused contraction of her brows which, to my shame, I now preferred.

"How did the match go?"

"We won, naturally," Scott said offhandedly.

"Behold the two heroes, Mother. I made a duck."

"Oh, you wretch, Harry. Never mind, you'll have tea with me when I've finished cutting." Turning to go, she said: "Then you may tell me all about it."

Scott led the way into the house, through the hall and along a passage at the back to a green baize-covered service door.

"Let's have a drink," he said, pushing open the door. "You won't mind coming in here?"

Gaily, in a free and easy manner, I followed them to the kitchen which was large, white tiled and well lit. At the window a smartly dressed maid was polishing silver while a stout cook, with her back to us, was at the stove bending over the oven.

"We'd like some ginger beer, Bridgie."

"Take it then," said the cook, over her shoulder. "But leave these pancakes be, Master Harry, they're for the mistress's tea."

Harry, who knew his way about, had supplied us with glasses of stone ginger beer, when the cook swung round and straightened, exposing to us a full red amiable face set with a pair of button black eyes. I stiffened, choked on my ginger beer. I recognized her instantly. Bridget O'Halloran, staunch devotee of St. Mary's and leading member of the Guild of St. Teresa. Did she know me? Idiotic, futile question. Had she not sat beside me in church, walked in the same procession, even passed me occasionally on her afternoon off as she went to the church and I emerged from school? If this damning evidence was not enough, her stare of wondering surprise that plainly said "What is *he* doing here, where he doesn't belong, with Master Scott and Master Harry?" would surely have convinced me. And now her expression had changed. I saw that she distrusted and resented my upstart appearance in a society so far above me, a sphere where as an old and privileged servant she had the right to feel at home. I was an offence against the sound established order that she believed in as firmly as she did the Communion of Saints.

She placed herself in a conversational attitude, one hand on her hip.

"You have a new friend, Master Scott?"

"Decidedly," he agreed, drinking deeply.

"That's nice. He'll be at the Beechfield with you?"

"No, Bridgie," Harry interposed. "For your private information, he has a weak chest and doesn't go to school at present."

"Indeed now, that's interesting. And where does he get his education like?"

"He has a tutor."

"A tutor is it?"

Disregarding Master Harry, who was now helping himself

to pancakes, she fixed me with a chilly, penetrating stare. Yet her tone was persuasive as, in a meditative manner, she queried:

"But surely . . . haven't I seen you in Clay Street with a school satchel?"

I affected an incredulous smile. It was a feeble effort.

"Of course not."

"Strange," she pursued. "I could have sworn it was you. Down by St. Mary's school?"

I was pale. The smile had stiffened on my lips. Ineffectually I tried an edging movement towards the door.

"I don't know what you're talking about."

"You're sure it wasn't you?"

"I'm dead positive," I said violently. "What the dickens would I be doing down there?"

She considered me for a long moment, then said slowly:

"And the cock crowed thrice."

Master Harry went into a fit of laughter.

"Silly Bridgie. And the cock crowed. Cock-a-doodle-do."

But Scott-Hamilton, unsmiling, was looking at me very curiously.

"Shut up, Harry. Let's clear out."

Tea in the drawing room where, basking in glory, I had hoped to shine, was a torment. Despite Mrs. Scott-Hamilton's puzzled efforts, conversation flagged and died. As soon as I could, I said that I must go.

"Must you?" said Scott, getting up immediately. "Pity you have to leave," he said with cold politeness, having escorted me to the front door.

"I have to meet someone," I said.

He raised his eyebrows with a faint, contemptuous smile.

"The tutor?" These were his parting words.

I went out of the house and along the avenue, past the two gardeners, the peach house, and the twin tennis courts. Sick with shame and blind with rage I saw nothing. All the hot bitterness of my burning heart was directed against Scott, against all the Scott-Hamiltons, against Beechfield, the cricket club, the entire world, most of all against myself. I loathed and despised myself with a searing and corroding violence that, while it must end in abysmal misery, kept me striding instinctively, in some such manner as the murderer is compelled to return to the scene of his crime, towards St. Mary's. Had Bridget's final words stung so fiercely as to stir in my perfidious soul emotions of compunction and contrition that could be assuaged only by a solitary visit to the church? If so, I did not reach that haven of penitence. Beyond the Victoria Library at the junction of the main road and Clay Street a game was in progress, a low, common vulgar game of "kick the can" played in the public thoroughfare by a ragged scattering of my schoolfellows. My eye dilated. Here, I thought, are my compeers. Welcomed by acclamation, unmindful of my patrician clothes, I flung myself into the game, running, sliding, kicking, falling in the gutter, shouting and sweating, revelling in the awareness that I was shedding the spurious veneer with which for the past two months I had encased myself.

In the midst of one hectic melee I heard a shrill exclamation of dismay. I looked up. An elderly lady in a spotted veil and a feather boa, with a bundle of library books under her arm, was gazing at me in horror. She was Miss Galbraith, one of Miss Greville's tea party friends who played the violin and painted nicely in watercolours, and to whom, not long before, I had made my bow.

"Laurence! What are you doing! With these dreadful little ragamuffins!"

"Playing."

"Oh, no, no, not with these frightful young hooligans. You must go home at once."

"I won't."

"Do come away with me, dear." She took my arm. "You must."

"No," I shouted, breaking free. "I won't come away. These are my friends. You can go to h—l."

The game proceeded until dusk. I did not give up until I felt myself completely purged. Then, pledging myself to more games when school took up next week, I set out for home, with a tear in the knee of my flannel trousers, exhausted, dirty, and sad, but for the moment at peace.

18

OH, THE dreariness of that ensuing winter when, under perpetually weeping skies, I passed, with lowered head, a shadow of myself, to and from St. Mary's School, travelling by the unfrequented back road, avoiding all that pertained to Beechfield in such a manner as my peasant ancestors had shunned the famine stricken, typhus ridden town of Bandon. Unhappily this alternative route presented me, on occasions, with a painful reminder of my fallen state since it was unpredictably the choice of the St. Anne's junior "croco-dile," thus confronting me at a turn of the road with a double line of young girls, swinging along in their fetching green uni-forms, aristocratic, arrogant, yes, all of them arrogant to the point of insolence, and to whom I must yield the pavement by stepping humbly into the gutter. As I stood there, an ignored obscenity, one in particular held my eye, a captivating little blonde with long double flaxen pigtails that swung with her dashing step. She it was who, by her fascinations, confirmed my outcast state. By chance I even learned her name. As she swept past with her indubitably snub nose in the air and never a side glance, her partner in the parade remarked, in the high, affected Ardfillan voice: "Oh, I say, Ada, how absolutely jolly!" Resuming my way, Ada became the touchstone of the unattainable, the token of my miseries, the central figure in fantasies which I created, not only by day but more often at night, in bed, before I fell asleep. Then Ada, dear Ada, watched rapturously, in company with Heston and George Gunn, while I carried my bat for a century at Lords. Permutations and combinations of my Ada complex transported me, the brilliance, the mutual admiration in our exchanges dazzled me. How often did she lean towards me and exclaim: "Oh, I say, Laurie, how absolutely jolly!" And on what flights was I borne by her daily letters.

Dearest Laurie,

How can I thank you enough for the exquisite orchids. And how splendid your being so friendly with Lady Meikle that she allowed you to pick them in her beautiful big conservatory. I will keep them as a constant reminder of your thoughtfulness.

Please don't imagine I didn't see you when I passed the other day. I had to pretend not to.

Have you been to the moor lately? It would be nice if we could meet there one day. But of course we are kept in very strictly at St. Anne's. That's why it is so jolly to be able to write you.

Affectionately yours,
Ada

I wrote these letters after my homework and dropped them into the letter box so that I should find them when I set out for school next morning. On my way to Clay Street I read them with a beatific smile fixed upon my lips, which, alas, slowly faded as cold reality dissolved a dream, springing not from any seductiveness Ada might offer, but only from a yearning for her esteem.

Fortunately, after some weeks I began to be bored with Ada. Perhaps she was tired of me, for her letters noticeably cooled off and eventually ceased. But it is truer to say that she was supplanted by a humbler being, possibly more worthy of my affection. I had fallen in love with Amoeba Proteus.

The chance discovery of an elementary textbook of zoology of Miss Greville's entitled *Pond Life* had sent me, idly at first, in pursuit of the protozoa. But it was a chase which, to my salvation, soon became a passion, supplanting my botanical researches of the past year, convincing me that I must become a scientist.

As spring came in I returned from my moorland expeditions not with a packed vasculum but with scum-filled jars that teemed with fascinating life and which, once my eye was glued to the tube of Miss Greville's Zeiss, gave me the entry to an unknown world peopled with amazing microscopic creatures whose elaborate activities, from the swallowing of diatoms and formation of food vacuoles to the halving of chromosomes and division of the nucleus in the final act of partition, filled me with wonder, an emotion that intensified as, passing from these primary cells, I came upon rarer and wilder inhabitants of this subaqueous jungle, the solitary volvox, the whirling rotifer, the shapely polystomella. And what joy when, one March evening, a glorious paramecium, with all its cilia waving, swam majestically through the green algae into my field of vision.

This was the interest that truly sustained me during a period of dulness and uncertainty when I felt that I was getting nowhere. I realized that St. Mary's could take me no further and that I was soon due to leave. Yet I dared not ask my mother what the future held for me. In her face now there was a reserve that forbade my question, an expression that I did not wish to read yet which instinctively I recognized as an omen contrary to all my hopes.

At first, through sympathy for her, and the general regard for Father, she had done well enough with the agency. But gradually the decline had set in, competition increased, and more and more she came back with a thinning order book and a set, harassed expression, the presage to increasing economies that dispelled the blessed ambience of security in which I had hitherto lived.

As the months went on it became more and more apparent how painfully short we were of money. Particularly in our diet was this stringency noticeable, for although worse was in store for me, Mother now concentrated on the cheapest and most nourishing foods, such things as baked beans, boiled salt codfish and cottage pie, which I accepted with an added sense of grievance, since it must now be revealed that those sustaining lunches with which Miss Greville had regaled my pampered stomach had practically ceased.

This, indeed, touched another of our problems, a mysterious enigma, surrounding my benefactress, that passed my present understanding. Miss Greville, caught up in new and unforeseen activities, was seldom in for lunch. When I came back from school at the midday recess, hoping against hope, I would be met in the hall by Campbell who, with a grim smile that made my heart sink, would remark: "Lunch is not being served today, Master Carroll." She gave always to the word "Master" an imperceptible sardonic inflection that, intensifying my sense of deprivation, wounded me deeply as, my nostrils dilating to the good smells of Campbell's own lunch coming from the kitchen, I slowly went upstairs where, on the alcove table, I would find a pencilled note left by mother: *Soup in the pot on the stove for you to heat, dear. And some cold rice pudding in the cupboard.*

What, I asked myself repeatedly, was happening to Miss Greville? Towards Mother and myself she was more forthcoming, more gaily affectionate, than ever. Yet it seemed as though in this effusiveness Mother found something oppressive. At first she had been pleased to be invited to those little tea parties, and even to play and sing there. But now, returning tired and dispirited from Winton she was apparently in no mood for such festivities, and only once during the previous six months when Miss Greville had entertained her few St. Anne's friends to a musical evening had she attended, with reluctance, and then because she felt it an obligation to play, or at least to accompany Miss Greville's performance on the 'cello. After this event she had returned depressed and with a disinclination for further social intercourse. It was difficult to escape the conclusion that the more Miss Greville offered intimacy, the more my mother had withdrawn from it, not obtrusively, but rather with discretion, as though anxious to moderate these approaches. I particularly noticed this reserve in Mother's manner on Sundays when, Miss Greville sumptuously dressed for church in a high waisted cream costume, an enormous exuberant hat on top of her chignon, a parasol in her white-gloved hands, and exuding a faint smell of Parma violets, came upstairs to be approved.

"Does this suit me? Will I *do*, Grace? Am I fit to be seen?"

Envisaging that full, richly moulded figure, Mother repressively replied:

"You will certainly be seen."

"I believe so." Miss Greville smiled confidently. "And why not, dear Grace?"

Of course Miss Greville had always been an assiduous church goer, and her penchant for remarkable attire was no secret to me, yet in these over elaborate Sunday toilettes there must surely be some meaning which so far had escaped me. Nevertheless I, as opposed to Mother, welcomed every sign and symptom, no matter how displayed, of Miss Greville's partiality. Not only did I admire her intensely — "look up to her" is perhaps the better phrase — I knew all too well what she had done for me. And I dared to hope that she would do more. Indeed, her interest in me now seemed the only chance of bringing me what I most desired.

This thought was in my mind when one March day, as still occasionally happened, I was lucky enough to find Miss Greville at home. Lunch was being served. Rejoicing that I need not, for once, face up to cold rice pudding, I washed and brushed my hair with unusual care before entering the dining room. She greeted me with a bright appraising smile. If sadness reigned in our part of the house, here surely the reverse held sway. Miss Greville, during these past deadly months, had been consistently animated.

"You are presentable, Carroll," she remarked approvingly, as I placed her chair. "Indeed, extremely so. Rather a different person from that scrubby little window breaker of . . . how long ago?"

"Four years, Miss Greville."

I do not recall how our conversation developed after that promising opening. I do not doubt that it was interesting, since this remarkable woman had an extraordinary gift of stimulating and often bizarre talk and had even taught me to respond in a civilized manner and, apparently, with intelligence. Today, however, I was at first too busily engaged with some excellent roast beef to give her my complete attention. But of the ending of that lunch my memory is exact, my recollection unforgettably clear. She had proceeded to the window with her cup of coffee according to invariable habit, and after remaining rather longer than usual returned to the table in a mood which I rightly judged to be communicative.

"You are remarkably discreet, Carroll," she began, looking at me intently, yet amiably.

"Am I, Miss Greville?"

"And, thanks to me, well mannered. So often, during our

moments of agreeable intimacy, you have observed me go to the window, yet never once have you chosen to inquire why."

"That would not have been polite." Falling into her mood I mouthed this appalling answer like a well-behaved little prig. For that roast beef, with my eye on a second helping, I would have made myself a triple prig.

"But you've been curious?" she pressed, unwilling to dismiss the subject. "Admit the soft impeachment."

Scarcely knowing whether it would be to my advantage to admit or deny I eventually inclined my head soberly.

"I *was* curious, Miss Greville."

"But you didn't guess?"

"I imagined you were waiting for a friend, who passed here regularly every day."

"Well done, Carroll!"

She seemed so pleased at my deduction that my inveterate wish to shine drove me to continue.

"And whoever it was would naturally see you there."

She smiled.

"It would be rather pointless if there were not an exchange of glances. The human eye, Carroll, as a means of communication is more expressive than the tongue. More subtle too, and truer. The tongue can lie, the eye, never. More beef?"

"Please, Miss Greville."

While I partook of another juicy slice she kept playing absently with her long chain necklace of ivory beads, that odd little smile coming and going on her lips.

"You know Mr. Lesly, of course. Our vicar at St. Jude's."

"Why, certainly, Miss Greville. I often see him in the street. And you remember he stopped and spoke to us that first day we were coming back from Glen Fruin. The day we found the *morio*."

"Of course. You liked him?"

"He seemed an awfully nice young man."

"Not nice, Carroll. Not that deplorable word. Charming, if you wish, intelligent, sympathetic, handsome. And not so young. He is coming to tea next Saturday. I want your mother to meet him."

A considerable silence ensued. When I finished rolling my napkin and hopefully putting it in its silver ring for possible future use, she was gazing at me benignantly.

"What age are you, Carroll?"

"Thirteen, Miss Greville."

"As I was saying, you have improved. I regard you, in a manner of speaking, as my own creation. And I wish you to understand this. Whatever changes may be effected in the immediate future I mean to do something for you."

All at once my heart came into my mouth. Did I interpret her meaning correctly or was I merely carried away by my own expectations? Surely asking how old I was had been significant. She had often said that fourteen was the proper age to . . . I did not dare ask, yet the longing in my soul made me falter out the words:

"In the way, perhaps, of sending me to a decent school, Miss Greville?"

She made a spirited gesture of acquiescence.

"What else, Carroll? A very good school." Then quickly, seeing an idiotic wildness in my eye: "No, not *there*, Carroll. You would not, I fear, be altogether comfortable in that establishment. You must go to one of your own persuasion."

"Rockcliff . . . perhaps . . . Miss Greville?"

"Why should we send you to Ireland? If you insist on the Jesuits, you'll do better in Yorkshire at Amplehurst, which is not a bad little institution in its own way."

Amplehurst! Beyond question the best Catholic public school. Stricken dumb, I gazed at her with glistening eyes.

That afternoon I could not be still, could not think of returning to imprison my bounding spirits in my malodorous Clay Street classroom. I simply played truant, put on an old pair of shorts and a jersey and went out for a long run in the rain. I liked to run and believed, with some justification, that I could run fast. Miss Greville had encouraged me to take these cross country chases and, like the morning cold bath which I shiveringly endured, they had become not the expression of my devotion alone, but of the authority she exerted upon me in forming a regime, quite foreign to my nature, that I had now come to enjoy. As I flashed along the sodden byways, leaping the puddles as though each were a Beecher's Brook, I wished, though vainly, that I might encounter Scott-Hamilton to convey to him in that brief moment of transit the brilliant change in my fortunes.

Mother was annoyed with me when I got back. She had returned by an earlier train and was at the stove making our supper.

"Oh, Mother, not beans again!" I protested.

She looked at me coldly.

"Where on earth have you been? And soaking wet, too."

"Don't be cross," I told her expansively. "I'll go and change. Then, Mother dear, I have some rather interesting news for you."

A few minutes later, when we were seated at our narrow table in the alcove, I related, with impressment, my conversation with Miss Greville. Mother, gazing over her cup, from time to time taking sips of tea, heard me in silence. But when, finally, or perhaps as a kind of postscript, I conveyed Miss Greville's invitation to her for Saturday, she gave a short disturbed exclamation.

"Mr. Lesly is to be there?"

"Of course. Why are you so surprised? Don't you know that

Miss Greville and he are great friends? Why, every day at lunch they smile at each other through the window."

Mother made to speak, but checked herself and was silent. But her expression remained decidedly odd. This, and the manner in which she had received my announcement, offended me. I did not offer to wash the dishes and instead went into my own room.

What could be wrong between Miss Greville and Mr. Lesly? It was painfully evident that Mother was upset by the idea of this invitation and had no wish to accept it. Naturally, I was not blind to Miss Greville's oddities. These, especially in the early stages of our relationship, had fascinated me. Her unusual personality awed and stimulated me so that I had come to regard her as a brilliant eccentric, and for this reason was prepared to accept her unconventional behaviour. But having her vicar to tea was not unconventional. Why then, all this fuss? I should not have been at all surprised if she had asked someone like Buffalo Bill, or Harry Lauder, rather than the estimable Mr. Lesly, the more so since, despite my pretence of ignorance, I had sensed that she valued him.

Nevertheless, when Saturday came a vague uneasiness creeping over my skin made me want to be out of the way that afternoon. It was fine, a good day for another run, I told myself, especially since the Harriers were out in a paper chase to Stair Head. These Harriers, made up of young men who were clerks, apprentices, shop assistants and the like, were now, more properly, my friends, and in the previous autumn I had established myself amongst them by winning the Junior Steeplechase open to boys under fourteen. After Mother had made me a scrambled egg on toast I slipped out of the house in my shorts and jersey. I was late. The meet had started at the edge of the Darvie Woods and soon I was amongst the pines following the paper trail that had been laid down. The excitement of picking up the track, losing it, then striking it again soon absorbed me. A thrill of pride shot through me as I overtook some of the club stragglers, and with my chin up and elbows pressed in, ignoring the stitch in my side, left them floundering behind. Yet the very merit of my speed proved my undoing. When, still trotting and spotted with mud, as the afternoon drew to a close, I swung into Prince Albert Terrace, I saw that I had misjudged my time. The door of No. 7 was open, revealing Miss Greville and my mother with Mr. Lesly in the very act of leaving. He was a handsome, measured kind of man with an exact middle parting of his hair, who looked rather like an actor. But now he appeared flushed and terribly uncomfortable as he hurriedly shook hands, and he almost stumbled as he came down the porch steps. Contrary to his usual civil habit, he did not recognize me. Perhaps he did not see me. If ever a man seemed anxious to expedite his departure it was the Vicar of St. Jude's.

I went into the house. Mother and Miss Greville were in the hall and, as I slipped past hurriedly, for somehow the situation appeared to have got out of control, Mother, in a low tone of remonstration, said something which I did not hear but to which Miss Greville replied, with a burst of joyful animation:

"It's not what was said, dearest Grace. Did you not see how he looked at me!"

Mother was a long time coming upstairs. When she came she sat down heavily at the table and put a hand to her brow. She alarmed me. I had been sweating and now I began to shiver.

"Mother, what's wrong?"

She raised her head slowly and looked at me.

"It will never end for us, Laurie. Never, never. Miss Greville is going out of her mind."

19

HOW STRANGE were the months that followed, for me so unreal as to maintain me in a perpetual daze, and for my mother so charged with an ever growing anxiety, the extent of which I did not realize till later, that her nerves were worn to shreds, causing her to start and turn pale whenever some unusual sound would reach us from the main part of the house. Even now I can scarcely bring myself to re-create the pitiful disintegration of a mind that I had always regarded as cultured and superior, the more so since that mental dissolution shaped itself ostensibly in the pattern of farce, the spinster's infatuation for the young clergyman, subject for the music hall stage, for vulgar laughter provoked by a cheap comedian with baggy trousers and a red nose. For us, it was far from funny but a reality with which we lived and suffered. That Miss Greville, of all people, should be the central figure, the victim, of such a spectacle — I could not believe it.

Yet, although of course I could not know this, Miss Greville's condition was one now well recognized in psychiatric medicine and not at all uncommon in women of her age and condition who have slight paranoid tendencies. In such subjects at the involutional period a flood of libidinal impulses, hitherto repressed, or sublimated, or dealt with by other mechanisms of defence, is released with specific imbalance of hormones and resultant delusions which are frequently centered upon a favourite physician or clergyman. This absolute and utter certainty that they are beloved and to be married is explained by the most cryptic indications, yet in a supremely reasonable way.

This to me was the most perplexing feature of Miss Greville's behaviour, the rational manner in which she gave effect to her delusion. Her preparations for marriage were proper and well considered. The additions she made to her wardrobe, no longer exuberant, exhibited a severity which, as she informed my mother, befitted the clerical status of her future husband. The plans she outlined for doing up the vicarage could not have been bettered, and the materials she had already bought for new curtains were all in quiet good taste. Her activities in all directions were endless, she seemed always on the move, going to and coming from the town, and when she found time to sit down she would take up sewing, or start cutting out and shaping patterns, with commendable industry.

Most baffling of all was the manner in which she received every attempt to dissuade her. At first my mother had been diffident, tactful and discreet in her approach, but as time went on and all her efforts failed she had come to speak in the strongest terms and to use outright and forceful arguments which no one could reject. Miss Greville rejected them. With her calm and confident smile she would listen, amused almost by Mother's intensity, then, with a shake of her head, would dismiss the most irrefutable logic: "You don't understand, Grace. There are reasons for everything. *I know.*"

These two final words, absolute conviction of inner knowledge, were unassailable to reason. Mother was at her wit's end. From whom could she seek advice? Those acquaintances at St. Anne's, familiar with Miss Greville's previous foibles, were disinclined to take Mother seriously and advised against action on the grounds that this new manifestation would pass. In any case, from their position with the school, it was apparent that they had no wish to be drawn into the affair. Campbell, with whom Mother tried to take council, was not helpful. This deaf, taciturn woman had from the beginning resented our presence in the house. She considered that she had prior rights on her employer and was not prepared to divulge the address of Miss Greville's brother in Kenya when Mother proposed writing to him. The difficulty presented by any course of action seemed insuperable, since the first sign of interference on our part would undoubtedly precipitate a scandal in the town. There was nothing to be done but wait. And so there ensued a period of suspense during which Mother often exclaimed, in a tone of gathering foreboding: "How will it end!"

I must confess that the bizarre aspect of the situation with its suggestion of further awfulness had a morbid excitement for me, stimulated by the changes developing in Miss Greville's personality and physical appearance. Phrases of unprecedented frankness startled and embarrassed me. Her bust and hips were fuller and she had a new way of standing with her legs apart, and what I took to be her stomach but was undoubtedly her pelvis, thrust forward. The fascination of these transformations was, however, dulled by persistent intrusions of a most depressing thought. If Miss Greville did not resume her normal state, if she continued to deteriorate, how could she fulfil her promise to send me to school? What of my giddy aspirations then? They would never be realized. Never. My heart sank at the dismal prospect. I would be lost.

It may be imagined then how anxiously I studied Miss Greville on the occasions when we were together. These were diminishing, since in the evenings Mother kept me closely by her side. Nevertheless, lack of opportunity did not debar me from hoping and fearing, nor my spirits from rising and falling, like a barometer. In the main, I was optimistic. This can't go on, I told myself, it must pass. Nothing will come of it. And if we can last it out for another six months all will be well. Alas, I was deluding myself. Other factors were already operating, contingencies I had not even contemplated. All my thoughts and efforts had been concentrated on Miss Greville. I had forgotten about Mr. Lesly.

It was a wet Saturday afternoon and Mother was reading the *Ardfillan Herald* which always appeared at the weekend. Suddenly I heard her exclaim, in a startled voice:

"Merciful heavens!"

She had changed colour, yet she did not put down the *Herald*, but went on reading almost desperately. Then she let the newspaper slip from her hands and lay back in her chair staring unseeingly at me. This could only mean disaster. Already my scalp was beginning to creep as I put that too familiar question.

"What's wrong, Mother?"

She did not answer, did not apparently discover me within the remote field of her vision. Her lips were moving not, experience told me, in prayer but because, silently, she was talking to herself. I was about to repeat my question more pressingly when, as though breaking through the sound barrier, these words escaped her.

"She's bound to see it . . . or to hear of it."

"Mother." I had to shake her arm. "What has happened?"

She had to find me before she answered.

"Mr. Lesly is going to be married." She paused. "On the fifteenth of next month."

As though unable to continue, she handed me the paper. A paragraph in the Social and Personal column was headed: *Popular Vicar to Wed*. And beneath in smaller type: *Nuptials announced of Mr. H. A. Lesly and Miss Georgina Douglas.*

Reading on, I was not long in discovering that Miss Georgina was none other than the sister of the spin bowler, my late cricketing acquaintance, in whose conversation that twin-funnelled steam yacht had largely testified to parental wealth. Hurriedly I skimmed through the rest of the paragraph: a long standing attachment . . . sudden decision on the part of the happy couple . . . welcomed by their numerous friends and wellwishers.

"But this is wonderful," I cried. "It settles everything."

Mother eyed me silently.

"Don't you see, Mother, when Miss Greville sees he's going to marry someone else she'll know he can't marry her."

"That will be a great help to her, poor creature."

Mother's pale, sad smile disconcerted me.

"You mean, she won't . . ."

"I don't mean anything," Mother said firmly, with an air of terminating the conversation. "But I don't want you to go down to her for a bit. Not till we see how things work out."

All that evening Mother and I kept very quiet. The house was quiet too. On the following morning we went out to the ten o'clock Mass. Occasionally on Sunday we had an invitation from Miss Greville to have midday dinner with her. Today, when we returned from church, there was no invitation, and Miss Greville had not gone to St. Jude's.

The house was still quiet. I forget what Mother made for our lunch because, for once, I certainly did not notice what I was eating. Afterwards Mother lay down for an hour, while I did my weekend homework. At four o'clock I made the tea. We were now so under the spell of this perpetual stillness that we were talking almost in whispers. I took the tea things to the sink, glancing at Mother while I washed and dried them. I could see that she was terribly on edge, she kept walking up and down our little corridor, but softly, in her indoor slippers, listening all the time with her head to one side.

It was getting dark now and it had begun to rain again. Suddenly, as I was about to light the gas, there came a knock at our door.

Visibly, Mother started. I looked at her, with questioning alarm.

"Shall I open it?"

She shook her head and, moving to the door, threw it open.

Campbell stood there, a sudden apparition, her thin, black, angular figure ominous in the dusk. But her expression was as withdrawn, as impassive as ever. Her hands were folded in front of her starched apron.

"Madam would like to see you," she said formally.

"Yes," Mother said slowly. "I'll come."

"Madam wishes to see you both," Campbell said, in the same manner as before.

There was a pause.

"I don't think," Mother began, turning towards me.

"It's all right, Mother." I interrupted. "I'll go with you."

Nothing heroic prompted this declaration. My heart was beating fast and my knees were uncertain, but I did not wish to be left out of this. I felt indeed that Miss Greville, facing a crisis in her life, might well be impelled to a vital declaration upon my future.

Mother hesitated. I sensed that she wanted to question Campbell, to glean some information as to the present state of affairs. But Campbell was not one to be questioned. Already she had begun to move off. We followed her. Outside Miss Greville's bedroom she paused and, always correct, opened the door for us.

It was a large room with a double window opening on to

the front terrace, but now the lined silk curtains were drawn and the gas lamps lit. I had never been in this room before and would have been curious to examine its furnishings had not my attention been immediately rivetted to Miss Greville. She was sitting at a long sofa table, not fully dressed, but wrapped in a fringed bath robe, and writing so industriously that as we entered she did not look up. Four letters had apparently been written — instinctively I counted the stamped envelopes that lay on the table — and now she was busy on a fifth. She seemed calm, indeed perfectly composed, and although her hair was in some disorder, the normality of her appearance gave me a quick glow of reassurance.

"There!" she exclaimed at last, putting down her pen. "Do forgive me for keeping you."

She folded the letter, tucked it in an envelope which she then sealed, addressed and stamped. Gathering all the letters together she made a neat pile in front of her and sat up, erect and competent.

"Well, Grace," she remarked, mildly, "I suppose you have seen the paragraph in the *Herald*."

There was no point in denying this and Mother did not do so. I could feel her relaxing with relief at Miss Greville's reasonable attitude. Not a sign of frenzy, hysterics or delirium.

"I thought at first that I should ignore it," Miss Greville went on, "since it is, at best, a clumsy device. But on considering the matter more fully I have decided that action is necessary."

Mother had gone rigid again.

"You realize, of course, that *he,* poor man, had no part in this. The whole scandalous affair is an intrigue, instigated by that woman with the connivance of the editor of the *Herald* and, in all probability, the provost of the town."

Brushing aside Mother's attempted protest she continued, as moderately as before, but with a new note of gravity.

"So I have written these letters . . . which you will be good enough to post for me, Carroll." She held them out and I found myself accepting them. "One is to Mr. Lesly, another to his Bishop, the third to the editor of the *Herald* and the fourth to the town clerk. The final letter is to that woman." She paused, glanced significantly towards her dressing table. I felt Mother start. The foils had been brought up from downstairs and their end buttons removed. "Yes, Grace, I have challenged her to a duel."

"Oh, no," Mother cried. "You simply mustn't do that."

"Even if I must not, I will." Miss Greville smiled, and in its vacuity, its total blankness I knew it was the smile of an utterly demented woman, even before she added: "Naturally, dear Grace, I am relying on you to be my second."

I don't know how we got out of that room. The moment we escaped Mother went straight downstairs to the telephone and rang Dr. Ewen. He came in about half an hour. By that time, overcome by a sense of utter desolation, feeling like an idiot myself, I had retired to my burrow in the kitchen alcove. There I remained during the doctor's visit, emerging only as I heard signs of his departure. As I looked down over the bannister of the stairs into the hall below I heard him say to Mother:

"She will have to be certified and removed at once."

20

HREE MONTHS later, sitting opposite Mother in the Winton train, I examined her covertly, trying to read her face. What I saw there gave me a sinking in my inside. I sensed that desperate measures were in prospect for us. Several times, in the hope of discovering the secrets that sealed her brow, I had made an effort to draw her into conversation and presently I tried again, using the visit we were now making to Castleton Asylum as an opening gambit.

"Do you think Miss Greville will be better?"

"I hope so, dear. We shall soon know," she answered, and lapsed again into silence.

Defeated, I turned and looked out of the window, blind to the fleeting vista of the river shipyards, seeing instead the sequence of events that had brought us beyond the edge of disaster.

Not long after Miss Greville's removal her brother had arrived — tall, lean and bronzed, with a commanding manner and an appearance formidably correct. He had immediately taken charge and, after visiting his sister, and several interviews with her doctors, had terminated the lease of the maisonette and ordered the removal of the furniture to a depository. Towards Mother he was at first polite, then coldly polite, and finally merely cold. Campbell had his ear, he relied on her, the old family servant, and Campbell had never liked us. We had come solely on Miss Greville's invitation, and Mother, even when we were living from hand to mouth, had never failed to pay her rent, yet we were made to appear as interlopers. In the end, just three weeks ago, a lawyer's letter had arrived curtly giving us a month in which to vacate our apartment.

True, with Miss Greville gone, and with the main part of the house dismantled, there was nothing to keep us at No. 7. But as the period of our notice began to run out, the uncertainty of our future increased. While maintaining a disturbing reticence, Mother was unnaturally active, not at the agency, where her work seemed almost to have ceased, but in sudden sorties to unknown destinations. Never before had I known her write so many letters: to Uncle Simon in Spain, to her brother Stephen who now had an appointment in the Civil Service in London, to Uncle Leo in Winton, and others to people I had never heard of in places as distant as Liverpool, Nottingham and Cardiff.

A sudden blackout of the landscape, as the train roared into the low level tunnel, indicated our approach to the Central Station. In a few minutes we were making our way up from the smoky platform, sunk in the very depths of the city, to Union Street and the yellow tram.

It was a long, slow ride to Castleton — in those days, although the Corporation trams ranged far and wide, their speed was not excessive. But the day was sunny, and as we left the drab core of Winton, passed through the scattered suburbs, and emerged to the pleasant open countryside beyond, my spirits, always responsive to a prevailing green, lightened considerably. Castleton, still untouched, was a pretty little village. At the Asylum entrance, where the tram conductor put us off, two massively ornate gates were flanked by twin lodges set in the high surrounding stone wall. I felt a strange emotion, half anticipation, half dread, as I pulled the wrought iron handle of the big jangling bell.

Mother had a pass which she showed to the lodge keeper, and when it had been carefully scrutinized, he went to a wall telephone, whirred a little handle, and spoke.

"It's very hard to get in, Mother," I whispered.

"But harder to get out," she answered sombrely.

Eventually the keeper came back, smiled and nodded, the gates were unlocked.

As we entered and began to walk up the broad sanded avenue that wound between tall beech trees towards the castellated mansion on the hill, I gave an exclamation of wonder at the extent and beauty of the estate. On one side a broad orchard of apple and pear trees was in full flourish, through which I made out a model farm with barns and haystacks, while on the other a rising stretch of parkland, studded with specimen chestnut trees, gave way at the far end to the more formal garden that fronted the house. We passed a croquet lawn, a row of tennis courts, a trellised shelter set between double herbaceous borders blooming with pink tulips. There seemed nothing to offend the eye until suddenly, on the skyline, I made out a long dark procession of plodding figures, some grotesquely bent, others gesturing, all exercising slowly, like a string of prisoners, with a nurse in front and another behind.

At the main entrance we were now expected and admitted by a sister in dark blue uniform. Using a key, which was chained to her belt, with the dexterity of long practice, she took us through a series of doors, all without handles, along a wide thickly carpeted corridor embellished with ornate gilt furnishings and set at intervals with other heavy doors, all shut, then into a small end ante-room where she paused and, looking at me without enthusiasm, spoke in an undertone to Mother, who turned to me.

"Sister thinks you had better wait here, Laurence."

Although I wanted to see Miss Greville, at least the real Miss Greville, restored to herself, I was not sorry to be left behind. This progress by key, locking us in, away from the bright outer world, the strange sounds, mumblings and shufflings, muted by heavy doors, the atmosphere, tainted by the commode, of discreet morbidity, even the black convoluted ornate furniture of the reception room in which I now sat — it was Buhl, a variety I had never seen before — all conspired to send a shiver down my spine, a sensation heightened by a sudden shriek, instantly suppressed, that made me jump from the spindly velvet upholstered chair in which I had cautiously placed myself.

Mother was a long time in coming back, but at last she reappeared. In that instant through the open doorway I caught a sudden fleeting glimpse of a narrow corridor leading to another room, the door of which the sister was in the process of closing, and there, framed in that narrow aperture, was a strange, flaccid face, the hair cropped to the skull, the eyes staring yet vacant, meeting mine in a frightening exchange, without a shadow of recognition. The shock of that unknown, unearthly face still vibrated along my nerves as Mother took my arm. I could not speak. I knew that I had seen my good friend Miss Greville, and that I would not see her again.

Outside, Mother drew a long deep breath of the fresh spring air and, having thanked the sister and said goodbye, began to walk down the drive, still holding my arm. When we reached the trellised summer house she said:

"Let me sit here, Laurie. Just for a little while."

We went into the summer house. Although I knew, I had to ask.

"How is she, Mother?"

"Hopeless, quite hopeless."

"What was she doing?"

"Drawing up petitions, all day long, petitions that no one will ever see. And writing letters that will never be posted." She added, after a pause, as though to herself: "Now at least I know where we stand."

She rested her head on her hand and sat silent. I watched her uneasily.

"If we stay here too long we may not get out."

She looked at me and smiled. I was amazed. Her expression had altogether changed, a transformation that seemed to wipe out that fixed distress, the disquiet and indecision not only of today but of all these past troubled weeks. She stood up and to my further surprise, for I knew how hard up we were, very cheerfully declared:

"Let's go, darling, and have a real, slap-up tea."

Outside the gates, in Castleton village, there was an excellent tea room above the local baker's shop. Here Mother ordered tea and all the things I liked, hot buttered toast and a new laid boiled egg, fresh wheaten scones, honey, and a plate of cream cakes. While she sipped the hot tea she kept pressing me to eat so that, under this repeated prompting, I ate all the cream cakes. She had watched me with a hovering smile but now, glancing round to assure herself that we were still alone in the room, she turned to me seriously.

"Laurence," she said, "your mother is a failure."

A silence followed during which I felt extremely uncomfortable. Yet there had been no misery in her voice, merely a firmness that sounded almost defiant as she resumed.

"The agency is finished. It was a wonderful idea of your father's and now it's gone. The mistake I made was not to sell it and realize something as your Uncle Leo suggested." As she paused to take a sip of tea, I had a sudden, fleeting vision of Mother and me singing for our supper in a wet Winton street.

"I'm not going to weary you with my difficulties over the past years. I've always tried to keep them away from you. But you must have guessed them. It was no work for a woman, at least not for me. Sympathy doesn't last for ever. It's not a business asset. So all I have to tell you, and I must tell you, for you're a big boy now, we have nothing left, nothing but our furniture, for which I've an offer of forty pounds."

My lavish meal may have given me courage to withstand this shock. Perhaps that was why Mother had fortified me. I felt nothing more than a queer blankness which drew from me, involuntarily, the only possible response.

"So what are we going to do?"

"You are going to your Uncle Leo, and I am going to Wales."

This, being quite incomprehensible, was much worse. My expression must have warned Mother. She leaned forward, drew her fingers softly across my cheek and began persuasively, undramatically, to explain how extreme was our situation and how, after considering every expedient, this was the only way she could resolve it. I must leave school, at least for the time being. Uncle Leo had promised to take me and teach me his business so that at the worst, I should at least have something to fall back on. Her own case was more difficult. She had no qualifications for business, music was her only asset, and even so she had no teacher's diploma, and now would never get one. Yet Uncle Simon, writing from Spain, had managed to obtain a place for her as music mistress at St. Monica's Convent, a girls' school in Monmouthshire. Here, in her off duty, during the next twelve months, she would have the advantage of attending special classes in Cardiff. She was going to take an intensive course and pass the examination to become a public health visitor. Four of these appointments, a new departure open to women, were to be made in Winton and, through the intervention of a friend of Stephen's on the City Council, she had been promised one of them if she could take her training and get her certificate within a year. She would then be sure of a regular salary in a position for which she felt herself fitted. We would be together again, and if I did not wish to remain with Leo, she would be able to send me to a tutorial college to renew my studies so that later on, I could sit the bursary examination for the University.

Finishing on a high note of encouragement Mother looked at me entreatingly, while I tried to recover myself sufficiently to grasp the implications of this staggering proposal. I did not like it. Yet, through all the confusion of my mind, I could not fail to see how hard and painfully she must have tried, enduring all sorts of rebuffs, to put this plan together as a last resort. This, in part, tempered my resentment, as I said:

"Why can't I go with you to Wales?"

"It's not possible, dear." Mother forced a placating little laugh. "Not in the convent. You'll be better off with Leo."

The possibilities of being with Leo in a real business had already flashed intriguingly across my mind, but I would not admit this, saying instead,

"Uncle Leo is a queer fish, Mother."

"Yes, he's perhaps a trifle odd in some ways. But I'm inclined to trust him, if only because he doesn't promise us the earth."

"Wouldn't Uncle Bernard help us?"

"Never," Mother said shortly. "And I would never ask him."

She was right. Bernard, with the best intentions and tears in his eyes, *would* promise us the earth and completely forget about us next day.

A silence followed during which I examined our predicament, looking for an escape hatch through which we might both get out of it.

"Mother," I said at last, though hesitantly, for this was a forbidden subject, though I had to broach it. "Wouldn't it be possible for you . . . I mean didn't you have a long letter from Stephen last week . . . couldn't we go to your parents, your own family . . . ?"

I broke off, stopped in my tracks by the sudden colour that rushed into Mother's face and then as quickly receded, leaving her paler than before.

"Yes, Laurence, I had the chance to go back . . . but on conditions I could never accept."

I had a great curiosity to know what these conditions were but I did not dare ask. Instead, rather dismally, I began to reflect on our coming separation, which made me ask:

"When is all this going to happen?"

She took a quick breath and exclaimed spiritedly:

"Not until we've had a jolly good holiday together."

I stared at her in stupefaction. Had misfortune turned her brain? And now she was smiling at me, with that same challenging, almost reckless expression, carefree too, as though a load had fallen from her shoulders.

"Yes, I mean it, Laurie. We'll go to the Highlands. We both deserve a holiday and need it. I'm taking the offer for the furniture and we'll spend every penny of the forty pounds on ourselves. After that we'll be all set up and fit for anything."

Before I could say a word she took up the little bell from the table and summoned the waitress by ringing it like mad.

21

As we came out of the railway station Fort William lay under a raw mist that blanketed Ben Nevis and dripped from the slate roofs of the town. Looking about me while Mother arranged with a porter to deliver our luggage by hand cart in the afternoon, I became afflicted by a strange, sinking premonition that this Highland resort boded ill for me.

Ardshiel, the boarding establishment of our choice, stood half way up the hill, a small, square, red sandstone house set behind a prodigious monkey puzzle tree, in a neat garden overlooking the loch. Mother had favoured it because it was kept by two sisters, maiden ladies who advertised its virtues, and their own gentility, in one telling word — *select*. Indeed, Mother's judgement seemed justified by our rooms which, though small and on the top floor, she pronounced to be of an exemplary cleanliness. No sooner had she concluded her examination, which began with the bedlinen and ended with the water in the ewer, than the gong boomed startlingly for lunch.

We went downstairs. Not more than ten people were seated at a long mahogany table in a bay-windowed room cosily furnished in worn red plush. At the head of the table a tall angular woman in black rose to greet us, explaining that she was Miss Kincaid. She then introduced us to the other guests, and to her younger sister, Miss Ailie Kincaid, who sat at the foot of the board. Seating herself again, she bowed her head, said grace devoutly and began to carve the joint. This I soon found to be the standard procedure, while Miss Ailie, at the other end, dispensed the vegetables, and later, the semolina pudding and prunes.

Despite its plainness the food was good and hot, a welcome discovery corroborated by Mother's quick communicative glance. I already liked the smaller, softer Miss Ailie, and although I was rather wary of Miss Kincaid — a totally unjustified prejudice — I saw nothing wrong with the other guests. All were decent Scots, middle-aged or elderly people and all, with two exceptions, women. Of the males, seated beside me on my right was a short, thickset, red-faced man whom I had heard addressed as Baillie Nicol. He had a salmon fly, which I recognized as a Jock Scott, stuck in his lapel. And next to Miss Kincaid a little ghost-like old man with white hair had flitted in noiselessly in felt-soled slippers. During the meal he remained completely silent, keeping his eyes upon his plate and having considerable difficulty in controlling his false teeth. It took me some time to discover that he was Miss Kincaid's father, and stone deaf, but in the meantime I was inclined to regard him as something of a phenomenon.

Another curiosity which took my eye was a china pig with a slot in its back that stood in the centre of the table.

"Are you wondering about our wee porker?" Miss Ailie was smiling to me. "You see, we like everyone to be served properly while the meals are hot. And that means punctuality. So the rule is that if one comes late one must put a penny in the pig. Naturally, it's all for a good cause — our cottage hospital."

I looked across the table at a vacant chair.

"That person will have to pay up?"

"Oh, no," she laughed. "That's Mr. Sommen's place. He's gone off to Ballater for the day. To the Highland Games."

"I never knew anyone so taken on with the Highlands as Mr. Sommen." A stout lady opposite took up the conversation. "For an Englishman, I mean. He fair dotes on the tartan."

"I hope it's fine for him at Ballater," rejoined Miss Ailie, glancing out at the weather. "He was so looking forward to the step dancing and the reels."

"Had he the wee plaid on him when he left this morning?"

"He had indeed. And very braw he looked in it." Miss Ailie sighed. "Such a nice gentleman. What manners!"

"Aye, you don't often see the like. And forbye, the life and soul of our little party."

At this point my Baillie neighbour cleared his throat noisily, as though something had gone the wrong way, and changed the conversation. Doubtless he had seen me coveting his Jock Scott, for he turned abruptly and asked me if I liked to fish. He told me he came every year to spin for salmon in the Spean, and when he promised to show me a pool where I might catch brown trout, my spirits improved further. I nodded to Mother, indicating that after all Fort William was not a bad sort of place. She and I would certainly go together to the pool and she could knit and watch me while I fished. I gave no thought to the absent Mr. Sommen, or if I did it was in the vague yet optimistic expectation that he too, being the man he was, would contribute further to the satisfactions of our holiday.

At five o'clock that evening, while the others were finishing tea, I had gone to the front door to unravel a gut cast my new fishing friend had given me and which I had already succeeded in tangling, when an open carriage rolled up to the porch and a man sprang out briskly, paid the coachman with an added,

"That's for yourself, chappie," then bounded up the steps towards me. He was of a neat medium figure with a pale, glossy skin, large dark eyes, and a narrow black moustache that curved thinly and stylishly, like an extra eyebrow, across his upper lip. He had on a sporty check suit, a rakish balmoral with the ribbons sweeping across one shoulder, and over the other a short tartan plaid pinned by a silver dagger studded with a large cairngorm.

"Well, well, well, young fellow-me-lad." He greeted me genially. "You a new arrival?"

"Yes, sir."

"With your parents?"

"My mother, sir."

"Pater still turning the wheels of industry?"

"My father's dead, sir."

"Oh, sorry, old chap." He was immediately contrite. "Fearfully sorry I dropped a trick. No idea. Not the foggiest. Come and have some tea."

I told him I'd already had my tea.

"Then come and have another go of cake. Can do? Good. Fill the aching void." With an arm companionably round my shoulders he steered me into the drawing room where, sweeping off his balmoral, he bowed elegantly from the waist.

"Am I too late for the cup that cheers but not inebriates, ladies? If so, just say the word and I'll apologize, depart, put sixpence in the pig, abscond, in other words, buzz off, anything to make amends."

When several voices reassured him he advanced, accepted a cup from Miss Ailie and having implemented his promise, with a wink, by back-handing me a thick slice of cake from the tray, took his stand by the fireplace.

"Well, ladies, I suppose yours truly was never missed, that

absence did not make the heart grow fonder, and you haven't the slightest interest in his adventures at the Games, even though he did brush shoulders with none other than Royalty?"

"But we have, Mr. Sommen. Do tell us."

As I ate my cherry cake I gazed at him in wide-eyed admiration. He was so much at ease, so fluent, never at a loss, so amusingly at home with everyone and above all so dashingly good looking, with his pale skin, small neat features, stylish little moustache and dark engaging eyes. When he concluded his racy description of his doings during the day I was especially struck by his manner when, taking advantage of the pause, Miss Ailie introduced him to Mother. All the jocularity vanished from his expression, he was immediately serious, correct, respectful. He bowed again, talked with her for a few moments and, with a companionable glance that lightly comprehended me, wished her a top hole stay at Ardshiel. Then, as a kind of afterthought, he added:

"After supper we have little musical evenings here, just by way of entertaining ourselves, if you care for that sort of thing?"

Mother admitted that she was fond of music.

"Perhaps," he ventured, "perhaps you play a little . . . or sing, yourself?"

To my chagrin, Mother said that she would really prefer to listen. So acute was my disappointment I forgot my shyness and exclaimed:

"Oh, no sir, Mother plays the piano awfully well. She played once at a concert before hundreds of people. And she sings too."

He looked at me with such pleased approval that I reddened with gratification. Removing his gaze in a well-bred manner from Mother, who had blushed too, he said quietly:

"Well spoken, old chap. Perhaps between us we may be able

to persuade your mater to oblige the company. And now, if you'll excuse me, I must be off for my tub. Nothing like a tub after a day in the open. Au revoir then, till we meet again."

Mother was cross with me as we went upstairs.

"I hope your tartan friend isn't going to be a nuisance, with his little musical evenings. He is rather a gusher, isn't he?"

Nevertheless, I noticed that she put on her best dress, red with a lace collar, which she had sponged and pressed before we left Ardfillan, and extremely nice she looked in it.

When the gong boomed us down for supper Mr. Sommen was already in the dining room standing rather absently in a welcoming position with his hands behind his back, wearing a snowy white shirt set off by a black bow tie, well creased black trousers and a poplin tartan jacket. I thought he looked terribly smart, and so did the others. The jacket, which was apparently new, evoked murmurs of approval. Assiduously placing chairs for the ladies, he modestly admitted he had bought it at Ballater after the Games.

Only one of our company seemed openly at odds with this general adulation and when we had begun on some excellent tomato soup, with the kind of lentils in it that I liked, Baillie Nicol, after darting several caustic glances from beneath his bushy eyebrows at the new garment, suddenly remarked:

"Ye know, of course, sir, that the tartan ye have on is the Mackenzie."

"Is it, by gosh? Delighted to hear it."

"And the plaid ye wear is the Macgregor. While that strip on your balmoral is the Royal Stuart. It looks as though before you've done ye'll be a regular one man 'Gathering o' the Clans.'"

"Well, good luck to them," Sommen said airily. "I like gatherings and from what I saw of these Highland lasses at their eightsome reels I jolly well like the clans."

"But apart from the fact that it's almost illegal to sport a tartan ye're not entitled to, what's your object, man?"

"When in Rome do as the jolly old Romans." Sommen laughed with perfect good nature, not a bit discomfited. "That's my motto when I travel. Last summer I took in Switzerland. When I stepped off the last mountain you couldn't have told me from William Tell. Not bad that, eh? Told, tell!"

The Baillie persisted, inquisitively.

"Ye must have a grand business to be able to get away so much."

Sommen inclined his head, answered with a sudden note of gravity.

"Yes, sir, my family are perhaps the oldest tobacco merchants in the city of London. We are cigarette manufacturers, sir. May I show you our product?" He took out a morocco leather cigarette case and pressed it open, revealing a row of long, flat, elegant looking cigarettes. As it was passed from hand to hand I saw stamped in blue on each, "C. R. Sommen. Special No. 1."

"May I offer you one, sir?"

"Thank you, no," the Baillie growled, thoroughly put out by this demonstration of solid worth. "I have my pipe."

After these exchanges in which the cigarette maker had clearly had the better of it, supper proceeded with renewed amiability. When Miss Kincaid formally gave the signal to rise we went into the drawing room, or as Miss Ailie named it, the "best parlour." Here the curtains had been drawn against the evening chill and a cosy fire of peat was glowing on the hearth emitting its aromatic moorland scent. While coffee and shortbread biscuits were handed round, Sommen advanced to the piano and, standing over the keyboard, played "Chopsticks" with one finger.

"Excuse my humble overture, ladies and gentlemen. We

are now exceedingly fortunate to have a real genuine top notch pianist in our midst and with her kind permission I'm going to ask her to start the ball rolling."

He came forward and crooking his arm in invitation, exclaimed amidst appreciative laughter:

"Madam, may I have the honour of escorting you to the instrument?"

Now I must confess that by this time, I was beginning to be considerably bored by our new friend. His attentions to Mother at supper had been rather too marked and now this cheap gallantry seemed to confirm her own worst fears. I glanced at her sympathetically but, to my surprise, she did not snub him. Instead she rose, yielding without protest, indeed rather gracefully, to this unwelcome foolery.

She played a Chopin prelude then dashed into "Danse des Echarpes" with great brio and finished to sustained applause. I saw that for once Sommen was quite taken aback, as though, unexpectedly, he found himself in an element totally foreign to him.

"I say," he said, almost with deference, "that 'ad real class." Then, recovering himself from that fearful missing aspirate: "Absolutely topping. Good enough for the Albert Hall."

"Nonsense." Mother laughed, and went on rather as if poking fun at him. "Now it's your turn. Let's hear you sing. If you can? I'll play your accompaniment."

After much turning over of music, the song "The Mermaid" was selected. To my disappointment, he had not a bad voice, a light tenor, and he put great dramatic feeling into the words:

> *And down he went like a streak of light,*
> *So quickly down went he,*
> *Until he came to a mermaid*
> *At the bottom of the deep blue sea.*

The effect of this double display of talent upon the company was so pronounced that, to my annoyance, there arose a general demand for a duet. Surely now Mother would refuse, draw the line, put her foot down firmly. But no, still in the same lively, challenging way, almost, one might have thought, with enjoyment, she had already selected "The Tarpaulan Jacket," the first line of which, "A tall stalwart Lancer lay dying," gave me such a thrill of anticipation that I had come to regard the ballad as my own special property. They began. I wished I might have stopped up my ears. At least I kept my eyes on the ceiling and refrained from joining in the prolonged hand clapping.

By this time the singing, talking and laughter, the growing sense of camaraderie, above all the patter and too pressing urbanities of this bogus clansman had, in a manner I scarcely realized, made me extremely hot under my collar. I decided that it had gone far enough and should be terminated. Seizing a rare moment of silence I called out:

"I think I'll go upstairs now, Mother," imagining, naturally, that she would come with me.

Instead, still bent over the music with Sommen, without even turning round, she replied:

"Yes, do, dear. It's past your bedtime. I'll be up soon."

As I was already on my feet there was nothing for it but that I must go. And she did not come soon but late, much later than I had hoped. Still, the desire to express my conflicting emotions had served to keep me awake. I sat up in bed.

"You were right after all, Mother. It *was* a nuisance, wasn't it?"

She smiled at me. Her eyes seemed bright and there was colour in her cheeks.

"Oh, I don't know, dear. In a way it was really rather fun

and goodness knows neither of us have had much of that lately."

"But Mother, it was all so . . . so cheap and nasty."

"Was it as bad as all that?"

"*He* was, anyhow, the cigarette maker."

"Well, perhaps he is rather officious, dear, but I think he means well, so we mustn't be too critical. Let's just remember we're here for the one holiday we've had in four years and try to make the most of it."

This was not the kind of response I expected from my mother. Turning on my side I gave her a brusque good night.

However, next morning my sense of injury had gone and after breakfast, carrying my fishing rod and a picnic lunch, I set out with Baillie Nicol for the Spean. Mother, seeing us off from the porch, promised to join me in almost an hour. The pool the Baillie showed me was not far up river, a deep brown tarn among pine trees, fed by a rushing waterfall and contained by ledges. Having seen me settled he went off up stream to his own beat, having finally averred with a pessimistic survey of the clear blue sky that it was not an angler's day.

Certainly I did not look like having much luck. In the space of two hours I caught a three inch parr, which of course I unhooked carefully and returned. As nothing seemed to be taking, I began more and more to look for the appearance of Mother. What on earth was keeping her? Could my Ingersol be wrong? No, from the sun, directly overhead, it must now be noon. My neck was stiff from craning towards the path through the wood and the roar of the waterfall had made my head swim. I reeled in, retreated to the pines and ate my share of the lunch. Still not a sign of her. Angrily, after only a moment's hesitation, I ate her lunch as well. She would not deserve it when she did come.

With nothing else to do, I resumed my fishing, but in so spiritless a manner I permitted an eel to take my hook unnoticed and to digest my bait so thoroughly that it had to be destroyed, in a slimy mess, before I could recover my tackle. After that, as the afternoon was well advanced, I decided to give up.

I had trudged to the end of the wood and was on the road that led up hill from the river, when an approaching figure became visible against the skyline. It was she.

Immediately I threw off my despondency, set my expression to an injured and resentful coldness. Ignoring her too cheerful greeting, I said accusingly:

"You didn't come."

"I'm so sorry, dear." She smiled, breathlessly. "Our plans somehow seemed to get upset."

Apparently, though I gave her no marks for that futile and belated effort, she'd been hurrying.

"You see, there was such an interesting expedition arranged to Banavie. Somehow I was persuaded to go along."

"Who persuaded you?"

"Why . . . Miss Baird."

Had she hesitated before answering me? Miss Baird was the stout woman who liked Sommen.

"So you and she went off all by yourselves."

"Good gracious, no, dear." She made the idea seem ridiculous. "Two women, all alone! Your friend Mr. Sommen went with us. In fact he organized the trip and took care of everything most handsomely."

That evening at supper I studied him, viewing him after the manner of Scott-Hamilton with a critical, appraising eye. What a clown he was, or rather, what a cad, monopolizing the conversation — keeping things going I suppose he would have called it — and showing off in every direction. Why, at this moment, as Miss Kincaid, having sliced the boiled ham, seemed to be having trouble carving one of the chickens, and with a reproachful glance at Miss Ailie, had murmured that the carver was not sharp, he had the colossal cheek to interfere. I could scarcely believe my eyes when this bounder leaned over, with a "Permit me, madam" and taking the knife from her hand began to carve the bird. I longed for him to make some horrible gaffe that would draw down on him the laughter and contempt of everyone. I hoped the chicken would squirt off the platter to the floor or, better still, bounce up and hit him in the eye. But no, with unsuspected skill and a dexterity I believed impossible, he had it sliced and sectioned perfectly. This was too much for me and apparently for Baillie Nicol too. He kept muttering under his breath and glowering at our enemy. I was glad to accept his invitation to a game of draughts in the smoking room; I felt I would do anything to avoid the entertainment in the parlour.

The Baillie was not of a talkative disposition, but as we set out our men on the chequered board, he fixed his gaze on me and said:

"You seem a decent sort of boy, and your mother looks to me a sweet little woman. If I were you, I would just drop a word in her ear against the counter jumper of a cockney. I may be wrong, but for my part, I wouldn't trust him as far as I could throw him."

The warning alarmed me. And as the next few days passed, there was no longer the least possibility of doubt. This man, this Englishman, this tartaned Sommen, was — I sought a phrase that would not wound me too deeply — "making up" to my mother. Despite the deceptive mildness of these two words they sent a hot flush over me. And it deepened at the thought of Mother's response. At first she had merely seemed flattered: a natural reaction which I had persuaded myself was pardonable in a woman whose life had lately been so dull and hard. But gradually she had warmed to these hateful attentions and now, in her glance, her gesture, in her whole being, she could not conceal from me, nor from others in the boarding house whom I had heard whispering, the change that had come over her. She looked younger and prettier, with a strange attractiveness that exuded and bloomed upon her skin. She had a new liveliness, an unnatural vivacity, a sense of letting herself go that I had never known before. Worst of all was her change towards me: that excessive solicitude and open show of tenderness, which I felt to be propitiating, even insincere, since most of the time, to be free of my questioning eye, she kept avoiding me, or pushing me off to fish, so that she could go off with *him*.

At the start of the second week, as I sat at the Spean pool, I decided I wouldn't put up with it. I would not be cast off. Burning with indignation, I reeled in my neglected line, from which the worm had long ago been devoured, and set off for Ardshiel.

Mother was on the porch, but not as though expecting me.

"Any luck?" she exclaimed with specious brightness.

"No."

"Never mind, dear. I'm sure you'll catch something when you try again this afternoon."

I didn't answer. My mind was made up. I ate my lunch with apparent calm. Immediately the meal ended I excused myself, got up, and disappeared. I had not returned to the river. I was in the shrubbery at the edge of the garden.

They did not keep me waiting long. My heart gave a big, extra thump as they emerged, Sommen in his idiotic tartan get-up, Mother wearing her brown tweed costume and a new gay scarf which she certainly had not bought and which therefore he must have given her. Together, yet discreetly separated, they sauntered down the hill towards the town. Gazing from between the laurel branches I allowed them a fair start, then, with a casual air, though my pulse was throbbing like mad, I cut round the side of the garden and went after them.

The bitter excitement of the chase made me want to run, but I knew I must keep a safe distance behind them. Out of sight of the boarding house, they had drawn closer to each other. They reached the town and turned the corner into the main street. Trying not to hurry, I followed. It was market day and the town was busy. For a minute I couldn't pick them out, then I saw them on the opposite side of the street looking into the window of a shop that sold Gosse china and other tourist souvenirs. He was gabbing, as usual, and pointing in a persuasive manner, but Mother shook her head lightly and they moved off. A rush of traffic held me back, but when I crossed the street, out of the corner of my eye I saw them veer right into the Mealmarket, a narrow wynd leading to the old part of the town.

Now I increased my pace and sung into the Mealmarket. They were not in sight. With a catch of anxiety I pressed on, moving in and out of the stalls that crowded the narrow wynd, seeking everywhere, like a hound at fault. Minutes passed, five, ten. Not a sign of them. Had I lost them? And then, as I came out of the far end of the Mealmarket into the cobbled square that faced the open loch, my eye was caught by a rowboat moving easily on the sunlit water only a few hundred yards off shore.

I took a long breath. Now I had them, and I could wait. Slowly, without removing my gaze, I walked down to the stone jetty from which the boats were hired and took up my stand behind one of the bollards.

He was at the oars, alternatively sculling and drifting, while Mother sat facing him in the stern. When he leaned forward to make a stroke the intimacy of their positions stung me. I choked with jealous rage, invoking all the powers of light and darkness to work a miracle that would make this dandy, this bogus Clansman, this cigarette maker, catch a crab and somersault backwards into the water, where, strangled by the strings of his balmoral and shouting vainly to me for aid, he would sink in all his finery to the bottom of the loch which I knew to be fabulously deep.

At last they came ashore. Instinctively I crouched low, hiding under the edge of the pier. Now, although I could not see, I could hear. I heard the bump of the boat against the jetty, his step ashore and then his voice as he assisted her to land.

"Dear Grace, give me your hand."

The words made me wince.

Now I heard footsteps on the stones above and judged it safe to raise my head. Mother had taken his arm and was smiling up at him as they moved off. I folded my arms and in that dramatic attitude, with the frozen immobility of the betrayed, watched them go.

When I returned to Ardshiel I revealed nothing of the treachery I had witnessed, merely maintaining an attitude of stoic coldness. All that evening I confronted Mother with my silence and hostility. She had now begun to look at me reproachfully, and after supper tried to induce me to come with her to the drawing room on the pretext that there were to be parlour games. Games, indeed! I resisted, saying that I was tired, and went upstairs to bed where, as I lay awake, the misery of the afternoon was re-created by their intermingled voices ascending in another hateful duet. When she came up, quite late, I closed my eyes and pretended sleep.

Next morning came clear and sunny. Mother, eager for reconciliation and with the faintest hint of guilt in her manner, was all sweetness and light. After breakfast she came out to join me in the garden where already I had taken up a strategic position by the gate.

"Darling," she smiled placatingly — ah, I thought, the Judas smile! "Mr. Sommen has suggested taking us for a drive this afternoon. Along the coast to visit Onich Castle. But I daresay you can't be bothered with sightseeing."

"Why not?" I inquired.

"Well . . . you're such a fisherman I thought you'd surely want to go to your pool again."

"Considering that I've gone to my pool for the past week and caught nothing, doesn't it occur to you that I might prefer to go sightseeing. Especially," I added, with heavy emphasis, "as there will probably be plenty to *see.*"

She flushed slightly and was silent.

"Then you'd . . . you'd really like to come?"

"Yes," I said, not looking at her. "I definitely and positively would."

The carriage arrived at two o'clock. The cigarette maker who, while we waited in the porch, had been jocular with me in his best "old chap" manner, through which I detected a strain of unease, now gave me a hand up beside the coachman before taking his place with Mother behind. We set off with a slow clip-clop of hooves. I could not observe the pair at my back but at least I was with them and I swore that this time they would not get away. Never again would Mother have the chance to be alone with all that charm.

Partially reassured, I almost enjoyed the drive. The sun shone, the sky was a duck egg blue, the little waves lapped along the shore. It was good to be seated so high, and the coachman was friendly, pointing out places of interest with his whip. If only this interloper had not been with us. His intrusion was a profanation of our existence.

Too soon we arrived at the clachan of Onich and drew up at the little harbour where a few small blistered fishing smacks lay moored against the pier. In the foreground, high up on a cliff, was the castle. As I climbed off my perch the cigarette maker assisted Mother to alight.

"I say," he suddenly exclaimed, looking down, "what a spiffing day for a cruise!"

Two fisherboys in rubber boots and blue jerseys were hoisting a lug sail.

"Would you like it, young fellow-me-lad?" he said, turning to me. "Don't you think it a good idea?"

I thought it an excellent idea. How better could I keep them under my eagle eye? I nodded stiffly.

"Come on then," he cried gaily, leaping down and speaking to the boys. When I followed he helped me aboard solicitously, then, still on the pier, and before I knew what he was about or could collect my scattered wits, he had pushed the boat off, the sail caught the wind and I was out of the harbour and away while Mother, with a despicable pretence of affection, took out her handkerchief and waved to me from the shore.

I turned wildly to the bigger of the two boys.

"Go back. Go back to the pier."

He shook his head. The "gentlemans" had hired him "py the 'oor." He let out more sail and the boat took an unbalancing heave. Weak with rage and distress I collapsed in the thwarts. Yesterday they had been in the boat and I on shore. Now, precisely, the positions were reversed. This was the final treachery. They had begun to walk arm in arm along the cliff towards the castle. Yes, I had always thought him a cad, and

now I knew him to be a cheat as well. As for Mother's . . .
duplicity . . . oh, dear, the wind was making my eyes water.

For more than the specified time we tacked monotonously
up and down outside the harbour. My captors had practically
no English but they had the Gaelic and in this, to me, out-
landish tongue, they conversed continuously in low derisive
voices, gazing from me to the castle, then back again to me.
Although I could not understand a word of their ghastly
lingo I sweated with shame, fully aware that they were discussing me, my correct attire, my pallid looks which, because
of the movement of the boat, betrayed that I was on the verge
of nausea, above all — and this was the hardest to bear — the
obvious beastly reason why I had been shanghaied by the
gentlemans.

At last there came a hail from the beach. The despicable
couple had reappeared, and with a final sadistic tack into the
wind to prolong my misery, I was returned to the harbour.

"Have a good time, old chap?"

"Yes, thank you." I met his ingratiating gaze with the prim
unsmiling politeness I had resolved to assume.

Mother, who seemed flushed and agitated, was looking at
me nervously yet with an earnestness that told me her one
desire was to make up with me.

"I don't think you'd have liked the castle, dear."

"I don't think I should."

"It was very old.'

"It looks old."

"And damp."

"I thought it might be."

"You weren't too cold on the water?"

"Not at all, thank you."

"Were the boys nice?"

"Delightful."

There was an awkward pause before our unnatural dialogue could be resumed.

"Well," exclaimed Sommen, with an effort at heartiness, "it's about time we were off. I'll go and dig the cabby out of the pub."

On the way up from the pier Mother tried to take my arm but I pretended to stumble and kept away from her.

We got into the carriage and drove off. Up on the box again I decided that neither of them were quite themselves. Something undoubtedly had happened. Even now they were unusually silent. Was this an omen favourable to me? I longed to turn round but pride forbade me, though I kept my ears well cocked. And still they weren't speaking, no, not a word. They've quarrelled, I thought, with a surge of joy. I could resist no longer. Cautiously moving my head I squinted over my shoulder. The cigarette maker, leaning towards Mother, with an arm round her waist, was kissing her. Oh, God, my own mother spooning in the open, in full public view, with that cad . . . I nearly fell off the box.

When we got back to the boarding house I removed myself in silence and went directly to my room. I was seated on the edge of my bed staring at the faded roses on the wallpaper when I heard the handle of the door turn and hesitantly, almost timidly, Mother came in. She sat down beside me and put an arm round my shoulders. From her manner, her apologetic caress, I thought for one wild moment that she had repented and was going to ask my forgiveness for the injury she had done, not to me alone, but to our love. Instead she said:

"Laurence, dear. Charley . . . Mr. Sommen has asked me to marry him."

I did not answer for some time. Shock had silenced me. I felt a fearful burning in my heart that made me want to cry out, abjectly: "Don't, Mother, I beg of you, for pity's sake. You know we have always been together, how much we mean to one another. Don't, please don't let anyone come between us."

But the vision of that hateful public embrace choked back the words. It hardened me.

"And will you?" I said coldly.

"I think I should, dear."

"Why?" My tone was slightly contemptuous. "Are you what's called in love with him?"

"I like him, dear. And I think he is in love with me. Of course, he's a queer sort of chap, not altogether what you might call a . . . well, the sort of person you're used to, but he's generous and kind. He's so gay too, and that's good for me. He's got a good heart. Besides, it would be so much better for our future, yours as well as mine. It's been hard for me, trying to keep things going, alone. This way, we wouldn't have to separate, you needn't go to Uncle Leo. We could be together, in London. Charley, Mr. Sommen, says there are all sorts of good schools for you there. He likes you, dear."

"I don't want him to like me. I hate him." I disengaged myself from her arm, and although my breast was torn with wounded love, I stared at her cruelly. "He's an utter bounder, an absolute outsider, a common masher. What's come over you, a woman of your refinement! Baillie Nicol says he's nothing but a counter jumping cockney. I suppose you know that the whole boarding house is talking about the way you're behaving, and how silly you are, running after a man younger than yourself, and all heated up about it."

"Laurence!"

"And what do you really know about him beyond the fact that he's got a cigarette factory and flings his money around like a would-be lord. Two weeks ago you didn't even know he existed. And what have you told him about us? Is he aware that we're practically in the poorhouse?"

"I won't have you speak to me like that." She had drawn back to the end of the bed and was facing me with a look of pained anger. "Mr. Sommen would never dream of asking me about our circumstances."

"Well he as good as asked me," I sneered. "Not long after we came he tried to pump me about Father's business. I bragged of course, and said Father had built up the finest yeast agency in Scotland. So he probably thinks the sweet, soft little widow is rolling. And that's why he's swarming all over you." My voice broke suddenly. "I saw him in the carriage, the vulgar cad."

Provoked beyond endurance, Mother gave a little moan and struck me a ringing box on the ear that almost knocked me off the bed. We stared at each other in a terrible silence. I could not remember that she had ever hit me before.

"You're a wicked boy," she gasped. "A wicked, wicked boy. Trying to spoil the one little bit of happiness I've had since your father died. And in spite of all you say, and all the fibs you tell, I'll do exactly as I please."

I stood up. Through the singing in my head I shouted:

"Go ahead and do it, then. I'm only warning you. You'll be sorry."

I walked straight out of the house, my ear burning and hurting like mad, and although I hated the place now, somehow I found myself at the pool. I sat down on a rock, and clamped my head between my fists. This woman, sole possessor of my heart, whom I had loved exclusively from the moment I first opened my infant eyes, or perhaps when first she offered me her breast, had betrayed me. My immediate impulse was to desert her, to inquire the road to Winton of the first amiable stranger and set out by forced marches for Uncle Leo who, after all, expected me. Yet there was a flaw in this course of action that held me back. I wanted justice, and more, I wanted revenge. Revenge on Mother and on this . . . this mountebank — the word consoled me slightly — who had supplanted me. If only there was someone to whom I could turn for help. I racked my brains, dismissing one after another the Carroll relations, all uninterested, inept. I even considered the possibilities of Baillie Nicol. And then I thought of Stephen — safe, sure, reliable, Stephen could always be depended on. And Stephen, now established at the Ministry of Labour, was in London.

The possibilities of my idea sent a shiver down my spine. I bounded to my feet. Hurrying back to Ardshiel I begged some notepaper from Miss Ailie, then locked myself in my room. Stretched out on the floor I took a pencil and dashed off a letter to Stephen. Within half an hour I had posted it in the town. I even remembered to send it express.

When all this had been accomplished, a sudden calm descended upon me, perhaps the realization that, whatever the outcome, I had displayed determination and resource. In the days that followed I maintained a steady reserve. Although I watched "them" secretly at meal times, I assumed indifference, and when they went off on their excursions I no longer shadowed them, I could afford to wait. On several occasions Mother attempted to reopen the matter, and to break down the barrier I had erected, but always without success. I refused to allow myself to be cajoled.

Yet I was anxious, beneath these pretences, and as time drew on with no word or apparent sign of action from Stephen, my nervousness increased. Ardshiel, being some distance from the center of the town, was served by only one delivery of mail and every afternoon towards three o'clock I hung about the porch, waiting for the postman. At last, one wet afternoon, a letter was handed to me. Yes, it was stamped with the London postmark. Feverishly, I locked myself in the downstairs lavatory and tore it open.

Dear Laurence,

It was extremely awkward for me to take time off but, as I judged your letter important, I have done so.

The telephone directory revealed five Sommens, of whom one was listed as Tobacconist & Newsagent, at 1026a, The Mile End Road, E.C. I thereupon took a bus to that unsalubrious quarter — not quite a slum, but almost. The shop proved to be a small drab affair, newspapers, including racing sheets, on one side, cigarettes on the other. I entered and bought — guess what? — the News of the World! I was served by an elderly arthritic dame in a worn spencer, buttoned up to the neck. In the back shop a girl — dark, untidy hair, wearing a grubby overall — was rolling cigarettes on a small hand machine. Emerging, I entered the nearest pub — very near, three doors down, where information was readily forthcoming.

The father is dead, the business, negligible and declining, kept going, barely, by the widow. There are three daughters, one of whom is the cigarette maker. Father had some connections for this brand, now practically nil. Debts were mentioned. Mother, girls and the son all live above the shop.

The son, your man, takes no part in the business, is described as a good sort, generous, would do anything for a pal, but flash, a fancy dresser, and soft. Bit of a singer and performs at "smokers." Likes to bet, which he does with occasional success, and when he pulls something off, takes a holiday in style. His job — he is a waiter at the Metropolitan Sporting Club in the West End.

I trust this information will quash the incipient romance. Give my love to your mother and tell her please not to be foolish.

Yours,
Stephen

A thrill of fearful joy electrified me. Holding my breath I stared at the damning words — a waiter at the Metropolitan —

then turned and rushed towards the staircase. I could not wait an instant before avenging myself for all I had suffered by delivering this fatal blow, not only to my mother's hopes, but to her pride.

During the past two days of rain Mother had drawn more within herself, resting and reading in her room after lunch. I knew that she was there now. A cruel, an unholy triumph intoxicated me, sent the blood rushing to my head as I knocked at her door, with the letter in my hand.

"Come in."

She was not reading, but standing at the window, wearing that look of abstraction, a kind of meditative sadness, which, in later years, came over her more and more. She half turned, ventured a smile.

"Mother . . ." I went forward. Her expression, tender and, for some reason, forgiving, unnerved me. Not only that, before I could prevent her she actually took my hand and pressed it against her cheek. Yet I was not to be deterred by such sentimental tricks. I was trembling now and sweating all over, but I made myself go on. "There's something I have to show you . . ."

"Yes, Laurie, dear."

Still holding my hand she was again looking out and down. Instinctively my gaze followed hers. A station cab stood at the front door and luggage was being heaped upon its roof. Then, hurriedly, bent as if to avoid the plashing rain, a figure, familiar though untartaned, emerged from the porch and dived into the cab. The door slammed, the cabby mounted the box and drove off.

There was a mortal silence in that little bedroom.

"He's gone?" I stammered.

She nodded slowly and turned to me.

"I've sent him away."

"Why?"

"There was your father, Laurence. And now there's you. I suddenly discovered there wasn't room for anyone else."

Something in my throat tied itself into a knot so that I could not speak or swallow. I stared at her, then in my free hand I crushed the letter to shapeless pulp and blindly flung myself upon her breast.

22

THE HABITAT of my Uncle Leo was a four storey warehouse somewhat peculiarly named Templar's Hall and
situated in that unsalubrious district of Winton known
as the Gorbielaw. The building, which occupied one corner of
two mean, narrow cobbled streets, was old and in poor repair
with the side windows plastered over and painted a dingy
black, but as it stood in the centre of the city, adjacent to
Argyle Street and convenient for the docks, it presumably
had for my uncle advantages of a commercial nature. As a
residence it had less to offer. The top floor, consisting of a
long dark passage with a great many rooms opening off on
either side, served as the living quarters. However, as I had
arrived late the night before I had as yet no idea of the nature
of these rooms, only that my own, furnished with an iron bed,
a washstand and a burst cane chair, was at the far end of the
corridor, and the kitchen, where a sort of general servant to
my uncle, Annie Tobin, had given me bread and cheese for
my supper, at the other.

I had slept intermittently, disturbed by the clanging of the
Argyle Street trams and by an unmanly heartache for my
mother, whom I had seen off at the Central Station on the previous afternoon. The prospect of a separation for at least a year
— despite Mother's assertion that it would quickly pass — had

made it a difficult parting. But the morning brought the promise of new experiences. I got up, washed and dressed, then, opening my door, moved circumspectly in search of breakfast.

Mrs. Tobin stood at the kitchen stove. She was a shapeless woman of about fifty-five with a bright red face, pitted by acne, small deep set blue eyes and wild grey hair that seemed to be standing on end. An old brown wrapper was tied about her middle. Scuffed carpet slippers adorned her feet.

Apart from her blowsy appearance, her strong Irish accent and familiar manners had already offended me and I had quite decided that I should not like Mrs. Tobin at all.

"Is my uncle not up yet?"

She turned and considered me goodnaturedly.

"He's up and out a good hour ago."

"Has he gone to Mass?" I inquired, conceiving no other reason for so early an excursion.

Mrs. Tobin burst out laughing. When she laughed her stomach shook and her blue eyes dissolved completely in folds of inflamed red skin. Good heavens, I thought, she seems to be enjoying some kind of joke.

"My dear lad," she replied at last, "that fellow hasn't seen the inside of a church for more nor thirty year. He's a black atheist, none other. But you'll soon get used to his comings and goings, though God Himself wouldn't know what he's up to, or after. A gombeen man, no less. Are you wanting your breakfast?"

"Please," I said coldly, determined to repress all familiarity.

"Then you shall have it, my lad," she replied agreeably.

"Where is the dining room?"

"Just here, dear, none other. Kitchen, drawing room, dining room combined. So take a seat and be easy."

As with some reluctance I sat down, she removed a china

bowl from the shelf, half filled it with a yellowish mealy powder and stirred in boiling water from the kettle on the stove. The result was a sort of muddy brown porridge which did not smell at all good and which, with a cup of bluish milk and a spoon, she placed before me.

"What's this?"

"Just a kind of stirabout, only made with pease meal. Your uncle favours it, and gets it wholesale by the hunderweight bag."

I picked up my spoon and took a mouthful.

"You don't fancy it, dear," she said sympathetically, studying my face. "Still, as there isn't much else, if I were you I'd sup it up."

"It would taste better with a lump of butter in it," I said demandingly, with a grimace.

"Butter, dear?" Her twinkling eyes began to disappear again. "You'll not get as much butter from Leo as you could put on the end of a bumbee's arse."

Naturally, as far as I was concerned, this vulgarity was the end of Mrs. Tobin.

Nevertheless, anxious not to offend my uncle, since it was his choice, I supped the stirabout up, meanwhile reflecting gloomily on all my mother's appetizing breakfasts, not to speak of the delicious luncheons provided me by Miss Greville. When I had made my way to the bottom of the bowl Mrs. Tobin remarked:

"If you're not full, I'll give you a cut off my loaf."

"Your loaf!" I exclaimed, exploding with indignation.

"Well, yes, lad. I do buy myself a few things now and then, just by way of what you might call an extra."

Her tone was so mild and with that constant hint of laughter lying behind, ready to spring up and make light of any difficulties, I felt obliged to hold back my resentment. Besides, cradling the loaf in the crook of her arm, she was sawing off a thick slice of sweet-smelling fresh bread and spreading it generously with dripping.

I accepted it in silence. After the stirabout it tasted like real food. I was still chewing when steps sounded on the stairs and my uncle came into the room.

Although it was more than four years since I had first encountered Leo at my father's funeral, I now found not the slightest change in him. He presented to the world the same tall thin figure, almost emaciated, in the tight shiny navy blue suit, the same long, smooth, pale, expressionless, self-contained, unreadable face. Leo was an ageless man who remained fixed permanently, as by an effort of will, in the same changeless mould, and when he died, some thirty years later — worth, incidentally, three quarters of a million sterling — I felt convinced, although I was then four thousand miles away, that he had expired inscrutably in precisely the same form, and was buried in the identical blue suit.

Meanwhile, putting a hand on my shoulder, he had made me welcome, pleasantly enough, although with a deprecating shake of his head he seemed to take exception to my slice of bread.

"That bleached white flour rots the coating of the bowel, Laurence. But I see you've had your pease meal. That's the stuff that'll really stick to your ribs. You'll soon get used to our ways. We're careful what we put in our stomachs here. Now if you've finished I'll take you downstairs."

We descended by the stone staircase to the first floor, then, selecting a key from the shiny bunch secured to his braces by a thin chain, he opened a door and led me into the stockroom. This was a long hall which ran the entire length of the building, and so high — it contained both the first and second storeys — as to produce a faint echo when we spoke. In this lofty and extremely dusty repository a double row of trestle tables was laid out, leaving a passage in the middle which was covered by a strip of frayed red drugget, while on the tables bales of cloth were piled and strewn in some disarray.

"Now," said Uncle Leo, in a confidential manner, so plausible it would have deceived the entire College of Cardinals, "you'll begin to learn your trade."

After testing my knowledge of linear measure he presented me with an inch tape, which I assumed had got into the establishment by mistake since as he draped it professionally over my shoulders I saw on the reverse side, in plain black letters, "Property of Morris Shapiro Tailor." He then began to take me round the tables, stopping at each to instruct me in the goods displayed. First the saxonys, then the cheviots, next the angolas, the broadcloths, the tweeds — Donegal, Harris, Shetland. To each bale a ticket was attached on which was marked the price, not in figures but in letters, and glancing down at me obliquely with a deepening of his confidence and flattering implications of my fidelity, Uncle Leo entrusted me with the secret of his code. It was simple, a reversal of the alphabet in which Z stood for zero, Y for one, X for two, and so on back to Q which represented nine.

All this would have impressed me more but for the unworthy suspicion that those materials, which my uncle spoke of and indeed caressed with a proprietary touch as though they were rare and precious fabrics, seemed rather more shop soiled, ill used and exhausted than I, even as an untrained neophyte, would have expected — seemed, in brief, scarcely to merit the high sounding titles and rich encomiums bestowed upon them. Indeed, while I hesitated to mention the fact, my eye had more than once been attracted by other tickets, unrelated to Uncle's code, but crudely stamped in red with such devices as: *Bankrupt Stock, Sale, Job Lot,* and finally a fearfully incriminating tag on which was scrawled in blue pencil: *Knocked down to Pinchpenny C at 50% off.*

When our circuit had been completed Leo drew up at the last trestle.

"You understand, Laurence, that in the ordinary way I would expect a premium from an apprentice. And a handsome one at that. But blood is thicker than water. We'll let you off the premium. You'll have your board and lodging, and over and above I'm going to give you sixpence a week for your pocket."

Mother had told me that Uncle had promised to pay me wages, but this seemed very little. Still, I managed to say:

"Thank you, Uncle Leo."

Perhaps he noticed the hesitation in my tone for he went on quickly:

"What's more, if you need anything, and I think you need a suit," he paused, with an air of serious liberality, "I'll give you it." I looked at him gratefully, I undoubtedly had need of a suit. In the past few months I had shot up, and out, of my present garments so that my trouser ends were well above my ankles and the sleeves of my jacket failed to cover my wrists. But before I could express my thanks Leo went on: "Now here's a lovely piece of stuff."

The cloth he displayed, with a professional toss that unwrapped the bolt and spread it hurtfully before my eyes, was a strong pepper and salt check, of a pattern so vivid I would have judged it suitable only for gentlemen of the most pronounced sporting tastes.

"Isn't it a trifle loud, Uncle?"

"Loud!" He dismissed the idea. "This is a classic, Laurence, and the only piece of it I have. As for wear, it stands by itself.

It'll last a lifetime. I'll get Shapiro up to measure you this afternoon."

I was quite overcome, but whether by his generosity or by the design of the material I scarcely knew. While I remained silent he drew a large silver watch from his waistcoat pocket and thoughtfully consulted it, an action which, as I soon discovered, was the usual prelude to his sudden and mysterious departures.

"I have to go now," he said. "If anyone comes in call down Mrs. Tobin or just say I'll be back soon. Meanwhile, I'll give you some work to keep you busy. Come into the office."

I followed him through a door I had not previously observed, into a small room furnished with a flat desk, a single chair and a large green safe. The bare floor boards were cluttered with a great many packages and cardboard boxes, some open and disclosing to my gaze a varied assortment of attractively labelled tins, bottles and jars. Hustling through some papers on the desk he found a magazine which had the title *The Health Food Bulletin*. Turning the pages he indicated a number of advertisements, each of which he had marked with a cross.

"You write a pretty fair hand, I hope?"

When I had assured him on this point the instructions he then gave me, though astounding, were precise. Thus, five minutes later, when he had departed, I found myself seated at the desk, pen in hand, inditing a letter, the first of a series, which ran as follows:

Mr. Leo Carroll presents his compliments to the Ocean Seaweed Food Company and requests them to forward to his business office at the above address, liberal free samples of their product Sargossa as advertised in The Health Food Bulletin, for his personal use and possible future commercial orders.

When I had finished the letters, all addressed to patent food companies, it was almost noon and no customers had as yet appeared. I went through the warehouse and opened the door to satisfy myself that a queue had not formed outside. It had not. Then, as I turned, I saw pinned on a panel of the door a cryptic notice which read *Call again. Back at two. Leo.*

The realization that my uncle had so little faith in me caused my spirits to droop. I went back and stared through one of the front windows. Masked by the grime on the panes the narrow street nevertheless revealed itself mercilessly: mean little shops, a public house, a short string of hucksters' barrows, and at the far end, the familiar three brass balls of the pawnbroker. I could not comprehend why my uncle should have chosen to live in such a locality or to own so vast and dilapidated a building in order to carry on his business in so small a part of it. How could I guess, in those early days, his astute precognition that changes in the city planning would raise the value of this property to fantastic heights?

A sudden laugh from behind disturbed my brooding and made me spin round.

"The sight of you there with the inchtape on you!"

Forgetting that I had made up my mind not to like her, I felt surprisingly relieved to see Mrs. Tobin.

"I thought I'd see how you were getting on. Anyhow it's time for your dinner." She added: "Such as it is."

She locked the outer door and we went upstairs to the kitchen where I was not long in perceiving that my dinner was to be derived from a large pot of boiled potatoes and a wedge of Dunlop cheese. However, before this was served Mrs. Tobin set a frying pan on the stove and, almost from nowhere, by a kind of legerdemain, shot into it two fat sausages which immediately began to sizzle and to emit a seductive aroma that brought the water to my teeth. While she tended them she kept watching me with a broad, suggestive smile until I could no longer contain myself.

"Yours, Mrs. Tobin?" I queried.

"Mine," she agreed and, lifting the pan from the stove she forked one of the sausages on to my plate and placed the other on her own.

"This looks awfully good, Mrs. Tobin."

"Annacker's," she replied succinctly.

I was hungry. Despite Uncle's assurances, the stirabout had not stuck long to my ribs. Several minutes elapsed before I added:

"And these potatoes are beautifully floury."

"I have the knack of the spuds, dear, like most of the Irish. And don't call me Mrs. Tobin, just Annie."

"Does my uncle not come in to dinner?" I inquired, with my mouth full of hot sausage and mash.

She shook her head.

"In the first place he hardly eats what would feed a sparrow. In the second, except when he's messing about here in the evening with his patent foods and what not, he takes his meals in the Vegetarian Restaurant in Union Street."

"Good gracious. Is he really a vegetarian, Mrs. Tobin, I mean, Annie?"

"He'll not put meat in his mouth. Sure, if it was raining pork chops he'd only use the fat to grease his boots. Fornent which, he doesn't smoke. And as for liquor, and this is the quarest of all, he's never had a drink in his life. Leo's a quare fellow, dear, and *deep*. He never lets his right hand know what his left hand's doing. But you'll soon get to know him," she added slyly, "if you haven't already."

"It does seem to me," I spoke interestedly, anxious to pursue the subject, "that my uncle is not very well off."

If I had made the wittiest joke of the century the effect on

Mrs. Tobin could not have been more pronounced. She literally rocked with laughter. When finally she had composed herself she wiped her eyes and said:

"What makes you think that, dear?"

"Well," I reasoned, reddening with embarrassment, "Uncle doesn't seem to live very well here. I mean, the food isn't too plentiful. And, as a matter of fact, this morning not a single person came to the showroom to buy cloth."

"Oh they'll come, dear, they'll come," she said mildly. "In the afternoon when himself is there. And even if they didn't what's the odds?"

"The odds, Mrs. Tobin, Annie?"

"That little bit of a shop down there isn't but a fraction of Leo's interests. He has property all over the city. If you'd walked like me up and down the tenements at Anderson Cross collecting his rents you'd know to your sorrow just how much he has. And that's not the big thing."

"What big thing, Annie?" I gasped.

"Whisky!" she proclaimed, enjoying the effect of that omnipotent word. "Whisky in bond. Barrels and barrels of the stuff, all sealed by the revenue, maturin' and maturin' and gettin' dearer and dearer all the time. You'll know about that too, my lad, when we come to the next bottling day."

I looked at her dazedly, all my notions of Leo whirling around in a haze of amazed uncertainty. What was I to make of this uncle of mine who was so outrageously rich yet starved himself, and me, on pease meal stirabout? I didn't dare pursue the matter for fear of further revelations.

When dinner was over and Mrs. Tobin had refused my subdued offer to help her wash the dishes, I went pensively down to the shop to ensure being there when Leo returned.

He arrived punctually at two, seemed pleased to find me on

duty and even went so far as to congratulate me in restrained terms on the manner in which I had written his letters. He then took off his jacket and put on a waistcoat with black alpaca sleeves, then, still wearing his bowler hat, which indeed he rarely removed, indoors or out, went into his office, where for some time he was busy, alone, working over some stiff-backed ledgers. But these were restored to the safe as his customers began to arrive. What surprised me was the number of poor women, some even draped in shawls — sure emblem of the slums — who came in looking for what they described as "remnants," and which I soon discovered to be end pieces of the material just short of an adequate length. A few of these were apparently tenants of my uncle, for they addressed him as "Leo" but despite this familiarity and the cajoleries, usually prefaced by the exclamation: "Ah, Leo, for the love of God . . ." he remained unfailingly polite, merely pointing to one of a number of cards prominently displayed on the trestles and marked *This house does NOT extend credit.*

It could however be said for Leo that when they did buy he courteously presented them with a pattern from *Weldon's Home Dressmaker* on the back of which was stamped "Free Sample." But in the main his customers were cheap, single-handed tailors in a small way of business, some of them foreign, and many of Jewish persuasion. Mr. Morris Shapiro, entrusted with the honour of making my suit, and who came into the warehouse towards the end of the afternoon, was unquestionably in this category. A frail, cadaverous, ill-looking little man, pale faced, with enormous dark shadowy eyes and a plastered streak of black hair across his yellowish skull, his manner towards Leo, expressed in fluttering gestures, was painfully ingratiating.

Nevertheless he seemed to betray some misgivings when he was confronted by the chosen material. He looked at it, fingered it, looked at me, then at Leo.

"The young gentleman likes it?"

Too shy to speak, I permitted Leo to incline his head without a rebuttal.

"Not a trifle flash?"

"No."

Mr. Shapiro hesitated, then picking a single strand from the web of the material, he struck a match on the box he took from his pocket, lit the strand and brought the charred end to his nose. He then looked up at Leo again.

"Short on wool," he said.

"Perhaps," Leo said, turning away with extreme coldness. "But it will wear."

"And make up lovely," Mr. Shapiro agreed hastily. "It will hang a treat."

When he had measured me, he bundled up the material and tucked it under his arm. Then, as he hurried off, he took a cautious side glance, cupped his head and literally hissed in my ear:

"He's been trying for years to get rid of it."

Although Leo could not possibly have heard, I sensed that for some reason unknown to me the incident had upset him. He paced up and down, glancing at me from time to time, as though about to refer to it. But, in the end, he did not. When I asked if I should light the gas, as it was getting dark, he shook his head. Inspecting his watch, thus again signalizing his immediate departure, he came forward and put his hand on my shoulder.

"You're my nephew, boy, you know I mean to do the right thing by you. You've done well for your first day and we'll see how you get on. But always remember that money is hard to come by here." He gave me an approving pat. "Now I have to go out to see a man. It's time to close up."

He locked the door with the key from his bunch and went quickly down the stairs while I went slowly up to Mrs. Tobin. It had been for me a strange, unprecedented day and my head was spinning from it.

23

DURING THE weeks that followed it became evident that my uncle meant to keep me fully occupied, and as we were frequently together in these endeavors I had ample opportunity to observe this truly extraordinary man.

In the morning, on his instructions, I wrote most, though not all, of his letters. There was of course no typewriter in the office, recording machines were not at all to Leo's taste. Moreover, despite the diversities of Uncle's business, his correspondence was relatively modest, since the major portion of his affairs was conducted by word of mouth. Nor when he wrote did he trouble the penny post. I was sent to deliver his missives. When not engaged on such forenoon errands I remained on duty in the showroom draped in the inchtape and with a pencil behind my ear. I was now allowed to sell to the odd customer who came in at that hour, provided ready money was produced on the spot. But the expeditions which I took in Leo's company were the most revealing of all.

Why did he take me? While using me to his best advantage I believe that a residual spark of conscience, faint survival of his early upbringing or perhaps a reluctant sense of obligation to my mother, induced him to try to give me some grounding in a commercial career or the "art" of business as he practiced it. Thus, while so far he had excluded me from the rent collecting, managed by Annie and himself, he permitted me to accompany him to all the auctions he attended, and to the bonded warehouse at the docks.

At the right price Leo would buy anything, not bankrupt or salvaged stock of cloth alone, but any article whatsoever on which, immediately or in due course, he knew instinctively that he could make a profit. Standing beside him in the crowded, raucous auction marts that opened off Argyle Street I would gaze in wonder at his pale impassive face as with an almost imperceptible blink of his eyelids he increased by sixpence his bid for some incongruous object which if portable I must carry back to join the jumble in the storage rooms upstairs. These rooms, on both sides of the upper corridor, were so choked to the ceilings it was difficult to open a door without being crowned by an outrush of piled-up furniture.

The auctions eventually proved wearisome to me, but I was never bored by our visits to what Leo referred to simply as "the excise." To enter our door in this building, which was officially sealed, two keys were necessary, one from Uncle's bunch, the other kept by the revenue officer. The array of barrels revealed in the dim light of the frosted windows confounded me at first, not only from the number and size of these deep-bellied receptacles, but because I had naturally expected Uncle's whisky to be stored in bottles — a view which he soon dispelled by explaining that the spirit would never mature unless contained in sherry, or seasoned casks.

Here, then, was Leo's main business, his capital, his source of future profits. He bought whisky, bought at the right time, stored it free of excise duty, and as it ripened watched its value steadily increase. He was not only a shrewd buyer but a thoroughly expert blender. How often I watched, fascinated, as he took half Highland and Lowland malts, a "taste" of Islay, and mixed these with a patent still whisky the name of which he refused to divulge. Then, taking a measured sip, he would sample the blend by rolling it round his mouth and tongue, gargling almost in his throat, and finally, with a nod of approval and a hoarse expectoration, blow the whole swill out. As Annie had told me, he never let a drop down his gullet.

Even in those early days, Leo undoubtedly possessed unique and amazing foresight. He anticipated the danger of currency depreciation and placed his trust in property and whisky. Yet, as I became aware of his present and potential wealth, I couldn't help asking myself what on earth he got out of it. His life was a model of the dullest, most stringent and most utterly miserable austerity. Then it dawned on me that for Leo the supreme enjoyment, the pinnacle of inner delight, lay in the secret knowledge of his own worth, *under this pretence of penury*. I have said that he never smiled. Yet sometimes when in conversation during some business deal he would emit a typical phrase, such as "I'm a poor man" or "I couldn't afford it" or "you could buy and sell me," I would observe a twitch, that faint transient convulsion of the lips, as though with immense difficulty he was suppressing delicious gusts of internal laughter. Strangely, although I saw or surmised all this, and despite the exactions and deceptions he imposed upon me, I could not dislike him. Instead, as I gazed at his pale, peaked face, I felt an unaccountable rush of sympathy, and was disposed to pity him. This precisely was the emotion he sought to inspire, the triumph of all his guile, for it established and confirmed the character he had created and within which the real Leo Carroll lived.

While life with Leo was not too onerous, my main problem centred on food. Uncle himself, apart from the patent pabula towards which his faddism directed him, seemed to exist almost without sustenance. He took his breakfast alone very early before I was up, his lunch was enwrapped in equal mystery and when he came in late at night he would go to the stove and, still wearing his bowler hat and with a look of abstraction, stand silently concocting himself one or other of his messes: Gluten Groats, Arrowroot, or Sandfood Rusks and stirabout.

Certainly, he kept us on preposterously short commons, and as I was growing rapidly, I almost constantly felt hungry. I should have fared badly but for Mrs. Tobin who had an undetermined arrangement for board wages with Leo which, while lapsing periodically through Uncle's protests that he was short of ready cash, was eventually forthcoming when she threatened to give notice. This pittance enabled her to supplement the bare necessities of our diet by what she called "her extras," all of which she shared unhesitatingly with me. Indeed more often than not when it came to a matter of division it was I who received the larger portion.

Nor was it solely through my stomach that my first impressions of Annie were reversed. When my new suit arrived, its atrocious pattern threatened to condemn me to endless misery and shame. But one Saturday night, after a week of anguish during which I felt myself the object of every laugh and stare in the city of Winton, Mrs. Tobin removed the offensive garments, dyed them a dark inconspicuous brown, dried and pressed them, and by Monday morning presented me with an outfit that was at least respectable.

Annie was without exception the most obliging, cheerful person I had ever known, seldom put out, a fount of amiability, always ready to laugh off her troubles and mine. To her most things, even my uncle's incomparable stinginess, seemed good for a laugh, and although she would explain this to me with the most devastating clichés, such as "life's a queer business, dear, we've got to face it with a smile" or "laugh and the world laughs with you, weep and you weep alone," these were merely the expressions of an untaught mind. Nothing could detract from a nature that exuded generosity, honourable decency, and in which there was not a single streak of malice. When she told fortunes — she greatly liked to "read the tea cups" — she always predicted favourable happenings, never ill tidings. In all our association I did not once hear her make a mean or uncharitable remark. Even Leo, who surely merited her worst reproaches, she dismissed with a commiserating laugh. "You can't help but be sorry for the poor man. Faith, he's harder on himself than he is on us."

She was a widow with four surviving children, all sons. Three were in the British Army — she never said "the army," invariably prefacing the qualification as though her boys were in the service of a foreign power — two in India, one in Singapore, and the fourth had emigrated, but without success, to Canada. Although she seldom heard from them and then only briefly, she would sometimes speak of them to me, recalling some incident of the past with a reminiscent smile. On the mantelpiece of the kitchen, beside the glass bowl in which she affectionately maintained a rather senile goldfish, was an old postcard with a moonlit view of the Taj Mahal on which was written: "Dear Mother, I hope this finds you well as it leaves me. Your loving son, Daniel." When it would catch her eye she would smile at me and begin: "Danny was always a good boy though a trifle wild at times. I'll never forget the day he fell off the pier at Dunoon . . ."

But mainly, during our long evening conversations, she had most to say about her husband. She called him "Da." I must confess that I had slight interest in these family reminiscences, but as I had become extremely fond of Mrs. Tobin I made myself listen with every appearance of sympathetic interest. Usually they went like this:

"Da was a good man, dear. Intelligent too. But he never had

a trade. He'd get a job for a couple of weeks then be knocked
off. He was too much of a gentleman, in his own way, for
the labouring. He bought a horse and lorry, but the horse fell
down on us. Yes, dear, it died on him. Still if he'd got paid for
what he did, we'd of been well away. But making money
wasn't in him. It wasn't his line. Oh, he was popular. When he
died the whole street turned out. A lovely funeral."

Annie herself was deservedly popular among the group of
Irish expatriates in the district who congregated, usually on
Tuesday nights, at a public house kept by one of their number and named, with nationalistic spirit, "The Shamrock." Not
infrequently these were festive occasions for me. When Annie
had a few extra coins in her purse or when she had backed a
winner, since she was not above having threepence or even as
much as a shilling on a horse, she would put on a man's cloth
cap which she secured carefully with long hatpins and take
me first to Bonelli's fish and chip shop for a fried fish supper,
then, although I was still under the legal age, smuggle me in
with her to the snug of "The Shamrock." Her entry was invariably greeted with shouts of welcome and when she had
ordered a Guinness for herself — she never drank more than
one — and a ginger ale for me, there would be cries of "Give
us a song, Annie." After an exchange of chaff and without the
least self-consciousness she would oblige with "The Minstrel
Boy" or "Tara's Halls," followed, as an encore, by a great
favourite which I think was called "The Wearing o' the
Green."

> *Oh, Paddy dear and did you hear*
> *The news that's goin' round,*
> *The shamrock is forbid by law*
> *To grow on Irish ground.*

Then a chorus, in which with tremendous feeling, everyone joined:

> *The dear little shamrock,*
> *The sweet little shamrock,*
> *The dear little, swe-eet little, shamrock of Ireland.*

Despite these pleasures, or perhaps because of them, I could not blind myself to the fact that circumstances had reduced me to a submerged level of existence. For all practical purposes I now lived and worked in the slums of Winton. The change was alarming, the locality deadly. Back to back tenements surrounded us, interspersed with narrow streets and mean alleys in which one saw exhibited every sign and symptom of poverty and misery — the shawled women, idle men, and worst of all, the ragged, rickety, deformed children. Perpetually noisy, dirty and choked with traffic, Argyle Street seemed to me a running sore. Saturday night on its crowded, flaring pavements was saturnalia: drunks rolling around, lying in the gutter, or being frog-marched to the police station, sailors on leave from the docks looking for trouble, factions of the rival football "brake" clubs fighting it out with fists and knives after the match, while with a clash of cymbals, a thump of the drum and a blare of brass that heightened the pandemonium, the Salvation Army paraded up and down, pausing from time to time to sing a hymn, preach the terrors of damnation, and pass the tambourine.

In all my daily contacts, human and inhuman, there was nothing to improve or stimulate my mind. When, driven by the afternoon vacuum in my stomach, I slunk into Bonelli's for a penny plate of chips only to be met by a rush of broken English from the back shop: "Chipapotata no ready. Green pea ready. You wanna green pea?" I felt bitterly that my star had waned since those days of happiness and promise when Miss Greville, discoursing on the *Orchis maculata* in an ambience of Eton, paused to address me across the impeccable table: "Another cutlet, Carroll?"

I knew now that my mother couldn't have had the faintest precognition of what lay in store for me. Those earnest conversations with Leo, while she anxiously studied his sad, pale, plausible face, must have induced in her an entirely false impression of the prospects he could offer me. Yet I could not bring myself to write and reveal the truth. This would alter nothing of my situation, and from her frequent letters, Mother had trouble enough fulfilling her teaching obligations at the school in time to take the train journey to Cardiff to attend her all-important night classes, which, she had confided to me, were proving harder than she had foreseen, with many technicalities she found difficult to understand.

Nevertheless, as I felt myself slipping into a kind of bog, stifled by the prevailing smoke and grime, I tried to brace myself by striving again for that elusive Greek ideal which I had pursued in the past, a physical adequacy which was so far not reflected in my attenuated form. The solitary bath in Leo's establishment served at present as a repository for an accumulation of useless household rubbish, old door handles, bent nails, broken picture frames, bashed cardboard boxes and the like, which Uncle had not allowed to be thrown out; but aided by Annie I cleared away this debris. Although the enamel was chipped and rusted the antique tub held water, and thereafter, every morning when I got up, I did fifteen minutes of body building exercises, then took a cold dip. In the evenings, which had begun to lengthen, I returned with joy to my old love. It cost only a halfpenny fare to take the yellow tram from Argyle Street to Kelvingrove Park on the western outskirts of the city, but as I often lacked that coin I did not

mind walking all the way along Sandimount Street and Western
Road, since I was wearing my old gym shoes which made me
feel light and full of springiness. At the Park, which extended
in a series of tree-lined avenues and curving drives beneath the
University, I would pause to gather myself, then begin to
run, through the gathering twilight, on the circuit I had
mapped out for myself. Except for an odd couple spooning on
a bench, few people were about at this time. The sense of
freedom and inexplicable delight which I experienced in this
swift transit through the cool air, still luminous with the fading sunset, afforded me an escape from all my woes which, as
though blown away by the wind of my speed, fluttered and
fell behind me.

After I had spent myself I would sit and rest looking up at
the University, the old noble building outlined dark and towering against the western sky. The chances that I should ever
study there were now depressingly remote, yet when my
breath came back, impelled by an ineradicable longing, I
climbed the hill and wandered round the precincts. Passing
through the deserted cloisters I read the names above the lec-
ture rooms, drawn always to the Department of Biology where,
lingering outside the locked door, I sniffed the aromatic odours
of carbofuschin and Canada balsam. Then indeed, turning
away to return to the city, I felt that I had fallen on evil days
and that my life had sunk to a dull and profitless routine.

24

ONE AFTERNOON as I walked up Union Street rather slowly, returning from yet another of Leo's commissions, a young man, bareheaded, and of extreme elegance, came out of the Criterion Hotel accompanied by a stylish but rather over-dressed woman somewhat older than himself. I knew him instantly and, as his eye met mine in mutual recognition I instinctively called out "Terence."

He did not appear to hear me. Avoiding my glance, continuing to address his companion in the liveliest manner, he passed me as though I did not exist while, cut and humiliated, I stood staring like a fool. A few paces up the street, opposite the entrance to the hotel grill, an open red Argyle car upholstered in padded red leather was waiting with a chauffeur in attendance. Towards this rich vehicle Terence escorted his lady friend, saw her seated with every sign of solicitude, then after a vivacious and tender farewell, watched her driven off.

As he turned I stirred myself and began to move hurriedly away, confronted suddenly by the recollection of that moment eight years ago when in Terry's company I had repudiated Maggie. Now she was avenged. At that moment, however, a piercing whistle, such as might be used to summon a cabby, made me spin round. Terence was coming towards me in leisurely fashion, handsomer, more charming than ever, not a hair out of place and immaculately got up in striped trousers and a dark jacket, a regular fashion plate. As he looked me up and down I quivered slightly. In the face of such sartorial, mannered perfection it was impossible not to blush for my own inadequacy.

"Well, well, well. What a long drink of water you've turned into," Terence said slowly. "What are you doing up here, man?"

The total absence of communication that now existed between my mother and Lochbridge had left him in ignorance of our present situation. When I explained he emitted another whistle, but in a low and meditative key.

"So you're working for that skinflint. I never pass him in the street but I want to spit in his eye. Why didn't you come to me, man? I always liked your mother. A nice little woman. I'd have straightened you both out in no time. No time at all."

"Why . . . what are you in, Terry?"

"The hotel business. Learning it on the inside. I'm the receptionist here at the Cri."

Deeply impressed, I looked from Terence to the pillared marble portico and through the wide glassed doors to the vista of rich carpeting and gilt chairs in the foyer beyond. The Criterion was a new hotel with a sophisticated Continental atmosphere, not large but exclusive. In Winton it touched the heights of fashionable opulence.

"I suppose Leo feeds you well," Terence said suddenly, examining me sideways with a satiric eye. "Or could you do with a bit of a snack?" Before I could answer he went on. "Well, then, you nip round to the back of the building and I'll let you in at the other entrance."

The service entrance was easily found and Terence, already at the door, admitted me to a long passage which led into the hotel kitchen, an enormous lofty chamber, dazzling the eye with its display of shining metal and gleaming white tiles. A young man in a white apron and puffed cap was reading a newspaper.

"Tony," Terence said, "I've just discovered a long lost starving relative. Can you knock up something for him?"

Tony lowered his newspaper. He did not look particularly pleased.

"Three o'clock in the afternoon. And me the only one on duty."

"That's why we're here."

When Terence smiled no one could withstand him for long. Tony put down his paper and got up.

"What does he want?"

"Something with beef in it. And plenty."

It was a relief to find the staff dining room, into which Terence now led me, completely empty. Here, after a surprisingly short interval, Tony brought me a large helping of what looked like stew.

"That suit you?"

"Oh yes, thank you."

As I began to eat Terence took a chair opposite me and lit a cigarette.

"Heavens, kid," he said, after a few minutes, "you've got a swallow. You must be famished."

"Not really, Terry. It's just that this is the most delicious meat I've ever tasted."

"It ought to be. It's Boeuf à la Bordelaise. As a matter of fact, my friend, Miss Josey Gilhooley, had some for her lunch today in the grill."

When he said this in so conscious a manner I felt some response was expected of me. I could not well say that she was pretty, since even in my brief glimpse of her I had been struck by the prominence of her nose. So I said:

"She's very smart, Terry."

He nodded complacently, with a gratified proprietary air.

"Was that her car?"

"Her old man's. Gilhooley the builder. They're rolling. For your own information, kid, and strictly on the q.t., Josey and I are as good as engaged. At least, it's not official yet but she's practically my fiancée."

"I always thought you liked Polly Grant," I said, unthinkingly.

The nearest possible approach to a flush passed over Terence's face, confirming those early rumours of his frequent visits to Ardencaple.

"That was just a flash in the pan. This is the real thing." He added after a pause: "Don't you ever go out with the girls yourself?"

The idea was so preposterous I merely shook my head.

"What!" exclaimed Terence, "you haven't got a girl yet?"

I felt myself redden. I had no wish to enlighten Terence on my longings in that direction defeated by an abysmal shyness — a state of inner conflict only maintained in balance by the discipline I inflicted on myself.

"I'm not interested in girls," I lied, bravely.

"Then what in God's name do you do with yourself?"

"I'm kept busy all day," I said, defensively. "And at nights I go out to the Park and run."

"You do?" For the first time Terence seemed interested. "I remember you were pretty fair." He seemed to make a joke of this, then considered me thoughtfully. "Have you done any serious running — at sports and such like?"

"Oh, yes, I went out often with the Ardencaple Harriers,

and won the under fourteen steeplechase two years in succession."

"You did." He regarded me even more thoughtfully. "One of these nights I might come out and clock you. I still keep up with the track, although I've too much on my mind to go in for it myself."

"I remember you telling us how you won the hundred yards at Rockcliff."

He looked pleased.

"Sure. I left them like they were standing still. I was the champion there, man, or near enough to it. A pity you never managed to get to Rockcliff."

I acquiesced sadly, adding under my breath: "I'd still give anything to go."

"Well, who knows?" he said encouragingly. "It's not too late. There's ways and means. As I mentioned before, I have connections. Gilhooley is a big man. A strong Catholic too and Irish as you make them. Don't give up too easy. Why, speaking off hand, it just occurs to me that the Bursar there now, a fellow called Phelan . . . or is it Feeney, was a pal of mine. He took the collar. I might write to him, he'd do anything for me. Or even the Principal, they remember me there, I can tell you."

Terence's expansive attitude quite lifted me up. My eyes glowed as I murmured my gratitude.

"Say nothing of it." He pushed back his chair and got to his feet. "I must get back to the reception now. We've some important guests coming in this afternoon. But keep in touch with me. I want to time you on the mile. If it works out it might do you some good. Don't forget now."

"I won't, Terry. I'll come to the service door."

"That'll be easier for you," he approved. "By the way, did you know that Nora was in town?"

"No, Terry."

"Well, she is, and doing famously for herself."

"In what way?"

"She's junior assistant to Miss Donohue, the buyer in Earle's. The Donohues are good friends of ours, old Donohue and my old man were pretty close at one time, so it was all fixed up nicely for Nora to train under her. You know what a buyer is, don't you?"

I did, more or less. And as Earle's was the leading establishment in Winton for women's fashions I knew also that Miss Donohue's position must be a good one.

"Nora's always asking about you," Terence went on. "Why don't you look her up. She lives with Miss D. I'll give you the address. It's in Park Crescent."

He took a gold-cased pencil from his waistcoat pocket and wrote it down.

I could not thank him enough. Indeed, when he had shown me out by the back door, I went on my way rejoicing in the fortunate chance that had reintroduced me to my own people. I had been so long without proper human companionship that the prospect of friendship with Terence and Nora excited me. And more: the subject of Rockcliff had been raised. What might Terry, or Terry's friends, do for me? The name Gilhooley, linked to that splendid car, to say nothing of the dashing daughter to whom Terence was affianced and soon would probably marry, suggested possibilities which, while as yet undetermined, seemed almost unlimited.

25

FOR SEVERAL days I waited hopefully in the expectation that
Nora would get in touch with me. I was reluctant to take
the initiative and Terence must surely have spoken to her
of our meeting. But as no word came from her, on the following Saturday when I was free I wandered in a desultory fashion
towards Park Crescent. The afternoon, I remember clearly,
was mild, still, and sunny, full of a delicious promise of spring.

Park Crescent was situated in a favoured residential district on the west side of the city. It stood high, a quarter circle
of tall Georgian houses, now converted to flats, overlooking
Kelvingrove Park. Already discouraged by the superior atmosphere of this locality, which contrasted markedly with the
crudities of Argyle Street and Templar's Hall, I barely paused
outside No. 9 and did not arrest my self-conscious transit until
I was fifty yards further down the Crescent. Here, with the air
of a disinterested observer, I leaned over the railings and sur-
veyed the Park beneath me. Should I, or should I not advance
boldly and ring the bell? The spears were breaking on the
chestnut trees, yellow forsythia was already in bloom, perambulators were circling on the broad path where I took my
evening run. Nora could not possibly wish to see me. Yet I
had liked her when we last met and now I wanted her as a
friend. Half turning, I perceived that the street maintained a

total emptiness. At least I should be unobserved if I were rejected and thrown out. Bracing myself, I turned back, mounted the portico steps of No. 9 and went into the long entrance hall. From a variety of doors, peering in the semi-darkness, I selected one on which was tacked a visiting card with the name: Miss Fidelma Donohue. I straightened my tie and, reminding myself that I was fairly presentable in my soberly dyed brown suit, pressed the bell.

The door was smartly opened by a short, tight, bustling little woman dressed for the street in a stylish hat and coat who, in a well-corseted attitude, her head thrown back, appraised me with a hard, bright, competent eye and inquired:

"Well, young man?"

"Is Miss Nora Carroll in?" I murmured. "I'm her cousin, Laurence Carroll."

She relaxed immediately, her expression altered, she smiled a welcome. At ease, she had a full, rather humourous mouth, richly embellished with a gleaming double set of false teeth.

"Come in. Why haven't we seen you before? And why didn't you give us word you were coming?"

As I entered she put a hand on my shoulder and continued to look me up and down.

"Yes, you're a regular Carroll. I knew your father well, poor lad. So now you're making your fortune with your Uncle Leo." Without giving me time to deny this suggestion she went on, impelling me towards a half open door. "Nora's in there. Hurry in now and get acquainted, for as bad luck would have it, we've both got to go out. But don't forget to come again."

I saw that, like a fool, I had come at the wrong time and was prepared to apologize and retire. But, under her propulsion, I entered the room she indicated, a small feminine bedroom, done up with flowered chintz curtains and chair covers of the same material.

My cousin was seated before the looking glass of her dressing table. She turned, and we gazed at each other. Although I knew she must be my cousin I scarcely recognized in this alarmingly attractive girl the skinny child who had butted me at my father's funeral. For there was no doubt about it — Nora was a beauty. Not only so, but untouchably smart, wearing an embroidered silk blouse, dark green pleated skirt, and a necklace of speckled green beads, exactly the kind of girl for whom, with a lowered glance, I hurriedly stepped off pavements, lest my contaminating presence should offend her. Yet she was smiling to me, and her dark eyes, with their thick fringe of long curling lashes that seemed darker against her fresh delicate complexion, sparked with pleasure and mischief.

"Oh, Laurence, what a fine tall boy you've grown into! But oh, dear, I can't help thinking how I treated you in the hen house. Do you remember the egg?"

"Of course, Nora."

"Anyhow, it's done wonders for your hair. You've lots of it, and such a nice chestnut shade. But oh, dear, I did bang you against that wall."

She came forward, put her arms round me and gave me a full long kiss.

"There!" she said. "That makes up for it. After all, aren't we cousins?"

At that soft warm pressure I felt a kind of shock as though something within me had given way.

"Oh, Nora," I said faintly, "it's a treat to see you again. I've wanted to."

"Then why didn't you before now, you silly fellow? No,

no, it's really my fault. We're an awful family, the way we don't keep up with one another. Of course Simon's in Spain, and Leo is impossible, but we shouldn't have lost touch with you. We'll have to make up for it now. Stuck all those months with Leo can't have been any fun."

"No, not much, Nora. But then I'm not much of a one for fun."

"We'll have to go into that. And into all that's been happening to you." She had taken up her hat from the dressing table. It was a little chip straw with a single rose on the brim. "But not now, dear Laurence. It's a great shame, but Miss Donohue and I have an engagement that just can't be put off."

"I'll clear out at once," I said hurriedly.

"Oh, dear, aren't we touchy!" She finished putting on the hat at the mirror and swung round. "Now tell me, is that becoming? Be careful, it's a model borrowed from the show room." She burst out laughing. "Oh, Laurie, you are a funny chap, but if I'm any judge, a nice one. Now listen, we're all going, Miss D., Terence and I, and some others, to the second house of the Alhambra on Saturday night, and you're coming with us unless," she looked at me mockingly, "it will make you even more miserable!"

"Oh, no, it won't, Nora."

"Then meet us at the stalls entrance at nine o'clock. We'll have the tickets."

I left the house walking on air in a trance of happiness which, as I turned instinctively into the Park, was succeeded by a surge of restless exaltation. How kindly Nora had received me, how naturally and affectionately I had been accepted, invited to another meeting, made to feel that I was wanted. No one had ever kissed me like that . . . never, never in my life. The soft warmth of those lips pulsed and persisted in my guileless blood, and in a slow, delicious expansion I felt my heart go out towards my cousin. Sudden recollection of my absurd fancy for Ada, with whom I had not even been privileged to exchange a word, made me blush. That had been mere childish play. This was the real thing. I was grown up now. I understood life. And as I hacked along at a pace that made me sweat, I began to picture a future in which Nora and I would constantly be together. I no longer felt alone and Winton had ceased to be a wilderness.

Suddenly, as I came along the river walk, sharply intruding upon this blissful reverie, a static object, peculiar yet strangely evocative, caught my downward abstracted eye. Surely, in the remote past, I had been familiar with that short ebon stump, terminating in the angle iron that affixed it to the thick-soled surgical boot. I stopped instinctively and raised my head. Seated alone, on the park bench, a little shrunken man in a black bobtail suit, celluloid dickey and string black tie was regarding me with a benevolent half smile.

"Laurence Carroll," he said.

That he should recognize me, in my present state and after an interval of seven years, struck me with such force I dropped out of my dream and responded involuntarily:

"Pin Rankin!" And then, hurriedly apologizing: "Oh, I'm sorry, sir. I was so surprised you knew me it just slipped out."

"I'd have known you anywhere, Laurence," he said amiably, making a sign that I should sit beside him. "As a matter of fact, despite your elongation, you haven't really changed one iota."

Dubious as to whether this was complimentary or disparaging, I accepted his invitation and sat down. He continued to inspect me.

"Were you walking for pleasure or for profit?"

I had a wild and frantic desire to reveal myself, to tell him about Nora and of the splendour that had gloriously changed my life. Fortunately I was now sufficiently sane to restrain the impulse.

"Actually for neither reason, sir. I was on my way back to Argyle Street."

"Why Argyle Street, of all places?"

"That's where I work."

"Work? In what capacity?"

"Well, sir, I'm a sort of apprentice in a wholesale warehouse."

"You mean that you have left school?" When I nodded he looked at me quizzically and murmured: "Then we are in the same boat."

"Have you retired, sir?" I asked tactfully.

"In a manner of speaking," he said. "I have, in fact, been pensioned off. But I am still active, thank God, in a personal and particularly interesting way. I am compiling the Annals of Ardencaple parish, Laurence. I have access to all the records in the University Library, and as I now occupy a quiet, decent room in Hillside Street quite near, I have every facility for what one might well term a labour of love."

He was still the same mild, prosy little man, characteristically making the best of his present situation, which did not strike me as particularly entrancing, and with my mind too overcharged to allow me to appreciate our meeting properly, I had begun to seek some means of escape when he said:

"Now tell me about yourself."

With some reluctance I set off on a bare outline of the events since my father's death, of which he had heard. But he would not permit this brevity and kept drawing me out, pressing for more information, interspersing my answers with barely suppressed exclamations of interest and regret, until he had squeezed me dry of my entire history.

When I had done, having eventually warmed to my subject, I looked for some expression of sympathy by way of reward. Instead, with his head cocked at a sharp angle, he began to tug at his little pointed grey beard. Finally, in an absent manner, he said:

"And your poor mother was such a douce, happy little body." Then, before I could recover from the shock of this remark which, from Pin, seemed almost indecent, he glanced at me then away again in a manner which made me feel he was bringing himself to say something unpleasant. "I'm bitterly disappointed in you, Laurence. I thought you were a bright boy. I never imagined I'd find you clerking in a warehouse."

"But how could I help myself?" I protested.

"In a dozen different ways. Most of all by showing some gumption. You want to go up there, don't you?" He cocked the little beard upwards, not of course suggesting that heaven was my destination, but in the more immediate direction of the University which, from our position by the river, towered on the hill above us.

"I've wanted to go in for science, or even medicine, for long enough," I answered shortly. "I've wanted a lot of things I never got."

"Then why don't you try a little harder? There are scores of University bursaries, especially in classics, open to clever boys. You are clever, aren't you?"

"I don't know. I hope I am."

"Then let's see, right away, how we stand." He spoke with enthusiasm and, while I gazed wonderingly, fumbled in the inside pocket of his braided jacket and produced a thin, black, worn morocco booklet, rather like my prayer book.

"This is my New Testament, Laurence," he said briskly. "Just open it at random and construe."

I opened at random then, after a blank pause, attempted a feeble joke.

"This is Greek to me, sir. I don't know a word of it."

"What, no Greek? Oh, dear, that's a blow!" He paused, frowning at me. "Then how are you in Latin?"

"I've gone through 'Selections from Ovid,' and all of a book called *Pro Patria*, and, well, I sort of started a bit of Virgil."

"Started a bit of Virgil," he repeated, making a clicking noise with his dentures which appeared to express the ultimate in dissatisfaction.

Again there was a silence. Then he said:

"Define the fifth proposition of the third book of Euclid."

Hot with embarrassment, I faltered: "Afraid I haven't been taken beyond the second book."

Even then he did not give up. There, on that park bench, while the perambulators rolled past and a park attendant watched suspiciously as though we were conspiring to pillage his flower beds, Pin put me through a comprehensive examination and when it was over he gave out a kind of hollow groan.

"Who has been teaching you? Or ruining you?" He tugged at the straggle of beard as though trying to uproot it. "You are utterly and completely uneducated."

"No, I'm not," I said angrily. "I know lots of things about botany and zoology, perhaps more than you do, sir. I'll bet you can't tell the difference between the four different species of Erica, or how the chromosomes fission in an amoeba's nucleus."

He considered me with a wan, compassionate smile.

"My poor boy, these are precisely the subjects you would take, and doubtless excel in, *after* your admission to a scientific curriculum. But to gain that admission you require knowledge of a totally different kind, a standard text-book proficiency, which you simply have not got."

There was nothing I could say to this. Suddenly I looked up.

"Couldn't you . . . I mean, as we're both in Winton . . . couldn't you coach me, sir . . . ?"

At once, and with fatal certainty, he shook his head.

"Impossible, Laurence. You're so far behind you need at least two years hard and constant study. I'll not be here more than six months. On your side and mine it would be hopeless."

A long dull unhappy silence followed this extinction of my one sustaining hope, always at the back of my mind, that I would somehow break through my difficulties to a brilliant, scintillating career.

"It's a great pity, Laurence. You were such a promising pupil. Don't you remember those little sagas you produced for me when I set the weekend essays? They were uncommonly good. You had such an unaccountable sense of words. I used to read them to the class." He paused suddenly, reflectively, looking at me in a manner which struck me as odd. He murmured a word, to himself, which came to me indistinctly. It sounded like Elison. Was it a final benediction? Then, rather undecidedly, he said: "I suppose there's no harm in our keeping in touch. Have you a pencil? Take down my address. Two-twelve Hillside Street. You might come and see me one evening next week. And now I mustn't keep you. I'll walk down with you to the tram stop."

I answered sulkily. "I don't take the tram."

"But I have to, Laurence," he said mildly.

We walked together to the Park gates. His progress, conspicuously slow and more ungainly than before, attracted curious and often vulgar stares. On the inclines he was audibly short of breath. In a bad, sullen mood it did not please me to be publicly identified with him, to be an adjunct to this freakish, hobbling progress. He had not helped me in the least, but had merely cast me down. When, at last, he hoisted himself to the step of the tram and called, "Mind now. Come early next week," I barely answered before abruptly turning away.

At least he had not robbed me of all my future. I still had Nora. And as I went on towards Argyle Street I began to think of her again.

26

THE SECOND "house" of the Alhambra opened at nine o'clock, but on Saturday night, as could be expected, I arrived outside the entrance to the stalls well before that hour. I was in fact so early that the outrush of the audience from the first performance almost swept me off my feet. Thereafter, a cold wind blowing fog from the river made standing a chilly business. With an eye on the Central Station clock I paced up and down, warming myself, less with this activity than with the prospect of seeing Nora. But time was going on. Ten, five, three minutes to nine . . . now the curtain must be going up. I began to worry. Had I mistaken the date, or come to the wrong door? Fifteen minutes late, as I was on the point of leaving, they arrived.

The party was larger than I had expected: Terence and Miss Josephine Gilhooley, Nora, Miss Donohue, and a hard-looking young man in an expensive suit who turned out to be Miss Donohue's brother. They were all in a mood of combined and well-established gaiety which induced the belief that they had probably had dinner together. The suspicion that I had been excluded from this prior event was confirmed by the effusiveness with which, by way of compensation, they greeted me.

"I do hope you haven't caught cold, dear," Miss Donohue exclaimed, clutching my arm.

"Just had to step in and see a dog about a man," Terence explained. "Josey, this is Laurence."

"Pleased to meet you, I'm sure. I always say that any friend of my friend's is a friend of mine, only they ought to have told me about you sooner." Miss Gilhooley, who was wearing a rich-looking fur coat and swathes of mauve tulle round her head and neck, joined in the attempt to make amends. She pressed my hand, leaving on my palm an imprint of perfume that persisted throughout the evening, and added: "I hear you're a great runner. You look it too. I always say you can tell by the look."

"We think he might be good," Terence said judiciously. "Martin and I mean to give him a try-out one of these days."

So far Nora had not spoken. Now, though still silent, she smiled to me, a smile of recognition and acknowledgement, with, I thought, a hint of intimacy that more than made up for all my waiting. Better still, as we went into the theatre she said quickly in my ear, explaining everything:

"It was Miss Gilhooley's party, Laurence. So I couldn't very well invite you to the Criterion. But next time you'll be sure to come."

Unfortunately, in the disturbance created as we crushed our way into the centre of the stalls, I lost my place so that Terence, in the lead, sat with Miss Gilhooley, then came Martin with Nora, while I, at the end, was left with Miss Donohue. This arrangement did not at all suit me. In my disappointment, I looked along the row hoping for a commiserating glance from Nora, but with her usual animation she was talking to Donohue. On the stage a juggler was tossing balls in the air.

"The opening turns are never much good, dear," Miss Donohue whispered in my ear. "But just wait till you see Hetty King." She had unwrapped a large box of chocolates and having offered me my choice placed the box conveniently open on her lap. "Help yourself when you feel like it, dear."

These repeated endearments from Miss Donohue, in which I detected a note of compassion, were making me feel like an orphan charity boy at a free treat. A man in a small bowler hat, with a red painted nose, was now singing a song at which everyone seemed to be laughing but me.

"He's a scream, isn't he, dear?" Miss Donohue giggled.

I forced my stiff features into a concurring smile, taking, at the same time, another glance along the row. Miss Gilhooley, lying back almost in hysterics and showing all her gold-filled teeth, was clutching at Terence for support. Then, with an inward sinking, I perceived that Martin was holding Nora's hand. At first sight I had not liked Donohue, who had not spoken to me, merely favoured me with a cold hard look, and that impression was now strongly reinforced. He was too good looking, in a raffish, morose, dangerous way. With his prominent cheek bones and slightly flattened nose he had the appearance of a boxer.

"Look, dear, the Simultaneous Brothers."

Obliged to give some attention to the miming of these integrated twin-like figures, in flannels, striped blazers and straw hats, I nevertheless could not remove my troubled gaze from that other pair. The unnatural position thus maintained, with one eye on the stage and the other along the row, at last attracted the attention of Miss Donohue, who asked in an undertone:

"Have you twisted your neck, dear, you seem to have a crick in it? Or don't tell me you have a squint?"

With an effort I returned my eyes to their normal focus and hastily reassured her that I didn't need glasses.

The fall of the curtain for the interval saved me. Terence and Donohue immediately rose to go out to the bar and, as Miss Gilhooley stretched across the intervening space to talk to Nora, I turned to Miss Donohue with rare determination.

"I haven't had the pleasure of meeting your brother before, Miss Donohue," I remarked, conversationally, with a painful attempt at subtlety. "Does he live in Winton?"

"Well, part of the time, dear. But then he travels round the country a lot."

"On business, Miss Donohue?"

"Naturally, dear. He's a commission agent."

"Do you mean a commercial traveller, Miss Donohue?"

She studied me commiseratingly.

"You are green, aren't you, dear? Still, I like you for it, you're a very sweet boy. No, dear. Martin's a bookmaker. Not making books to read, you understand. Taking bets. A bookie, if you've heard the word. He has a stand at most of the race meetings and is in the way of building up a fine connection. Have a chocolate, dear, one of these, I don't like the caramel centres, they get in my dentures."

"It seemed to me, Miss Donohue, that he and Nora are pretty good friends."

"You might put it rather stronger than that, dear," she said, giving me a queer look. "There's what you might call an understanding there."

"An understanding, Miss Donohue?" I forced the words out from between my teeth.

"They're not exactly engaged, Nora's too young yet, only seventeen you know, and I want to bring her on for a year or so, at Earle's, so she can have her own business when she settles down. But take it from me, dear, already it's a settled case."

That there was no engagement might have afforded me

some solace but, while I did not precisely understand its mean-ing, the word "case" had a fatal sound, made worse by the fact that it was settled. I gazed at Miss Donohue in silent misery as she went on.

"Nora's a lovely girl. A trifle wild maybe, it's the Irish in her, too full of mischief. But a dear girl, I'm very fond of her."

"I'm sure we all are, Miss Donohue," I croaked, in a vain effort to save face.

The rest of the show was dust and ashes in my mouth. Even Hetty King failed to stir me despite Miss Donohue's impressive whisper that her hit number "Oh, You Beautiful Doll" was King Edward's favourite song.

As the final curtain fell and the orchestra bashed off a few bars of "God Save the King," I had a melancholy sensation of relief. In the general scurry Terence and Donohue hurried to the bar for a last quick drink, while the two ladies, with a conscious air, retired to Cloaks. At last I was alone with Nora, waiting in the emptying foyer. She came close to me, so that her eyes looked straight into mine. They were serious, yet her mouth, so mobile, so warm when it had pressed against my cheek, had a humourous twist.

"You haven't enjoyed yourself," she said accusingly, yet with a note of sympathy, as if to indicate that she understood me. Indeed, when defensively I protested that I had, she shook her head. "No. You thought it was pretty crude, and perhaps it was. This isn't at all the kind of thing you like."

I felt, then, in sudden desperation, that I must unburden myself.

"I would have liked it, Nora, if I'd been sitting with you."

"Then why weren't you?" She widened her eyes. Her breath, as she stood close to me, was warm and sweet. "It would have been nice."

"I thought you wanted to sit with Martin."

"Martin!" she exclaimed. "I get enough of him. He's much too pressing. I was wanting you to be beside me."

My heart gave an enormous, joyful bound. Freed of my load of misery, I felt the blood run into my face.

"But, Laurence," she was looking at me provokingly, "Terry says you don't care much about girls."

"I care about you, Nora. If you want to know, I've never cared about anyone the way I do you. I like you very much."

She smiled and I thought she would go on teasing me. But after a moment her expression changed, a soft look came into her blue-black eyes.

"Well, I like you too," she said. "I really mean it. And I want to see a lot of you, show you around a bit, take you out of yourself. It's a hard world, Laurence, and if you'll forgive me, I think you could do with a little more experience of it. You've got to learn to mix with people and to have a bit of fun now and then. Am I offending you by saying all this?"

"No, you're not, Nora."

The others were approaching, and she went on rather quickly.

"Then I tell you what. Next Sunday Mart and Terry are going to be away. So you come up to Park Crescent and we'll do exactly what you want."

"Oh, Nora," I breathed. "How perfectly wonderful. Shall I come in the morning?"

I thought she was going to laugh. Her lips twitched and her eyes, under those curling lashes, screwed up into sparkling black slits.

"Come when you're ready," she said. "But not too early or you'll find me in bed."

I was alive again, quite ready to smile when the others reappeared and pretend gaily that I'd had a wonderful time, to exchange hearty goodbyes and thank Miss Gilhooley when she said she wanted me to come to her next party, all of which was a performance completely foreign to my nature but which I now accomplished because I knew that Nora truly cared for me.

When at last I left them, I walked on air all the way back to Templar's Hall and the clanging of the trams made music in my ears.

27

PART FROM my mother's regular weekly letters, I had nothing to expect from the mail. The postcard which arrived by the morning delivery on the following Wednesday and was handed to me at breakfast by Mrs. Tobin was therefore a surprising event. It came from Pin, and it said briefly:

Why have you not come to see me? I shall expect you Wednesday or Thursday of this week without fail.

Now, I had already given Pin up. His appraisal of my ability, or lack of it, had left a sore spot on my mind, and I had no wish to be catechized and dismissed again. If my prospects were as bad as he made out he could clearly be no possible use to me. I would not go to him. Any action to improve my situation must await the return of my mother.

Nevertheless, as the day wore on, I kept pulling the card out of my pocket and staring at it. After all, it was a rarity. And I began to ask myself if some sense of urgency might not be detected in the message. Then, after all, I did owe an obligation to my old teacher. In the end, with characteristic inconsistency, at seven o'clock that evening I stood knocking at the door of 212 Hillside Street.

It was a boarding house, of a noticeably modest class, a fact which I deduced from the smell of boiled cabbage in the bare little hall and the cracked linoleum on the stairs leading to Pin's lodging, a bed-sitting room on the second floor back. He was there, reading at the window, but obviously expecting me, and he received me without reproach. Over his shoulder I saw immediately that he had provided for me, obviously from his own purse. A bottle of lemonade and a plate of sweet biscuits had been set out on the round table by the window.

"Laurence," he began, when he had seated me. "I had a thought the other day which might or might not be a happy one. Since then I have made it my business to pursue it."

"Yes, sir," I said dutifully.

"First of all, let me offer you some refreshment."

He poured the lemonade and pushed the biscuits hospitably towards me.

"Won't you have some yourself, sir?"

He smiled and shook his head then, after watching me for a few minutes, he said, with a certain impressiveness:

"Laurence, I want to talk to you about the Ellison."

"The Ellison," I repeated blankly.

He nodded, and pressing his finger tips together, so that his hands formed an inverted V, he leaned towards me.

"As you probably know, there are all sorts of foundations, trusts, scholarships and the like endowed to the University. Some of them are unusual, and while perfectly acceptable to the Senate you might even call them peculiar — in as much as they reflect the character of the donor." He paused, holding me so tightly with his eye that I forgot to finish the biscuits. "Now John Ellison was an odd sort of man, Laurence — a Forfar grain miller in a modest way of business, not particularly literate, but a perfervid Scots nationalist with a passion for Scottish history. I'm led to believe that he went every year to

Bannockburn on the anniversary of the battle. At any rate, when he died, at the age of eighty-three, he left all his estate to found a scholarship, thirty pounds a year for five years, open to students bent on entering the University, for the best commemorative essay on a Scottish historical character, the subject to be set unseen by the Professor of Divinity, the essay to be written in the space of two hours in the University Hall on the last day of the first week of August. That's just about three months from now." Again he paused, then said mildly, but with a certain impressiveness: "Laurence, how would you like to spend those three months cramming Scots history, and sit the Ellison at the end of it?"

I gazed at him stupidly. My reaction, beyond the initial surprise, was mainly one of instinctive rejection. The idea was so utterly unexpected, the basis of the scholarship so preposterous, verging even on the absurd, and my competence for the undertaking so manifestly questionable, I shrank away from it, like a rabbit bolting for its hole. I knew that I could not do it, that it was all quite beyond me, and I immediately set about arranging my refusal, logically, and in terms least likely to hurt Pin.

"It's kind of you to bother about me, sir. But when you speak of time you forget I have a job already, that keeps me occupied most of the day."

"I was speaking of your spare time, Laurence. In the evenings and possibly the nights at your disposal you could, with my help, steep yourself in history."

"But where would I get the books?"

"With my present facilities at the University Library I could borrow all the books you need, and more. Rare books, splendid, interesting books." He added pointedly: "And you know how you used to love to read."

That stung me — it was months since I had nourished my

faculties on anything more substantial than Mrs. Tobin's weekly copy of *Tit-bits*.

"In any case," I said, "you have no guarantee that I could do the essay, beyond those early compositions, which were only childish efforts. And you've already informed me that I'm only half educated."

"Nevertheless, you're clever, Laurence," he countered dryly. "Besides, I doubt if literary ability is the main criterion in question. The judges will be looking for national spirit."

"National spirit!" I protested. "I'm half Irish!"

"That gives you the imagination to transpose yourself and become more Scottish than the Scots."

This gentle yet insidious pressure was getting me down.

"No, I really don't feel up to it, sir. I'm too young to go to the University. I'd rather wait till my mother comes back. Her course finishes in September. When she gets her appointment in Winton she means to take rooms, or a small flat. Then I may be able to go to school again."

"You're not too young for the University. You'd be past sixteen if you entered in the autumn. And that's too old to think of school, at least the kind available to you." He went on accusingly: "As for your mother, wouldn't it be a great thing if you were able to tell her that you'd tried the Ellison, perhaps even," he paused, "that you had won it. In that event, what a joy, what a relief for her. You starting at the University with more than enough to keep you there. Thirty pounds a year guaranteed for five solid years. Think of that, Laurence. And don't forget, I'd help you."

Whether deliberately or not, he was pulling out all the sentimental stops, evoking tenderness for my mother and contempt for myself, playing so unfairly on my emotions that an angry flush came into my cheeks and I could find nothing to say.

He glanced away, tugging at his beard, appearing not to notice my humiliation, but not before, in a subdued tone, he sounded the last outrageous, unpardonable chord.

"I suppose you can imagine what it would mean to a useless old man like me if I coached you through to win the Ellison."

Was he play-acting, descending to these base ends to win me over? Pin was a scholar, a classicist, and a man of culture, yet in his veins there flowed a strong infusion of kailyard sentiment. I believe now that he meant and felt every word he said. Then, it was enough for me to know that I was defeated. And he knew it too. Rising spryly, he hopped — being at ease in his slippers and divested of the stump — towards a cupboard in the wall.

"You can't drink that now, it's gone flat. I thought you'd manage another bottle. I have it in the press." He produced fresh lemonade and decanted it into a clean tumbler. "There's more biscuits too if you want them."

I wanted neither biscuits nor lemonade, feeling that, having elevated me to manhood, he was now treating me as a child. But I accepted them to gain time to collect myself, and disposed of them in downcast silence. No one could have been less elated at the prospect of our enterprise than I. He must have sensed this, for he addressed me in a different, authoritative manner.

"Now pay attention. You will come here to this room at seven o'clock three nights a week, when we will spend at least two hours together. I have drawn up a schedule of your reading. Here are your first two books, the first Hume Brown's *General History of Scotland*, the second Duncan's *The Border Wars*." He handed over one of the volumes and turned the pages of the other at random. "You don't realize what a splendid time you are going to have . . . the amazing people you are going to meet. And to think that I had to drag you to it. Take this Earl of Angus for instance, named Archibald Bell-the-Cat, he was a character, I can tell you. Draw your chair nearer and we'll go over him together."

We began to investigate the heroic eccentricities of Angus, head of the Red Douglases, how he hanged the King's musicians and earned the nickname of Bell-the-Cat. In spite of myself, I became interested. Whatever Pin might have been in the pulpit he was always a sympathetic and engaging teacher. I was sorry when at nine o'clock he ended the session.

"That's enough for a start. Now apart from the reading I've set you, I'll expect a short written account, say five hundred words, on what we've just been over. Bring it when you come on Friday."

I stood up, trying to find a proper expression of willingness. How could I have been so obstinate, so timidly averse? But he checked me.

"I know you, Laurence. No raptures, please. Hard work."

With the books under my arm I took my usual sprint through the Park and then, so eager was I to resume my acquaintance with the Border Reivers, I continued my run all the way to Templar's Hall, chosing the back way by the river, speeding along deserted side streets and ill-lit alleys, hearing my footfalls echo behind me between the dark sheds of the docks, until at last I was in my own room, propped up in bed, with the candle lit and the book open on my knees.

28
❧❧❧

SUNDAY, so eagerly anticipated, came at last. Although I was up and about by seven, I went out as usual to the ten o'clock Mass at St. Malachi's with Mrs. Tobin. St. Malachi's was our neighbourhood church, serving the poorest district in the city, and remains associated in my mind with rows of women in shawls and the perpetual sound of coughing. But Mrs. Tobin liked it, she had friends in the congregation, and I always went with her. Actually, on this exceptional morning I had thought of going to the nine o'clock, so that I might arrive at Park Crescent about ten, but reflecting on Nora's hint that I should not come *too* early, I decided that I ought to get there around eleven o'clock. Although this, perhaps, on second thought, seemed rather late.

The University clock was, in fact, booming out eleven strokes as I pressed the bell of No. 9, spruced up in the best I had, and nervous of course, but alive with anticipation. My dedication to the Ellison was now a settled thing, but it was still a long way off, and nothing would have made me miss the chance of a day with my adorable cousin.

Perhaps the bell had not rung. I pressed it again and waited. There was no response. Once more I had my finger on the button when sounds reached me from within, then the door was opened, partially, but enough to reveal Nora in her nightdress and dressing gown. She blinked at me, with a vague expression, only half awake. At last, not particularly pleased, something seemed to strike her.

"It's you, Laurence," she said. "You'd better come in."

Tightening the cord of her gown and scuffing along in her feathery mules, she led me into the kitchen, sat down on the edge of a chair, and with difficulty suppressed a yawn.

"Oh, Nora," I exclaimed grievously, yet fascinated by the picture she made. "I'm afraid I've disturbed you."

She looked at me, meditatively rubbing her shoulder under her nightdress, then suddenly began to laugh.

"Don't worry, man. I was a bit late last night, out with the gang. Seeing Miss Donohue off. She's away to Perth with Terry and Martin. But if you'll put on the kettle and make me a cup of tea, I'll be ready in two shakes of a lamb's tail."

When she had shown me the pantry cupboard and retreated to her bedroom, I decided to make her a proper breakfast. Life with Mother had made me fairly expert at improvising a meal. By the time she came back the tea was infused and I had made a rack of toast and plenty of scrambled eggs.

"Well I never." She viewed my preparations set out on a checquered table cloth. "This is luxury. Beats the Criterion. You'll have to share it with me."

"I've had my breakfast, Nora."

"What did you have?"

"Oh, mostly the usual stirabout. That's a kind of porridge, Nora."

"Then you can stand another. That Leo should be shot. Dead."

She brought out another cup and poured the tea. We started on the toast and scrambled eggs. I had never imagined that breakfast with anyone could be so agreeable. My cousin, now fresh as a daisy, was prettier than ever. Although still barelegged and in mules, she was wearing a soft white blouse and a short tartan skirt that had a lot of yellow in it.

"It's the Kerry tartan," she explained, smoothing it over her knees. "If you're Irish you've got to be proud of it. Now tell me straight, Laurence, what you'd like to do with me today."

It was her colouring, I decided, the dark hair and eyes against the creamy skin, that made her so enchanting. I loved to watch her wide soft mouth sipping the tea, and as she crunched the toast, her small even teeth were as white as my father's had been — the good Carroll teeth.

I took a big breath.

"I'd like best . . . that's to say if you'd like it . . . if we could go somewhere into the country."

"Ah, you're not a city boy."

She glanced out of the window. The sun was shining on the white wall of the courtyard.

"Still, not a bad idea. Winton's ghastly on Sunday. Suppose we take a run down to the houseboat."

"The houseboat?"

She was enjoying my surprise. That, I thought suddenly, was Nora's special charm — her capacity for enjoyment.

"Lots of people have houseboats on Loch Lomond. Martin . . . and Miss Donohue . . ." she added, "have one, not far from Luss. For holidays and so on. It's fun. We'll take the bikes, you can have Miss D.'s, and we'll be there by one o'clock."

This prospect, after months in the purlieus of Argyle Street, was a real excitement. I could hardly wait to be off. I jumped up.

"Let's start soon, Nora. I'll hurry up and wash the dishes and make some sandwiches, if you like."

"No sandwiches, man. They're deadly. And never mind the

dishes. If you want to go now, we'll go, but first let me get my stockings on. Hand me them. Over there."

A pair of lisle stockings had been washed and now hung, dry, two slender filaments, on a rail by the kitchen range. As I brought them to her they were light as gossamer.

Sitting there, she began to draw them on, watching me out of the corner of one eye with sheer mischief and something else, a sort of beguiling inquiry that came from beneath her lashes, meanwhile, as I stared fascinated, affording me fleeting yet generous glimpses of white beneath the Kerry tartan.

"There!" she declared casually, rising and shaking herself down. "Once I get my shoes on we'll be off."

"Thank you, Nora," I stammered. This idiotic remark, which may have sprung from my subconscious as an appreciation of her performance, sounded so pointless that I flushed. To my relief, she did not appear to notice.

The two bicycles were in the basement cellar. We wheeled them out through the yard and set off.

Miss Donohue's machine, an old model with high handlebars and a fixed low gear that had no free wheel, made me work hard. I had to pedal twice as fast as Nora to keep up with her. Going down hill she would dart ahead and turn round to mock me as, perched on the high saddle with my feet on the front fork and the pedals spinning wildly, I rattled behind her. I felt sure Miss D. hadn't used the machine for ages. But the exercise was just what I wanted, the roads had a Sunday freedom from traffic, and the open country, already tender with the green of spring, was a sheer intoxication. The hawthorn was bursting into bloom, I sniffed the sweet perfume as we swept past. In the meadows lambs were bleating after their mothers. Primroses and cowslips were already showing under the hedges. When we came to the Loch, winding

along the lovely curving shore, Nora began to caper on the
bike.

"Look, Laurence, no hands."

Then she started to sing. It was not Hetty King's song but
one rather like it, beginning:

> *You called me baby doll a year ago,*
> *You told me I was very nice to know.*

This violation of the Sunday stillness had an unaccountable
effect on me. I liked it until suddenly it made me remember
that Nora had not been to church that morning and that I was
undoubtedly to blame for this omission. I pedalled up to her
and exclaimed in consternation:

"Nora, you didn't get out to Mass this morning. And the
way I rushed you off, it's all my fault."

She stopped singing.

"Yes, Laurence," she said gravely. "That's a bad sin on your
conscience. I didn't want to bring it up on you, but it's been
worrying me a lot."

"Why didn't you stop me, Nora? I'd have gone out with
you to the Jesuits, on Craig Street. It's my favourite church."

"You didn't give me a chance, man. You had me on the bike
and out of the city before I rightly knew what day it was or
where I was."

"Oh, dear," I mourned. "I'm terribly sorry, Nora."

"Well, don't upset yourself, my lad. Maybe it's not mortal,
and if it is, there's some I've heard of that are a lot worse."

As she spoke she jumped off her bike. We had reached a
quiet cove with a pebbled beach on which a small dinghy lay
moored to a stake by a rusty chain. Some fifty yards off shore
a curious yet inviting white-painted structure with windows
and a door that in miniature exactly fulfilled my conception of

Noah's Ark floated gently at anchor. It was the houseboat.

Nora took a key from her bicycle satchel and unlocked the padlock on the dinghy's chain. We pushed off and, each taking an oar, rowed to the houseboat. Inside, it was exactly like a little house, with a bedroom, a sort of lounge that was the sitting room, and a kitchen fitted with a metal stove. It was also in a state of extreme disorder, the bed unmade, newspapers and dishes cluttering the table, an empty bottle lying on the floor.

"A bit of a mess," Nora said, looking round and wrinkling her nose. "Well, never mind, that's not our problem. What would you say to a bathe?"

"I'd love it," I said, longingly, for I was hot and dusty. "But I've no pants."

"Who's to see you," she answered coolly. "I'll not look and even if I did, aren't I your cousin? Go in off the top deck. But mind you, it'll be cold."

A ladder staircase led to the top deck, which was flat, surrounded by an ornamental balustrade. Woods enclosed the cove on two sides and beyond, the lake shimmered in the sun. In the distance the Ben was bluer than the sky. I threw off my clothes and, still dubious of my total nudity, hurriedly dived in.

The shock of the snow fed water was breathtaking. I came up gasping, but as I struck out my circulation came back to me with an exhilarating rush. I had been swimming for some time when an unexpected splash made me swivel round. My unpredictable cousin had joined me in the lake. Impossible to discern whether or not she had on a bathing suit. Only her head was visible as, with a fast breast stroke, she bore down upon me. But the thought that, like myself, she might be in a state of nature stung me. I took off like a frightened trout, making instinctively for the shore. But she had anticipated this and cut me off. I turned. She followed, a maddeningly persistent mermaid. Only with an effort that left me gasping did I reach the opposite side of the houseboat and haul myself out to safety.

A towel had been placed beside my clothes. I rubbed myself down and got into them like lightning. Five minutes later she appeared, dripping, shaking water from her hair and, to my immense relief, adequately covered.

"Why didn't you stay and let me duck you? Really, Laurie, you're so shy, it's painful. Don't be so serious, man. Let yourself go. You're far too nice to be a stick. Do you know what? I took a wee peep at you in your birthday suit and, to put it mildly and not to swell your head, you've nothing to be ashamed of."

"But, Nora, I only thought . . ."

"You think too much. That's just your trouble. Anyhow, I'm too hungry to argue, we both need something to eat."

"If you've anything to cook . . ." I muttered helpfully. "I could light the stove . . ."

"When you know me better, and I hope you will, you'll discover I hate cooking . . . about as much as I hate sandwiches. In any case, there's nothing to eat on this tub but tins of sardines and mouldy abernethy biscuits."

I started to tell her that these would do, but she had already started to go below, saying:

"I'll be ready in a tick. Then I'll tell you what's on the cards."

She was not long in coming back. Then we got into the dinghy and under her directions I rowed about half a mile up the lake and into another bay where, on the shore road, there was an inn with the sign: *Inchmurren Arms. John Rennie, Proprietor.* We disembarked at a little wooden jetty. Here I hesitated. Truth must be spoken.

"Nora . . . I've no money."

"What!" She affected an exaggerated surprise. "Not even a round O for Paddy Murphy? Then we're stuck."

As I reddened she burst out laughing.

"Don't worry, dear Laurence, this is my treat."

Nora was apparently a fairly regular customer, the pub-keeper knew her at once and shook hands with her.

"Mr. Donohue not with you today, miss?" He then gave me a long stare followed by a dismissive turn of his head, and said: "There's chicken, roast beef or boiled mutton with apple dumpling or curds and cream to follow. You'll have the Snug to yourselves." As a kind of afterthought, he added: "The wife will be sorry to miss you. She's down the village at the daughter's."

The Snug was not a particularly good room, the table covered with oilcloth, and spitoons on the sanded floor. A sad stuffed pike in a glass case swam over the mantelpiece. But the food, when it came, was the best country fare. We had the roast beef, thick slices pink in the middle and charred at the edges, with floury potatoes and greens. With this Nora ordered a glass of beer. I took lemonade. Then the homemade apple dumpling with lashings of thick fresh cream. I had a second helping. Finally, a round of sound yellow Dunlop cheese was put on the table. Sitting back and finishing her beer while she nibbled a sliver of cheese, my cousin viewed my activities on a much larger wedge with a faint smile.

"We'll do this again, won't we, man?"

"Oh, Nora, if only we could . . . This is all . . . so perfect."

"There's just one thing we need to top it off. Remember the sup of port I gave you in the bar when we were both kids? We'll each have another sup now."

She got up and went out of the room to fetch it. After a longish time, she came back with a glass in each hand.

"Rennie tried to keep me talking about horses," she said. "Martin usually gives him a tip."

At the mention of that name the sweetish port tasted slightly bitter. Even so, it was giving me courage.

"Nora . . . Do you come here often with Martin?"

"Well, occasionally. And with Miss D. too."

"I suppose . . ." — I was developing a way of going round this painful subject — "it's only natural that you're fond of Martin."

"Sometimes I like him a lot. Other times I hate him. I'm out with him now."

"I hope you stay out with him."

"Why?"

"Because, if it won't offend you," the port was helping me, "I'm terribly fond of you myself."

"Why should it offend me?"

"Well," I muttered deprecatingly, "I'm not much, you know, Nora."

"For God's sake, man!" She sat up. "When will you stop running yourself down? You don't think enough of yourself. If you want to know, I'm liking being with you in a way I never thought I would. Do you hear me? I'm enjoying this every bit as much as you are. You'll see, I mean it. Let's go back to the boat."

As I got up a delicious euphoria pervaded me, induced by the lunch, the port, and this warm expression of her regard. Decently, under the pretext of discussing horses, Nora had already paid the bill. Outside, as we came through the inn garden, the velvet wallflowers, hot in the sun, distilled their faint delicious fragrance. It was a beautiful still afternoon. We reached the houseboat, tied up the dinghy, and went inside. Nora was looking at me with that faint suggestive smile I had noticed when she drew on her stockings. Yet somehow it had changed. She was no longer mocking me. Instead of mischief in her eyes there was warmth and a strange, sweet, vague allurement. She gave a little laugh.

"After that gorge, I feel like a nap. Don't you? We could stretch out there."

Following her gaze I saw that the bed had been made up. She must have done this when she was changing after the swim.

"But it's such a lovely day, Nora. Wouldn't it be nicer lying on the top deck?"

"I've tried it." She gave me a slight endearing grimace. "It's awfully hard."

"I could take these cushions off the settee."

"Well . . . if you like." She gave in. "But it's not half as cosy as the bed."

I gathered all the cushions and carried them up. They were rather knocked about, exuding feathers, but seemed soft enough when I spread them on the deck and we lay down on them. It was blissfully warm. I shut my eyes. Even through my closed lids the sun made a radiance that matched my state of mind.

"Are you comfortable, Nora?"

"Yes," she said. "I never thought of the cushions. That was clever, Laurie. But where are you?"

She stretched out an arm. Still with blind eyes I found her small warm hand and held it. She began to tickle my palm with the tip of one finger.

"I'm so happy, Nora. Thank you so much for everything. And especially for being with me."

"You're still too far away. Come nearer."

As I turned on my side her arm encircled my neck. I opened my eyes. Her face was ravishingly close to mine. I could see the blue specks in her dark eyes, the mole on the angle of her cheekbone, so exactly placed it became a beauty spot. A tiny bead of perspiration glinted on her upper lip. Her skin, usually creamy pale, had a slight suffused flush. A strange and scented warmth came from her nearness. It made my heart flutter and miss a beat.

"Shall I tell you something, Laurie dear?" Then she spoke slowly, with a pause between each word, as though to bring its meaning home to me. "I like you very, very much."

"And I like you, Nora dear," I breathed. "In fact I absolutely love you with all my heart."

"Then love me, dearest Laurie."

She drew me tightly to her and put her open lips against mine. A great wave of sweetness passed through me. In all my life I could not wish for anything more than this. I felt carried away, out of myself, borne on a stream of the purest most powerful emotion, a feeling so utterly detached from my body that it was like a rapture of the soul.

Alas, poor simpleton, I did not dare presume that my cousin was in pressing need of my assistance. My capacity to cooperate was not in question, heaven knew I had trouble enough steering my way through the devious paths of puberty. But Nora was to me mysterious, exceptional, almost angelic. Not only would I have died rather than offend her, my exalted mood restrained me from the earthy fumblings of an act which then seemed a sordid and indecent business. Was I an utter ass, a prig perhaps, or simply a soft, inexperienced, idealistic youth? Do I merit the contempt of the present generation of knowing adolescents who set out on such excursions with bored assurance and a pocketful of contraceptives? And would I, in fact, have sustained my seraphic attitude to the end? Whether or not, at least I am now spared the obligation of providing my history with that most banal of all performances, the loss of a youthful virginity, for as we lay together, blissfully, breathlessly, in each other's arms, there came a loud arresting shout from the shore.

"Miss Nora, I've brought you some flowers to take home."

"Oh, God," Nora groaned. "It's Mrs. Rennie from the inn, blast her."

"Some for you and some for Miss Donohue," came from the beach again, and turning on my elbow I saw a stout little woman waving masses of daffodils at us.

"I'll go for them," I said.

"No, stay here. Don't move an inch. I'll get rid of her and be back in no time at all."

She got up, though with reluctance, shook back her hair, and a moment later I heard the plash of the dinghy's oars. Presently the sound of amicable greetings, of voices in conversation drifted over the lake. Mrs. Rennie was a talker and less easy to get rid of than Nora had hoped. How wide the sky was, and how drowsy the slow lapping of the lake. I began to feel that I was floating dreamily through the clouds, floating more and more dreamily until, in the end, the long bicycle run, the stupendous lunch, the port, and the hot sun had their way with me. To my everlasting shame, I fell asleep.

When I awoke it was cooler, the sun was beginning to go down and Nora was not beside me. I sprang up to find that she was below, and had actually made tea. She greeted me not, as one might expect, with reproaches or disdain but tenderly, and with a certain new, and to me puzzling, clinical interest. She kissed me cherishingly on the cheek, uttering words of commendation which I thought strange.

"You're a doat of a lad, Laurie. Such a gorgeous day, and not a thing to reproach ourselves with."

"Did you have a sleep too?"

"No, lad. I had another swim to cool off, then I put the kettle on, sat down and had a bit of a think to myself."

"About what, Nora?"

"Ah," she smiled. "I'll tell you some day."

When we had drunk the tea, which I found most refreshing, we locked up the houseboat, rowed ashore and, having padlocked the dinghy, set off unhurriedly on the bikes for home. Nora rode very close to me, often putting a hand on my shoulder so that we could talk. Indeed we talked most of the way to Winton. I told her about the Ellison and she urged me to work hard for it. Other advice she gave me, warning me not to let Terence take advantage of me.

"Terry's a good sort, there's not a bit of harm in him, but he'd wile the bird off the bush. As for Donohue, that fellow would skin his own grandmother."

It was late when we reached Park Crescent. My lamp had gone out and we had walked our bicycles up the last part of the hill. I took Nora's from her and said I would put both machines in the cellar. As I stood in the darkness she gave me a quick hug and kiss.

"Good night, dear Laurie. And bless you for being yourself."

Then she ran up the stairs and was gone.

29

I T WAS four o'clock on a hot Saturday afternoon in mid-July,
and Mrs. Tobin had brought a cup of tea to my room. Before going out she shook her head at me as I sat behind a
pile of books at the wicker table I had rescued from Leo's
junk rooms.

"Education's a wonderful thing. But if I were you, I
wouldn't keep at it that hard."

"But I have to, Annie," I agonized. "Time's getting terribly
short."

"Well." She considered me. "Don't give yourself brain fever,
like Mrs. Finnegan's lad when he failed for the Post Office."

I was too strung up to treat this as a joke. For more than two
months I had been grinding steadily under Pin's direction,
and had worked myself into a state of nerves. From those early
appetizers, Hume Brown's *General History of Scotland,* and
The Border Wars, I had progressed to more solid reading:
Barron's *Scottish War of Independence,* Skene's *Celtic Scotland,* Gregory's *The Stuart Kings,* and was now absorbed in
The Thistle and the Rose. Apart from my real objective, in
which I scarcely dared to hope, I had become interested in the
subject for its own sake. At night, my best reading time, I
would find myself so caught up in such excitements as the
feud between Rothesay and Albany, leading up to Rothesay's

mysterious death at Falkland, that only the final guttering of my candle — an illumination surely in keeping with the fourteenth century — brought me to a halt. I now went to Pin four evenings a week, a truly heroic devotion, less on my part than on his. Often my thoughts went back to the days when I foolishly pretended to have a tutor. Now I had one: a patient, admirable teacher. His main concern centered on my lack of literary style, a defect which he constantly tried, by correction and advice but with slight success, to improve.

"You write from the heart, Laurence." He would shrug regretfully. "Not from the head. We'll have to leave it that way."

I turned to Mrs. Tobin's kindly offering. As I drank the tea, which had begun to get cold, my gaze returned, not for the first time that afternoon, to the postcard. It had come yesterday and now lay, too conspicuously, on the table beside my notes on the regencies of Murray and Lennox. Frowning, I took it up and, as if to deduce some meaning that had hitherto escaped me, read it through once again.

Meet me under the clock at Central Station 5 o'clock Saturday without fail. It will be very definitely to your advantage.

Terence

Of course, I would not go. I had made up my mind not to go. Time was too precious now to waste on futile meetings. Above all, had not Nora, my dear Nora, distinctly advised me to be wary of the elegant Terry. Yet that final sentence had an alluring ring. *Very definitely to your advantage* — soundlessly my lips formed the words. If, indeed, this should be a real opportunity, and my thoughts went back to my conversation with Terence in the kitchens of the Criterion when he had spoken of his influence at Rockcliff, then how badly I should feel if I missed it. While I finished my tea I debated the problem first one way then the other. In the end, I jumped up, seized my cap, and set out for the Central Station.

When I arrived it was ten to five. This was a favourite meeting place, and others were waiting beneath the big clock. I joined them. At five minutes past the hour, striking a note of unusual punctuality, Terence appeared, carrying a small Gladstone bag. He was not alone. Donohue was with him.

"Good, man, you're there. And looking great." Terence greeted me warmly. "I hope we haven't kept you."

Donohue was smiling too, at least his contained, morose face was fixed into an expression of unusual affability, all the more surprising, since until now he had practically ignored me.

"We can't talk here," Terence said. "Let's go into the buffet."

We went into the first class buffet.

"What'll you have?" Donohue asked, hospitably. "This is on me."

Commendably turning the offer to my advantage I said I would have a ham sandwich and a glass of milk. They both had Guinness.

Terence waited until we had been served, then, having inquired of me solicitously if everything was all right, he took a pull at his stout and made the following announcement.

"Now, man, you've often heard me say I wanted to clock you on the mile. Well, it's today we're going to do it."

I ought not to have been surprised since the matter had indeed been brought up before more than once, in Terry's half serious, half jocular manner. But the suddenness of the proposal did take me aback.

"Why today?" I asked warily.

"We'll come to that all in good time," he said, with an intimate, knowing look.

"But I haven't been doing much serious running lately. I'm rather out of form."

"Ah, a fit young fellow like you is never out of form. Is he, Mart?"

"Shouldn't be," Donohue replied noncomittally. "From what I see, there's not an ounce of fat on him. Still, I'm not convinced he can stay."

"Don't worry. He'll stay all right."

"But has he the speed?" Donohue looked at me doubtingly. "He'll need that for a fast finish."

"I'll guarantee it," Terry said emphatically. "Haven't I told you how he sprinted me practically level when he was a kid."

Donohue waved away the argument.

"That was years ago."

"Maybe so. But there's his two big wins with the Harriers this year and the year before. Laugh that off, D."

"Mm, yes," said Donohue, as if half convinced. "Well, I suppose we may as well give him his chance."

"And a real chance it is." Terence turned to me. "It's all fixed up, man. The togs are here for you. My own Rockcliff kit, if you please." He tapped the Gladstone bag with his toe. "And I've arranged for us to try you out at the Harp ground."

"But why, Terry?" These preparations, the interest displayed in me, and the manner in which Donohue had been unwillingly won over were extremely flattering, yet I was not to be taken in by them.

"Later, later, man. What's the use of going into it till we see what you can do."

"No," I said determinedly. "I have to know how it'll effect me."

"Didn't I tell you on my card?" Terence exploded. "It's definitely going to be a good thing for you. Provided you're all we think you are, which now I'm beginning to doubt."

That note of scepticism decided me. I agreed to go. Actually, I saw no harm in the expedition. And now I did want to show them what I could do. Because I disliked him and resented his association with Nora, Donohue especially I wished to convince. We left the buffet and got into a taxi from the rank outside the station. Trust Terry, I thought comfortably, to do things in style. My cousin had again impressed himself upon me with his charm and self-sufficiency.

Our objective lay quite far out in an eastern suburb of the city. After a drive of some twenty minutes it was revealed as a football ground belonging to the Harp Juniors Club. The neighbourhood, dominated by two huge gasometers and the contiguous gas works, was poor and stank, not unnaturally, of gas. I had never heard of the Harp Juniors, and their domain, surrounded by a rusty corrugated iron fence in the process of falling down, enclosed an extremely worn football pitch and a small wooden pavilion. Surrounding the pitch there was, however, a cinder running track.

"Here we are then," Terence exclaimed enthusiastically, telling the taxi driver in an aside to wait. "You stop by the track Mart, and I'll go in with Laurence."

We entered the pavilion, which was even less impressive than the ground. The floor boards were bare and broken, a few old striped jerseys hung on pegs, dust was everywhere, also a strong odour of stale sweat, beer and urine.

The bag, when snapped open, revealed shorts, singlet and spiked running shoes. Solicitously aided by Terence, who had constituted himself my valet, I began to change. Everything fitted well except the shoes which were too long, leaving an inch of soft leather beyond my toes. I pointed this out to Terence.

"It's not a bad thing," he said, with an expert's judiciousness. "It'll give you more spring."

We went outside. Donohue was strolling up and down, with his hands in his pockets and an air of expectancy. He had lit up a sporty looking cheroot.

"There he is," Terence exclaimed, pushing me forward. "And doesn't he look a runner, every inch of him."

"By God, he does. He has the height. And look at those legs."

Donohue's tone, in which I sensed a grudging respect, was highly gratifying. Actually in this lightweight kit with the Rockcliff colours I felt that I should not disappoint them. I took a few preliminary paces.

"That's right, limber up, man."

"Only don't weaken yourself," Donohue said, momentarily choking over his cheroot.

"Now, Laurie," Terence, with a glance that seemed to repress D.'s enthusiasm, put one hand on my shoulder. In the other he held his watch. "Four times round this track is exactly one mile. Are you ready?"

"Yes."

"Then get set." He stood back, eyes on the watch. "Go!"

I made a good start and, doing my level best, went round the track four times. The sandwich I had just eaten troubled me somewhat on the final two circuits and Terry's shoes, while bending freely on the hard cinders, had less spring in them than he had promised. When I drew up, pale and panting, I felt dissatisfied with my performance. Apparently I was mistaken. Bent over the watch Terence gave out a whoop of delight.

"Well run, man. I knew you'd be right for us, and you are."

Not a whit behind, Donohue slapped me heartily on the back. Still gasping, I flushed with pleasure.

"What was my time?"

Terence put a finger to his lips.

"Not a word about that at the moment. You'll see why. Now away and change. The water seems cut off in the pavilion but give yourself a good rub down, there's a towel in the bag."

Ten minutes later we were in the taxi on our way back to the city. As we rolled along Terence turned to me in an extremely confidential way.

"Now listen to me, man." He spoke in a guarded tone, as though he feared the driver might overhear. "There's a sports meeting coming up beginning of August at Berwick-on-Tweed. It's a small country affair and its mostly no account clod hoppers who enter for it. But," he eyed me keenly, "there's a lot of betting goes on and Martin, as you know, is in just that line of business. Our idea is to enter you for the mile. We've studied the local form and from what you've shown us today we're convinced you can do it."

"Win?" I exclaimed.

"The cup." Seriously, he inclined his head, adding even more impressively, "and win a packet as well. We'll take care of the money angle. Martin'll handle the bets. And you'll be ten quid to the good."

"Ten pounds!" It was more than tempting — a dazzling amount. "But, Terry, I'm taking my examination the first week in August. On the seventh."

"The sports are on the fifth. Two whole days before. It's no more than a three hour run from Winton and we'll get you there and back the same day. What's your worry?"

I bit my lip in agonized indecision. I wanted to win that cup, and I particularly wanted the ten pounds. My mother, in a recent letter, mentioning the flat she would take on her return, had bitterly regretted having sold our furniture when we left

Ardfillan. Ten pounds would buy furniture, might even furnish a whole room. But how would Pin regard such an expedition, practically on the eve of the Ellison?

"Why, it'll do you a world of good to have a bit of a break before your exam." Donohue must have read my thoughts. "Of course, if you want to throw good money away I've another fellow in mind who'd jump at the chance."

The thought of being supplanted was too much for me.

"I'll do it."

"Good, man." Terence shook my hand in congratulation. "You'll find you won't regret it. All you have to do is keep your mind easy and do a little light running of an evening. Don't overtrain. And if you look in at the back of the hotel occasionally I'll see you get a few good steaks."

Familiar thoroughfares were being traversed. I saw that we had passed the North British Station and were entering Mortonhall Street. Donohue lowered the window and dispensed with his cheroot. He glanced at me.

"Where would you like us to drop you?"

I judged it must be well past six o'clock, almost time for me to be starting for my session with Pin.

"Anywhere near Hillside Street."

Obligingly, Terence told the driver to make a sweep round the Park. The taxi stopped at the foot of Gilmore Hill, not far from the University, and I got out.

"I'll be keeping in touch with you, man," he shouted, as they drove off.

I walked towards Pin's lodging, still rather excited and with a pleasant feeling of importance. It was flattering to have been sought out by Terence, and to have confirmed my innate belief in my own exceptional fleetness of foot. This awareness of my own speed, first implanted in my consciousness when I ran for the doctor for my father, and fostered by my own efforts to maintain myself in condition, was well supported by material evidence, since when I trained with the Ardencaple Harriers I had twice won the race for boys under fourteen at the end of the season Annual Sports. Yes, this was unquestionably a special gift, comparable almost to the capacity for levitation bestowed by heaven on some of the rarer saints. Indeed, when I ran, in the rush of air occasioned by my transit, I not infrequently had the impression that I had temporarily lost contact with terra firma. In view of all this it seemed only just that I should capitalize on my advantages. Terry's handsome proposal was perfectly legitimate, and if Donohue wanted to bet on me that, too, while entirely his affair, was a permissable proceeding. Nevertheless, in its bearing on the Ellison my conscience was not altogether clear, and as I arrived at Hillside Street and climbed the stairs to Pin's room I decided I must let him have the final word. He was already seated at the table, waiting for me, and turning over a sheaf of papers with every appearance of interest.

"Laurence," he began immediately, motioning me to the other chair. "I've been fortunate enough to get hold of the Ellison exam papers for the last ten years. They make advantageous reading."

"Do they, sir?"

"In the first place, in six out of ten occasions the essay set was devoted exclusively to a Scottish historical character of the sixteenth century. In the second place, I observe that it is exactly ten years since the character selected was Mary Queen of Scots."

"What does that mean?"

"Nothing probably." He smiled, tugging at his beard. "Still, as a guess, I've an idea it would do us no harm to pay special heed to the fifteen hundreds with a little extra attention to that unfortunate young woman and her immediate circle.

Andrew Lang would help us there. I got his biography from the Library today. And how he favours the poor creature."

He was opening the book when, anxious to clear my mind, I spoke up.

"Just one thing before we begin, sir."

I told him that my cousin had asked me to take part in a sports meeting in Berwick two days before the Ellison and that while I had provisionally accepted, if he thought this in any way likely to impair my chances I would immediately withdraw.

He considered, gazing at me with kindness. His face at that moment had a simple dignity that outweighed his absurd deformity, prosy sentimentality and old-maidish ways, and all at once I felt how much I liked him.

"Why, Laurence, I believe it would be the very thing for you. I always advise a break just before an exam. And a day in the open air would be perfect."

This reasoned approval was a great relief. With renewed ardour I joined Pin in a fresh and more intensive examination of the character of Queen Elizabeth's half sister.

30

THAT SAME evening, when I finished my session with Pin and came out of the house into the street, Nora was not there. Quite often, when the weather was fine, she would walk across the Park to meet me and I would find her waiting under the lamp outside No. 212. Then, arm in arm, we would stroll back to the Crescent where Miss Donohue, who fancied her talent in this direction, and enjoyed a tasty bite, made welsh rarebit on toast, to which we drank cocoa. The concentrated application demanded of me by Pin had prevented further excursions to the country, nor had Nora herself proposed them. Although I sensed it only vaguely, never having grasped the full significance of those abandoned moments on the houseboat deck, Nora's attitude towards me had undergone a suttle yet material change. I felt that she was fonder of me than before, not quite in the same casual and mischievous way, but always encouraging me, and telling me how she hoped I might win the Ellison. She seemed suddenly to be older, more restrained, and while we kissed with tenderness, something I could not define was missing — solicitude had taken its place. Lately, indeed, I had begun to imagine that something was worrying Nora. Although she denied this and brushed aside my inquiries she often had an absent look and at times appeared thoroughly depressed. As it was more than a week — an unusually long interval — since I had seen her I decided to call in at Park Crescent on my way back.

Here, however, I was unlucky. There was no answer to the bell and though I took trouble to go round to the back court no light was showing in any of the windows. I hung about for a quarter of an hour vainly hoping that Nora or Miss Donohue would turn up. Then I set off along the Crescent towards Craig Hill. This was by no means my shortest route to Argyle Street, yet Craig Hill held a special attraction for me in the shape of a Jesuit church which, contrasting with the many conventional Pugin chapels of the city, was outstandingly attractive, at least to my mind, in a grim Romanesque style. Partly this was due to lack of funds, since the original design to marble the interior had been shelved, leaving stark arches and pillars of brickwork that cast mediaeval shadows across the nave. Moreover, in the late evening the church was usually empty, darkish and very silent, all of which I liked, and I will confess that I had the habit after leaving Park Crescent — it was in any case the nearest church — to enter this sanctuary not from pure religious fervour, which I could never claim, but, with a trusting heart, in order to solicit heavenly aid for success in the Ellison, without which I felt I would not have a chance.

This evening when I entered, I proceeded to my favourite side altar where there was a replica of Simone Martini's Madonna that I enjoyed looking at, which usually put me in a proper petitioning mood and induced me to part with a penny, if I had one, for a candle. Tonight, however, I could barely see it; all but one of the surrounding votive lights had gone out. A woman, opposite me, was presumably responsible for the single candle, since it was newly lit. Most holy women who lit candles were invariably discovered on their knees with beads between their fingers. But this woman, who was young, merely sat, staring straight ahead, as though hypnotized by the tiny flickering flame she had herself created. Surprise, rather than curiosity, caused me to concentrate my vision through the intervening gloom, then, all at once, with a start of pleasure and surprise, I saw that it was Nora.

I could scarcely believe it. Nora was not devout. I had now discovered that she was careless about such things as not eating meat on Fridays and her Easter duties. Indeed, she was apt to make jokes about holy water and holy smoke that worried me. Yet what happiness it gave me that, aware of my evening habit to light a candle, she should tonight actually have forestalled me and herself made the votive offering for my intention. My heart swelled with love and gratitude. Still unseen, I contemplated her with a rapture that here I usually reserved for heaven. Yet she too, against the background of the altar, her pale, pure profile, softened and made serious by her mood, was like a little madonna. I could wait no longer. Tiptoeing forward, I bent towards her and whispered.

"Thank you, Nora. Thank you for the candle . . . and everything."

"Laurence," she said, turning sharply.

"It's the nicest thing you could ever have done. I'll always remember it."

She looked at me.

"Will you?"

"Yes, I will, Nora. Even if I don't get the Ellison. What made you think of it?"

She looked away.

"It seems I just did. I was sort of in that kind of mood. Strange, isn't it?"

"No, Nora. I believe it will help."

"I hope you're right," she said.

There was a silence.

"Do you want to stay longer?" I asked.

She shook her head. I smiled at her.

"Then let's go together."

Outside, as we came down the steps of the church, I took her arm.

"What a lucky meeting, Nora. I called at the flat but there was no answer. And it's ages since I've seen you. Shall I walk back with you now?"

She stopped at the foot of the steps.

"I'm not going back yet. I've a message to do . . . for Miss Donohue."

"Where, Nora?"

"Why . . . down by Mortonhall Street."

"I'll come with you."

I spoke eagerly, prepared to step out. But she seemed to hesitate and I wondered if my inadvertent discovery of her offering for me had annoyed her, until a moment later she said:

"Aren't you tired? You must be. After all that study and everything."

"I'd never be too tired to walk with you, Nora."

"Oh, very well, then," she said, after the slightest pause. "Come along."

We set off. Had there been the faintest note of impatience in her tone? Impossible. Yet, glancing at her sideways, I had the impression that she was not quite herself. The city was enduring a midsummer heat wave and the evening was still and stifling. Under the street lamps she was pale, with a distant expression and darkish patches under her eyes. She was also unusually silent. But I was dying to tell her about my eventful day.

"I don't suppose you know that I've been running. And that I'm entered for the Berwick Sports."

"Yes, I did hear that was coming off. Apparently we're all supposed to be going in the Gilhooleys' car."

"You too?" I cried.

"It depends. To tell you the truth, dear Laurie," she turned to me, "I've been a little off colour lately."

"I'm terribly sorry. What is it?"

"Oh, just a bit out of sorts. I'm sure I'll be all right soon."

"Then do come, Nora. The trip would be good for you."

"Well, then, we'll see."

We were at the end of Craig Hill and had turned into Mortonhall Street, crowded, as usual, and thick with traffic. Not far from Market Cross, near the Market Arcade, she disengaged her arm.

"This is as far as I'm going."

We stood on the pavement opposite the Arcade, a covered passage way occupied by odd little interesting establishments: a herbalist's, a queer sort of chemist's, even a fortune teller and a naturalist's shop with live tortoises in the window. It was here that Mrs. Tobin bought the ants' eggs for her goldfish.

"Before you go, Nora." It was difficult, I didn't want to keep harping on the subject, but I simply had to get this out. "Thanks again for your candle."

Again I thought I had offended her. But no, as she stepped off the pavement she gave me a faint, wry smile.

"Well, Laurie, as you probably know, I'm not all that religious, but when you want a thing badly enough you'll try anything."

I could not speak for an overflowing gratitude. Her man-

ner, the very words she used, told me how much she was behind me in my effort. I waited till she had crossed the street,
then, still uplifted, took my own short cut to Argyle Street and
the Templar's Hall.

31

At half past eight on the morning of Saturday, August 5th, I set out for the Criterion Hotel. Although the sky was still grey, the softness in the air was refreshing after the recent heat. I had said nothing to Uncle Leo of my plans. The good news from my mother made me hope that, if all went well, I should not be with him long. Her appointment in the Department of Health was now assured and she expected to be back in Winton within the next few weeks. She would then surely terminate my stop gap arrangement with Leo.

Although Terence had insisted on an early start I expected that I should have to wait, but when I approached the hotel I saw that the red car was already drawn up outside the entrance with Terence in the driver's seat and Miss Gilhooley beside him.

As I hurried forward Terence waved his arm in greeting.

"Glad to see you, man. How do you feel?"

"Fine thank you, Terry."

"Hop in the back then. The others won't be a minute, Nora's just gone in for a coffee."

As I stepped into the rear seat Miss Gilhooley half turned and exposed her gold teeth in a welcoming smile. She had on a showy check coat and a flat saucer hat secured with her

favourite pink tulle. She might be Miss Donohue's best customer, and undoubtedly her expenditure in Earle's was lavish, yet I had never known anyone who contrived to look so
garish, an effect which she intensified by a variety of vulgar
affectations. She was always fluttering about, primping herself, touching up her hair, powdering her nose, looking in
her handbag, patting herself in unexpected places, examining
her finger nails, straining her neck, gesturing with genteel
flicks of her wrists or demanding unnecessary attentions from
Terence with an air of languishing feminine charm. Miss
Gilhooley was neither beautiful nor youthful and her preten-
tions to these attributes together with her habit of prefacing
every other remark with the words "I always say . . ." seriously offended me, even though she now greeted me with
gracious condescension.

"Good morning, young man. I hope you're going to make a
nice bit of cash for me today."

"Are you in need of cash, Miss Gilhooley?"

Terence gave a loud laugh.

"He had you there, Josey. We all know what the name
Gilhooley stands for. But what's keeping Nora?"

"She must have had a rush getting here," Miss Gilhooley remarked. "I always say you should never rush. She looked
quite faint too, the love. Pale as paper."

A moment later Nora came through the swing doors of the
hotel followed by Donohue. Urged on impatiently by Terence,
who now got out and took up the starting handle from its
leather strap, they joined me in the back of the car.

"Take the rug, Nora. There . . . on the rail. It may be
chilly. Wrap up well, I always say, before you start." Miss
Gilhooley offered this advice as Terence, after several swings,
started the engine and, resuming his place at the steering
wheel, set us in motion.

Nora, who was sitting in the middle between Donohue and me, spread the rug over our knees. As she did so, she smiled at me, but did not speak. The car moved off.

Actually this was my first experience of a private motor and as we rolled through the main streets of Winton towards the Edinburgh road I gave myself up to the smooth luxury of our progress. Terence was an excellent driver, it seemed likely that he had driven this car many times, and I could now surmise why Miss Gilhooley possessed attractions for him beyond her rather meagre physical charms. They were both in a festive mood, laughing and talking with a vivacity that contrasted notably with the almost total silence in the rear.

Now it was impossible not to recognize that the split between Nora and Donohue had widened. While he did, presumably for the sake of appearances, address an occasional perfunctory remark to her, she barely answered, but continued to look ahead with a pale, set face. This did not suit Donohue at all and presently, with a shrug, he abruptly gave up this pretence and, leaning forward in his best manner, began to devote himself to Miss Gilhooley, whispering in her ear, making her laugh, and competing with Terence for her attentions.

Nora gave no sign, her expression did not change, but after a time her hand moved under cover of the rug and sought out mine. Her fingers were so cold I began to chafe them.

"Are you all right, Nora?"

She looked at me and nodded.

"I've been a bit off lately, but the fresh air's helping me. I just wish I hadn't taken that coffee."

The others were so engaged, and Miss Gilhooley's spasms so shrill, there was no danger of our being overheard.

"Do you feel sick?"

"Just a little. It'll pass."

I gazed at her with concern. She did not look herself at all. Had Donohue's defection upset her to such an extent?

"If you don't feel well you shouldn't have come."

"I couldn't bear hanging about all day alone. Miss D.'s away buying in Manchester. And don't forget, I want to see you run."

Did she really mean this? In her present state of mind I doubted if the race was even remotely in her thoughts.

At this point a diversion occurred. Terence had mistaken our route and now discovered, on consulting his map, that a wrong turn beyond Dunbar had taken us about fifteen miles off the direct route. Rather than risk getting lost in country lanes, it became necessary to go back to the coast road, a divergence which raised the question as to whether we should arrive in time for the start of the Sports at two o'clock. Conversation was now reduced as Terence pushed the car to its top speed, and with such effect that at twenty minutes past one we slipped through a narrow stone archway and entered Berwick-on-Tweed.

This was an old grey border borough, straddling the river Tweed where it entered the sea, with cobbled streets and twisting wynds, ringed by a mediaeval wall, with ramparts that overlooked the harbour. As we passed through the old arched gateway I felt at once that it would be a delightful place in which to wander round and dream. Today, however, it presented a scene of activity that was clearly unusual, the main street alive with people, the central square crowded with cars, wagonettes and farm carts, the entire town in a state of commotion that, from their comments, proved highly gratifying to Terence and Donohue.

"We must get a paper," Terry said, drawing up beside a newsboy and tossing him a coin. It was a small double sheet —

I saw the name: *Berwick Advertiser* — and Terence scanned it quickly.

"Is it in?" Donohue asked, craning forward.

"It is," Terence answered. "And it's good."

They both examined the page with every appearance of satisfaction until Miss Gilhooley, peeved at her temporary desertion, exclaimed:

"Look here you two, when are we going to get lunch? That looks like some kind of a hotel over there."

"No, Josey dear," Terence said. "The food there would kill you. We'll run down to the sports field, have a drink and a snack in the marquee, and on the way home we'll stop in Edinburgh for a big blow-out at F. & F.'s."

I experienced a premonitory thrill. F. & F.'s, the smart name for Ferguson and Forrester's, was the most famous restaurant in Edinburgh. Terence was certainly going to treat us well. Before starting off again he turned and, with a smile of approbation, handed me the paper, pointing to the centre of the page.

"Take a look, young fellow-my-lad. That'll show you what they think of you here."

It was a conspicuous box paragraph in a section devoted entirely to the sports, giving the times of the races, the names of the runners, and the probable betting odds.

A Dark Horse for the Mile

The general belief that the Open Mile lies between Peter Simms, last year's runner up, and the present holder, hardy veteran Harry Purves, may be rudely shattered just after 4 p.m. today by a young stripling from the West in the person of Laurence Carroll. This ex-schoolboy, who will be in the Rockcliff colours, was recently timed over the measured distance at the ground of the Harp J. C. and rumour hath it, much to the annoyance of his trainer, that young Carroll showed a clean pair of heels to the record. This will not be a long shot now, but for my money it's the best thing on the card.

Glowing with pride, I lowered the paper. I wanted to show it to Nora, but now, bumping over a rough track, we had joined the crowd already making for the Sports field, and she was leaning forward, supporting herself against the handrail on the back of the front seat. I folded the paper carefully and put it in my pocket. I would show it to her later; in any case, it was something I wanted to keep.

Presently we came to the field, an expanse of flat, cropped downland stretching along the cliffs, neatly railed off, marked out with limewash and gay with flags, marquees and a variety of booths that gave the place the air of a county fair. On one side was a small golf course, on the other the open sea. The situation appealed to me and the fresh breeze blowing in from the ocean stirred my blood. I knew that I could do well here. I jumped out of the car and, while Miss Gilhooley and Nora went off to the refreshment marquee, began to help untie the gear from the luggage grid. Terence had not parked the car in the regular enclosure but behind the row where the bookmakers were putting up their stands. And now, as Donohue began to set up his board and a kind of platform made of sections that fitted together, Terence said:

"Mart, don't you want a sandwich first?"

"Later," Donohue said. "You go . . . and take him."

As the principal participant in the great event of our day, this oblique and somewhat slighting reference to myself was not particularly agreeable. When I went off with Terence I said:

"I daresay I should be careful what I eat. And not too much, either."

"All you'll get here won't hurt you."

The truth of these words was borne out when we joined Nora and Miss Gilhooley at a long crowded bar. Miss Gilhooley had an outraged air.

"This is the giddy limit, Terry. What a low down mob. And there seems to be nothing but sausage rolls."

"Just put up with it," Terence said, placatingly. "You'll have lobster and champagne tonight."

"Tonight's a long way off. And here's Nora, sick as a dog, she ought to have a cognac. I always say there's nothing like cognac to settle the stomach."

"Do you want a brandy, Nora?"

She shook her head. She did look sick and unutterably miserable too.

"If I'm to have something I'd rather try some gin."

"All right." He pointed to a table in the corner of the tent. "Both of you go and sit over there."

Terry, who was extremely good at that sort of thing, managed to get two plates of assorted food and some drinks. Between us we carried them over to the table. Nora drank the gin but did not eat anything. Miss Gilhooley ate half a sandwich, then, with an air of wounded refinement, discarded the other half. I had a couple of sausage rolls, sanctioned by Terence, who finished what remained of the sandwiches, even absently consuming the half left by Miss Gilhooley. He then produced a round competitor's tag and handed it to me.

"That'll take you into the changing tent. I have your togs in the car. Get there in good time." He got up. "Come along, Josey dear, we'll go out for a breath of air."

As they went off together, I tied the tag to the lapel of my jacket. I was glad to be alone with Nora, anxious to discover exactly why she was so upset. Then, raising my head, I saw that Donohue had come into the marquee and was advancing towards us. He sat down, and glancing at me as though he wished I weren't there, said, uncomfortably:

"I'm just going to start work. I thought I'd see how you were first."

I thought Nora wasn't going to answer, but after a moment she said, stiff lipped:

"Aren't you a bit late? If you do want to know, I'm feeling awful."

"Can I get you something? A gin."

"I'm sick of drinking gin. I seem to have been living on the blasted stuff. And you know I hate it."

"Now, Nora . . . pull yourself together. Things may not be as bad as all that."

"I'm glad you think so."

I wanted to get away from this quarrel but the bench Donohue was sitting on wedged me in. I had to listen as, trying to control his temper, he said:

"Don't be a bloody wet blanket, Nora. For God's sake make an effort. The party tonight will buck you up."

"I'm not going to the party," Nora said.

"What!"

"No, I'm not. I'm going to stay here in this marquee and if I don't feel any better I'm not going back by car. I'm going to take the train home."

"What train?"

"The ten to six express. Yes, I mean it. I thought I mightn't stick it out all day so I looked up the timetable before we left."

"You're not coming back with me?"

"No. And don't look at me like that."

"Not so long ago you were glad enough for me to look at you."

"That's all finished now. And you are too. Finished and done with."

Donohue was silent. Then he gave her a long hard stare.

"Well," he said. "If that's how you want it, go ahead." He stood up and pulled at my arm. "Come on, you. It's time I got you over to the secretary's office. I don't know why the hell

everything falls on me. If we don't confirm your entry, that'll
be a washout too."

We left Nora and went to the office, a square tent near the
finishing line. Outside, Donohue paused and said, warningly:

"Don't let on who brought you here."

"Why, aren't you coming in too?"

"I've got my book to make," he said. As he was turning
away he suddenly stopped. "And listen, if they ask you what
your age is, you're sixteen past."

"But I'm not sixteen till the second of next month."

"You are now, you stupid young bastard, or you'll be dis-
qualified before the race. And if that happens I'll break your
bloody neck."

I stared after him in angry dismay. What right had he to
treat me like that? And what was all this pretence about my
age?

Still indignant, I went into the tent. The secretary was a
short, red faced man, wearing a Hawick tweed knickerbocker
suit and a club tie. He made no disagreeable inquiries, indeed,
when I signed my name in the book he looked at me with
interest and held out his hand.

"We want more of your sort here." He smiled, salving my
damaged pride. "Good luck."

When I came out, Donohue had gone to his stand. Terence
and Miss Gilhooley were still not in evidence. It was almost
two o'clock and all the bookmakers had begun to call the odds.
I walked slowly along the line, noting that the prices for the
main event, the mile, were already chalked up on the boards.
My self-esteem was further restored as I observed that I had
been made joint favourite with Purves at evens, with Simms
at two to one behind us. Indeed at one board I was quoted at
evens with Simms and Purves both at two to one. I had now
had quite enough of Donohue, I did not go near his stand,

but from the crowd around him he appeared to be doing a roaring trade.

The report of a pistol shot split the air. The first event had begun. Pressing forward to the rails I saw that it was the first heat of the hundred yards. Almost at once the second heat came up. I wanted to go to Nora, she was terribly on my mind, intermingled confusedly with a number of other worries that had begun to trouble me. Yet I felt that she wanted to be left alone and that any interference on my part would only make things worse. A strange passivity had come over me, an indefinable impression that I had been caught up by circumstances in which I could do nothing but submit. I remained at the rails and continued to watch the races.

As time went on and one event succeeded another, my nerves tightened. Restlessly, I moved my feet, and bent my knees, restoring elasticity to my legs. My moment of truth was approaching, I must not be late. Edging out of the crowd I retrieved the Gladstone bag containing my togs from the car, then walked along the bookmakers' row to the changing tent, encouraged by the fact that I was permanently installed as favourite at evens. More people than ever were gathered round Donohue now, hands reaching out, clamouring to place their bets. Curiosity alone caused me to glance at his board. I could not believe it. With a painful shock I saw that, chalked up in plain figures, he was giving odds of five to one against me. Even as I went by, he rubbed out the five and made it six. At that, the crowd around his board increased.

I entered the tent in a state of absolute incomprehension. The thing was meaningless. Had Donohue gone out of his mind? From the outset, every step taken had been premised on the certainty that I would win and now, if I did, he would pay out six times what he took in. Suddenly, as I stood in a maze of mystification, a hearty grip brought me to myself. A lean elderly man, bald as a coot, with a thin weather-beaten face, wearing a red and blue striped jersey and old washed out tight trunks that clung like a second skin to his sinewy legs, was shaking me by the hand.

"I'm Purves." He grinned, nodding towards the bench at the back of the tent. "And that's Simms. I hear you're going to knock the stuffing out of us old timers."

Simms, in the process of stripping and practically naked, came forward. He was a much younger man than Purves, about twenty-six or -seven, solidly built, with short muscular limbs and a thick chest covered with a moss of matted black hair. He did not look particularly dangerous, he was altogether too heavy. As for Purves, why the thing was ridiculous, he was virtually an old man.

"Well, good luck, youngster," Simms was saying, goodnaturedly. "May the best man win and devil take the hindmost."

"Better get shifted, lad," Purves said. "The bell will be going soon."

I began to change. Some others were on the benches pulling on singlets or lacing up running shoes. A lanky youth, addressed as Chuck, whom I guessed to be about seventeen, was the only one near my own age. Most of my rivals seemed on intimate terms and, from their jocular references to past events, regular competitors at all the Border meetings. Beyond that I scarcely noticed them. Out of the turmoil in my mind one clear certainty had emerged. Whatever trickery Donohue was up to would be scotched if I won the race. I took a long deep breath. I had come to win, I had promised to win, and by heaven I would win!

The clanging of a bell summoned us from the tent. When we filed out I counted the runners: we were eight altogether. Outside, we drew lots from a hat for positions. My slip, number 4, was at least moderately good. Then we came through a narrow opening in the railings into the arena. Hitherto I had not realized the full size of the crowd; now, with intimidating force, it struck me as enormous: a great massed ring of watching faces. But strangely, that ring receded as we lined up on the curved white starting line. Leaning slightly forward, my eardrums tense for the starter's pistol, I was conscious only of the sun shining on the grassy track stretching in a wide oval before me, and of the fact that three circuits made the mile.

Crack! I was off with the shot, sprinting across to the inside of the track and, as I had intended, taking the lead from the start. The rapid pad of footsteps behind did not disturb me. I was ahead and meant to stay there. Moving freely in the cool fresh air, I felt I could go on like this for ever. How quickly the first circuit was completed. And now, as from a distance, but deliciously, in a foretaste of triumph, I began to hear my name shouted and repeated. I was half way round on the second lap when a runner, neither Simms nor Purves, but an unknown and unfavoured contestant, unexpectedly thrust past me by a good three yards. Impossible to submit to such an insult. To the accompaniment of further wildly excited shouts I spurted hard, and with a burst of speed left him again behind.

But now the air was suddenly less cool and the movements of my limbs scarcely so elegant or easy. Nevertheless, the second circuit was achieved, I was still ahead, and only the final lap remained. Head up, heart pumping, I pounded on, conscious that I was flagging but praying that I could hold my lead. Alas, that prayer produced no answer from the celestial powers to whom it was addressed. I was no more than half way home on the last round when, with a tremendous rush, Purves shot past me, his leathery legs going like pistons, elbows flailing the air. Slogging along closely behind him came Simms and two others. I tried but could not match this mass assault. My own legs, if indeed they now belonged to me, for they were entirely without feeling, would not respond. My lungs were bursting, my throat choked and raw. I knew that I was done. My name, no longer shouted, sunk in obloquy, was lost in the roar, dimly heard through the red haze that swam before me, of "Purves, Daddy Purves!"

Still going, but blindly now, I had the vague consciousness of more shadowy forms gliding past me. As I staggered across the broken tape, only a single runner, one lone laggard, the youth called Chuck, was behind me. I had finished second last.

Mercifully the changing tent was near. Beat to the world, humiliated to the verge of tears, I tottered into it and hid myself. As I sat, bowed, with heaving chest, on the bench, Daddy Purves tried to console me.

"The mile's not your distance, boy. You'd have done well in the half. But never mind, you've years ahead of you."

I felt his kindness but could not respond to it. What a fool I had been, Terence too, to imagine that at my age, untrained, out of condition, I could compete with men, experienced runners, who did the Border Circuit, who were in a sense professionals. At last I pulled myself up, got into my clothes, flung my sodden togs into the bag and went outside.

Immediately, I ran into Terence. He had been waiting for me and before I could utter one word of abject apology he took me by the lapel of my jacket.

"What a time you've been!" he exclaimed, urgently, and before I could speak went on: "Now listen, Laurence. You're not to come near Donohue or any of us. Don't come to the car. Not on any account."

"Why not?" I faltered. "Because I didn't win?"

"No, you idiot!" He hesitated, looked about him, and lowered his voice. "As a matter of fact, there's been a spot of trouble over the bets. And it's much safer for you to keep out of it. It's all that damned Donohue's fault. What I thought was just going to be a lark has turned nasty. So what you'll do is this . . . you'll walk quietly into the town now and wait for us at the Archway. Remember where we came into the town."

"Yes."

"Right, then. We'll pick you up there with the car in less than an hour. Here's a pound note if you want to have a snack or anything while you're waiting."

"I'm sorry I lost, Terry." Anguished, I managed to get it out at last.

He stared at me in a curious manner then, without a word, swung round and hurried off.

For a moment I stood watching him disappear in the crowd then, with bent head, carrying the Gladstone bag, I slunk out of the ground by the golf course exit and started to trudge along the field road towards the town.

32

THE ROAD ahead, to my relief, was almost clear. Since the sports did not finish until five o'clock and the time now was not more than half past four, only a few spectators had begun to leave the ground. Dead tired, I walked slowly, so sunk in my own gloom that at first I had no consciousness of the figure, walking with equal languor, not far ahead of me. But suddenly, I saw who it was and, hurrying forward, called out:

"Nora."

"It's you!" She had turned, surprised. "Have you left the others?"

I nodded miserably.

"Terence told me to keep away from them. I'm to meet them at the Archway in the town."

"Why to keep away from them?"

"They're having trouble over my bets."

She considered me palely, but with compressed lips.

"Did you win the race?"

"No, I didn't, Nora. I was practically last. They were all men, far older than me. I didn't have a chance, in spite of all it said in the paper."

"What paper?"

We were now moving along the road together. I took the

Berwick Advertiser from my pocket, unfolded it and showed her the box paragraph.

She read it, looked at me, read it again, then stared straight ahead. Under her breath she murmured something with such anguished bitterness, I felt relieved not to hear it. After that she was silent for a moment, then she seemed to draw herself together.

"My poor Laurence. You're not going to meet them at the Archway. You're coming home in the train with me."

This was an unexpected, brightening prospect.

"But won't they . . . keep on waiting for me?"

"They won't. Don't worry about them, for they aren't worrying about us."

"When is the train, Nora?"

"Ten minutes to six."

"Won't we have to change at Edinburgh?"

"No. Luckily, it's a through express. Before we leave we'll have time to get you something to eat."

"You, too, Nora." When she did not answer, I added anxiously: "Are you still sick?"

"I'm not altogether at the top of my form, dear Laurie. But I'm doing my best to get over it." She moistened her lips and made a fair attempt at a smile. "We've both been messed about a bit lately, but if we stick together we'll come out of it all right."

Taking it very slowly, for Nora apparently did not wish to hurry, nor for that matter did I, we reached the town. I had thought that all of Berwick had gone to the Sports but here the streets were swarming with people, many of whom appeared to have come in from the surrounding country, and in an open space near the central square a sort of fair, with roundabouts, had been set up.

"It's fearfully busy," Nora said. "It must be some kind of holiday."

Looking around for a place where we could have a meal, she stopped outside a small restaurant with a bill in the window marked: *Tweed Salmon, Boiled or Grilled, ⅙ the cut.*

"You'd like that, wouldn't you?"

"Very much," I said. "Especially grilled." I had not tasted salmon since the days of those affluent lunches, now seemingly so distant, with Miss Greville.

We went inside. It was a simple eating house, steamy from the kitchen, and so full that we had difficulty in finding places. Nora ordered salmon for me and a pot of tea for herself.

"Eat something, Nora," I begged her. "Please do."

She simply shook her head.

While we were waiting to be served, I said:

"I still can't understand why Terence said they were in trouble."

"Laurence, dear," she said. "We won't go into it now. It was simply a dirty little trick to make some dirty money. They knew all along you had no chance of winning. But don't blame Terence too much — he's soft and selfish, but he's not a bad sort at heart. It was just fun to him. Donohue's the one who's to blame. He thought it all out." Her voice hardened. "I hope he gets well beaten by the crowd. But he won't. He'll get away with it, as usual."

She took out her handkerchief and wiped her forehead. She was breathing quickly.

My salmon came at last. Served with a dish of potatoes boiled in their jackets, and slapped down before me by a man in his shirtsleeves, it was a noble cut from as good a fish as ever came out of the Tweed. I suddenly discovered that I was starving, and for a brief but active interlude my troubles receded. Only when I had practically finished did I observe that Nora had pushed her tea away untasted.

"It's so hot in here," she said, by way of excuse. "I think I'll go and wash."

I watched her with concern. She was so unlike herself, even in her way of walking, that I decided that the sooner we were in the train the better. While she was away I asked the man for the bill. This came to 2/9 and I paid it with the note Terence had given me, adding a threepenny tip from the change.

We started up the main street for the railway station. Unfortunately, this was situated at the summit of the incline on which the town was built. Although she made no remark, I could feel that Nora did not like the climb. But presently we arrived and found the booking office open. I told myself that she would be all right when we were in the train.

Nora took out her purse and asked for two third class singles for Winton.

"Thirty-two and ninepence, please."

The clerk selected two pasteboard tickets from the rack, twirled the little black stamping machine on the ledge and was about to snap the two tickets into the slot when he looked up.

"You want them dated for Monday? The early train leaves at seven fifteen A.M."

"Monday!" Nora exclaimed. "We're going with the ten to six train tonight."

He shook his head.

"There's no ten to six tonight."

"But there is," Nora protested. "I looked it up specially in Murray's Diary."

Silently he produced a timetable, leaned forward and, removing the pencil from behind his ear, pointed to the page.

"You see that little star, miss. Except Sundays and bank

holidays. And today, Fair Saturday, is the biggest bank holiday of the lot."

Watching Nora anxiously, I saw what a shock this was to her. She seemed to shrink into herself.

"Surely there's another train?"

"Nothing, miss. And nothing tomorrow either." Detaching himself from us completely he began to add up figures on a pad.

Nora supported herself against the ledge. I thought she was going to faint. An icy shiver contracted my skin.

"Nora, we'll have to hurry back to the Archway. Terence might still be waiting there."

"No," she said, hopelessly. "They're sure to have gone."

"We must try. We must."

The Archway was not far from the station. We were soon there and for nearly an hour we stood waiting, straining our eyes for the red car, never speaking a word, elbowed by the passing crowds, while the holiday traffic of the main street rolled and rattled past. Now it was almost dark.

"It's no use." Nora spoke at last in a beaten voice. "They probably had to run for it, and they have."

"Then what are we to do?" I said, desperately. "Can we hire a car to Edinburgh? And take a train from there."

"Even if we could, I couldn't stand the journey." All at once she broke down and began to cry. "Laurence, I've kept up all day feeling like death, but I can't, I can't go on any longer. I've got such a bad stitch in my side if I don't lie down soon I'll drop. We must find some place to stay the night."

A sensation of unutterable consternation left me dumb. All sorts of weird contingencies flashed through my mind. Would that booking clerk allow us to stay in the station waiting room, or could we perhaps find some sort of shelter in the local Park?

Then I saw her look of collapse as she stood with one hand pressed against her side. I knew that she must find a room in a hotel.

The hotel in the main square behind the fair ground, despite Terry's slighting comment, had seemed altogether reputable. I took Nora by the arm — she now seemed incapable of voluntary movement — and brought her down the street to the square. The hotel had a sign: "The Berwick Cockle." Streams of boisterous country folk were moving in and out yet I managed to steer Nora through the crush into the red-carpeted hall. After the street it seemed a blessed sanctuary. But the man in the little glass office scarcely looked at us. The hotel was full, he said, full to the doors, they had been turning people away all day.

We went out. Across the square was a much smaller inn, the "Masons' Arms." Leaving Nora outside, with instructions not to move, I squeezed my way into the crowded, smoke filled lobby. It was packed with groups of men standing with glasses in their hands, laughing and talking at the pitch of their lungs. No one took the least notice of me. I spoke to several men, asking for the office, before one pointed with his pipe to a plump, yellow-haired woman in a black dress who, from her general air of sociability, I had assumed to be part of this convivial gathering. I pushed my way towards her and with some difficulty succeeded in catching her eye. She had a red, amiable face that encouraged me. But my heart sank as she shook her head.

"You'll not find a room in Berwick tonight, lad. Not one."

"Is there no place you can think of?" I pleaded. "Anywhere at all."

"You might try Spittal, across the river," she said, doubtfully. "There's a pub there, just over the bridge, called the 'Drovers' Rest.' They might give you a bed."

"How do I get there?"

"Turn second on the right. Down Cooper's Alley. It's just over the old bridge."

Outside again, I took Nora's arm. She was silent, unresistant, almost lost, hand still pressed against her side. The town was now in a ferment, crowds milling in the square, the fair in full swing, music from the roundabouts splitting the night air. Twice I took the wrong turning and had to get back to the main street but in the end I found Cooper's Alley. And there at the foot of the hill was the river, dark and smooth, rushing out with the tide. We crossed a narrow humpbacked bridge and came to Spittal village. Here a merciful sense of quiet prevailed, a smell of seaweed and the blessed coolness of salt air. The masts of fishing smacks stood out against the glare of Berwick as I helped Nora long the cobbled quay.

Quite soon we came to the "Drovers' Rest." It was an old brick building, poorly lit and with few signs of accommodation. With nothing to distinguish it from an ordinary public house it did not give me much hope. Inside we were faced with a narrow stone passage that led to the bar. The sounds of voices, raised in discussion, emerged. I did not want to take Nora there. On the right was a door marked *Private*. I knocked, and presently an old man appeared. He was in his slippers, wearing a long knitted blue spencer and he had in his hand a dog-eared copy of *Chambers' Journal*. So overstrained were my sensibilities, I registered these unessential details as, simultaneously, desperately, I burst out:

"We've been to the sports and missed our train home. Please give my cousin a room. She's not feeling well. I'll sleep anywhere you like."

While, with palpitating heart, I held out the Gladstone bag conspicuously as evidence of our respectability, he examined us over his spectacles. He glanced from one to the other of us and I knew in my bones that he was about to refuse. I saw it in his face.

Just then a woman came out of the bar. She was about thirty, plainly dressed in a blouse and skirt, carrying an empty tray under her arm. She had a decent, competent look.

"What's the rub, Father?" she asked.

"This pair want a room."

"What!" she exclaimed, shocked. "Together?"

"No, m'am," I burst out. "Only for my cousin. I'll walk about outside if you like."

There was a silence.

"Ye say you've been to the sports," the old man said.

"Yes, sir." To authenticate the fact I martyred myself. "Harry Purves won the mile."

The woman had been looking at Nora, then at me.

"They're all right, Father," she said suddenly. "She can have Number 3, and the boy'll shake down in the boxroom. But no tricks, mind you, or I'll throw you both out myself."

My chest heaved, I gave a great gasp of relief. Before I could thank her she had gone back into the bar. The old man shuffled into the room and brought out a key. We followed him upstairs where he opened the door of a small single room. It was a poor room, sparsely furnished, with faded wallpaper, and a cracked ewer, but the floorboards were scrubbed and the bedlinen fresh and clean. Altogether my survey assured me, with relief and pride, that in our extremity I had done well for Nora.

"You'll sleep well here," I said, forced to keep my tone impersonal. "And be all right in the morning."

"Oh yes, thank you, Laurie." She managed a faint, pale smile. "Just to be able to lie down and rest."

"Don't you want to leave that with her?" The old man was eyeing the bag, which I still clutched in a permanent spasm.

"Yes, of course," I agreed hurriedly, though it was no use to either of us.

I wanted to say more to Nora, beyond everything I longed to kiss those soft blanched lips, gently, with all the tenderness of my loving heart. But the old man still had his eye on us, though now with less suspicion. I simply said good night, and went out of the room with him. As we moved along the passage, I heard the closing of her door.

33

MY FUTILE exertions in that disastrous race and the
struggle to find a lodging had left me almost dead
with fatigue. The mattress on which I lay, on the
floor of the boxroom, was not uncomfortable. Yet I couldn't
sleep. Round and round, inextricably tangled, the events of
this most unnatural day kept spinning inside my head. What a
fool I had been, what a *soft mark*, so easily, so willingly duped,
flattered into the belief that I was a paragon who must win
today. And what ironic diversion my idiotic credulity must
have afforded Terence and Donohue as, from that first farcical
trial at the Harp football ground, they led me on, with serious
faces, stuffing me for the slaughter. Why did I lack the common sense to see that while I might run well enough for my
age, competition against seasoned professionals who habitually
made the rounds of all the Border sports was lunacy? From
the beginning it had been a hoax and it ended as a swindle.
Donohue had planted the paragraph in the local paper and by
offering excessive odds against me, had cashed in heavily on
my defeat. If only I had won, and made him pay out five
times over, ruined him in fact, what a triumph it would have
been, not for me alone but for Nora too, since from her own
words, I knew that she must hate him. But that, like most

other things I had wanted in my life, was beyond me, an achievement realized only in my dreams, never by accomplishment.

Tortured by my own inadequacy I turned restlessly on the mattress. It was evident that I had been born to fail and to be imposed upon. A sudden recollection, as from a distant world, of the Ellison added to my distress, less on account of the difficulty in getting to the University on Monday — the early train would be in Winton at least by noon — than from the settled conviction that, as I had failed in the race, I would fail there too. Pin had led me on, not like Donohue, but from the best motives, merely to improve the standard of my education.

At this point, I drifted into a troubled sleep, but not for long. Suddenly my brain snapped back to consciousness with the startled impression that someone was calling my name. I raised myself on my elbow, listening in the darkness. Sounds from the bar beneath and the distant hum of the fair in Berwick both had ceased. The faint scratching of a mouse somewhere in the room intensified the stillness. I was about to lie down again, convinced that I was mistaken, when again I fancied I heard someone call.

I jumped up, knocking my shins hard on the sharp edge of an unseen object, and felt my way to the door. Undecided, I stood there, listening with my ear against the panel, but hearing nothing. Yet if someone had called me it could only be Nora. Guardedly I opened my door. The corridor was in darkness, but half way along a faint sliver of light showed beneath the door of her room.

I had not undressed, having merely taken off my jacket and my boots. Now, moving softly in my socks, I advanced to the lighted door and tapped on it with a finger nail. There was no response.

"Nora," I whispered. "Are you there?"

Her voice came back to me, indistinctly yet with an unmistakable appeal. I turned the handle and went in.

She was lying sideways on the bed with nothing on but her chemise, which had rucked up above her knees. Her eyes were shut and her hands half clenched. The sheets and blankets of the bed, tumbled in a heap, were bunched in disorder on the floor. Worst of all was the strained, sunken greyness of her face. She looked older, almost ugly, scarcely recognizable.

"Nora," I faltered. "You called me."

She half opened her eyes.

"I couldn't stand it alone any longer. I've such a pain."

"Where, Nora?"

She made a gesture towards her stomach, but lower. She was obviously in severe pain. A fear that had hovered in the back of my mind during the day now took formidable shape. I might be a fool and a failure but, thank God, I had enough sense to know about appendicitis. I went forward to the bed.

"Do you still feel sick?"

"Yes. I feel awful."

"Nora." I tried not to alarm her. "We'll have to get help."

Still pressing her side, she did not answer. I took her free hand. It was hot, the palm moist with sweat.

"We've got to find out, it's dangerous not to. You must have the doctor."

"Oh, not yet." She gasped in another spasm. "We'll wait for a bit."

"We must." I pleaded.

"It's the middle of the night. You'll get no one to come. I'd rather stick it out by myself. Just stay with me."

"But, Nora . . ." I broke off, aghast that she wouldn't let me go for assistance.

"Please stay. If only you'll get me up to walk about the room, that might get rid of the pain."

She raised herself on one elbow and put her other arm on my shoulders. While I supported her, I was conscious of a bad, unhealthy smell in the room. Then I noticed that the Gladstone bag was open and empty. My white singlet and shorts were lying, sodden and terribly soiled, a dirty brownish colour, in the corner.

I thought she had been sick on them and that decided me. I put her back on the pillow. Without a word I went out and downstairs to the room marked *Private*. I knocked hard on the door, then, as no one answered I turned the handle and went into the room, found the switch and put on the light. I was in a small comfortably furnished sitting room. A clock, ticking on the mantelpiece, caught my eye. The time was half past two o'clock in the morning. Another door, almost hidden by a curtain, led me into the kitchen where, starting up from its basket before the red embers of a fire, a small dog began to bark and growl at me. Suddenly a sharp voice called out.

"Who's there?"

I called back, saying who I was, and that I needed help at once. For some minutes nothing happened, then, to my immense relief, the woman, who was the old man's daughter, entered the kitchen. Still tugging at the cord of her wrapper, she quietened the dog and stared at me angrily, her eyes swollen with sleep, her hair, in a thick plait tied at the end with tape, hanging down her back.

"My cousin's terribly ill and in great pain." I got it out before she could start on me. "I'm sure it's appendicitis."

This silenced her: she was still angry, but could not quite bring herself to abuse me.

"Oh, Lord," she groaned. "Why did I ever let you in?"

"It's awful to have to trouble you. But please come and see her. Or phone for the doctor now."

Another silence, then she said:

"I'll have a look at her. Go on, you clown. Don't keep me standing here all night."

I led the way upstairs and opened the door of Nora's room. The woman went in, at least she paused, one step beyond the threshold. Her gaze took in Nora, the disordered bed, the tumbled blankets, my soiled singlet in the corner, even the half full chamber pot and some alarming stains on the sheets, which I had not noticed before. Then, in quite a different manner, a voice that suddenly chilled me, she said:

"Go to your room, you. And don't stir an inch out of it till I send for you." She shut the door in my face.

I could not disobey her, yet, back in the boxroom, I sat close to the door, in the darkness, listening, with every sense quivering and alert, afraid, dreadfully afraid for Nora. I shivered as I thought of her chalk white face, so drained and sunken. I prayed that the doctor would come quickly. The operation for appendicitis was in itself serious and I knew also that if an inflamed appendix was not quickly removed it would burst, with fatal consequences.

The woman was still in the room with Nora; for perhaps ten minutes she had been there. Suddenly I heard her go downstairs. The boxroom was directly above the lower passage, and its old floor boards bare of any covering. Flattened out and straining my ears, I heard her go into what I guessed was the sitting room. Almost at once she began to talk and although I could not distinguish the words I gave a quick sigh of relief. She was telephoning for the doctor. This went on for some time and when it ended I heard her come upstairs again.

An interval elapsed, insufferably long, before the doctor

arrived. He was not long in Nora's room. Almost at once he went down to the telephone. I knew, with a slight shudder, what that meant. Then I heard him on the stairs again.

Now a few streaks of dawn were beginning to creep into the boxroom, revealing a dusty clutter of boxes, mops, pails, odd pieces of broken furniture and other lumber. I went to the single window to watch for the ambulance. But when it swung into the still, grey street, I could bear it no longer. Retreating from the window I listened to the sounds of Nora's removal. I could not bring myself to look.

At last all was quiet again. I put on my boots and jacket, and half opened the boxroom door. I could hear nothing. Surely I couldn't be expected to go on enduring this suspense. Cautiously I came along the corridor. The woman was in Nora's room, with her sleeves rolled up and her hands on her hips, surveying a scene of appalling disorder.

Only one thought was in my mind. I said:

"Will she be all right?"

She spun round. Her face was a deep red, mottled and distorted with anger.

"I don't know and I don't care. You young blackguard, bringing that slut in here, messing up all my bedlinen, mucking the room so it must be scrubbed, and keeping me up half the night, and all for a two-faced little bitch you pretended was your cousin. I ought to turn you over to the police, that's what I ought. And I will too. Just like they'll be after her."

I might be scared, yet I had to stand up for Nora.

"She couldn't help it."

"Couldn't she? I'll swear she brought it on herself."

What on earth did she mean? She must be mad with rage.

"Brought on what?"

"You young twister, don't pretend you don't know. She's had a filthy miss."

I did not understand.

"A what?" I said.

"A lowdown dirty abortion from taking pills." She shouted and caught me a stunning box on the ear that nearly knocked me down. But the brutal force of her words stunned me worse than the blow. Unable to speak, I stared at her dully, so shocked I lost all sense of where I was, or what was making me shake all over. Then something within me gave way. I covered my face with my arm and leaned against the passage wall.

34

THE TRAIN, gathering speed after its stop at Glaisend, was on the last stage of its journey to Winton. Alone in the corner of the end third class compartment I sat with commendable stillness, my hands on my knees, devoid of all sensation but that of profound apathy. For three hours I had been sitting like this, looking fixedly out of the window, dulled by the swift, confused passage of the landscape which served to block off or at least submerge the sluggish current of my thoughts. I hoped this state of blankness would not leave me. I encouraged it, when the scenery failed me, by staring at the advertisements on the opposite side of the compartment until they merged gradually into a mesmerizing blur. Now I'm looking at nothing, I thought, as though this sensation of visual and mental vacuum represented the summit of achievement.

Yet this stupor, a defence against the state of acute shock that I was in, did not always save me. And from time to time, fragments of fear and horror floated up like foul refuse to the surface of my mind. Then, the experience to which I had been subjected struck at me again. The net of deception that had entangled me was not the hardest to bear. Worse than that, worse even than my interrogation and detention by the police, when everything had come out, even the faking of the race, was the thought of Nora. I shuddered as once again the woman's voice rang through my head: "Good for nothing little slut . . . fetch the police . . . tampering with herself . . . a mucking abortion . . ." Life was sordid and hateful, could I ever believe in anyone or anything again?

The suburbs of Winton were now drifting past, the train had begun to slacken speed, and the ticket inspector, sliding open the corridor door, was again in my compartment. With a start, I surrendered the ticket the police sergeant had given me that morning and which had already been punched three times.

"Winton next stop." He was disposed to talk, since obviously he did not know that I had spent Sunday in Berwick gaol. "You've had a long journey, lad. And an early start."

I had to think a moment before I could find an answer.

"You have too, Inspector," I said at last.

He laughed.

"That's my job. Are you going on holiday?"

"No," I said, immediately, as though a button had been pressed, releasing the fixed idea in my mind. "I'm on my way to the University to sit an examination, at two o'clock."

"Are you now?" he said, impressed.

"I am. I've been working for it for three months."

"I thought you looked a bit hard done by. Well, good luck to you, lad."

I thanked him. He gave me a friendly nod and went out.

It was true, and I felt a strange relief to have openly established my intention. Perhaps, in my present state, this was no more than an obsessive compulsion, the reflex to those months of constant preparation. Yet I knew that I had given my word to Pin, and after the shambles of that shameful weekend I must try to keep it. Nevertheless, while I understood what I must do, while my movements were directed almost involuntarily towards that objective, I occasionally had difficulty in identifying myself with the individual who must perform them. This tendency of my personality to fade out into a sort of exterior wasteland was a frightening sort of thing in which I seemed to lose myself completely and to wander alone, all indentity gone, in a strange shadowy landscape. Yet it was not persistent, and when it passed, as now, I was again Laurence Carroll, possessed by the necessity of attending the University Hall, Gilmore Hill, W.1., at two o'clock precisely this afternoon.

The engine, with a last hissing expulsion of steam, jerked to a stop in Winton North British Station. Obscurely, I felt relieved that we had not come into the Central. I got out of my compartment and walked along the platform to the Queen Street exit, taking pains, as I did so, to confirm that the train had arrived at 12:40, only five minutes late. I had no need to hurry, everything would be performed in a well regulated manner. Although my ticket had been given up, I still had some coins in my pocket and, as it seemed correct to sustain myself before taking the examination, it became obligatory for me to have lunch. Not far down, on the other side of the street, I saw a Rombach, one of a chain of modest Winton restaurants. I crossed over and entered.

The menu, in light blue typing, offered a choice of mutton chop, boiled ox tongue, or steak and kidney pie. Unhesitatingly I selected the chop and, when it was served, with peas and mashed potatoes, I ate it as though complying methodically with a fixed routine, quite unconscious of any appetite or sense of taste. Although I could not realize this, all my actions were now controlled by an automatism, certain prelude to nervous disintegration, which, even had I tried, I could not have resisted. A clock on the wall of the restaurant above the entrance kept me informed of the time and at twenty past one I asked for my check, paid it at the cashier's box and went out.

A green tram would take me to the foot of Gilmore Hill. They ran frequently on this route and presently one appeared. Although it was crowded with workers going home for lunch, I boarded it handily. But I had to stand during the journey and when we arrived at Gilmore Hill I was not feeling quite so competent, particularly in the management of my legs. I climbed the hill slowly, from necessity rather than choice. It had apparently turned warmer and I was also experiencing a strange retarding tightness at the top of my head. Even when I reached the coolness of the cloisters this feeling persisted. The clock in the tower struck two o'clock as I entered the University Hall.

"Cutting it a bit fine, aren't you?" the man at the desk said as he ticked my name off on the list. He handed me the test paper, gave me an odd look and pointed to a vacant desk. I sat down and glanced about me, observing that the other competitors, about twenty in number, contorted in assorted attitudes of concentration, were already writing hard. I refused to be hurried. In an orderly manner I opened the exercise book on my desk and took up the test paper to study the question.

The Ellison Essay

Write an apologia of not less than two thousand words exonerating, as best you can, Mary, Queen of Scots, for her conduct in relation to Lord Darnley and with particular reference to the night of February 9th 1567.

I might have smiled — the temptation was almost irresistible — not because, at the back of my mind, something, or perhaps someone, had suggested that this, or a comparable subject, might turn up, but solely from the absurdity of the idea that in my present state I could ever bring myself to defend that royal adventuress, even if it were to win the Ellison for me a hundred times over.

Calmly, aware that I was wrecking my chance of success, I dipped my nib in the inkwell and began to write. I did not hesitate, words flowed from my pen, and every word I wrote sprang from the hurt I had received. The period in Scotland covering the fifteenth and sixteenth centuries had been my special study, I knew the full history of the unhappy Queen and now, invested with this urge from my subconscious, almost with malice, I scarified her mercilessly and with a subtlety of which I could not have believed myself capable. Under the pretence of defending her, one by one favourable arguments were advanced, then ruthlessly demolished, extenuating circumstances suggested, only to be crushed by the hard facts of history.

In this manner I made it obvious that her misguided marriage to the youthful, foolish Darnley, ostensibly a love match, had been conceived for no other reason than her ambitious hatred of her cousin Queen Elizabeth — only one year later the outlawed Earl of Bothwell was her adulterous lover. Estranged from her husband — who lay ill and disfigured, longing for a reconciliation, in the city of Glasgow — was it wifely solicitude that caused her to decree, after a secret meeting with Bothwell, that he might more conveniently recover his health in the lonely, half ruined house of Kirk o' Fields? Once Darnley was installed, not with comfort perhaps, for it was a miserable dwelling for a sick man, nothing could have been more virtuous than the assiduous attentions of the young and beautiful Queen who devotedly sat through the day with him on her red velvet cushion and at night slept in a bed in the room below.

Unfortunately, on one particular night, the Saturday night of February 9th, she could not well be there. A promise to be present at a masque and ball following a wedding had been given, the royal word could not be broken. She kissed her husband good night, saw that his candle light was trimmed. One last touching, pious gesture before she went out. She handed him his book of Psalms. Strange that Paris, Bothwell's servant, soiled with gunpowder, should pass her at the gate. Strange the locking of doors, the dismissal of the few attendants. Strange too, that tremendous explosion, almost a royal salute, while she danced the night away.

For more than an hour I had not once looked up, while my pen travelled to and fro across the white pages with a robot regularity. Devoid of conscious thought, it was automatic writing, nothing else, and no planchette could have more relentlessly evoked the past. But gradually, as I approached the final description of Mary awakening on the morning following the murder amidst the silken hangings of her great bed and, already contemplating her marriage to Bothwell, sitting up to enjoy her favourite breakfast of a soft boiled fresh egg, my bitterness seemed to flag and to be replaced by an extraordinary sensation of lassitude which obtruded itself in a manner so peculiar as to compel my attention. The lines were now wavering on the page, patches of shadow floated before my eyes and when, in an attempt to adjust my vision, I raised my head and looked about me the tightness previously experienced at the top of my skull was transformed to an actual vertigo. At the same time, giddily, it dawned upon me that most of the other candidates had handed in their essays, the time allotted must almost have expired. With an effort I completed my final paragraph, blotted the page, and closed the book.

What next? I supposed I should hand it in. But that seemed

altogether pointless, and besides, I had a strange disinclination to stand up. Now that I had expelled my venom, rid myself of that fearful sense of outrage against decency, like a devil cast out, I felt weak and limp, altogether spent. The examiner, if that was the term I should apply to him, was leaving his desk and advancing slowly towards me. To my surprise, as he drew near and I could see him better, he appeared to be a clergyman, long, lean and saturnine, complete with dog collar. Had I noticed that when I came in? Surely not.

"You are the last." He was addressing me mildly, in a speculative way. "Have you finished?"

"I believe I have."

"Then may I take your book? It's just after four."

I gave it to him. He was watching me out of the corner of one clerical eye.

"You've written a lot," he said rather ironically, turning the pages. "I trust you've been kind to the poor woman."

"No, I haven't. As far as I'm concerned she was just *a two-faced little bitch*."

"Indeed!" He raised his eyebrows, and said nothing more.

Holding on to the desk I stood up. I was reluctant to leave it, but somehow, with a pretence of normality, I got out of the hall. Outside in the cloisters someone was waiting. It looked like Pin. If so, he was in a state of fearful agitation.

"Laurence! I've looked everywhere for you. Where were you?"

I put my hand to the top of my head to see if it was still there.

"I can't exactly remember."

"Can't remember?" He was weaving in indistinct outlines, as though seen underwater. "Have you done a good essay?"

"No, a damned bad one. I answered it all the wrong way. And I told the examiner so."

"The examiner! Oh, heavens, that was the Professor of Divinity himself."

"Well, I don't care. It was the truth."

"Laurence, are you ill?"

"I don't think so. It's just that my head aches. I feel not myself any more."

"Oh, dear, what have you been doing to yourself? Where did you sleep last night?"

"I remember now. In gaol."

"Good God, boy!"

"Oh, they let me go this morning. Said there was nothing against me. The sergeant even gave me breakfast. But it was all hateful while it lasted. They had thought I was the cause of it all . . . and of Nora. That I was . . . I was . . . I was . . ."

He began to weave more and more, growing larger and larger, like some queer aquatic monster, and finally faded away altogether in the wave of universal darkness that swept down and absorbed me in its black, rushing tide.

35

It was past four o'clock in the afternoon some six weeks later. I had been lying down but now I was up and moving about the still unfamiliar flat my mother had rented. At last I was beginning to feel better, dimly to realize myself again, to know that I was making the journey back, out of that dark and spectral country in which my breakdown had so long confined me. It was not easy to forget the fear and horror of that shadowy period wherein my mind, narrowed to a single minute focus, was fixed in tormented apathy. The paths of my return had been tortuous and difficult, yet this morning the doctor had said to me: "You're out of the woods now, my boy, and soon you'll be clear of the undergrowth." The most joyful symptom of my escape was my ability to look outwards, away from my imprisoned brooding self, and to see things with an eye in which a spark of interest had begun to glint.

Thus, again, I examined the flat. It was small and very empty, made up of no more than a kitchen and a single front room with a tiny bathroom between, but it pleased me. The front room, which I occupied, was furnished with nothing but an iron bedstead, one chair and a rickety folding bureau, but the wallpaper was new, in colour a warm rich red, and when the evening sun came in, as it did now, the room glowed with a rosy flush that flooded and filled its emptiness. The kitchen, into which I wandered now, had the usual fittings, sink, built-in cupboard and dresser and, in the curtained alcove, that unique Scottish feature, a concealed box bed.

But the main attraction of the flat was its height. Situated on the top storey of a working class tenement recently erected by the Winton Corporation on Clarkhill, it afforded a sweeping open view of the roof tops and even, on clear days, of the Ochil Hills away to the west. Later I was to learn that in securing it my mother had been specially favoured by virtue of her new appointment with the city.

The nickel alarm clock on the mantelpiece told me it was not far off the hour of her return and, in the new lightness of my mood, I asked myself if I might not attempt to prepare our evening meal. Although the woolwork tasks I had been set had improved my sense of coordination, this had not been fully restored. I was afraid that I might drop things, and our store of crockery was not large. However, I succeeded in nerving myself to begin. Slowly and carefully I filled the kettle and, surprised by its weight, put it on the stove. I then spread the table cloth and began to set out the tea cups. I found the loaf in the cupboard and the bread knife in the drawer. There was no disguising the fact, however painful the admission, that this big serrated knife frightened me. No one who has not experienced a breakdown can remotely realize the agonizing phobias it may induce. Earlier in my illness, I had been mortally afraid . . . and of what? — the small wooden bureau in my room. Invested with every sinister attribute, it had terrified me. I could not bring myself to look at it. Here, surely, was an indication of what I had gone through, and the abysmal state to which I had been reduced. But now, shame and the will to prove that I was well again forced me to grip the knife and cut some slices of bread. But my heart was still racing as I set them under the gas ring to toast. All that remained was to cook the sausages, a rare treat in store for us tonight, and the gift of my faithful visitor. Annie Tobin did not bring flowers, she had a practical mind and knew my fondness for "Annakers." She brought also news which, while surprising, touched me not at all. Nora and Donohue, constrained perhaps by the ecclesiastical powers, were to be married. It meant nothing to me now.

A sense of accomplishment pervaded me when I had finished grilling the sausages. I felt that Mother would be encouraged by this evidence of my recovery. It was not that I particularly wanted to please her, although in our earlier days together this would certainly have been my motive. Our relationship was not the same. No longer did I feel for her that intimate, all suffusing, all encompassing jealous love. The cord was severed. I respected and trusted her, I was fond of her, but whatever the inflictions I had suffered, these had killed the passionate complex of my childhood.

Perhaps my mother's altered attitude, still affectionate, yet restrained, had contributed to the ending of those transports. Although this change had begun, insidiously, after Father's death, her sojourn in the convent had markedly altered her. She had become more serious in manner and disposition, and in a striking way, altogether more religious. In our early days at Ardencaple she would go to church on Sundays uncaringly, with a sort of lighthearted complaisance, and solely to please my father. Now, every morning she rose at six o'clock and before going to work went out to Mass at seven, taking daily Communion with every evidence of sincere devotion. No doubt conventual discipline had imposed its pattern upon her. Yet the change in her nature was deeper and more fundamental in its origin. Estranged from her own family, and with our Carroll associations now irrevocably severed, she must have felt herself a solitary figure, compelled by unhappy circumstances to stand against the world alone. Still, the moods of sadness that later afflicted her, and which eventually settled into a permanent melancholia, had not yet asserted themselves. She knew how fortunate she had been in receiving the Corporation appointment and was especially happy in her new work, which had to do mainly with the inspection and rehabilitation of ricketty slum children. In Winton the numbers of undernourished, verminous, deformed children suffering from this disease had become a national scandal.

Although she gave no apparent sign of this, I could not fail to realize that Mother's main anxiety was centred upon me. What on earth was to become of me? Through my mad efforts at the Ellison I had thrown away my one slight chance of attending the University. At the age of sixteen a return to board school seemed equally out of the question and if it were not, how could I expect my mother to support me for another two years with no assured prospects at the end of them? What a mess I had made of my life! My future seemed dim indeed.

A step sounded on the outside staircase and I heard a key turn in the door. Mother came into the kitchen wearing the navy blue coat and skirt and the neat turned-up blue chip hat with the Winton Corporation badge, all of which made up her new uniform. She smiled and exclaimed:

"Why, Laurence, you've made the supper."

"The sausages seem all right. But I've very cleverly burned the toast."

My reply seemed to please her.

"That's how I like it."

She went into the bathroom and I heard her shaking herself in the empty bath, an essential routine procedure to rid her garments of the fleas she invariably acquired in her daily pilgrimage amongst her unfortunate children.

While she was changing I went into the front room to

straighten my bed. As I folded the coverlet at the window I saw that Pin, who not infrequently came at this hour in an effort to console me, was stumping towards the common entrance to the flats. He had completed his "Annals of Ardencaple," but alas, no publisher seemed to want the book, and soon he would go back to the village to finish his days on his meagre pension. When I finished folding the bed cover the sharp staccato of Pin's peg on the pavement was still ascending to me and I saw that he was pacing to and fro in a manner manifestly indecisive and disturbed. It puzzled me. Then all at once I understood the reason of his reluctance to come up. This was no surprise at all and caused me no distress. It was part of my recovery that I could feel sorry for Pin in his disappointment with me. I went into the kitchen.

"Mr. Rankin is outside. Shall I call him up?"

"Do, Laurence . . . but first put on more toast."

I went and put two slices of bread on the stove. When I returned to the window Pin had gone. Apparently he had decided to depart. I just caught sight of him as he turned the corner of the street. And yet, mysteriously, some ten minutes later, when we had begun our meal, the bell of the flat door rang and there, when I answered it, was Pin.

"Laurence," he said at once, "I've been waiting for your mother, outside, and at the tram stop, but she seems to be unusually late."

"She's here," I said. "She came back early."

He appeared somewhat disconcerted by this information. Indeed, when he came into the clearer light of the kitchen, I saw that his general air was disturbed. He seemed obliged to find an excuse for his condition by remarking:

"I'm not so good at the stairs as I was."

"Be seated then," Mother said. "You'll have a bite with us."

"No, thank you, no."

"Then let me give you a cup of tea."

"No, no . . . well, as you're so kind."

He sat down and accepted the cup that Mother handed him. His hand was slightly unsteady, so that some of the tea spilled into the saucer, but he was becoming more assured. He gave me a sidelong solicitous look.

"How are you today, Laurence?"

"Much better, sir." I almost added: And quite prepared for your bad news.

"Good . . . good," he said.

His habit of repeating the word suddenly annoyed me. I knew exactly what he wanted to say and I wished to heaven he would get it out. I said:

"If there's anything on your mind I'm quite able to hear it."

He gave a sigh of relief.

"In that case I'll go ahead. I did think of speaking first to your mother. To see if it might set you back. But now I may as well admit that I've just come from the University and as you've guessed, the results of the Ellison are out." He took a slow drink of tea and went on, in a flat voice, not looking at me: "You probably remember the nature of the question, an apologia for Queen Mary, and I can assure you that most of the candidates fell over themselves to gild the lily. They didn't see the catch in the question, in the words "as best you can," and by heaven I didn't see it myself. They fell into the trap and practically beatified her, and with a panel of judges made up of two Presbyterian ministers and a Divinity professor by the name of Knox, they were dead from the word go." His voice was rising and becoming so hoarse, he had to gulp down tea. "By some chance, however, some turn of the unpredictable, there was one candidate who, unable to sustain any favourable evidence, found himself forced to condemn, in the strongest terms. I understand that his essay was an immense satisfaction to the judges, a vindication of their own belief, and the subject of the highest praise. They've given him the Ellison, unanimously."

I began to feel queer all over. There was a strange, strained expression on Mother's face as Pin went on:

"Laurence, there's supposed to be someone up above who looks after fools, especially if they're young fools with some sort of ability."

He could contain himself no longer. Jumping up suddenly, knocking over his cup, he flung his arms about my neck, hopping with me in a kind of one-legged dance. Half stifled, I scarcely heard his shout of victory. But I knew that by an amazing fluke, a freak of circumstance over which I had no control, I should go to the University after all.

At that exultant moment everything seemed settled. Our future was assured at last. The thought of the long and wearing struggle that must lie ahead never entered my mind. Yet for the next five years we were to fight a battle with circumstances that wore us to the bone. While my mother's position with the Corporation was assured, her weekly wage was pitifully slender, scarcely enough to provide us with the bare essentials of life. Yet somehow by a miracle of economy and self-denial she managed, and all without assistance, except from Simon, who himself had so little, yet who sent an occasional small contribution from Spain. From the other relations nothing was asked or given. Bernard continued to muddle along in great comfort in the condemned Lomond Vaults, somehow evading all orders for their demolition, while Leo silently and implacably went on to amass a stupendous fortune. In that laudable process his meanness and parsimony increased to such a degree that Annie finally left him and sailed from Greenock to join her son in Canada. It was a sad moment for me when I saw her off on the *City of Montreal.* On the rare occasions when I passed Leo in the street he pretended not to see me. Even then I was struck by his look of emaciation, and when he died, years later, completely alone in a miserable room in the Gorbielaw — Templar's Hall having been sold for some fantastic sum — there was more than a suggestion that death was due, at least in part, to starvation. In his holograph will, from which health food societies were the main beneficiaries, there was a clause specifically dispossessing his nephews and niece from any inheritance whatsoever.

The only one to suffer from this manifestation of family feeling was Nora. By that time my own medical practice was flourishing and Terence, shelving Miss Gilhooley in favour of the proprietress of an old established Dublin hotel, was then extremely well off. But Nora's marriage, arranged in an atmosphere of reparation — a futile idea on both sides of straightening things out — was a disaster. Donohue could never be anything but Donohue, he was seldom at home, and when he finally disappeared Nora was left stranded in Liverpool with three young children to support.

All this, of course, still lay in the future and meanwhile Mother and I were struggling along on shillings and pence. It is sad how little I then thought of her heroic self-sacrifice, and how often our relationship turned strained and difficult. As a student of comparative anatomy I was not now devotionally minded, while her religious fervour had become intense. On other matters too our ideas were in conflict and we had periods of estrangement when to me her withdrawn, tight-lipped silences had the semblance of martyrdom.

I am sure I was to blame. Yet amiability and good temper do not come easily when one is hungry, ill clad — for years

I remained garbed in Shapiro's camouflaged effort — isolated by an obvious poverty, and worried to death by the constant threat of failure. Although in my first two terms the record shows that I took honours in botany and zoology, every succeeding examination loomed as a terror from the knowledge that if I did not pass I was finished. The lush state assistance of later years did not then exist for impoverished students and my bursary, barely adequate, could never have afforded me a second chance. I can still see myself with my elbows on the desk and my head in my hands poring over Quain's *Anatomy* while Mother went out just before the shops closed on Saturday night to bargain in the cheapest market for a miserable scrag of meat, or on her return suffered the insults of some brute who had called for our overdue rent.

But at last, slowly and wearily, like a storm-beaten ship staggering towards the shore, we came in sight of the promised land. I passed my final examinations, the graduation day arrived, and Pin came from Ardencaple to join my mother at the ceremony. As I pushed my way out of the Bute Hall to meet them at the Union where, to avoid the crowd, I had told them to wait, I drew a long, deep, triumphant breath, conscious of my new personality: strong, reliant, and successful, equal henceforth to any emergency. Now I knew that the ingenuous softness of my youth was gone. Never again would I permit myself to be imposed upon. Never, never would my heart get the better of my head. The Greek ideal of my boyhood had been achieved at last.

At that moment when I had almost reached the doorway, I felt a touch on my arm. Despite the grey hair, which aged her markedly, I knew her at once. Miss O'Riordan. She had seen my name amongst the list of successful candidates and had wanted to see me capped. When we had talked for some minutes — she would not come with me to the Union — she placed a small, religious looking leather case in my reluctant palm. Impossible not to know what it contained.

"I'm sure you've broken the one I gave you. Or lost it. So here's another. So you don't forget."

After she had gone I glanced at the case with mixed sensations, mindful of my soulful performance at the presbytery so long ago, and only too well aware that when I got home I would drop the beads in a drawer and never give them another thought. Suddenly, under the pressure of my fingers on the soft leather, I felt a faint crackle. I opened the case. Yes, the rosary was there. But Miss O'Riordan had tucked in beside it a neatly folded Bank of Scotland five pound note.

Oblivious of the press around me, I stood there, quite motionless, so overcome by this opportune kindness which would enable me to get the few instruments I needed to apply for an assistantship, that slowly, inexorably, against all my efforts, my throat tightened, my vision was blurred with moisture.

No, it was no use — I had not changed, and never would. There was a soft spot in my nature, a strain of weakness, a sensitivity that would never harden. All that I longed, and had striven, to be — cool and stoical, detached and aloof, a true Spartan — was beyond me. Marked ineradicably by my singular childhood, by an upbringing in which too many women had participated, I was, and always would be, the victim of every sentient mood, the unwilling slave of my own emotions.